On the Horizon

Other books by the same author

Poetry

Yakhal'inkomo (Purple Renoster)
Tsetlo (Ad Donker)
No Baby Must Weep (Ad Donker)
Behold Mama, Flowers (Ad Donker)
The Night Keeps Winking (Medu Art Ensemble)
A Tough Tale (Kliptown Press)
Third World Express (David Philip)
Come and Hope With Me (David Philip)
Freedom Lament and Song (David Philip)

Novel

To Every Birth Its Blood (Ravan Press)

Essays

On the Horizon (Congress of S.A. Writers)

Gods of our Time

Mongane Wally Serote

RAVAN PRESS

First published 1999
Ravan Press
P O Box 145
Randburg
2125

ISBN 0 86975 521 8

Typesetting and design: Pat de Zeeuw cc
Cover illustration: Sfiso ka Mkame 'Letters to God'.
Permission granted by the South African National Gallery, Cape Town.

Printed by Creda Communications,
Eliot Avenue, Eppindust II, Cape Town

To my late friend, Djibril Mambeti,
one of Africa's finest film makers.

ONE

A bell rings. Then there is dead silence. And then, as if many, many stones are rolling down and hitting against each other, a sound comes. Running footsteps. A song. Yelling. It is about five-thirty in the morning. The night has gone. The day comes to prisoners. A scream. A cough. A yell. Rolling footsteps. Running water. The smell of food and the smell of fresh shit. The feeble lights. The shiny floors. The shining boots. Naked buttocks. Eyes, full of contempt - smiling, angry, staring. People come and go. Hundreds come - pass law offenders. They look sheepish. They undress, they run, they vanish into this room, they come out wet. They shiver. They dress. They run. They duck – a yell, the dull sound of a boot on buttocks. A slap.

The Saturday afternoon prison pace is much slower. Prisoners agree this is the most painful period of a jail term – weekends. The routine is the same. The difference is that most doors of the prison are closed, and there is too much silence. Now and then there is a cough; and then a sneeze, from somewhere, behind a closed door. The weekend pace in a prison is much faster: by 1.30 pm everyone has had supper. And there is something else: it is quiet, silent, yet there are about 10 000 people in here somewhere. Footsteps. Shower water. Smell of tobacco. A dog barking in the prison yard. Visiting hour:

"Hullo …"

"Hullo …"

"How are you?" The eyes meet. For a second, there is a terrible silence. The warden is watching. You can't touch. "I am fine." The eyes drop to the shiny floor, the floor is like a mirror, it is as if it has water on it. Who shines it like this? Whose voices are those? Why is it as if everyone is running, but you don't see

1

anyone running. You feel watched? They tear open the bread you brought, they examine the milk container closely, they look at you, with their green eyes, straight into yours, and they are talking softly, firmly, and then ...

"Skopendonner! Skopendonner! Skopendonner! Skopendonner! Skopendonner! Sabela igama lakho!" The man comes walking slowly, yellow in complexion, dry watchful eyes, jacket collar turned up, all in green, even a green hat.

"Hullo ... Lindi."

"Hullo ... Justice." Their voices seem to echo.

"How are you?" A stare, a watchful stare.

"I am fine." A sigh. "How are you?"

"Sweet." Silence. "How are the kids?"

"They are fine, they are always asking after you."

"Do they still go to school?"

"Yes."

"How's the old lady?"

"Fine."

"Is she still with Jonas?"

"Yes."

"How's Jackie?"

"He lost his house."

"Why?"

"The superintendent."

"Why? He's been in that house for ten years."

"You know, love . . ."

He looks down to the floor.

"So where does he stay now?"

"With his mother."

"In that crowded house?"

"Yes." She looked at him.

"In Alexandra?"

"Yes."

"How are you?"

She looks down. He stares at her. Slowly her head rises, their eyes meet.

"I am fine."

Silence. She picks up the paper bag. One by one, she takes out the things in it – toothpaste, cigarettes, bread, a huge packet of fish and chips. He receives these in silence. Their eyes meet. She sees he is wearing his frown. She knows that frown. It makes him look like a trapped animal. His jaw is tight. He stares and stares and stares.

"Love, I love you," she says, she is about to cry now, "don't do anything foolish."

He is quiet, he is looking away, his head drops.

"You must go now," he picks up his parcel and goes away. It was when she went down the stairs, holding her black umbrella, that she wondered if she could take it any more . . .

In the past, she had often passed through Pretoria. But this time she had had to search for this huge building housing 10 000 men only. That meant she had to walk, from one street to the other, very, very carefully. Watching the cars ... watching the uniformed white men: policemen, soldiers, God knows what else. Thus did Lindi walk the streets of Pretoria. She was uncertain whether what she was thinking was correct. No, not the attitudes of the white faces she saw but, the attempt to understand them, and as a result, to understand her life. There had been something called the Treason Trial – she was about fifteen when that happened. Yes, she remembered, she was then learning how to carry her child in her arms, and play hop-scotch when her mother was not looking. Little Thoko, with eyes like a cat watching and expecting you to throw the piece of meat you are preparing for its supper, was about to mew, but not yet mewing.

Babies don't have the ability to be understanding. Everything centres on them; their little mouths, their little stomachs. They wail and wail if you don't feed them, and when they wet themselves, they cry at you as if to say how come you do not realise that they are wet? Lindi smiled at this thought. No, Thoko had been, at times, a very sweet child – whatever that means for a mother of fifteen.

It was at that stage of her thoughts that she stumbled into Pretoria Central Prison.

She mused. Audiences are a funny lot. They are like children. Selfish. The song that Lindi had taken to the University Great Hall at Wits that night, for its whites-only audience, if there is such a thing, was a song about her life. There is something about a piano which touches Lindi's essence, daring a very intense struggle inside her.

When she arrived on stage, walk-running, the curtains, like death snatching its victim away, slowly cut the thin space between the audience and the performers – the audience a large hole, a space expecting to be filled. She stopped abruptly at the edge of the stage, where it suddenly becomes the long pit of the auditorium. One day, just one day, she would not stop, she would walk-run into the pit, smash her head, and break her neck; it would be so silent after that! Lindi gestured to the pianist.

A piano must be in the right fingers. It was this time. John Molamu was the pianist that night. In the past he had attempted to define what a piano is, or rather, what it can do; he talked about it as thunder, as a storm, as a loving woman, as God, as a piece of shit. That night, he played it like rain falling on a roof of a house in which lovers lie, eye to eye, face to face, flesh to flesh – and in full command of themselves, masters of being gentle and tender to each other; old, old lovers, who are together once more, after a long, long time. It was dead silent in the hall. A mixture of rich perfumes reached Lindi, far away, under the bright lights on stage. She had frozen, dead still, mike in hand, staring at the many white faces, men, women, girls and boys – hundreds of pairs of eyes, gaping mouths – the song came:

> *darling, I asked you whether the sky must fall*
> *or the earth make deep, deep holes*
> *so you can believe me, believe me*
> *when I say there is no other man in my life ...*

Lindi has a certain laughter, which reveals that she has become very knowledgeable about the game of losing. That is alright. But this laughter also tells you that it does not matter any more what it is that she still has to lose, since she had to lose it once, and if you ask her about that, you will have no illusions about what she will ask of you.

She laughed. The audience applauded. For a split second, with the raising of her arm, silence fell immediately – and she took the song:

>*darling, I asked you if I should take lightning in*
>*my hands,*
>*or allow the flame to eat and eat my body*
>*so you can believe, believe me*
>*when I say there is no other man in my life ...*

>*you've come home now*
>*it's been a long time since you were away*
>*come*
>*let's close the night and the noise out*
>*come*
>*darling, I ask ...*

Hope, we must say, can be stubborn as the will of the sun to rise; it can be as strong as a tree trunk – and, it is human. Now, here comes the lady. And we must try to keep a sharp focus. Lindi, when was she born? One has heard of that time. Old people – since we keep throwing stones into the pond, and the ripples form, we must follow each ring – old people, I know, say nothing nice about life. The old people, who were young men and women when Lindi was a little girl, talk a lot about that time. There is something about their faces, which have been able to weave fear and love together, something one picks up from the way their eyes light up, as their faces wear shadows or light, and from the tone of their voices, something that keeps saying the worst is borne by the oldest.

Msinga is a village in Natal. History has ripped it into ribbons. The people from this area are an embattled people. They make guns from bicycle frames. The guns load bullets made from the legs of huge three-legged pots. God knows what primes the bullet, but these have been used in battles against cops and their helicopters, and Msinga is a feared place. This is where Lindi was born. She knows very little about the village. The only thing she remembers, and this must be said about a great many South African children, black children – they left the village one day, they arrived at a strange place where there were no houses. The strong emotion she remembers about that time, is that of fear: it was on everyone's face – and so was anger, it burst out through gestures, looks and tones. It was here, in Masakeng that Lindi learnt about stories of her past in Msinga.

The only way to describe Masakeng is to compare the area where this bloody place was situated with the sea. The open vast sea, with millions of ships, sailing, millions of sails, blown in the wind. This is how the houses were in Masakeng. If a strong wind came – and it came often – the houses were blown away.

That is where Lindi spent her childhood, and early motherhood. This Masakeng is a place of sacks. Houses had no cement walls; their walls were sacks. Lindi gave birth here. She learnt to sing here. She learnt about womanhood here. It is this place also, which instilled Lindi's rebellion. She was not going to work for no white people, and wear clothes which they chose. The clothes, with their colours and their brand names written on them, marked you. You were branded by those colours and branded forever to work for white people. To work for white people, you lost your age, your name, your being and your humanity. You became their property. No, Lindi was not going to wear colours which the people chose for her. She will wear her own. As we entered the café to have lunch, the floods of people, workers, in colours of the rainbow arrived.

Lindi and I had no colours, that is, no visible colours. The café was noisy. We started to eat, sitting on a cooldrink box.

"If I were a man, I would think that is a nice lady," Lindi said, wearing a mischievous smile.

I laughed. I did not want to look at whomever she was pointing at.

"She's fat, juicy and has a doll face, don't you think?"

I broke the bread. I dipped it in the gravy. I chewed.

"Why, how come, why don't you look at women? Are you well?" she asked, looking all serious, "you must not be forever serious, it's bad for your heart you know?"

I chewed and chewed and chewed.

"How old are you?"

"Does it really matter, Lindi?"

"Maybe it does not," she said, and laughed loudly. Everybody

6

looked at us. Well, everybody knows Lindi, and, I think, they expect her to do that, to be half crazy, not because she needs help or that it may be there is something wrong with her, but – this lady sings, don't you know?

"Sweetheart," Lindi said, walking towards the girl she had been talking about, "come here awhile." Her eyes were gentle as she held her by the hand.

"What's your name?"

"Magnally."

"Where do you stay?"

"Orlando."

"You work for OK Bazaars?"

"Yes."

"I think you are a sweet child," Lindi said pulling her gently towards her, "what else do you do besides OK Bazaaring?"

"Nothing," she said.

"Sure you have a lover, please say yes," Lindi said smiling.

"Oh my God," Magnally said laughing, "sis-Lindi, what are you saying?"

"I am saying there is nothing nice about working for OK Bazaars, so you must at least do something nice, like having a lover? Why are children so serious nowadays?"

For a while, we all had nothing to say. Lindi was still looking straight into Magnally's eyes, holding her hand.

"You know," Lindi said at last, looking at me, "I have forever wanted to write a song, a very, very beautiful song about black women, a very beautiful song – I hold them, I touch them, I talk to them, just for a clue, maybe a word, a gesture, something, just something, I am not a man you see." She looked at me with terrible eyes.

"I have forever wanted to write a song. So I can sing it – I sing you know – so I can sing it for the black women, not to despair. I do not mean that they despair – but they don't know that I want to write a song, get a good band, a piano, a bass, and me – simple, and we sing and sing this song ..." She let go Magnally's hand. People were beginning to trickle out of the café, lunch-time was up for most of them. Outside the traffic was thickening. I knew from its roar. Magnally said she had to go now. Lindi stood up, hugged her, and said: "It's alright, be sweet, you are sweet, does your boy know that?" Magnally smiled, and said, bye ...

There were just the two of us in the café. Us and the bread and the gravy. The Portuguese – or Greek? – shopowner banged and rang the empty Coke bottles as he packed them into crates. He was whistling some song, which reminded me of the ringing of bells around the necks of sheep and cows as they clumsily, slowly, walk to the river. And then suddenly, that part of Johannesburg became very quiet.

How come Lindi has said nothing about her brothers or sisters except to refer to them in passing? I can't remember if I ever asked her about them. Maybe it did not matter, maybe it did, but it is not easy to sort out rubble, especially if that rubble, that debris, breathes, is hot. Today, there is something called Soweto, which, as the whole world knows, is threatening to make a deafening noise, even though it is the pride of its creators. Soweto is the result of places like Masakeng. Masakeng, Pimville, Sophiatown, Alexandra, Dendela, all of them have become one word: Soweto.

Soweto is too far beyond Lindi's time. It has never heard Lindi sing 'Stormy Weather', 'Phalafala', 'Tamati Sauce' – it has never seen the theatre of song when people sang, mimed and danced at the same time, expressing the story of their lives. In those days, when Lindi and others did this, they expected to be given a penny, sometimes a shilling; and the Queen of England was on the penny and the pound and the shilling which hit the Masakeng street and made bus-fare for the dump-hill. In those days, when someone was getting married, or at a birthday party, even at a funeral, Lindi sang: Masakeng was preparing a lady who sings, who would in a while sing for the world.

Lindi and I sat in the cafe, knowing full well that the world had not known what to do with her. The world took Lindi from Msinga to Masakeng to Pimville and then to Johannesburg, and then to England, and then to the USA, and then threw her back to this café of a lost Portuguese who is singing his song and packing crates of bottles; here, where we ate bread and gravy, and thought about Magnally. The world had nothing to offer Lindi except a penny. What does one do with things like that?

8

My first encounter with Lindi had been in an interview. Some magazine, probably chasing a scoop, had found Lindi and asked her how come she no longer sings.

"Fuck the fans!" she said. I had no clue what that meant. I came out of Tembisa. I searched for Lindi. *reporter*

I searched and searched for her until eventually I began to sus*reporter* pect that I was not clear about what I was looking for. Lindi had disappeared. However, that search, in the bright hour and the dark hour, began to ask me, what are you looking for? Why are you looking for it? There was nobody who was going to stop me looking for Lindi. Scoop or no scoop, story or no story, I was going to search. But in time I gave up the search, and all that remained was: "Fuck the fans," a very favourable phrase.

Lindi and I walked out of the café. We hit the streets, and their pedestrians, and their traffic, and their lights, and their hoots, and their neon lights – a mess! It was dark. I rushed for my bus, she rushed for her train, we would meet some other time, we sure would.

This story is hard to tell. But it must be told. It is hard to tell because, given my country, and my countrymen, we have worked ourselves into becoming extremely careful. That is what Lindi says. That is how she explains the silence which both of us have come to agree, does not exist. There is a silence here. It is a silence which will not be broken by the roaring cars, the shattered glass, the deafening and deadly sound of the rifle – it is a silence as still as a tree when there is no wind blowing. But since we discovered this silence it is no longer there, it is now too loud.

On this day, Lindi and I were in her house. Cat-like she sat curled and sprawled on the sofa: one leg folded, one foot under her buttocks and the other stretched out, its toes tapping in the air. She was bare-headed. She had on a loose red woollen dress and a very careful face. Now, thinking back to that day, I know she must have realised that I had made lots of decisions and that I had come to the point where I did not care.

Lindi was still on the sofa. She watched me, with her great big eyes, with a calm face. She bit at her red nails. She kept spitting out something after biting her fingers. She looked down for a long, long time. And then she took me by surprise. Her hoarse voice, wearing thousands of accents, which were dominated by a Zulu one, burst the silence very quietly.

Where do we start? She said Lady was a good lady indeed. She did not mean to be mean when she built a house, bigger than a church with hundreds of little rooms which knew no day, rooms which housed hundreds of sexless, groaning men and women.

Place-of-sorrows, the house that Lady and Rocky built, had an eerie aura about it. People said so many things about it! It was built long ago on the corner of Second Avenue in Alexandra. A man and a woman with the hopes of all women and men – to build a house, to have children, to be a family and to be part of the world – had built it. It was a massive house with six bedrooms, a large sitting room, a dining room, a lounge, unfinished toilets, a bathroom and a pantry. The woman of this house, in those early days, earned herself a name: Lady. The man was simply known as Rocky. When Rocky died very few people went near the house, only Lady went in and out of it. People whispered things about her. They pointed at her when she was not looking. They stealthily walked away from her as she approached. As it is with secrets, it's those who hold them who think that no-one else knows about them. But Lady knew what people were saying about her. She expected them to point at her, behind her back. She expected them to whisper things about her – she had made up her mind though, that she would go about her life as usual. Father Zulu was the first to ask for a place to stay.

Lady looked at him, "Why?" she asked.

"I have nowhere else to go," he said.

"But is it not true that every time Zulu had to say mass, members of the congregation carried him from a shebeen to church on a wheelbarrow?" I asked Lindi.

"That is true, but this is no reason for the house of God to leave its child to the dogs," she said, and she looked like a child when she said this. I have never stopped being amazed by this. Lindi has a way of becoming almost criminally naive, of being very innocent, like a child, through her eyes. I suspect that it had to do with the fact that she can also be a ruthless fighter.

"I sensed how it came about that Zulu landed up where he did – the same reason that put you there too."

10

"But I am only a bitch, or I was only a bitch by then – but a priest!"

"What's the difference?"

"He had a church."

"You had halls and audiences, and like him you went to the US and England, the works …"

"But I was only a singer!"

"He was only a priest!"

"I was not in love with Goddammit!"

Silence

2

TWO

Nomvula was sitting on the bed, keeping an unconcious rhythm with her whole body, partly putting the baby on her back to sleep and partly keeping pace with the many thoughts which raced through her mind. It was very quiet. Not so long ago, the guns, the running footsteps, the songs, the lorries had made too much noise, and so, at one point, had the heart. Nomvula knew, she just knew as she sat there, that the baby on her back was the only one she had now. She knew this. This knowledge brought no tears to her; she had cried and cried some time back. She could not any more. All she had learnt to do in the past few days and months was to wait, and once the news came she would act from some strength which the times had given her; some strength which had built up as she realised and understood, from watching, hearing, ducking, fighting – and simply concluding, there is no point in being fearful or crying. She had chosen to fight now. Where would she take her last child? Unconsciously, she was now humming a song. You could still hear distant voices, roaring trucks, a yell, and the air smelt of teargas. The small candle flame seemed to stagger under the weight of bad air. It seemed to help Nomvula to wait. She was waiting for her little boy to sleep. She would then put him on the bed and put more blankets over him. It was at this point that her mind leaped, to struggle with time. Her mind was tired. It could not go back to trace how she had come to believe, how she had understood that there is nothing which goes on forever. That everything comes and goes.

Something seemed to give in right inside her: an emptiness. She began to fight, she had resolved that she was going to fight, she began to fight the vacuum, the pain she was feeling inside; she stood up and began to walk up and down. How do those in prison fight? How do they fight, year after year after year for twenty years? How do they keep intact? They are without their wives, their children, without friends, without the freedom to walk down the street, to look at people or to talk to a neighbour or be greeted by a stranger – how do they fight? She must fight. She had resolved she must fight – how, she did not know, but she must fight, fight for what? For freedom; what is that? That which those in prison on Robben Island fight for. The many freedom fighters who have fallen, killed in strange places, far from their friends or family, sometimes in foreign countries; the many people, leaders, children who are dying in the streets of Kwanobuhle, Uitenhage, Tembisa, Elsiesriver, all over the land life is being swept away like dirt, into the ditches, in dusty streets, burnt in the veld. She had, though, resolved to fight – this she knew. There was a light knock on the door. She started to the door, her big eyes glued to the wooden frame. She put the child on the bed, and quietly walked to the door. She opened it. Thuledu looked at her, their eyes met briefly. Nomvula could see, she knew from Thuledu's eyes. She held her by the hand, past the open door, shut it. "They have killed Sipho," Thuledu said.

"Where was he killed?"

"Near the bottle-store."

"Look after the child," Nomvula said. She unwrapped a blanket from her waist and quickly put her doek on. "You must wait till I come back," she said and closed the door behind her.

It was getting dark. The air was filled with tear-gas smoke, she could hear the strange sound of the hippos, casspirs and trucks in the distance. There were very few people in the street. She walked quickly. She knew no-one, no-one on earth could stop her. From where she was she could see the roof of the bottle-store. She smelt gun-smoke, dust, and in spite of the sounds made by the hippos and trucks, it was very quiet, her footsteps were very loud. She turned the corner. She heard running footsteps, she stopped and looked back, forcing her eyes to tear the thin shadows of the night. Young boys and girls came running towards her – two, no three, four.

"Ausie-Nomvula, here is a blanket for Sipho," the little girl said as, breathless from running, she gave her the blanket. Nomvula looked at them, one by one; they were silent, staring

13

back at her.

"Cynthia, take her half-way," one of the girls said.

"Is that Joyce?" Nomvula asked.

"Yes."

"And is that Steve?"

"Yes."

There was a silence.

"Let's go," Cynthia held Nomvula's hand, and began to walk. The others, just as they mysteriously emerged from the dark, so they disappeared into it. Nomvula knew that wherever they had disappeared to, they were watching her. Cynthia walked very quickly through short-cuts and helped Nomvula over fences. Then she stopped.

"I cannot go further than this," she said, "they will shoot me. Walk straight to those two figures, tell them you want to cover Sipho's body." Cynthia disappeared.

Nomvula focused her eyes in the darkness on the two figures. One of the figures was smoking. She walked toward them, unwrapping the blanket so that it dangled over her arm. One figure lifted its gun, pointed it towards her, "I want to cover my child with this blanket," she said to the darkness. She stopped.

"Drop that blanket."

She dropped it.

The figure began to walk towards her, still pointing the gun at her.

"How do you know it is your child?"

"It does not matter."

"What?"

Silence.

"I said, how do you know this is your child?"

"That does not matter."

"Voetsek! Voetsek … !"

Silence. She was dead still.

"Fuck off …"

She could see he was white.

She stood dead still, looking at the dark figure. She heard a sound, made by the gun.

"Fuck off!"

14

"Piet!"

Piet looked back.

"Don't shoot her," said the other dark figure who was smoking.

"Fuck off!"

Nomvula picked up the blanket, walked past Piet towards the other figure, and then she saw Sipho, sprawled on the dusty street, lying on his side. She walked straight towards the body of her son. It was dead quiet, but for her footsteps. She covered her son with the blanket and sat down next to the body in the darkness.

Piet walked back to his colleague. They stopped a while, silent, looking at the two figures below them. Jaap nodded his head that they should go. Nomvula heard the click of the gun once more, and then the footsteps as they walked away from her. She knew she was getting cold, but she did not feel it; she knew that Cynthia was somewhere waiting, but she could not see her; she looked at the covered lifeless body of her son, she knew that she must not cry. The footsteps died. It was very dark now. All she could see was the body of her son, and not very far away.

"Rest yourself," the old lady said. "Put your head on my lap." She pulled the blanket from her shoulders, folded it into a pillow, and placed it on her lap.

"Are you sure?" Nomvula asked, sighing, looking the old lady in the eye.

"You are tired, and you must be cold, lie down and let your body soak the heat of the sun," the old lady said.

"Did you drink anything since the morning?" another old lady, Morula, asked.

"Yes, the children have been so good to me."

"You know these children, these children ..." she stared into the distance.

"They say twenty other children have been shot and killed since sunset yesterday," Nomvula said.

"The night has been roaring like thunder," said Morula, "the whole township is smelling like a chemical factory, smoke is biting into the nostrils and eyes."

"We are at war, there is no other way," old lady MaNhlapo said.

There was silence among the three women. The heat of the sun

15

was burning on their bodies; there was no breeze; occasionally a shot rang in the distance, and there were sounds of running horses, trucks and casspirs – the police were still making death; the people of the township were assigning themselves tasks; some, like old Morula and MaNhlapo, helped those who sat by their dead, others watched the smoke and fire and listened to the crash of glass. They spoke in whispers to others; the young were busy, jumping over fences, from one yard to the other, evading death, resisting, surging forward. The men, smoking pipes, whispered to the young, they walked quickly, they stood at corners, watchful, disappearing, regrouping, separating and listening to the tearing gun shots. Women's skirts were filled with blood, soot, were torn, the cold night had made them all wrap blankets around their waists; the busy day did not give them a chance to wash or change their clothes; time, this acid which cannot be touched and which alone can touch and eat into life, had assigned them a role, and they embraced this role with their lives – they refused to give death any recognition, they walked straight from the world of the living, crossing between death's speedy bullets into the world of the living, and were getting ready to bury their dead – their children, brothers, husbands, sisters – once and for all, and return to the shattered day and night of the township.

"Here," Morula said, stretching her hand to MaNhlapo, giving her a piece of bread which she had taken out of a paper bag, and roughly broken.

"That's too much for me," MaNhlapo said, breaking it up into more pieces. "You must have some, Nomvula," she said, almost pushing it into her mouth, denying Nomvula any chance to turn her offer down. "Your heart has been hurt, but you must allow it to beat still, we need it too, if anything, you must help us bury other children," she said, and began to chew, looking into the distance.

"MaNhlapo," a voice said, and the three women looked to where it came from. It was Cynthia – none of the three had seen or heard her come.

"MaNhlapo, Steve says he feels we have taken too much bread from Mlambo's shop, should we try Lucas?"

"No, no, I don't know where you will get more bread, but def-

16

initely not from Lucas, no!"

"The other thing, you remember Joyce?"

"Joyce ...? Who is Joyce? Joyce?"

"The one you were with last night," Nomvula asked.

"Joyce, Joyce ... who is Joyce?" MaNhlapo kept saying, thoughtfully glancing up and down, wringing her hands. She knew what Cynthia was going to say about Joyce, and she was searching and searching for the little girl's face – for Joyce's face.

"Joyce, Ma-Moeng's daughter," Cynthia said.

"Oh, yes, yes, Joycy, that one, yes, the pretty little girl with a naughty laugh, yes of course I know her, I know her very well ..."

Silence fell among the women. Cynthia looked at Sipho's body covered in a blanket. She stood up.

"I must go now," she said.

"My child, what about Joyce?" MaNhlapo asked. Cynthia fought back her tears. She looked at MaNhlapo.

"They killed her?" MaNhlapo asked.

"Yes," Cynthia said.

Silence.

"Don't go anywhere near Lucas, Cynthia, you hear me?"

"Yes."

"We would rather starve than take bread from a sell-out!" MaNhlapo concluded.

Cynthia turned, and walked away. It was broad daylight, as the saying goes. The sky was blue and bright, watching. Tembisa had been hit by an iron fist. Its streets were being walked by strangers, carrying guns, riding horseback, casspirs, hippos and trucks. Its inhabitants, with stealth and care, walked its alleys, seeking the stranger's back, seeking each other, crossing streets with great care, whispering to each other with such skill that even the age-old walls could not hear what was being said.

"I agree, I do," said MaNhlapo, almost talking to herself. "We must give Lucas a chance to turn a new leaf, but this is not the time, and we must not go to him cap in hand, no! we can't do that!"

She rolled her eyes in thought, she looked away into the distance, to the many, many similar houses, dust-burdened and seemingly deserted, to the dry, brown trees which stood lifeless under

17

the scorching heat, to some figures which came into sight suddenly and so disappeared. Without meaning to, she caressed Nomvula's face.

"We will devise a means of making him a complete friend, if he refuses, to go to hell for ever. We must, we will, he can't remain like that forever – surely he belongs somewhere, doesn't he? He does ..."

"Will he ever come right?" MaMorula asked.

"That is his problem, ours is how do we help him to make up his mind one way or the other, although I must say, if he comes right, as you say, we are the stronger, but if he weakens us ..." she looked at Sipho's covered body.

"Well ..."

Silence.

"You see, we must go to talk to Lucas; we must tell him that we are not happy that he blames the death of the dead on the dead; we must tell him that we want the army and the police to leave our townships, that if they leave, no-one will die; we must tell him that it is correct for children to demand that they want better education; that we are genuine and honest when we say this, and that we want him to support us; we must also tell him that we have learnt painfully that Botha, Malan and le Grange can't rule us, we have volumes of evidence to prove this, including his own life, you see ..."

"Yes."

"We must tell him straight that anyone who stands against this will be eaten by the fire."

"Does he know that?" Ma-Morula said.

"Perhaps he does," MaNhlapo said. "We are fighting for unity, we can't tire, we will fight and fight and fight for it, and those who stand against it, like Botha and his people, who believe in a disintegrated life, will be smashed; there is no other way for them, we must tell Lucas this."

"After we bury Sipho, I would like to go and talk to him, I will go with Cynthia," Nomvula said.

"I must talk to the other women first, I will also mention that you asked to be among those who go to talk to Lucas," MaNhlapo said.

"I want to be among those who go to talk to Lucas," Nomvula said. "Sipho wanted me to be involved, he trusted that I am strong and that I will learn and do good if I'm involved. I was hesitant, I always responded to him like my little boy Sipho, and he always told me, when he dies he would rest in peace if I were involved. He told me he is proud of me ...." She felt tears coming, she began to fight them. She looked away – how does one fight sorrow?

"Milner was very secretive, I never knew what on earth he was doing. I knew though that he was up to something. I fought him so!" MaNhlapo said. "Then he disappeared for five years. I never knew where he was. I had given up hope of ever seeing him. I had been everywhere, the police, mortuary, relatives, friends looking for him. I eventually decided that I must wait, whatever took him away will bring him back to me; it did. The police came and told me he had been arrested, he was a terrorist, he was going to hang. My mind went wild; I had heard the word 'terrorist' many, many times, even when I was searching for him, but that, I thought, can't be a word which describes my little boy ... I met him in court – he was still himself, my little boy, only, something about his eyes and face and shoulders told me he had grown up, and that I may never know what he knows. He smiled at me – I said, Milly, what have you been doing? I did not know what else to say. He said, nothing. I said, what do you mean nothing. He said, nothing bad I mean. What else could I say? I held him, and when he put his hands around me he reminded me of his father. I wept. He said, Ma don't do that, don't cry – if you do, you will break me. I have done nothing bad, I'm a freedom fighter. His voice was shaking as he said this. I knew I must not cry. I smiled – tears still on my face – I smiled; he looked at me, he just stared at me. I said to myself, I'm his mother, he is my son. I must not cry, because if I do, I will break him. Every day and night I said this to myself; they hanged him ... you see?"

"I remember that very well," Ma-Morula said. "I will never forget the song he sang when we went to see him for the last time and when, after that, we saw his coffin, his very, very awful coffin emerge, being rolled on wheels, dripping blood, and other coffins followed, and they were put on this truck, and we followed it. Many, many times lights went out of my eyes. I was dizzy. I felt sick, I felt my stomach contract, contract and I thought, what am I going to do?"

"But why do the boers kill, kill, kill, kill all the time? Why? What do they hope to get out of all these corpses, why are they unable to deal with life, what will they do with all this death?" Nomvula asked.

"We are fighting for freedom," MaNhlapo said. "We want a house, bread, water and happiness, that is all we want; in this time of aeroplanes and telephones, these simple things are very costly my child, they are bloody costly – you see, the day I want you to be my slave, to work for me, in the end, the only way this can become a reality is if I make sure that I make you completely uncertain about everything – I've got you then. But, you see, the day you say to me a house, bread and water are your right, what you are saying is that I have no right to make you dependent on me. You have made me believe that you can become free of me, and what this means is that you and I must share life, and the more you demand, the more I have to prove that you are wrong, till in the end, that, that is the only relation you and I have. I do everything in my power to say you are dependent on me, and you do everything in your power to claim your freedom. And this," she said, pointing at Sipho's body, "is the result." She began to rock to and fro.

"Here's Cynthia," Ma-Morula said. They simultaneously turned in the direction she was pointing, and saw Cynthia coming, with one more fence to go before she reached them.

"MaNhlapo," Cynthia said, breathless, "the Black-Maria has started collecting the corpses. We have counted forty bodies so far. Steve is with the reporters. He wants to know from you whether to give them a statement?"

"What statement? Tell Steve I said that it is important that out of this strange night, we emerge strong and united, let him allow Mlambo to make the statement. Mlambo stands for all of us now, we gave him the power, let him use it on our behalf; we will do the spade work for him. Tell Steve I think that is the best, give Mlambo the figures, also count how many houses, cars have been damaged, how many people injured – and don't forget to remind Steve to tell Mlambo that we want all the councillors to resign,

20

and we want the police and the army to leave our township alone. We want our leaders out of jail," she looked away. "That is all," she said.

"Ausi-Nomvula," Cynthia looked at Nomvula, "Thuledu wants to know whether it is okay to use the money she found in the wardrobe to buy milk, coffee and sugar?"

"I don't know anything anymore, please tell her to do what she thinks best," Nomvula said. Her heart was pumping fast; the word Black-Maria had sent her mind whirling – indeed Sipho is dead, the Black-Maria would be here soon, to take him away. She could hear the sirens in the distance. The sun was falling down. Thuledu, what has she been doing all this time, by herself with the child? She must fight, this is no good, she must fight, if she goes on like this, she will cry.

As the dust rose, so much dust, which also, suddenly, brought all these footsteps and voices, it seemed in its strength to take Cynthia also, who suddenly was not there. The Black-Maria had come; the boots, guns and voices, the stretcher, and the bloody blanket and in no time, Sipho, had gone – MaNhlapo saw the back of the Black-Maria, dust whirling behind it as it disappeared with its cargo into the distance.

She stood a while, watching the dust and the burnt-down bottle store, and then she began to walk away from the spot where Sipho had fallen.

21

THREE

At Lady's they made their own coffins. They bought planks and nails and a sheet. That is all you need to bury someone, apart from a hole, of course! In the three years since she and Lindi had been there, they had buried many people. Planks, nails, a sheet, and a hole – that is all you need. The corpses were very thin, lean as a rake, as they say. They had no hair any more, something had eaten their hair. The corpses were frightening because they sometimes had their mouths or eyes open. The blisters on their legs and hands and faces looked like holes. I looked at Lindi's legs, and saw black marks. But now she was fat and tall and had this very knowing smile.

"PW killed those people," Lindi said.

"PW? You talk like you know him," I said.

"I know what he has done. He is a cruel and dangerous man – and so are Vorster, and Jimmy Kruger, and Pelser, and Pik."

I bit an apple and it nearly choked me.

"You know, I told Skopendonner the boers were responsible for my not being a good singer, and for his being such a deadly criminal, and he would tell me he had nothing to do with politics."

"Who was the Prime Minister when Masakeng came into being? I don't remember, maybe Malan or Strijdom – I think Verwoerd came later. But why do they make a place like that?" she asked me.

"Do you like Soweto?"

"It's the only place I know in the world," she looked at her nails. "Where will I go if I hate it?"

"I suppose that is what that poor priest told you to say?"

"I don't think Zulu ever believed in God, that is why he left, he had to leave the church."

"Did he say that?"

22

"No, now I know."

"How do you know?"

"I just know it right now as I sit here," she said.

"But Lindi, we talk in circles, can't we talk straight?"

"I am not talking, I am thinking aloud. You help me, coming here and asking me about the past – God it's so funny!" A shadow fell on her face. She looked very old now. She sighed, sat up then. She straightened her face – like the moon, it seemed to appear from behind thick clouds. Whenever I looked at Lindi I thought of an energetic child on crutches, with both legs stiff in plaster of paris. She sat up, and with the greatest gentleness in the world, she wiped her eyes, her face, yawned, and watched me. She sighed like a puffadder. She threw her head back, not, this time, like the Hollywood stars are told to; it was, this time, Lindi Maboso, the girl from where the thunder touches trees, and lightning looks one straight in the eye at night, in the open veld. She threw back her head, she was tired, very tired, it was three in the morning, we had been there a long time now – too many coffees, the stomach rumbling and rumbling.

"Do you know what a man is?" she asked, and there was this great silence, the silence of cemeteries. "I have watched Skopendonner walk, run, leap, look, piss; I have watched him do everything, and I have wondered, forever wondered, what the hell I allowed him to come into my life for. The swine! Now look what he has done. For weeks, for years, he stayed home, taking me to the bus stop, fetching me from rehearsals, making fire, cooking, understanding, sleeping, from early evening reading his bullshit comics, listening to Dollar Brand, to me, me! To me – saying nothing, just listening, and when I came to bed, with cold feet and cold buttocks, and, like a tick, clung to him, he would be still, listen, say nothing – why couldn't he scream, just scream once and say, bitch, you're making me cold! How come he was so silent? Only that stare, sometimes cold like a dead person's, sometimes hot as if the sun had fallen to earth – you know, that dog! that swine! And then I asked him, is there anything wrong? Is there anything wrong? Is there anything wrong? No. That is all he would say. Now I go to see him in prison, the only thing I hear, eventually, when I am alone here thinking about him, is: Okay, I must go. He walks away, behind those doors, along that terribly shining floor, into that dark corridor, filled with these unintelligible noises – the swine! That man shot a white woman, he killed her, he stole, he robbed a bank. Yet, he is still so silent in prison. He is still feeling cheated. You know, I want that man, I want him to be mine. I don't want him behind those bars, and walls, and corridors. I want him to come here, and stare at me, and give me that silence of his. He is okay for me like that, but why did he do it? Christ, I know; but I also know many other things. I don't want him robbing banks, and killing people. I don't want him staying away so long, do you know what I mean? I am not scared at all of these white bastards. They can never touch me. I know they can't touch me. I know they can't touch me. They won't starve me. There is nothing they can do to me. I kept telling them this. I told him, if only he had an ear, he would trust, doesn't he know? I know him, he knows me, but he won't trust, he can't trust. I told him, let the whites go to shit forever, until they shit their intestines and their stomachs and their lungs, and their hearts, but we should not allow them to hurt us. I told him so many times, but he holds grudges. That is why he keeps so silent, and stares and cooks, and makes fire. It is a way of saying please be quiet, and now what did that help? I am quiet, he is quiet behind bars! A man is a funny beast! Just because I am a woman, he can't trust that I will feed him. I will look after him. He must stay home, read his comics, listen to Dollar Brand, drink his gin. He had such interest in my singing, he would criticise me, "We don't sing like that. Why do you put on an American accent in that song? Don't forget you are an African. Why do you believe that you are a superstar? We don't have things like that here. Now here at home, you are a good singer, believe me you are, and if you are yourself, you will be a much better singer."

"I tried, I tried, I tried to be a good singer, to be myself – I succeeded. I don't care who says what. I am a good singer. I am an African. I know it because I fought, I looked, I watched, I listened, very sincerely to Africa, to me, to him, I listened. He helped me. I love him, but why could he not trust me? I trusted him!" She looked at me as she spread herself on the sofa. I looked at my watch. Outside, the dogs were barking. Hundreds of dogs barking.

24

Dogs, as many as the stars; in the dust; in the dark in the streets, stared at by dark, blank, blind windows; in the thick darkness which was spotted like a leopard with hundreds of the white houses which have made Soweto so famous, so notorious; dogs – if, instead of barking they talked, what would we hear? They were barking the hell out of the darkness, whatever they were seeing. This being Soweto, for a moment the barking preoccupied our minds. I could see in Lindi's eyes, in her face, she was still. Listening carefully, then, with a sigh, and somehow, with a slight shake of her body, she came back to the room, to the flickering candle, the heat from the paraffin heater, the sofas, which had created this comfort. The sofas, the mat, the heater, the coffee, the now echoing hoarse voice, the tired face, the missing Skopendonner ... and the unknown. My lungs and throat were aching from smoking. "I must also be very honest," Lindi said, and laughed her laughter of ghosts, looking to the ceiling: "I love that swine," she said at last!

I sat there, feeling, I kept feeling, that after all this, after all that had been said, as she spoke, something was still missing. It felt like Lindi could change her mind, decide that she was no longer going to be nice. Hell would break loose. She would fight with her teeth, her red nails, her fingers, her legs, with all her might. Now that she was seated, sighing, her eyes rolling like that, shining, her voice strong, fighting to say what was in her heart, we were safe.

"It hurts to love someone," Lindi said, breaking the silence. She looked a mess now. It was as if she was like jelly, about to spill out of herself. The past years came rushing, mad, like angry water, and burst through her face. What is to be done? The dogs barked and barked and barked and barked. In the darkness of my closed eyes, my heart broke, my head rang and rang. What do I want with Lindi? Why don't I take my broken heart away, home, and forget her? This story is not about me. I will not go home. I must, I have to finish it. I must stay here with Lindi. And then?

Lindi had been to her rehearsals many times. I had rehearsed this story many times. Then, I met her again, in a park, Joubert Park, and we sat on a bench; already they had erased the "Europeans Only" sign on it. It was strange sitting on it. The bench was red. It had feet like those of an elephant, though it

25

spread them as if it were a male dog making a pee. Lindi and I sat on this bench. This is what we were given after June 16th 1976. And Lindi was looking at the trees, listening to the birds, watching the people, black, white, go by. I knew this is what she was doing because she was silent. Her eyes and head going this way and that, as she followed the movement of the people. She and I sat there for days. She had been to see Skopendonner. She had had many performances.

"I have sung many, many songs. I want to sing three songs now. One to a man, one to a child, and one to a woman," she said. "That is frightening because it takes a long, long time to make a song. Even one, it takes a long time to write it, to sing it, and then to take it where it belongs. It takes a long time. I am going to be a miser with instruments: a piano, bass, trumpet, drums, maybe a trombone – and me," she said. "I wish I could, I hope I have the strength. Miser!" she said, and laughed her laughter, "I use very fancy words since I have been with you, you talking and talking – by the way, where is your girlfriend?"

"She is in Tembisa."

"When did you last see her?"

"Two days ago."

"Look, I am a woman," she said. "I know what it is to be without my man, you must not do that, unless it is necessary." As she said this, I thought of my mother. She sounded like her. Telling me, don't slam my door! The way she used to say it, I knew I would never slam anyone's door in my life.

"Why are men like this?"

"Like what?"

"I am serious you know. I want to know, why are men like this? Whenever I saw Skopendonner walk, naked, in the house, from room to room, looking for his comics and playing with the record player, I thought, look, a child!" Lindi said as she laughed aloud. People looked at us. She was sitting, her legs apart, her back hunched, like an old lady, her wig ruffled. The sun was nice and hot. And the sound of roaring cars in the distance did not touch the silence here.

"Why did you put the wig on today?" I asked.

"I feel a little witchy today, I must say, I must confess."

"To quote you, it's old habits."

"That is nasty you know," she said, not looking at me. "Did you know Koos? Koos, the guitarist?" she continued, still not looking at me, "They say they can't cure his VD."

"Koos has VD?"

"Yes."

"They can't cure it?"

"Yes," she did not look at me. "He went to the hospital too late, he had been going to the witch doctors for a long time."

"Where is he now?"

"In the mad house." We spoke about many things. Eventually, I picked up my jacket and we parted. I did not look at Lindi walk away – I knew what she looked like. I walked on to the bus rank. I think she was going for rehearsals. Today, I am not going. There is no way I can go there. I must go back home. There were many people now. They spilled out of sliding, opening doors, gaping doors into the streets, into the traffic and the lights; they came and came and came, filled the streets, black faces, many black faces, women, men, footsteps, noise, cars, the roaring below. There is something funny about so many people. When they walk, it is as if they don't know where they are going. It is as if they are going to walk endlessly. Their noise, their manner says so. It is not until you look them in the face, in the eye, that you know, they come, they vanish, they are not alone, they are many – faces, eyes, noses, mouths. They have age. Their faces say it. Their hands, their clothes, their shoes – all this says who these people are. They are many, so many that if you were to light a match, they would ignite and no-one, no-one would be able to extinguish the flames. But no, their faces and eyes, even their clothes say it does not happen like that. It did not happen like that when the buses, the bottle stores, the offices, the houses, everything started burning in Soweto – it takes time! What is time? Time is not a box of matches. It is not a thousand litres of petrol in SASOL. Time is seconds, minutes, hours, days, weeks, years, generations upon generations. It is life.

FOUR

[handwritten margin notes: casspirs, hippos + trucks / repetition / silence - repetition / graves repetition / song repetition]

His voice joined the silence. The silence was as large as the world and the sky. The sky was blue, bright, leaving nothing in the dark. Everything was exposed. The sun, and its light, was bright, and its heat harsh. His voice seemed to join, to become part of, to be one with and to be all these. The silence persisted. A cough now and then. A sneeze. But the silence was as silent as the many staring and blinking eyes, with their dark pupils and their staring whites. The cars had ceased to purr. The buses and the trucks were silent now. Everything was still, dead still, even the leaves of the hundred and one trees which hovered above us looking on, looking on in a very familiar stare, looking upon us, the heaps of soil, the many six-foot-deep holes. And I started to count the coffins – twenty. Twenty young men and women and children, twenty, thirty, forty ...

There were many fresh graves to my left, where the children are buried, and I counted the coffins in that section: six. Six white coffins. Someone had decided that children take too much space. They decided that they should be buried in a mass grave. There were many of these mass graves. I wondered how many coffins each mass grave takes. Many of these graves still had fresh flowers on them, and toys which looked brand-new. The graves stretched the length and spread the breadth of the children's section.

A woman's voice took a song. I looked at us all. There were hundreds of us. There were here, many, many townships come together to bury the young. We were under siege. There were many, many casspirs and hippos and trucks filled with soldiers, who, besides looking bored like the trees, were, like them, looking on at us. Does this happen anywhere else in the world? If it does, what does it mean? If not, what does it mean? The song ended. His voice picked up the silence again. Someone began to cry. The noiseless heads turned to look in the direction of the sad weeping, and looked back at the holes in the ground. She was weeping now. Another joined. She kept quiet, he kept his peace. Bible in hand, clutched to his bosom in his left hand, he was silent now.

The body of the crowd moved a bit. And the soldiers and the police seemed a bit interested. The many coffins were dead still. I do not know what it is that happened. He began to speak again. The silence came back. It was joined by his voice and the weeping. I felt tears come to my eyes. I heard someone next to me give a loud sigh. We had all been there before. We had all done more or less this same thing. We had become a crowd which attends mass funerals. Throughout many past years, we had done this. Something was very familiar.

Another song. He stopped his sermon. *pastor Makone*

A senior soldier got off the trucks. Mokone went to meet him. The song was rising, becoming a storm. There were murmurs, and I became fearful. The soldier, with his cap under his armpit and his stick hitting the side of his trouser-leg, slowly, deliberately walked the distance between us and them. The song rose and rose. They met. Mokone looked back at us. I could see that he was straining, straining to hear, the soldier was talking to him. But the soldier did not seem to listen when he tried to speak. Mokone turned to face us. He lifted his hand. The song subsided. He *Child* walked back to us. He began to speak again. *Funeral*

"Friends," he said, "we meet once more after we have buried *speech* some of our best children, little boys and girls whose hearts were big and loving and kind, children who loved life, but could not live it; who loved their people, but were not allowed to learn from and teach them and grow among them; children who loved their country, and wanted it to be among the countries in the world which would fight for, sacrifice and contribute to peace among peoples and countries. They were not allowed to do this in life, but they will contribute to this in their death." He paused, looked around, he shifted, seemingly seeking to be comfortable in the way he stood, facing us – men and women, boys and girls whose silence like death created an uneasiness in the open sky. He looked at us,

29

wiping his forehead slowly, wiping his eyes and mouth, "We have come to bury our warriors, let them rest in peace for they fought and died for peace. We know that they have given us strength, for when they died, they were aware of death. They had seen it rage and wipe some of them from our streets. They faced it with absolute contempt, they hurled their lives so we can be free men and women. We must not, we must never forget them. They have given us strength, for we today, standing here, have learnt to be contemptuous of death. It is this contempt for death, and our strong belief that we are fighting a just cause which will ensure our eventual victory. If we cannot live as free men and women," he stared at the blank and blind face of the crowd, his eyes rolling, his face stern as he shifted, bending towards his listeners, "we will not live to be anyone's slave."

"Friends," he said, "their funeral has resulted in other deaths. Deaths, once more of young boys and girls. If this country can, without a blink, without a second thought, wipe children from the face of the earth with such ruthlessness and brutality and no regret, then, friends, all of us are in danger. We are in danger of being erased – but why?" he coughed, "we reject white domination, we reject being exploited by a few people while millions of us live in poverty, are illiterate, are hordes of cheap labour, are penned in dirty unliveable townships, and eventually die like dogs. We reject this state of affairs, and not only this, we will, as the young have, as we have throughout our history, we will fight with everything we have, to the last one of us, to wipe out white domination and to create a non-racial, free society. Those we bury, those who died after we buried others, did not do so for nothing. Once more, we await another mass burial of boys and girls, heroes of our struggle. We are going to bury them, and no-one will stop us. We will bury them as the soldiers they were, soldiers of the people. This, my friends, is not happening here in Tembisa only. It is happening throughout the length and breadth of our country. Young men and women die like flies before a frightened and ruthless lot who are armed and paid by Reagan and Thatcher and the western countries. When we say to them, take your monies out of here, stop giving these madmen guns, and stop making available to them modern equipment and know-how, they and their kind tell

30

us we do not know what we are talking about, for if they took the guns, the money, the know-how from the boers, we blacks would suffer. What suffering do we not know?" His hands gestured above our heads, over the coffins. "Friends, we here, with our Movement will liberate ourselves, no matter what double-talk Thatcher and Reagan and their like have mastered! What we know is that at this hour, as we are standing here, the streets of our townships are soaked with our blood. What for? You and I have to keep asking this question, and we must answer it. We are the gods and this is our time, we must make this world a better place to live in," he said.

"Friends, there are many of us who are in jails. Many of us are inside very cold walls, behind thick steel bars and doors in the hands of extremely cruel men, being tortured. This we know. But we will not endeavour to prove this to a disbelieving world. We know, for as I look around here now, I see many faces which have been face to face with Botha's police – and we know what takes place when we are in their hands!

"Friends, I have been on Robben Island. I know Mandela, Sisulu, Mbeki, and many others on the Island who have been in Botha's jails. I have been in the hands of Botha's people, as some of you have been in their hands. It is this knowledge which must inspire us to be tireless, to fight and fight and fight the system of white domination, knowing that we have been through a period when Looksmart, Timol, Biko and many, many others have been in the hands of these men. People like Mdluli, who, less than twenty-four hours after being in the hands of these men, were dead. Timol died, Looksmart died. Biko died in the hands of these men. Why are we being detained? Why are we being tortured? Why are our homes, our townships endlessly occupied by the apartheid army? Why is the army so brutal, so ruthless in killing our people?"

"There is a war here, my friends. Our land is at war. For what? Who is at war? What are we fighting for?" He seemed to be at a loss for words. He seemed to search for the answers to his questions on the ground, on the earth that we were standing on. His eyes lowered, seeming to be attracted by the many heaps of graves, the empty six-foot holes; he lifted his eyes, faced us, and began to talk again. "We want to make this country liveable and lovable. We want to make this country one that can be counted among those who fight for and contribute to peace and progress in the world. This we say now, and say it forever; we say it now while we are fighting and dying so that it becomes part of us. We have to say it forever so that no one among us will say he or she did not know that we believe that our country is not only beautiful and wealthy, but also brave and strong and can be a bastion of peace. My friends, we must never forget, that Kotane, Dadoo, J.B. Marks and many, many of our countrymen died far away from their homes and country because they believed that South Africans, black and white, are capable of building a powerful, free country." He shifted, and once more, moved back. "I know, as we come out of these bloody days, after burying so many young people, we are hurt. Our hearts are bleeding, but our minds are hard at work, trying to grapple with, to understand these our times. Our times, my friends, demand of us that we become courageous fighters, brave warriors who must smash oppression and exploitation, so that we may become liberators and builders of a great nation."

There was a movement among the soldiers and then, familiar sounds. Among us, a great silence fell. We hardly looked at each other. For a while there was stillness. Nothing moved. We heard the sounds from the soldiers. They were jumping off their trucks. Whatever they were carrying was rattling. Like us, the twenty or so coffins wrapped in ANC flags that now and then brought a glint into our eyes, were dead still.

I could hear the footsteps approaching. One among us, Mokone, moved. "Let us lower the coffins!" he said. A few young men and then many more, moved towards the coffins. Sounds of sods as the coffins were lowered.

"I will allow no more singing, no more speeches, and I want all, everyone to move from the graveside to your transportation," a megaphone voice said behind us. "Only those who are lowering the coffins and those who will cover them must remain. Reverend Mokone, you too, get into your car, I give all of you five minutes to do this."

Mokone signalled, and, like one body, we moved. Dust whirled into the sky, covering us, covering the sunlight. For the first time

32

I came face to face with soldiers. They spread out around us. Their rifles were at the ready. They stared at us. The megaphone man stood, watching. Something told me, these are very dangerous men. We vanished into the buses, trucks and cars that had brought us here. About fifty or so of us remained at the graveside. All the coffins were now in their holes.

"I want all drivers of vehicles to start their vehicles, and form a single file," the megaphone man said. Dust. Sounds of roaring vehicles, footsteps, took over the silence of the graveyard. There were army vehicles in front, behind and next to us as we moved away from the graveyard. Other army vehicles seemed to encircle those who remained to bury the dead.

Some distance from the graveyard the convoy was stopped. We were ordered at different places to get out and walk to our homes. It felt strange. We were used to going back to the place where we started the funeral procession. Now we were not allowed to go back there. Usually we would wash our hands. We would exchange condolences with the bereaved. We would eat together. We would sing. We would bid each other farewell. Now we were denied all this.

I felt anger. I walked down a street of Tembisa I had never seen before. I was among people I did not know; all of us had been told to get out of the bus and walk 'home'. The procession was broken. Buses and trucks took off in different directions, ordered by the soldiers who boarded them in groups of five.

Tembisa came out to watch. Men, women, children, came out of their houses, left their Sunday behind, stood at gates, peered through windows as, keeping their distance, they watched. Something no longer seemed to hold. I wanted to cry. I saw a man crying. I saw a woman crying. I held my tears. I walked on. I sensed that my back was broad, big, uncovered, vulnerable – a 'target', to use the language of the young. I walked on, now alone. I did not know where the others had gone. I was looking around, trying to find out where I was. I stopped at a yard.

"Good afternoon," I said.

The old lady looked at me, from my eyes down to my feet.

"Are you from the funeral?"

"Yes."

"Come in," she looked this way and that way quickly. As she did so, I thought, I am sure this is how an animal which senses danger looks, listens and moves. "Come in," she said again, moving backwards. Then she turned and went into her house. There, four men were seated at a table: empty glasses littered its surface. They looked at me, their eyes glued to me.

"I greet you," I said.

"Yes …" they said.

We looked at each other.

"Are you from the funeral?" one asked – perhaps he's the husband of the old lady, I thought.

"Yes."

"Who is going to bury the dead?"

For a while I did not know what he was asking me. I looked around the room.

"Did the soldiers ask all of you to leave the graveyard?" another asked, helping me out.

"No, a few remained," I said. I sensed – I do not know how – I sensed the hurt in the silence that followed. I wanted to ask them how they knew what had happened at the graveyard. But something told me it did not matter.

A radio blared music. Yvonne Chaka Chaka. Her lyrics were meaningless. But something, Yvonne's melody, the rhythm she created, merged with the two quiet voices in the room. Not only in the room, but also in the yard, throughout Tembisa. In a funny way even her voice, Yvonne's voice, blended with this moment.

I was thinking about Mokone. His stern face. His large frame. His slow manner of talking. His thick spectacles. His startled face as words came out of him, as if from his stomach. His flowing cassock; the Bible he seemed never to refer to, but held onto with his life, close to his bosom as if it were a crutch of sorts. How many young men and women had this man buried? The way he walked to meet the senior soldier – he walked as though he was going to ask the soldier what his business was on his property, the graveyard.

"What is your name, my son?" the old man asked me.

"Moses Motsamayi," I said.

"Motsamayi?"

"Yes."

"From where?"

"Kgatlamping."

"You are far from where you live. It is going to be very bad, very dangerous to walk, there will be no transport. It's going to be very dangerous," he said with finality.

"Yes, Tembisa is hurt," another said.

"Ma-boy," the old man said, "Moses would like some tea."

"I'm sure, can you give him some?"

"If you say so," Rra-boy said, standing up.

"How can you say he will use tea while you are seated there?"

Rra-boy

"No, no, I'm not fighting, I was asking."

"You are taking chances," she said.

"Ma-boy," he walked to the cupboard, brought out a cup and saucer, sugar, milk, "are you sure you should go to your woman's meeting?"

"Why not!"

"There is going to be trouble in Tembisa," he put the tray with the cups on the table.

For the first time I looked around the house. The blue, bare walls. The pink curtains. The burglar-barred windows, painted red and white. It's strange, poverty has a smell; the wooden rafters, and asbestos ceiling, the unbearable heat from the stove and steam of the cooking pots – something made poverty tangible. Even the clothes of the people, their hands which looked like steel or rough rock.

On a Sunday afternoon in Tembisa, in this house, with these old men, and Yvonne singing, "I'm burning out, my heart is on fire, I'm burning out …" what was I to do? I was, for some reason, overwhelmed. I must go home. I started to sip my tea. They produced their brandy bottle from underneath the table; Rra-boy poured first brandy into the glasses, and then water.

35

5

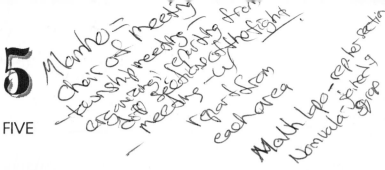

"I declare this meeting open, I will ask that each one of us give a report-back – if we have one – from our areas, so we know what is happening. After that I would like us to get straight into business, so that we can go back to work. MaNhlapo, can you lead us?"

"Yes, yes, first, I thank you Chair, and also, I thank all the representatives who are here. I represent the women of my section, Moeding. As you know, there, we have just buried eight children. All of the parents of these children have been met and discussions held with them. The mothers of the eight have now formally joined our women's section – we still have to decide what work they will do after they have made their recommendations. One of them, Nomvula, will be working with some youth and students who will be dealing with that difficult area of discussing with those who may be tempted to take an anti-people position. Already she has been to several of these meetings, and from reports, she is very strong, sympathetic and firm in her convictions. With most of the others we will have to wait and see. That is all."

"How strong is your women's section?" he asked.

"We have now about 300 women; I would say out of these, twenty are active."

"Do you have any standing projects you are working on?"

"Yes, and here I wish to get the advice of this meeting. Presently, we are discussing fund-raising. Nomvula reports that she wants to discuss fund-raising with Lindi, the singer, to find out if she is prepared to do a benefit concert for women so they can start the vegetable, sewing, and child-care centre, but we do not have experience in organising a thing of that nature; we shall need help from the youth."

36

"Lindi, the singer from Alexandra?" Cynthia asked.

"Yes, that one," MaNhlapo replied.

"I see," Cynthia said, and for a while she was quiet; everyone was looking at her, but she looked away.

"Do you have anything to say about this?" Mlambo asked.

"But Lindi is such a drunk!" Cynthia said.

"Are you saying she can't sing?" MaNhlapo asked.

"She used to be a good singer," Cynthia said.

"Does she still sing?" Mlambo asked.

"I don't think so, I have not heard her sing for many, many years," Cynthia said.

"No, but I saw a report in the paper that she has formed a new band," Lungi said, "and on the basis of that Nomvula thinks of approaching her."

"Well, there you are," Mlambo said, "if she has just formed a band, she must be approached – encourage Nomvula to keep close to her, remember everything we have must be used to bring the struggle forward. Let's give each and everyone something to do, something they can contribute," he said.

"No," Cynthia said, "that is not what I'm against, but I'm just thinking, you know, Lindi is such a drunkard, Lindi is the lowest type of musician, and I am not saying this to degrade her, I'm talking about tactics here; there are other musicians who are known, who have influence over a broad section of our people, who, if they come to this fund-raising event will pull lots of people along, people we may never have had the chance to talk to, and at the same time, we will be pulling in crowds for the fund-raising for the important projects which MaNhlapo is talking about."

"How does her being a drunk prevent her from pulling people to the show?" Steve asked.

"I'm trying to say she is not known, she has spent too much time, years at Bitch-Never-Phela …" everyone laughed.

"Where is that?"

"Bitch-Never-Phela is one of the shebeens where concoctions are sold at Lady's," Steve said.

"Yes, I'm saying she is no longer known," Cynthia said.

"She no longer sings, you mean?" Mlambo asked.

"But she has a new band," Steve said.

Aug. 9 - Soweto fundraiser.

"No, Cynthia has a point, what she is saying is, if we are thinking of pulling lots of people to the show, whom we wish to reach, through whom we want to raise funds, Lindi may not be the right person. That is what you are saying, not so?" Mlambo asked.

"Yes, that's what I'm saying."

"Do you have any other suggestions then?" Mlambo asked.

"Not right away, but I can talk to some people who can make suggestions."

"Okay, is that acceptable to everyone?" Mlambo asked.

"Let Cynthia ask other people, but let's not drop Lindi," Lungi said, "Soweto is organising on August 9th – let's invite Lindi there, to sing, even if we have to pay her for a start."

"Pay her!" Cynthia objected.

"Ja, let's do it; you know Lindi is one of our old, old musicians, it isn't her fault that she ended up at Lady's, it is our duty to help her up, to become part of us, let's do it."

"We will have to pay every musician we want to mobilise if we pay Lindi," Cynthia interjected, "we can't afford it, nor is it correct to do so. Why are you suggesting that we should pay her?"

"Well, maybe 'pay' is the wrong word, we must sponsor her, pay for her costs and talk to her."

"Let's not talk paying now, let's go to Lindi and put to her what Lungi has suggested, let's involve her in the discussions, problems and work of our struggle – we will see from there how she takes it, and what we can do," Mlambo suggested, "is that okay?"

"No problem," Steve said.

"I don't think we should talk about paying," Cynthia repeated.

"I agree, let's involve her," Mlambo said. There was a short silence and everyone looked at Cynthia. She looked back at Mlambo as if to say, you have passed a ruling – what do you expect me to say?

"That is all from my side," MaNhlapo said, "I take it I have to inform Nomvula to see Lindi, suggest to her to perform on the 9th of August at Soweto, and in the meantime, Steve and Cynthia will come to see the women about organising for the fund-raising show?"

"That's right. Are there any other reports?" Mlambo asked.

"Yes, as you all know I am from the youth, Cynthia and I have a problem, too many of our people are sought by the police. We no longer stay at our homes, we have nowhere to stay. At the moment, there are about twenty young people who sleep in pipes, broken cars, in trees, and in the veld; morale is low, some are talking about leaving the country, some about going to other townships and rural areas – if we do not intervene, we will be in trouble. Some are injured, two girls are pregnant and there is one who is ill and we don't know what the problem is . . ."

"She had an abortion," Cynthia said.

"Oh! I did not know that," Steve said.

"I found out yesterday, I forgot to tell you, we had to find a place for her at Kgatehaping section, where she is with a certain old lady. There is a nurse looking after her, who thinks she can find a sympathetic doctor to examine her."

"Are you through, Steve?" Mlambo asked.

"No, the other thing is that people feel very strongly that Lucas must be workshopped, we are almost unable to hold back some people ..."

"What do you mean 'workshopped'?" Mlambo asked. Steve, Lungi, Strike, Linda – the young people in the meeting – laughed. They were looking at each other, giggling.

"What does 'workshop' mean?" Mlambo asked again.

"Steve," Strike, who up to now had been quiet, said, "tell the old man," and he burst into laughter.

"It means they want to burn him," Steve said.

"We must burn Lucas," Strike said, "he gives the police and the soldiers tea in the morning. He calls us dogs, he says we are little boys and girls who have become lawless, so says Botha and that is why we are being shot and killed. Lucas must be 'workshopped'," he said.

"I have been saying to everyone that there is no-one who says Lucas should not be 'workshopped' – but when? – that is most important," Lungi said.

"Now," Mlambo shifted from the bed, leaning forward, arms stretched out, "you see ..."

All the young people burst into laughter once more.

"No, no, listen," Mlambo said, "we are going to talk to Lucas, if he becomes one of us we will be stronger, we must talk to him,

39

we have plans to do so, so let this 'workshop' business stop …"

"If he does not become one of us?" Strike asked.

"Look, we don't know for certain what he will say or do, so let's give him a chance to say it."

"But why?" Strike asked.

"Strike, we are fighting a just cause, because our grievances are legitimate; we would like as many people as possible to join the fight, so we can isolate and destroy the enemy. We lose nothing by putting in extra effort to win more people to our side — in fact, by doing so we ensure the shortest possible way to destroy the enemy, we ensure a long-lasting victory, let's give Lucas a chance. If he refuses, that is his problem, but let's do our duty," Mlambo said.

There was a finality in the way he said it.

"Lucas has been given too many chances, why do we want to expose people further to him, so he can tell his bosses who come to see him who said what?" Strike insisted.

"Strike, you are giving Lucas a prominence he does not deserve, you and I must agree to give him a chance. It is not as if, by 'workshopping' Lucas today, our problems will be solved tomorrow. We need to concentrate on the other point of Steve's report, can we do that?" Mlambo spoke softly and calmly yet firmly.

"Strike, leave it, my brother, I will talk for you …" Lungi suggested.

"No, talk here," Cynthia said.

"I am saying so because I think we will need lots of time to talk on this," Lungi said, "you can be part of that if you want, Cynthia."

"Why can't we talk now?" Cynthia asked.

"Because, as the Chair said, we must not give Lucas prominence he does not deserve, there are more pressing issues, like the twenty comrades, the injured, and those who have nowhere to sleep. If we solve that, we are sure to continue struggling in an organised manner," Steve said.

"Now let's get into that," Mlambo said, "you say there are people who are talking about leaving?"

"Yes," Steve said.

"How many?"

"About ten."

"Where are they going if they leave?"

"To join the Movement."

"Where?"

There was silence. Steve tapped his fingers, he was uneasy.

"They will reach it through one of the front-line states," Steve said.

"What do they want to do when they reach the Movement?" MaNhlapo asked.

"They want to join MK," Strike said.

"Well, okay, what I want to know is, do they think there is no other way to struggle but to leave?" Mlambo asked.

"They say they do not see how they will go on working if the police are looking for them," Strike said.

"Ja, but if they join MK they will be expected to work, and the police will still be looking for them," Mlambo said, "not so?"

Steve nodded.

"Anyway, I understand what you are saying. MaNhlapo I suggest we leave this matter and deal with it another time, what do you think?"

"Cynthia, okay?" MaNhlapo asked.

"Let's go to those who have nowhere to stay," Mlambo said, "I agree, let them look elsewhere for places, other townships. In town and even rural areas," he said. "Mandela set us an example, he lived underground, we also must if we can, but underground is not to hide forever and not work, it is a very difficult life, we shall help with that, not so, MaNhlapo?"

"Yes, I hear it is a very difficult life," MaNhlapo said, "we shall help with that."

"Now, the injured – at least it seems the one with the abortion is being handled ... Cynthia, what is her name?" Mlambo asked.

"Lerato," Cynthia said.

"Do I know her?"

"I don't know if you know her, you may have met her."

"Lerato – is she not the one whose sister was buried recently?"

"Yes."

"I see, I see, you must remind me to tell the women about her."

41

"Okay. Lungi, do you have anything to report?"

"Yes, not much though, we have been able to persuade some of the professional men and women to organise themselves, we will be meeting on the coming Sunday."

"Who are you with?"

"With James, Calvin and Bongi," Lungi said.

"That is a very important contingent of our people. They are our experts, we need them, they will also lead us to others, so do all you can to make that meeting a success. I am sure it is in capable hands," said Mlambo.

"How many do you expect at the meeting?" MaNhlapo asked.

"Six to ten," Lungi said.

"A good start," MaNhlapo said.

Too many hours had gone by. It was only now, at the end, that each became aware of where they were. A two-roomed mud house, filthy, with papers spread all over the floor, an unmade bed, the smell of socks, and a pin-up girl on the wall. The breeze and sunlight freshened the room as the group emerged from it, into the street.

Lungi — proffessional
quarto report.

SIX

I saw the long, colourful buses at the bus terminus which, at this hour of the day, are like a bush, in the midst of an attack by a storm. Everything was rattling. The orange, purple, red, blue, green colours of the kombis received the light, the red, yellow, blue light of the setting sun. The reflections bounced against the blue sky, the mauve sky, against black flesh and the hundreds of colours of doeks, berets, hats, shirts, skirts, trousers, dresses, shoes, and with the moving of heads, shoulders, hips, buttocks, feet, arms their buzz and buzz in a blaze which merged with their groaning. The rattling of the train below, and the thousands of pairs of eyes and mouths, and footsteps and screeching tyres and hoots, and the kombis with loads and loads of people, pulling out of the terminus, was a dazzling moment.

I was at the tail of a long queue, but it did not take long before I was part of its body. It would be a while before I'd be swallowed by the mouth of the kombis. The queue was slow. It did not move. It wove together footsteps, clothes, murmurs: soon the sun would go down, and the queue would be shorter, and silence would fall. Soon.

My kombi came. I sat down – just managed – and the kombi moved. Already, the neon lights, in their hundreds of colours, were singing. The street lights would soon light up. Everybody was talking in the kombi. The kombi was talking also. It turned and jerked, and stopped and moved, making different sounds. Along the streets, a few whites, and many blacks, criss-crossed. There were hundreds of cars, many of them carrying white people. They sat alone. They sat in couples. They looked neat, as if they were packaged in boxes. They almost all did the same things: reading a newspaper; sitting in the same car, yet looking as if they were not aware of each other; the cars moved. Stopped. Moved.

43

They turned. They came. They went. We left the city behind. Soon, the smoke would loom in the sky, from the many chimneys of Tembisa.

Today Lindi said she did not want to talk. She said that she was tired. She wanted to talk in the only way she thinks is left for people like her to talk. I am always suspicious when she says things that way. I know that this is when she feels she has the right to look for her hole, so that she can hide. The result was we walked, from our café, quiet. She did not care. She just walked. She crossed the streets. She beat the lights. And she swung her arms just like the other day, when she told me she was not scared of what white people could do to her. She wove through cars. I was content to follow her, though I took care of myself. We entered the room. There was a piano in the corner, battered chairs were scattered all over. A closed saxophone case and a closed trumpet case. Lindi and I were the only two in the room.

"Where is Esther?" Lindi asked. She was standing against the piano. She moved a little, to make herself more comfortable. She spread her legs and threw all her weight onto her arms which anchored her on the closed piano-top. She was looking at me, really glaring at me.

"I don't know," I said. Today, she has decided not to call Esther my girl friend. I have always wondered why she prefers to work in this state; she had on an old brown cotton dress which barely reached below her knees, showing all the scars on her legs – a dress that left her almost naked from the waist upwards; torn shoes, and bare-headed, with unkempt sparse hair. She looked tired. She was also very watchful.

"Tell Esther that I will come to see her on Sunday. She must not cook. I will cook. Tell her her elder sister is coming," Lindi said, and looked away from me. John came in.

"Heit!" he said with his soft, shy voice.

"Hoozet?"

"Lovely," he said, looking somewhere below my forehead, avoiding my eyes, as he sat on one of the broken chairs, like an old man. Silence fell.

"I keep missing Koos," Lindi said, "whoever it is, was a very cruel bitch to do that to him," she moved away from the piano,

44

looking like a strolling cat. "But I must not say this in front of Job," she said, looking out through the window.

Silence.

Somehow I believed her. I knew what she was trying to do. She was struggling to give up Koos. I knew though that Job would walk some distance with her, if he had the stomach. Job walked in, carrying his guitar and a beer can. He looked for a chair and sat down. He opened his guitar case. He kept sipping from his beer, the notes stalked us. Everybody arrived. Business started. It began strangely. It made me nervous. They eyed each other. They fingered, as if uncertain of their instruments. They stopped. They started. They stopped. They started. All this, just by looking at each other.

Now, the song, Lindi's, John's, Job's, is called 'Children'. The way it was being rehearsed, and as we stalked it, then, all of us were in great despair. The way it was being rehearsed left one feeling as if one were constipated. It was just not happening. And there was this smell in the rehearsal room. Bad socks? rotten rat? – I do not know what it was. No one seemed to care. So I held my peace too.

Lindi was singing:

Let the child be born and let it grow
With a heart and a mind
Ready like a mother's hand, to help the world grow
Then the mother and father of tomorrow shall live a
better life;

Does someone hear me
Can someone please say yes
Does someone hear me
Can someone please say yes

Let's make love and let's make children
With a heart and a mind
Nourished like a fruit tree, soon to bear red-hot peaches
Then the land and the sky tomorrow will ring with
laughter

45

I had heard those words, like the wheels of a train, rattle and rattle, on and on. The piano, sometimes like a mother, gentle, careful, soft and quiet, persuaded the song, the child, which had nothing but just bare words. The words were bare like the eggshell, so brittle. The words, now and then, carried the huge hoarse voice, spilled like jelly. Over and over, the trombone, like a whip, and sharp as a blade, and then blunt like a finger, and then blind like a door, kept embracing the words; and the trumpet, like the cry of a woman, hit the heart; the guitar, like the sea, seemed permanent and forever around the words – but there was something wrong. Lindi was sweating. John had become oblivious of everything but his fingers and the black and white before him and, I think, at a certain time, all of us waited and waited knowing that it would come; the voice: "stop!" and then she would turn away, to the window. It was a struggle – for what? She would turn back again, from the window.

"No, John, we are not crying here, we are trying to embrace the child, can't you see?" she would walk towards John, who would be staring blank, listening, trying to know. He knew, but was also trying to know how a child is embraced, through the whites and blacks of a piano. He looked with a blind man's blank face. She would get close to him, lean on his shoulder, support one arm on the piano, face him, almost to the point where their eyes would touch eyeball to eyeball and ask, "Sweetheart, we have cried, it's enough, this is our child you know. It is our child, we are aware that there is no love here, nothing. We have to make love out of rocks. You see, we have to make miracles, we have to, we have to let them go to the moon, we want to make miracles here, with our child, make love out of rocks, out of iron, out of steel and turn that into our child, you know what I mean, John?" John's face was blank.

He seemed to listen through the pores of his skin. When that happened, he seemed uncertain about everything. He looked lost.

"That piano is crying, and crying, it is wailing John, no that's not what we want ... how can I say this? I must say it, I must ... look," Lindi said, "here is Hector Peterson, he is about to go out into the street, to march, to demonstrate, you cannot stop him, there is no way that you can stop him, because you yourself have come to know that it is important that he go to the street to march. We, you, all of us know there is fire there. He must go through it. We cannot waste time by crying. We must know how to love him; can you make that out of the piano? Please, John, we must love Hector, hey, John, please man ..." Then there was a terrible silence in the torn room.

The tall windows, seeming to hover in the concrete, threw their gaze on the streets. Hundreds of people, their shadows and their reflections, bouncing from the windows, splashing and shattering on the concrete sidewalk. The elongated reflections of cars, with hundreds of colours, zooming in and out of the reflections of neon lights, with a thousand colours, everything gone mad. The siren of a traffic-cop screeching on the sky. The wheels of cars, the shoes, the voices, and the little white women, and then white men, walking blindly, straight, with force, like a locomotive. The little black men and little black women hurrying, flying out of the city, the gaping doors of cafés, and the crowd thickened into a solid block now, and the station opens, gaped, received us, we flooded, we flowed. Below the earth, the train. Trains, noise, shoes, laughter, voices, whistles, footsteps, cement, concrete, iron ... sweat, flesh to flesh, something smelling, rattling and rattling, iron on iron, to Soweto. Lindi is laughing. She is talking to someone, she turns to whisper something to John, to Job, to me ... someone greets her, she hugs him, she kissed a girl, young, pretty, smiling. Someone is laughing. Behind me there is an argument about a football match. On my right side, someone is talking about his employers, no, about white people, also about Cosatu. Someone else is talking about trains. The man in front of me is struggling to read a newspaper.

Like vomit, we get off at Phefeni. The train pulls out. It is as if it hardly stopped. Crowds have come out of it. We are in a hurry, we are flying, up the stairs, down, crowds, and crowds. In the streets: vendors, newspapers, oranges. A placard says Cosatu has called for a stayaway. The crowd vanishes. We are alone as we walk to the gate. Lindi unlocks the door, we enter. It is dark. The room smells of being empty. I search for the sofa. It is silent.

47

Light. Fire. Smell of food. Tea. We settle down now.

The way Lindi listens to music is like it is a big secret. We settled down. And then Lindi made me feel as if I was intruding. She was silent. She would not settle down. She sat down, went back to the kitchen, came back, then went to the bedroom, listened, quickly, biefly, to some tune from the radio, came back, put a cup of coffee before me, left. I knew I had to leave her alone.

The radio was too loud. She had made it so. She went out and came back with this big, fat, dirty old lady, who sighed herself into the sofa while Lindi was somewhere in the house, somewhere, I could only hear the sounds she made.

I do not know what happened yesterday. This morning, when Lindi and I came into town, it seemed we had nothing to talk about. She was very quiet. She had made a distance between us, answering questions in monosyllables, or shaking her head yes or no. Last night, I left her with the fat lady, and went to bed. I spent the night, almost all night, reading a strange book. From where I was lying, I could hear them talking. I don't know what about. I heard Lindi walk into her room and close her door when she went to bed. It must have been one in the morning.

She woke me up this morning. She was already dressed, in her loose dress and casual shoes and a hat; it looked like she was not going far, from the way she was dressed. She spoke quietly, hardly looked at me, and wore a sad face. The whole way, from her house to town, it felt like we were shadow-boxing. The city streets were empty. So were the trains as we were coming into the city. I said a lot of things to Lindi, which she ignored. Knowing that she can bubble with joy, this attitude I found totally intolerable. I tried to break it – eventually, it began to feel as if Lindi was faceless. I tried to search for her face. This made me feel as if I was running around, increasing my speed, running around her. She just walked on, turned, and walked until we climbed the stairs to the rehearsal room. We were received by a calm melody from the trumpet, trombone, saxophone, guitar and piano. Lindi stood a while at the door, waited, it seemed, quietly, to have the men finish their tune. She walked to John, sat next to him, and they talked, wrote something down; it took a while. Then she went to Job. She hugged him, sat very close to him, almost talking into his ear. She went out, and immediately came back, she kicked off her shoes, unbuttoned her dress, then took off her hat and threw it across the room onto a chair. She stood a while next to the window, did some breathing exercises, voice exercises, body exercises – and all the while the room was filled with different sounds from the horns. The guitar and the piano, and of course Lindi's voice, which was like hundreds of waves, climbing, breaking, gathering momentum, climbing, breaking – its sound was disturbing. It was a murmur that rose to become a muted scream, thunder, rolling, wailing thunder, then a murmur – on and on it went, and Lindi, sometimes dead still, at times walking around the room, her body at times like a frog, puffing up-down-up-down and to the sides, and then she would walk around the room, to the window, the door, stand next to John, to Job, her face close to their ears; and when she had held them, briefly, she would walk up and down next to the window, to the door. And then she sat down. She was sweating, breathing heavily. She sprawled on the chair, arms hanging, legs wide apart, her back sagging, and her head hanging. The guitar and the piano took up, in a conflict, a delicate conflict, racing, chasing, racing, chasing, moving together – Job was sitting awkwardly on a chair, his mouth open, his eyes protruding, watching John; Billy, on trombone, was a sound like death – a gasp, and the trumpet, in a thin melody, hung around the sound. The tune, or whatever it was, died down – the silence that fell was sweet indeed.

"I have a feeling that from 'Does someone hear me' to 'Can someone please say yes' – it overpowers all of us, is that not so?"

"Overpowers us?" John asked.

"Yes."

"How?"

"We give all we have to that, at least all we think we have."

"We are crying, is that what you want to say?"

"Yes, but we also give all we have to it."

"Like what?"

"Feeling it out."

"I see."

"What's this business about crying?" Job asked.

"Look, Job, any man's heart is full of all sorts of emotions,

49

happy, sad, we laugh, we cry, we are quiet – now which do you try to express through your guitar? What is the best memory you have of life, okay? And once you get what that is, find out which memory you associate most with music, right? Now, I am not asking for some emotion that you are an expert on – I don't trust that, I am asking you to realise that something has happened to children, what is it? Do you know? Do you?"

"You mean the school-children, and the kindergarten children, and the outcast children, and the dead children, and the unborn children?"

"That is tough."

"I don't disagree with you, but are we together?"

"I was not looking at it like that."

"I am asking you to."

"But how?"

"With your guitar – is it not the only thing you say you know? How can you know it if you can't play for the children? The children need you to play for them. They say you have played for everybody else – the bitches, men and women, the thugs of South Africa. You have played for all of them. You have also played for yourelf. But not for the children. They are asking you to play for them now."

"That is tall!"

"It is."

"Where do we start?"

"I ask you."

Without standing up, Lindi dragged the chair across the floor toward Job. She started to talk in a whisper.

"Okay, okay, why don't we start where we say, fuck everybody else that we have played for ... no, seriously, fuck them, let all of them, the rest, everyone we have played for so far fokoff, let them kak, from Botha down to everybody else ... let's start from there. But let's keep in mind that we are doing this because there are children we would like to play for ... remember Hector? If you dare say no, don't, I will ask every one of us here to throw you out of the window, I will also sing about how you forgot Hector everywhere that we played. I will say your name, address, everything. I shall have passed judgement on you, 'strue Job, I mean it ... you

50

*Hector = 1'st child
killed Jone 16 1976*

remember Hector?"

"The first boy to be killed on June 16th, 1976?"

"The first child, remember that, the first child," Lindi said, sighing.

Job put his guitar down.

"Lindi, look here, I came to play music here, what is all this you are saying? It has nothing to do with music!" He lit a cigarette.

"Who are you playing music for? You talk like these fucking politicians who don't know that they are fuckall without people. Their slogans and parties are fuckall without people."

"For myself Goddamit, Goddamit!"

"Not for yourself only, otherwise you would stay home and play and play and play – with you the only one listening – doesn't that seem ridiculous?"

Job walked toward Lindi, slowly, like a cat stalking a mouse.

"I have been playing music for years now, you hear? Don't you ever try to teach me how to play music, that is all!" Job said at the top of his voice, his face close to Lindi's.

"A musician learns music every day, from everybody, and you are no different, Job; here, today, we want to play music for children. We have come to realise that we don't know how to do it, so, we have to learn, stupid!"

"Lindi, don't say that, don't ever say that to me."

"Stupid, I say, and I repeat, musicians learn music every day."

Job stood dead still before Lindi. She was seated.

Now, I do not know what happened then. Job was on the ground. He was under Lindi. His legs flying in the air. He was screaming.

"I will take off my panty and pee in your mouth, stupid!" Lindi said, holding Job around the neck, and standing up.

"Lindi, Lindi, haai, wait man, what are you doing?" John said, walking towards her. He held Lindi, who was struggling – with her underwear, her thighs, her buttocks and everything showing. He pulled her aside. She staggered towards the door, against the wall.

"Don't ever try to throw your weight at me," Lindi said, "I mean it when I say musicians learn music every fucking day. I

51

mean it, I mean it! I know we have played music for the wrong people, for the wrong reasons, Goddamit yourself, Job! I will kill you with these bare hands if you keep going on the way you are, fuck, fucking your pride! What are you proud of? Who the fuck do you think you are?" Job stood up. He seemed lost. He walked toward the door. He turned back, put his guitar in the case and walked out the door. John sat on the piano stool.

"Fix your dress, Lindi, your panty is showing," he said, watching her.

"Thanks," Lindi said, as she loosened the dress from the panty elastic at the back, and sat down on the chair. "I still feel strongly about what I said." Someone laughed.

"You were saying children something," said Billy, who had sat composed while all the trouble raged. He had clutched his trombone to himself and kept shifting further away from the trouble. Something about Billy reminded one of a peacock.

"Look, Billy, I said that we have played music for money, for ourselves, for all the wrong reasons – can't we change?"

"The name of the song is 'Children'?"

"Yes, it is 'Children'."

"We are thinking about all children?"

"Yes."

"Black, white, coloured, Indian children?"

"Oh, I did not think about that – what do you think?"

"Well, watch it! I will soon pee in your mouth, too," Billy said, laughing.

"But that is serious, you know," Lindi said, "that is a serious point you are raising."

"Let's have in mind children in general, but black children specifically."

"But well, the world of the song is about children in general."

"Does that refer to black South African children only?"

"In a sense, it does."

"How?"

"I have a special feeling towards them."

"How do you express that?"

7

SEVEN

"We have just been with Mlambo, we have finally decided that Lucas must be boycotted," Steve said. "Lucas is stubborn, several people have been to him, they have talked to him, but he will not see reason. He says we must not forget what he is now, comes from nothing; he started as a 'soft-goods' hawker; walking the streets, he became a fruiterer; sold fruits and vegetables, sometimes sweets in buses and trains. He feels that all these poor people are lazy. If he could build himself from nothing, why can't they, that is his thinking, so what can we do, what can we still say to him?"

"He says poor people are lazy?" asked MaNhlapo.

"Yes," Steve said.

"I see," MaNhlapo said, as she looked away from Steve and Cynthia, "so the committee has decided that his shop must be boycotted?"

"Yes," Steve said.

"I see. Who went to see him?"

"Ma-Morula, Nomvula and Chakela; then I together with Lungi and Sarah."

"Did you discuss with him that our intention is not to destroy his business, that is the last thing we want to do, in fact, we want him to prosper. We are merely asking that he realise that he is what he is today because we buy from his shop, that we have declared war on the boers; that every single space here is a battle-ground, and that we need everyone to fight, in any way they think they can – did you tell him this?"

"He says he will not be intimidated by small boys and girls …"

"Did you tell him that it is not possible for anyone to sit on the fence?"

53

"We told him ... "

"Lucas must not be a fool ... poor people are poor because they are lazy? What does he meean by that, that there is no oppression, that there is no exploitation, that it is not true that in the past few days children, men and women have been dying because they have been demanding to have a better education so that they can work for themselves? That we have been dying because we say we are underpaid, we can't afford to buy food, pay rent, travel ... what does he mean?" She held the dress she was sewing high, measuring its hem with her eyes. She stood up, held it to her shoulders, sized it by looking down to her toes, "Well, Lucas has judged himself, we have tried all we can to make him see reason, the people who have been to see him are good people. They are not rash or flippant; besides, we have given him lots of time to see for himself, to think what role he can play, we do not believe that it is possible that he does not play any role. So be it then, but Steve, and you, Cynthia, you must listen to me carefully: first, why do we decide to boycott him and not petrol-bomb his shop? Why?"

"We would still like to persuade him," Cynthia said.

"Yes, we are a Movement of the people. We are asking him to disassociate himself from the boers. We hope he will learn, we do not think that he sides with the enemy, but we would like him to know that we mean it when we say we are going to determine our destiny, we want him to know that we have power and that we can use it if our interests are undermined. So, Cynthia, I want you to go to Mr Tholo, discuss what we have been discussing now with him, tell him that we need 5 000 leaflets, that they must be ready in two days' time, so that we can distribute them by Thursday morning. Steve, you must go to Mlambo, tell him I agree with the decision, and that I will pass the word to the women's committee. Both of you must come to see me tonight. I want us all to be clear, very clear, we are boycotting Lucas's shop – nothing else, I don't want what happened to Mrs Sonti to happen. When we say boycott, we do not mean that we burn down, if we want to burn down we will do so, if that is the only way left to us. Are we clear?"

"Yes." Steve said.

"Cynthia, are we clear?"

"Yes, we are."

"Right, let's meet here at eight tonight."

Cynthia left the house, using the front door, while Steve used the back. Both scaled the fence, Cynthia the one to the south, Steve the one to the north.

Tembisa, like many other townships, has assumed a different character from what it was three or four years back. Long ago, during the week, during the day, townships assumed a quite forlorn character, with the heat of the sun beating the empty streets which are faced by shut doors and windows of houses in deserted yards. Other yards would be engulfed by the voices of old people and little children, the ill, the mad, the unemployed, and occasionally a car would pass, a lone man or woman would go by, dogs would bark; otherwise it would be quiet. But now, it is no longer so. Angry flames have ravaged buildings and rendered houses, office blocks, shops, bottle stores and cars mere shells; buildings with charred walls, without doors or windows, stand by as evidence of activities which now preoccupy the minds of the people of the townships. Police cars and trucks, the ugly hippos and formidable looking casspirs buzz and roar along streets which have an eerie feel about them.

A very vague memory told Cynthia of a Tembisa of four years ago; she was more familiar with the Tembisa of now. She felt as if she had been alive a long, long time, although she was only eighteen. She was walking now, down the street, with a keen presence of mind. Although at eighteen her memory did not have to stretch far for things she had experienced, she felt she had been alive a long time; she lived in meetings, and distinguishing between the different days, at times even time did not matter, and sometimes whether it was day or night meant very little to her. She was thinking about MaNhlapo: is she going to be like her? Why does she go on at times as if she is talking to herself, giving little chance for others to talk, especially when she is angry? How old is MaNhlapo? Cynthia heard a familiar sound, she stopped abruptly, listening and looking for the vehicle – it must be a hippo; she quickly walked towards the nearest gate, opened it, and ran round the house. The noise stopped. She listened. The sound was rapidly approaching. It was here. A casspir drove past. She saw the

55

soldiers on it, their rifles pointed in front of them. She waited a little, listening carefully. She walked away from her hiding-place, stopped at the gate, listened, looked this way and that, then walked back into the street. This time she walked quickly. There could be other casspirs following the one that had just driven by. She walked close to fences, listening and watching. She could still hear in the distance the sound of the one that had just gone by.

"How is MaNhlapo?" Mlambo asked.

"She is well, Cynthia and I had a discussion with her, she said to tell you that she agrees with the decision regarding Lucas, she said she will pass the message to the women, she wanted us to make it clear to everyone that we want to persuade Lucas to be one of us, that we must not treat him as an enemy as we have no proof of his workings with the enemy," Steve said.

"I hear you," Mlambo said. "Well, we did all we could to talk sense into Lucas, he has a hard head, and so he has judged himself, we shall see. Tell me, how is Nomvula?"

"Nomvula is doing alright, she is going to the women's meeting in Soweto at Regina Mundi; she gave a good report the other day on that meeting she had with a new group of women. She says she met the singer, Lindi. They had a discussion with her, and it seems Lindi is prepared to come to Tembisa to stage a fund-raising concert for the women. They still have to finalise the details."

"Oh, she is mobilising already – that is good, that is very, very good. Lindi seems a very good woman, we must look after her. I must go to talk to the business people about Lucas; I agree with MaNhlapo, we must persuade Lucas. I hope you will make it clear to the students that insofar as Lucas is concerned, we would like to persuade him; we must not make the mistake we made with Ma-Sonti, we are not terrorists as the boers would like the world to believe, we are not hooligans or thugs, we are fighters for freedom, we are fighting a just war, we are fighting for the power of the majority, we use all peaceful methods to persuade people to see reason. Not that we are afraid to fight, we are not, since we are not afraid to die for our freedom, for peace, that is why we will never surrender, for if we do, we know we will inherit slavery. We can, we need to win even our enemies over to our way of thinking, or at least, render them neutral … but if all this has failed, we shall fight with everything we have. Please make this clear to the students. The Movement is the Movement of the people, it stands for them, they stand for it, it protects them, they protect it, and so it speaks for them and they speak for it. Lucas is in discord. We want him to at least not work against us, he can do whatever he wants to do, but he must not work against us. He refused to be neutral. If he gives tea and bread to the police and army and refuses to give bread and tea to our people when we are looking after our dead, then there is something wrong if we in turn support him by buying from his shop. We will not buy from his shop. That is all, we will not support him so that he in turn supports our enemy; it is like hitting one's hand with a hammer, and pushing the arm to hold a hammer so that one can knock nails and build a roof on one's house, that is not possible."

"I must go now," Steve said, standing up.

"Be well, Steve, look after yourself; I have to go to a union meeting. When will I see you again?"

"I have to see Lungi and Sarah, and then later in the evening, I'm seeing MaNhlapo and Cynthia," Steve said.

"If you can make time, not necessarily today, keep checking on Nomvula, will you?"

"I will, I know that Lungi and Cynthia keep in touch with her; I will, though … "

"Okay, okay, take good care of yourself."

"Stay well," Steve said, and shut the door behind him.

"I am wondering if we should not take this chance, to also talk to the taximen and the hostel dwellers; there is trouble there, and, if we do not nip it in the bud, it will be very difficult to control in the future," Tholo said.

"Ho, I do not think that we should combine them – the taximen are separate from the hostel dwellers. Lucas is like many other shopowners, only he has gone a step further in that he feeds the police and the army. But by dealing with him in the suggested manner, we will also be dealing with many other shopowners here, and not only here, but also in other townships where shopowners may be hesitant to support our struggle."

"I see," Tholo said, "that is how you look at it?"

"Yes, we have been discussing this in our women's group; I agree with this way of thinking."

"The taximen are not supporting our struggle, nor do the hostel dwellers, nor the shopowners, so why are we paying so much attention to Lucas? Five thousand leaflets on Lucas alone, and not only that, but Lucas has been the subject of our meetings over and over – what is so special about him? I am suggesting that we use one stone for these many pests. Lucas is being blown out of proportion, don't you see this, Cynthia?"

"No! I don't, I think he deserves all our attention. As I say, it is not Lucas alone we are looking at, we are directing our energies and time at him, but we are also doing so indirectly with many like him. Lucas is special, he is a successful businessman, he is indirectly influential with many shopowners who are undecided as regards support for our struggle, and he has gone a step further, he has become a rendezvous point for our enemy; he is testing our strength. Now, I agree with you that there is trouble brewing with the taximen and hostel dwellers, this is true, especially with the hostel dwellers, they do not have a conflict with residents, they can be used against us – it was done in Soweto in June '76. It can happen here – in fact, all signs are that it will happen. But I think that we should, as we say, use one stone to kill many birds. If all our attention is on Lucas, and he gives in, so will many of the shopowners, and, in fact, so will many business people; at least they will think twice before they go out in open support of our enemy. The taximen will learn from what we do to Lucas, but if we confront all of them at once, we are pushing them into a laager, we are forming them into a block opposed to us, and if that happens, we shall have created a base for our enemy which they will use against us. Lucas alone cannot defeat us, but Lucas, hostel dwellers and taximen can cause serious division among us, and we must avoid that at all costs."

"So Lucas is special then?"

"Well, you could put it that way."

Tholo, a short, dark man, who was known among his comrades for his stubbornness and hard-working habits, at his age – sixty – had amassed a lot of experience as a printer, and lately as a distributor of pamphlets and leaflets; he questioned every decision, argued with everyone, until he was certain he knew what was to be done, and why, and eventually could try to imagine the results of decisions. With some of his comrades, he was unpopular because of this, while others, especially those who were patient with him, found him lovable, dependable and reliable. Cynthia was one of these. He treated Cynthia like a little girl, in that he always saved sweets for her and teased her as he would his own daughters; he listened to her carefully when she spoke and thought her very respectful, though now and again he would bully her, scold her, and remind her that she was a little girl who had to listen and learn.

"You know," Tholo said, "I hear what you are saying. I tend to agree with you; sometimes I wish you were a boy – you would then go a long, long way, but well, as the Movement says, women are like men, and this coming time will also give you what it has given to men, it's okay … "

"Rre-Tholo, the Movement says there is no difference between men and women – what difference there is, is caused by society, and we want to correct that!"

"Okay, okay, I will not get into that; all I can say is that I agree with you, tell MaNhlapo I said Lucas will also read the leaflet in two days' time."

"But Rre-Tholo, you must correct your ideas on women."

"I'm old my child, what does it matter, I have nothing against women, they are lovely."

"And they fight," Cynthia said.

"They fight, okay, they fight, I have no quarrel with that."

"And they are equal to men," Cynthia insisted.

"Okay, you must go now," he turned towards the drawer and pulling it out, he turned and looked at Cynthia, "take this," he said, giving her a sweet.

"No, I am not taking it," Cynthia said, "I will never again take a sweet from you until you accept that women are equal to men," Cynthia said and stood up to leave.

"You are being silly, take this," Tholo said.

"No, bye now, I'll deliver your message to MaNhlapo," she walked out of the door.

"Remember, I still think you are a good, a very good woman," he said, and threw the sweet back into the drawer.

Besides being a shop steward and working at the printing plant, Tholo was slowly building a printing press in the back of his landlord's yard.

Meeting of Biz

"You know, I am confused, I no longer know what on earth we are expected to do," Albio said, "we can no longer think, you know, we act out of fear, like naughty little boys; we are told, close your shops, and then open them, and we do so; delivery vans are burned down, so our shops are slowly becoming empty. We do not know whether tomorrow we will wake up and find our shops burned down also; what on earth are we supposed to do?"

"Does anyone want to answer that?" Mlambo asked, looking around the room.

"Mr Chair, it is difficult, very, very difficult; I agree with what the speaker says, why are we boys and girls, today close, we close, tomorrow open, we open, today give petrol money, we give, tomorrow give bread, we give, all the money is going low, stock is going low, what is shop for? I want to know that!" shaking with anger, Molete sat down.

"Friends, two questions: the first is, faced with the violence of the police and army, what must we do? The second is, how can we run a business when we are in a state of siege?"

"No Chair, no, it is not a state, it is petrol-bomb, it is little boys and girls come ask, for petrol-money, for bread, for closing of shop, not state, why you turn what I say around?"

"Can anyone answer these questions?" Mlambo asked again.

"You know, Mr Chair, we must be honest with each other in these difficult times, for we need each other, we need to be together against these terrible odds facing us." Thembi, a fish and chips shopowner, said, "The questions which are being raised are genuine questions which need honest, straightforward answers; Tembisa is at war, people are dying daily, people are hungry, people are unemployed, we are surrounded by heavily-armed police and the army – what must we do? What have we done to deserve this? The question we must ask is, what is the cause of this war?" She sat down.

"Who is fighting who? Why is black fighting black? Why is it that it is black children who are not going to school? It is only us who are dying. It is us only who can't move because everywhere there are police ready to shoot. It is us burning our shops. It is us stopping the delivery vans – why is this?" Ngwenya asked.

"Friends, there are many questions being asked, genuine questions which need honest answers, as Mrs Moloi has said, but who is to answer them? I think this is why we are here, we are here so we can put our heads together and give answers to our problems; no-one is going to do this for us. We are suffering, we have to find a solution to the problems. Now basically, the question is, we as business people, we find that because we are in a state of siege we do not function as we used to do before, so what must we do? We have done the first correct thing, we have come together as business people to solve our problems. We intend to go out of here and say to the people out there this is what we can do and this is what we need. What can we do, what do we need?" Mlambo asked.

"Mr Chair, I agree with you, the questions are, given that we are embattled as a people, what is our role as business people, and what do we need from our customers?" Tsatsi looked down, pulled up his trousers, cleared his throat, "now the facts are, on the one side we as business people, regardless of whether there is a seige or not, we need to run our businesses, that is, we need our profits. That is one side of the story, the other side is that the people who are our customers have very little buying power, what must we do then?" he paused, looking around the room. "We as business people must come together, we must pool our resources and increase our buying power so we can buy more for less, then we can sell for less, are we able to do so, are we able to influence fruiterers to come together, dairy people to come together, grocers to come together, and so on, and then form a co-ordinating committee?"

Silence fell in the room for a while.

"How will that stop the violence that is going on?" asked Ngwenya.

"One person at a time, please," Mlambo said.

"Are we trying to stop the violence, or are we asking, as business people, what is our role in a township torn by violence?"

61

"We must not play around with words, we are in serious business," Ngwenya said, "can we make business in this violence?"

"Friends, what brought us together is that we as business people want to know what is our role in the struggle," Mlambo said.

"We will form the dairymen, grocers and fruiterers into a group, but where will the goods come from?" Ngwenya asked.

"Yes, where will the goods come from?" asked Mrs Moloi.

"The delivery vans can't come to townships, the boys and girls burn them," Molete said.

"Where would the delivery vans get the goods from?" asked Tsatsi. "We must start from where we can; let us come together as we have, let us reach agreements on what to do, let us find out what we can do now, and what we can't do now. The children who burn shops and delivery vans are our children, we can talk to them, we can tell them what we can do and what we can't, we can come to agreements with them," Mlambo said.

A figure wearing dark overalls emerged from a yard, stood at a gate, listened, peered into the dark morning, then, hearing and seeing nothing, walked out into the street toward the T-junction; he looked this way and that, and, seeing nothing, he lit a match and quickly extinguished it; another figure about one hundred metres away at an intersection emerged, looked this way and that, and lit a match. Between the T-junction and the intersection a third person emerged carrying a sack on one shoulder. He scooped up sand in one hand, quickly pulled out a batch of papers from the sack, put some on the street, then poured a little sand on them and ran forward. He did the same a little way ahead near the intersection, then disappeared into the yard, as did the two figures, one at the T-junction and the other at the intersection. They had been at it for over five hours now, it was nearly five in the morning. Somewhere in the distance, a shot rang, and another, yet another … otherwise, this morning was quiet.

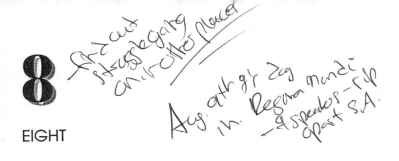

8

EIGHT

Too many things have happened now. They have happened because here, we are faced with a very strong woman. So much has happened because there has been a great urgency in our lives. Time – what is it? – has run madly over our lives. Job is back, in what is now called Sethulaphoko Free Band. He is still with the band, but has grown thinner, his whole frame seems to be dwarfed by the size of his eye balls. Billy is here too, with humour as sharp as a blade, and his shining trombone – it is not only the metal that glitters, but also its sound. *Lindi's voice.*

I am dead scared to attempt a description of Lindi's voice. But I must. This is also one of the things that has happened. The voice, Lindi's voice – this is what it said when it carried the words of the song, the harmony, the melody and the rhythym of the silence of the words: it was clasping the silence, the vast, the large, the heavy, deep silence of the sky, the voice said. I really don't know how she reached this beginning, what she did to herself, to her stomach, to her womb, to her breasts, to her womanhood, because everything in her, including her eyes, persuaded the words of the song to say it once and for all.

I was part of the audience that day. It was a very cold day, a very cold morning which grew to become a very hot day, as we shall see. This day – really, to call it a day is inadequate – but, this day, like many other days, has been taken from the South African calendar, by hurling life at them. As few as they may be, they are many, they are a beginning. But they are the end of one of the saddest stories of the world since Hitler. It is very difficult to say how the audience came. There were so many who came. Also, it is not easy to say anything about the mood of the audience, of the people, of the gathering, the mood of the day itself. It was a very cold morning. Soweto was sullen, with its monotony, its sameness –

sullen, as it was unable to lift the smoke-curls hovering over it, the smoke which stubbornly shaded the sun, the winter sun, and its rays, the light, the day. The streets were deserted.

It is August 9th – we have gone through March 30th, June 16th and 26th and have rapidly arrived at August 9th. Too many, just too many things have happened. Lindi will never ever be able to carry the load of what happened, alone, let alone be responsible for it. No matter how strong she is. I do not know where we did not come from. We came, watchful, uncertain whether the glittering snake was giving its last twist or rearing, once more, for a fierce fight. We had been fighting, and we were walking again, to the arena, to the open space, the deserted battlefield, aware, untrusting, the past days and months not just a memory, but a fresh experience. I saw little children. I saw young girls and boys, laughing still. I saw the old and the soon to be old. The cars outside were as numerous as stars. People shook hands, smiled and laughed, and walked on into the hall. The pattern of the many, many benches, chairs and whatever else could be sat on, had now been arranged. The many doors and windows which a little before may have been said to be gaping, were now choking. The audience flooded the hall, spilled outside to the grounds, flooded the grounds, spilled to the streets, flooded the streets, and spilled into yards and private gardens, flooded these, and seemed to flood every available space on earth, then, beginning to rise, it flooded the rooftops of houses …

I really do not know how an audience this big, this large, settles itself down. It soon became thousands of pairs of eyes and ears, still, silent like a mountain, except, now and then, for a cough, a sneeze – it was winter after all – then shuffling footsteps and the eternal echo in the hall. I saw a young man, maybe about nineteen, on stage, paper in hand. He stood a while staring at the audience, and soon silence fell. Indeed, I thought, we have come a long, long way. From the Kgotla, where women and children and young men knew their place, which was nothing but the function and silence of furniture in a house, to now, at this hour, when the young man stood before us to say:

"Comrades, friends, brothers and sisters, today is August the 9th, on this day in 1956 in our country, our people declared this day women's day … "

How does one make sense of this day? I kept asking myself this question. I really don't know what all the women who came on stage after this boy, said – it is impossible to know. I know one thing, though – as the total story of women unfolded, as one after the other came and went, in all shapes and sizes, in all the ages of the world, their smiles, sullen faces, their eyes, gait, gestures, their hundred styles and common style, their voices, their silence as they pondered a point – South Africa was stripped naked. Slowly it was undressed and each part of its body examined very, very closely, looked at with the greatest care in the world. As the women came on stage, it was time, our country's colours, its voices, its texture were laid bare – with the footsteps of women, as they came one by one, came, unfolded, enacting a system of breaking down South Africa as it had been known up until that hour. They came, in the colours of the rainbow. Even if they wore nothing, not a single cloth around their bodies, they would still have displayed the rainbow – I did not know that flesh could take on all those colours! So their eyes, so their lips, so their nostrils, the insides of their mouths, of their palms as they gestured, their hair, grabbed the rainbow and scattered its colours.

Something in the silence of the hall told me that, I myself do not know the story of South Africa. That is, I cannot tell it. The story of South Africa is still to be told. I agreed to this between the silence created by the last speaker and the shuffling made by the feet of the next who was going up the stairs. Her presence, that is, our realisation, the audience's realisation that she was going to speak, was expressed in a very loud silence. The audience sighed, relieved. She was not very old, nor was she young. She was certainly a stranger in this environment. That is part of the story. To relate the story further, let me attempt a description of her clothes: rolled-up brown balaclava, perched on top of her head; very grey, almost white, hard-looking dots of hair showing; a colourful blanket hanging from her shoulders, held in place by a neat knot to the right of her neck; a brown mochikisa, with white frills flowing to her ankles, brown shoes. She turned, after what seemed to be ages climbing up the stairs, to face us. She was thin, not tall. She was a beautiful old woman. She lifted her shoulder, adjusted

65

the blanket, cleared her throat, then cried:

"Amandla!"

"Nga'wethu!" the audience replied.

"Maatla!"

"Kearona!"

"I greet you all," she said. "I am very happy to be here. I have listened carefully to all the speakers before me. I am not lying when I say I know where I am. I know with whom I am. I hope to be able to let you know where I come from, who I am, and as a result, to say everything that needs to be said so that you know the people who sent me here. I come from the Orange Free State. There is a little town there called Marquard – you know it now; before, it was not known. I say you know of it, because, here I am today, from there, after somebody sent us word that we should send someone here to represent that town. I have been sent to do so." She smiled. Her eyes were bright and shining. "There are men and women there, as you would expect; they are farmers, or were supposed to be farmers, were it not for PW. We have fought those who were before PW and we are now fighting PW, and this is a long journey. It started as a very lonely journey, a very painful journey. When it started, we were not fighting to be farmers, though this does not mean we did not know that we were farmers. We started to fight so we could walk, for if we were not allowed to walk, we would not be able to eat, drink, or sleep. So we fought."

"Amandla!" someone said in the audience.

Silence fell again. The old lady looked like a stone. She looked like a rock. She looked like a mountain. She looked like all these things. Her scalp peeping between the furrows of her hair said so. Her face, steel-hard, grey, said so. Her hand, as she gestured as if to say Marquard was behind her, pointing over her shoulder as she mentioned that town, had been hardened and chiselled by the sun; it had been shaped by the cold waters of the Free State; her frame, the way she stood, still, humble, proud and stubborn, said so. She looked straight at the audience like the warrior she was.

"Our fight," she said, "is as old as us and as that town. We fought when it started and we are still fighting, and we will continue to fight. I hope that this is how you came to know of the

66

little town, Marquard. Now, that fight has brought me here to meet other fighters. I am a proud woman today. I have been honoured. That is why I glide over the past. We share a past. We need not dwell on it, though I must say, we cannot forget it. We know each other by the wounds in our voice – no-one will erase these! The people who sent me here asked me to pass their greetings to you all."

"Amandla!"

"They want you to know that if there is one thing you can trust in, it is that they are unshakeable in fighting for and together with the Movement, for, the fight for Marquard, the fight for the right to walk, we see it as the fight for the Movement to walk. We cannot, and never will, separate the two."

"Amandla!"

"When we fight so we can walk, we are also fighting so that we can have a new way of talking. I and those who sent me here want everyone to know that we are fighting so that one day, this country, if it cannot erase the words, Coloureds, Indians, Europeans, and Bantu – words it used to curse its children – we will not stop fighting, even if we are allowed to walk. If they say we can walk and they get rid of those words, we expect them to know that we are a majority, consisting of Africans, Coloureds, Indians, and Whites, who do not only want to walk in Marquard, in South Africa, but who want to vote. Not only that, but we want the Movement to walk this land – they said it cannot walk, we say it can; not only that, not only do we want to win this land, we want to share, all of us, equally, what this land can give, and I know that this land can give plenty."

"Amandla!"

"We want our children to be given a proper education. We want our own army which will protect and defend all of us, black and white, women and children, all South Africans. We want this land to be put back on the map of the world. We demand that we be a free people!"

"Amandla!"

"We want our leaders, leaders that we choose, because we know who they are, to lead us, we want them out of jail, back from those far lands, here among us – nothing less will satisfy us!

67

Amandla!"

"I want to tell you a secret. When I came here, I was fearful. Look, I come from the country. I have been around the town, and some of the things I've seen, I've heard our people do and say in towns, have shocked me. I must say this. So I was fearful. I wondered what you meant when you asked us from Marquard that we should attend this, one of our great days, 9th August, here in Regina Mundi. Women's day. We have heard that in other lands, especially those that eat with PW, women have made enemies out of men." She smiled. "But here," she gestured from one side of the hall to the other, "I see men and women, mothers and fathers and children, the family, the nation, all have come to celebrate Women's day — I withdraw my suspicions," she said, and laughed.

"Amandla!"

"Sometimes it takes seeing to believe. But also, I am very happy to see that women have come up, have gone to the front, are fighting. I am happy to see so many women. I have listened to what they had to say. They know what they are talking about because they have been shoulder to shoulder out there with the men, and the men with them. When we say we are a happy nation, a singing nation, a dancing nation, and a fighting nation, we are referring to each and every one of us. I saw that today. I have learnt, I will go back with many stories to relate. That is the end of my secret."

"On this day, we remember the many women and men who died so we can walk; who are in jail because we were not allowed to walk, who are in exile for the same reason, who have been gallant fighters – we remember, and pay tribute to our lovable, brave and stubborn young man, Solomon Mahlangu."

"Fanie, Wilfred and Humphrey and the many, many others who are dead, who are in jail, who are in foreign lands. I know, as I say this that the wombs of women contract as if to vomit, but also, I know that we will continue to give birth, all those who can, will. The double-edged blade is in our hands, it cuts the flesh of our palms, but we do not regret that we seized it and now hold it firm; no matter how deep it cuts, we will hold it until it cannot cut any more. We will twist the blade to the hand which holds it. Amandla! We warn Reagan, we warn Thatcher, we warn all PW's

Speaker from — Mapule
Marquard
Sechele

allies, that the trunk of an elephant, stronger than the neck of a cow, swifter than the legs of a springbok, will make them fall. They will fall beneath the weight of our arms."

I held Esther's arm, and asked who this woman was. She did not look at me. She nudged someone two people away from us, asked for a programme, and without looking at me, her thumb indicating a name on the programme, she held it to my eyes. Mapule Sechele – Secretary, Women's Organisation, Marquard, this was the name at the tip of Esther's silent thumb. Mapule was calm, like a bird in flight. It was evident that the stage was unfamiliar to her – it could not possibly be familiar to her. It was evident that everything else she had seen before. Her eyes were watching, so was her face. Her body was taut. Her flight was smooth. Unlike a bird, her vision came not just from her eyes, it was something deeper than that.

Time and stories are in perpetural conflict. Both are stubborn. Both are very demanding. How will I tell the story of that day? All of us, as we sat there listening, had seen everything. There was very, very little that we did not already know, and because of this, we knew that there was a whole lot to be learnt, we knew this. We had come to Regina Mundi in the morning. It was already late afternoon. After Mapule had spoken, we would go outside for lunch. We would then return and listen to Lindi.

I could hardly believe what I had heard before lunch. The young boy who had opened this "gathering" had said that we should know as we were gathered there, that other people throughout the country were doing the same. If those people were listening to similar things, wherever they were, then South Africa was a different place. It was different to those who were talking and to those who were listening – not watching, but listening. Yes, some of our countrymen were watching out there in the cold, some were here, watching, but the display was more evident outside. Everything was out there. Out there was bewilderment: bullets, tear-gas, batons, and bush clothes. We knew they were there, they knew we were here. We had separated them from us, and although now and then we talked about them, it was never to them. We talked about them when we needed to make something clear to ourselves; we talked about them in passing. But we talked mostly about us: a family affair, as one singer says.

"At this hour, South Africa is not different because it has changed for the better. No! It is different because it is breathless from a long, long fight. It is planning a better, a more fierce battle."

"We will not repeat how the weight of the hands which handle the blades in their palms will thrust their weight down. If those who are our enemies do not know, because they can't, they are unable to know; if they do not know, we shall give them the chance to know. PW will fall under us. So will all the oppressors! The people will win!"

Mapule began to walk down the stairs. There was a sound like rushing water as the audience stood up. Fists punched the air. "A-M-A-N-D-L-A! Ngawethu!" the hall echoed. The young boy came on stage to tell us to break. He also told us that there were shots outside. We walked out slowly, one by one. Up until we, Esther and I, got out into the light, I had been wondering what the loudspeaker was saying. Now I saw what it was saying. People were walking in fours, and the police were retreating. At some point, though, we were no longer in fours, and the police were close by. I held Esther's hand in mine. She held the wet cloths which we had brought with us, and which we had immersed in the basin of water put there by students. The students had also brought some cloths in case some people had forgotten – but it seemed no one needed these. I did not think about the bullets, but I was, like everyone else, armed against tear-gas. I saw a strange look on Esther's face.

She slowed down a little. I held her arm. I took the cloth from her. The look on her face was not strange in the sense that I did not know it. I knew it.

"What's the matter?" I asked.

"Where?" she said this with a voice that sounded like she held a blade in her palm, and she was defying the pain.

"On your face," I said.

"And on yours?"

"Okay." I looked around. Many, many, many people.

"You know what?"

"What?"

"I raised my fist, and at that moment, I got my monthly blood," she said.

I must have looked at the front of her dress or somewhere there …

"Don't be a fool!" she said, and stopped dead still, seeming to push her thighs together, and tightening her grip around my hand. I looked away. I stopped. Then I looked around. I was afraid to look at her legs. We walked into a yard. She went into a house. She emerged, looking shy, but walking confidently. We walked on.

"You made it sound so crude," I said, "monthly bloo … "

"Shut up!" she snapped. We walked on in silence.

9

NINE

Esther and I walked this same day to Lindi's house. We were going up a steep street and were in what can be called a valley, at a bridge. We were not alone. There were many other people, walking, coming from Regina Mundi.

Already, on the far distant hillside, there were crowds of walking, moving dots. Behind us, up another incline, there were hundreds and hundreds of these dots. Although it seemed silent, it was not. If it is true that eyes, when they see, and gestures, when they fly, make sounds, then it was not silent. There were too many eyes and gestures on this day. If what the little boy said was true, that what was happening in Soweto was happening in many other places in the country, then this was not a silent day.

Esther was silent. I was silent. We held hands. We walked. By now, we were part of the mass of dots going up the incline. There were others behind and ahead of us. We had ceased to be two lovers, two people walking up a hill. We had become part of a force. The terrible thing about all this is that once this happens, once people become part of a larger force, they sense it but can do little else. And as a result, it created too many unknowns, but that was because already we knew a lot. What did we know?

A people involved in struggle know everything. Esther and I have never been educated. Our country never intended to educate us. Our country had created a method by which it was going to have complete control over us. The methods were crude. They were sharp. They cut and cut and cut, forever cut, the mouth, the ears, the eyes, the hands, the legs, and then grope for the stomach, and with sharp, piercing fingers, reach for the mind, touch, wiggle, twist, tear, and then hold. Hold firm. Esther and I are mere examples. We are part of a whole, of the dots going up the incline, down the decline, onto the bridge, up the incline. A crowd consisting of individuals. Everything is here, threatening to be nothing. But it can never be nothing, for as soon as that threat becomes real, as soon as nothing manifests itself, everything, something, everything emerges. What is this force? Sometimes, for there are those times, we talk of mother, father, child, sister, niece, brother, grandfathers, grandmothers, and then, at times, there is worker, student, farmer, at another time, mineworker, factory worker, nurse, teacher and then women, children, men, youth, a community, a society, a nation, nations, a people, the world – alas, a people in struggle! The crowd, the dots, the moving dots are mum! I think of the woman, Mapule. A woman as hard and as thin as a stick. The many women of that day who came, one by one, forming a crowd, up-stage, coming, going, coming, going, coming, bringing with them the past, their lives, the lives of their communities, their gestures, their dressing styles, their eyes, the women brought with them everything they knew.

The women brought a long, long story. One by one, up and down, down and up, they came, every word, every gesture, every flicker of the eye, digging and digging the fathomless deep, deep and unreachable, a stubborn motion, backwards, forwards, up and down, a movement, its process enacted by footsteps, gestures, eyes in motion; its voice stung as only experience can sting. Every single person in the crowd had been to battle, the degree did not matter there. It was this fact which for that moment tore the day, creating, welding a deep ecstasy, a deep sadness – everything just at the brink of tears and at the brink of a gut-laughter. The air became taut. The sky was visible. The earth was firm under the feet. You stand, you learn to wait, you go past, you sense the distance. You sense the distance, you learn to wait, you learn to stand and that is because you have learnt to walk. The strength of the air, of the sky, of the earth, of the depth of the gut, is brittle, is strong, like the leg of a bird, like a wing in flight – it is the content of an egg contained in a shell. This Movement is as brittle as the skin of the eye. The skin, the women, the men, the children, the workers, the farmers, are thin, hard like rock. The Movement, the eye, looks and looks and looks. Who is the Movement? These dots? This crowd? People who are drowning must feel like this: space and space, substance and substance all around, but nowhere to hold –

73

life then thrusts, thrashes out, becomes alive like life itself. We rise as a people, we rise slowly, as slow as rain clouds. We rise, and rise, and rise.

Who is the Movement? My hand in Esther's was wet. I shook it. She loosened her grip. We walked. She by herself. I by myself. We entered the gate, the door, the house. Job was lying on the floor. I circled him to reach the sofa. It received me. I heard a door – possibly the toilet door – close. And I heard the water running. I dared not go to help. She would chase me away. Besides, this, whatever she was doing, was her business – it was her blood. It was her legs. Everything was hers, and she immersed it now at this hour in water. Job was snoring. I sensed that there were other people, besides Esther, besides me, besides Job. There were other people, somewhere in this house. There were people outside, walking. The dots, the walking dots. Everything was touched by August 9th – is this the Movement? The Movement for what? John came out from one room. He was wearing a suit. He was wearing a black striped suit, a tie and polished shoes. He wore a smile. I thought he might have mistaken this day, Women's day, for a funeral. Was he wrong? He walked quietly. He paced towards where Job was, snoring.

He touched him lightly, and in a soft voice said: "Wake up! We must go to play now!"

10

TEN

Meeting other Comrades

"Our position is clear," Steve said, "we want Botha to take out his army and police from our midst, they are dangerous to life, even peaches on a tree are not plucked at the rate which we die daily; also, we want all political prisoners to be released, we want the exiles to return to our country without fear of victimisation, we want all political organisations to be unbanned and we want the apartheid constitution to be abolished. Now in talking to you I say there is no contradiction between what I've said and what I said to you earlier on, that there is no way that everyone who supports our struggle will oppose your saying people will leave the country for military training – no-one!"

"Steve," Strike said, "you must not talk to me as if I'm a white man – I have never opposed the conditions for negotiations. I'm saying, why does Mlambo sound as if he is opposed to people leaving the country?"

"Look, Mlambo cannot support a position that propagates the conditions for our negotiations and at the same time oppose military training; they are one and the same, Strike, can't you see?"

"But he did oppose our suggestion that people should leave, didn't he?"

"When?"

"At the last meeting."

"No, he did not – in fact Strike, let us leave this discussion, we are not here for that."

"Steve, tell me, why do you say this?"

"Steve and Strike," Lungi said, "I think you should leave what you are talking about, we are here to talk to the other comrades, and instead, they are listening to you, you have hardly said a word to them."

"Comrades," Steve said, turning to face the twenty or so young

75

people who were seated on the floor, mattress, table and chairs, young men and women whose sweat-fumes filled the room – some unkempt, some half dressed. "I am sure that you have been following events as they unfold here in Tembisa and in our country generally. It is obvious that we will have to use new methods of struggle, as the boers are moving into more repressive measures to halt us. As I am talking now, I must say that it is wrong that we are in such a large group, also, most of you here are wanted by the police, some have been injured, others are ill, what must we do?"

"There is no other way," Strike said, "we must leave the country, we must go for training."

"That is one way of struggling," Lungi came in.

"That is one way, yes, but there are many other ways – as our leader Nelson Mandela has said, we must fight on many fronts," Steve said, "what other ways are open to us?"

"Comrade Steve!" Strike interjected angrily, "why are you avoiding my question?"

"Strike, Strike, you are out of order, you are not the only person whose opinion is sought here, there are more than twenty people here and we would like to hear their views," Cynthia argued.

"Why are you all suppressing me?"

"You are out of order, man, just be disciplined," Cynthia continued angrily.

"Allow Strike to talk," someone said from among the group.

"Yes, allow Strike to talk, you know I don't agree with talk talk all the time, it's a waste of time," another said, "I want action!"

"Viva action! Down with yes yep!" said another.

"We want to leave to train and come back to fight!" another shouted.

"Why do we throw papers at Lucas instead of stones or petrol bombs, are we playing games or are we fighting?" Jacob, a tall, thin boy of nineteen asked, jumping off from the table where he was sitting. "What are these papers going to do to him? You know, I want to be frank and honest with you comrades, you must remember that our brothers and sisters have been killed here, you know, you know, many people have been killed, you know, we must not play games by talking and throwing papers around".

Someone from the group laughed.

76

"I am serious, you know, you must not laugh, you know, it's serious business this, you know, don't laugh, or are you laughing at me? I'm not educated … "

"Haai Jacob, you are out of order," Cynthia said.

"Out of order? What do you mean by that, out of order? Don't say that to me, you know, out of order when I'm talking about dead people! What are you saying? You are too big for your boots."

"I say you are out of order!"

"Who do you think you are?"

"Who do you think you are?"

"I am out of order."

"Comrades, can we listen to each other?" Strike interrupted.

"This bitch must not … "

"Who is a bitch? A mirror in front of you will tell you who is a bitch … " Cynthia leapt to her feet lunging towards Jacob. Strike jumped up and stood between Jacob and Cynthia.

"You disrupt every meeting every time, Jacob, we are tired of your nonsense."

"You and … "

"Shut up, you must never call me a bitch," she darted round Strike, trying to reach Jacob.

"You must never … "

"What's wrong with you? You are out of order … " Strike was saying when Cynthia struck him across the face.

"No, no, don't do that!" Strike cried out, standing in front of Cynthia, "now you are out of order completely!"

Cynthia pushed past Strike, held Jacob by his neck and smashed her head into his face; Jacob responded, agile as a boxer, and soon Cynthia fell onto her back. Steve, Lungi and Strike watched all this, standing aside, as other people also gave way to the fighters; Jacob, bleeding through the nose, lifted Cynthia up and smashed his right fist into her face.

"Jacob, Jacob, haai, man, haai, that's enough," Sipho pleaded, pushing his way from against the wall where he was standing, "you can't beat a woman comrade like that … "

"Are you buying it?" Jacob moved towards him, the two met in the centre of the room, "are you buying it, I ask you? You know

77

Cynthia has contempt for me, she does not respect me, you saw what she did to me!"

"You called her bitch, you called her bitch."

"Come, you swine, finish me ... " Cynthia was on her feet once more, staggering towards Jacob.

"I will fuck you up," Jacob threatened as he turned towards her, "you must never ... "

"I said you called her bitch," Sipho said, pulling Jacob towards him. "How can you call her a bitch and comrade at the same time?"

"Leave him ... " Cynthia sneered.

"Sipho, leave Jacob," Steve stood up, "Cynthia, you must keep quiet now, and Jacob, I want to tell you, we cannot call her a bitch, nor, Cynthia, can we lift a hand against a comrade; the only people we have contempt for are our enemies. I suggest that we go on with our meeting, those who have other agendas must leave this room," he sat down. "We came here to talk about new ways we can devise to fight the police, the army and the reactionaries in Tembisa, comrades were saying that the most important way is to leave the country for training, some of us are saying that is one important way, there are other methods," he said. "Comrades, this is what our agenda is, there are comrades here – Eric, Sam, Thabang and others – who have been injured, Lulu over there is ill, all of us here know that it has become a great risk for more than twenty people who have nowhere else to sleep, to sleep in this house. There are immediate problems like these which we have to solve, there are long-term ones which I mentioned earlier on. Those comrades who are injured, I will ask to give their names to Lungi; Lungi, please discuss possibilities of them seeing doctors or nurses, Lulu must receive priority. I want to know, are there comrades here who have anywhere else to stay other than Tembisa?" For a moment there was movement and the shuffling of feet as the injured and Lungi moved to one section of the room. Then there was silence.

Cynthia had walked out weeping. Jacob seemed a little lost. Sipho and Strike stood together in the corner looking at Steve.

"I can move to Alexandra ... "

"Comrades, you don't have to mention the place you can go to,

78

all I'm asking is, do you have elsewhere to go? Those who do, raise your hands." Six more hands shot up.

"Strike and Sipho, divide the group into fours, each group will be led by two people who have somewhere else to stay." As they moved into groups Steve slipped outside to see Cynthia.

Facing her he said, "We have five groups in the house, the injured and the ill make one group, and four groups led by two people each who have alternative places to stay. Lungi is talking to one of the injured; Strike and Sipho have one group each of people who have elsewhere to go, you will take one group and I the other … "

"I am very angry with Jacob," she said.

"Cynthia, you must help arrest this bad situation which is developing, this is what the enemy will make mileage out of, we must stop it now, go in and lead the group that Paul has been put into." He slipped back into the room, "Comrades I'm taking my group to the veld, I would suggest, Strike and Sipho, that you meet elsewhere with your groups so we can leave Cynthia and Lungi with theirs. Jacob, in which group are you?"

"I have no group."

"Join this one, it is the one I'm leading, let's go." He moved slightly towards the door, turned, and met Jacob's eyes, which wavered – Jacob was thinking at that moment, maybe it is true that Steve had once left the country for training. He moved towards the door, showing all the signs of being willing to follow Steve. Six people, including Jacob, walked out into the dark streets.

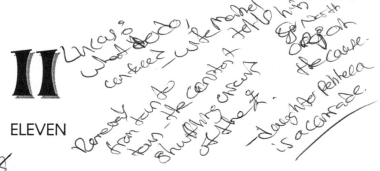

II

ELEVEN

Lucas Ngubeni, tall, heavy, with a bulging stomach, a bald head, a broad face and a charming smile, was born in the northern Transvaal, near Louis Trichart. He came from a family of fourteen, two girls and twelve boys. His father, a miner, and mother, a housewife, had brought them up on the wages from the mines and income from the land, cattle, goats and sheep. Lucas had left the northern Transvaal for the Golden City to seek employment, first in the mines, then in the city as a street-sweeper, then a hawker, and then he had settled in Sophiatown. After the Sophiatown removals he lived in Alexandra, and after the removals there he went to settle in Tembisa. By this time he was married with grown-up sons and daughters, two of whom were now in high school. Lucas, a shrewd businessman with a razor-sharp mind, had developed his business from hawking shoe-laces, sweets and cigarettes, to building and ably running a grocery shop, fruit shop and butchery; he was in the process of planning for a restaurant when the heat of the fire crawled into Tembisa, devouring people and buildings alike.

One of his daughters, Rebecca, now at high school, had on many occasions threatened to leave home if Lucas did not heed the voice of Tembisa. Lucas had responded with silence, close watchfulness and careful listening. Rebecca left home. Lucas knew Rebecca was somewhere in Tembisa among the stone-throwing youth, but where exactly he did not know. Now, seated at his home with a frightened wife and children, a lonely man isolated from the community he believed he was serving through his business, he wondered where Rebecca, whom he had made such plans for, was. Was she among the youth who had become the target of the police bullets? Did she not think of coming to see him, to talk to him when so much trouble had befallen him? What wrong had he done? Was it wrong to work hard and protect what one had worked for? He stood up, he could hear the gentle snoring of his youngest son, Moses, who seemed to be developing chest problems. He wondered what a petrol bomb was. What does it look like? He knew, he had seen what it can do. Where do the young people get this bomb from? The ANC? Why would the ANC leave a dangerous thing like this in the hands of young people?

Nomvula was also now talking like Rebecca. A cold fear hit him now, van Niekerk had asked him about Nomvula, and he had said to him, don't ask me that, she has just lost her son, the police shot him; good Lord, this place is full of evil, everyone has become so evil, petrol bombs and van Niekerk, police and soldiers, death all over the streets – why was he being pulled from all directions into this? All he wanted was to be a good businessman serving his people. Nomvula, she had said, when he said this to her, it is not you who are doing bad, it is not you alone who is being called upon to be with the people, all of us want to build a good place to live in and raise children, everyone, not only in Tembisa, but throughout the country is saying to the boers, we have had enough, and we are asking you, old-man Lucas, to support the voice which says no to the boers … van Niekerk, when he asked him why the police were shooting children like this, had said, to defend people like you, to protect the property of people who have worked hard building it, and these students and youth, instigated by terrorists, are tearing this country apart … He moved away from the table, aware of the deep quiet in the house, aware of the night, and fearful of sounds. He picked up the leaflet from the table, read it for the hundredth time, and put it back on the table. This, he thought, is in the hands of hundreds of people of Tembisa. These many, many people, now know him as a person they should have nothing to do with. It is difficult to walk the streets, no one talks to him, no one comes to the shop but the police … Suddenly his wife appeared before him, he had not heard her coming. He looked at her, her eyes were filled with fear …

"Lucas, why are you not coming to bed?"

He looked at his watch: 2.30 a.m. – he yawned, cupping his

face in his hands. "I'm coming."

"I have such a splitting headache, I can't fall asleep, even the tablets don't work."

"Please go to bed, I will join you," he turned away from his wife and opened the door to go out.

"No, no Lucas, don't go out, they will kill you, oh please, please don't go out … "

He turned back, shutting the door behind him. "Don't be like that, don't, you will break my heart, please go to sleep, please …"

"Lucas, I am not going to bed, I am staying here with you."

He sat down. She sat down. The night, the house, all but their eyes, were silent.

"I was not going away, I wanted to stand on the stoep."

"We can do that together," Mabel said.

He looked at her. He knew now he should stop talking about her going to bed.

"I am trying to think, Mabel. We can't live like this. You know I am being pulled from all sides. Van Niekerk this side, with his soldiers and police, and now look at that," he pointed at the leaflet on the table. "You know, no-one wants to speak to me, soon we will have to close the shops, maybe before we do that, even, the petrol bomb will come; we have lost Rebecca, what is all this, what must we do?"

Mabel sighed. Her head, eyes and body were a throbbing pain. She had not been able to sleep the past few nights. A slight sound, every sound, pulled her to her feet, to all the doors and windows, from where, she had heard, the bomb comes into the house. Even at the shops, where now the employers were no longer to be seen, she was restless at every sound and footsteps. "We must go back to the north."

"You think so?" Lucas had not thought about this, but something in him refused to accept the idea.

"What would we do there, why would van Niekerk and that paper not follow us there? We have worked here, we have lived here, what would we do in the North?"

"I am tired Lucas, I can't live like this."

"I know, but if this thing follows us to the North, what then?" he sat down on the sofa. "No, Mabel, we must face it, we must not run, what can we do, what are we expected to do, what have we done wrong?"

"It's that van Niekerk and the police and the soldiers who guard our shops. That's what called the wrath on us – also, you must resign as a councillor."

"Are you also blaming me?"

"I am telling you what wrong you have done."

"You mean, you also think I am as bad as these people say I am?"

"Lucas, your child is among the youth somewhere, you are busy gving fish and chips and drinks to the police, for free, are you not?"

"I said I don't want them guarding my house, my house is not a prison!"

"Well," Mabel said, "you are either with van Niekerk or the people, there is no middle road."

Lucas sighed. "What is going on? Why is everyone turning against me? What have I done? Was it wrong to have become a businessman? You also think I'm wrong?"

"Lucas, I keep telling you there is a war out there, people are fighting and dying, you are not the only one with shops, some have been burnt, others are not burnt. Your shops are shops like many other shops. It is your turn, either the shops are guarded and you are a community councillor to van Niekerk, or you resign as a councillor, and find out what all these people here want you to do." Mabel yawned loudly, stretching her legs and arms on the sofa, soothing her aching body.

"I did not know that by working hard I was going to wrong people. I did not mean to, also, I did not know that other people are entitled to live off the bloody sweat of others, but that is how things have come to be," Lucas said.

People in the townships, people who have grown up in the cities, have a way, their own only way of looking at things, very little respect for life, for other people's property, very little respect for anything; maybe Mabel was right, they should go back to Louis Trichardt, but what would he do once he was there? Start once more from scratch? He knew as he sat there, that he had no more strength for that. He sighed heavily, he could feel that he

83

was extremely tired. What had gone wrong with the children? It would be better to ask the ANC what exactly they were up to. He remembered that once, long ago, when Mandela was not in prison, he had a friend with whom he used to talk about the ANC, Baloyi, that was his name; Baloyi had left long ago, and Lucas wished he could go and ask him, what is all this? He would tell him what van Niekerk had said to him. Van Niekerk had said, although there are problems here, there and there with bantustan leaders, he should think about talking to them; he, Lucas, knew as van Niekerk said this, that he must never go to see those people, never. He had heard of the meeting at which it was said Mlambo was talking, but also, something had told him he should not go there. He resented the fact that Mlambo, it seemed, had sent those little boys and girls to talk to him. Why, why couldn't Mlambo himself come to him?

"Lucas, what are you thinking about?"

"Nothing."

"What are we going to do?"

Lucas sighed.

"We can't live like this, what are we going to do?"

Lucas felt deep anger engulf him. He did not want to look at Mabel. He hoped, with all the strength that was left in him, that Mabel was not going to ask that question again.

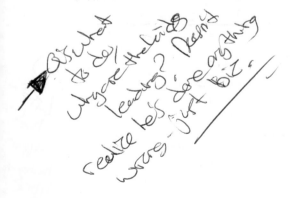

84

12

TWELVE

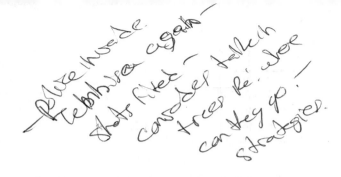

The night was dark and starless. The darkness blinded the eyes. It was dead quiet, except where they were now. They had brought with them the sounds of the streets from where they had come. The Western countries, a part of the earth which had gone through the madness of Hitler, talked on and on. What were they saying? Violence cannot be condoned. Yet they did not hesitate to use it when their interests were threatened, no matter where in the world they went, with fire and fury, they said if innocent civilians are affected, who does not know that war kills? Mozambique, Cuba … The young boys and girls now huddled under a tree, under a very dark sky, with nowhere else to go. The West, the world of Reagan, Thatcher and their friends, the world of greed and avarice and murder would never come to know that hate of oppression had become so ripe, it was hateless; suffering had been lived to its fathomless depth, and so had become non-existent, ignorance had embraced people with all its might and rendered itself powerless, and, as the Western world spoke and spoke and spoke about how, if Botha was squeezed, the blacks would suffer, about how surely, there were alternatives to the problems of South Africa, under this night and this tree, the truth was that any space, no matter where it was situated, would do for a meeting place. The lives of these six young people carried with them sounds whose touch took life, spilled blood, and left an eerie silence, a silence which forever threatened to break, threatened to come once more, a silence which forever threatened life. Life had stopped being lived in Tembisa, the Vaal, Uitenhage. In every single space of South Africa, except for that which was clutched and which clung to illusions – life was no longer being lived. Therefore, time, which can move as slowly as a million years, was slow in illuminating the existing gulf between blacks and whites – blacks who had

85

nothing to lose, having given everything, and whites who thought they had everything to lose, since they had taken everything.

Steve and his group, on leaving Cynthia, Lungi and the others in the house, had separated after agreeing where they would regroup an hour from then. Each had taken different paths and each, that night, had seen, heard and felt what he or she had seen, heard and felt once faced with the dark streets which the law had prohibited from being used after ten at night. They regrouped under this tree, under the starless night sky, knowing that once more, Tembisa was being invaded.

"We have to make a decision," Steve said. "One of us must go back and alert the two groups we left behind. There is no doubt the police and army are here to search."

The night, unable to conspire with sounds, told them so. For, far in the distance, casspirs, hippos, trucks and cars could be heard entering the sleeping town – if ever Tembisa was a town, and if at all, it could sleep. It was pointless to criticise whoever decided to plan and build Tembisa. There was no other way Tembisa could have been built except the way it was. It popped out from where it did into an empty patch, like so many other places of its type. And in time, spreading the length and breadth of South Africa, Tembisa, without consideration that children are born and people must live there, became a township. The history of these townships is as tragic as the history of South Africa. It could not have been otherwise. South African history had informed the planners of these townships that one day they would have to be attacked, and so they were built, and so it was easy to attack them. But then, no human being lives comfortably with the full knowledge that at any time he or she can be attacked, and does nothing about it. It is those who planned the townships and who attack who have a problem. For, in planning the townships as targets to attack, which are also places to live in, if those who are supposed to accept their traps as liveable begin to live instead in trees, in broken cars, and inside pipes and in holes, then the grand plan has failed. The grand planners then complain to the world that their targets are inhuman – how can they live in trees? – which is also a way of justifying and further believing that all means must be used to cow the madness of the blacks.

86

The third invasion of Tembisa by the police and army in less than six months was the result of what those who had been captured in the last two invasions had to tell their captors – that they were determined to stay alive, against whatever odds; so the invasion was going to pack the odds against life, and it would, they hoped, be more efficient than the previous two.

Steve, who had been away for over an hour, came back to the tree. He gave the signal and, as expected, the reply came from the top of the tree. He climbed up.

"Comrades," he said, once he had sat on a branch, having twisted his feet under it to make sure that he would not fall, "I think the other comrades heard the sounds of the coming boers. There was no-one at the house when I got there."

"Did you go into the house?" Thabo asked.

"No. It was dark and locked."

"Well, if they had time to switch the light off and to lock, they may be safe," Thabo said.

"Well, let's hope so," Steve said, "but listen, listen to that!"

The invasion came alive, combining the sound of the carriers and their cargo and the silence, the darkness and the intrinsic unknown which the night brings. Tembisa became a soft thunder of the night as the police and the army knocked and banged on doors and windows, shouting, while dogs barked and barked, and barked. From where Steve and his group were, they could see light spark to life at different windows of houses as if in rhythm.

In the tree, it was dead silent. Each person absorbed the meaning of what he or she saw. Each, perhaps, thought of a mother, father, now, once more, face to face with the might of the South African state. This might, once, long ago, was a mystery. It was a mystery and a feared might, because at that time, in that long ago time, in faraway countries, it used to bring the black townships and villages, without its being known or seen, very bad news indeed. News of death, brutality and ruthlessness, as it entered Angola, Mozambique, Lesotho, Botswana, Namibia, leaving behind, as evidence and proof, startlingly sprawled corpses of men, women and children, and, with pride and uncompromising frankness, the leaders of South Africa welcomed it back, announcing the results of its action, stating that there would be no hesitation in repeating the act, and that they hoped their boys had given some people, some nation, a very good lesson. The South African Defence Force had, once, long ago, been a mystery.

The majority of the oppressed in South Africa have never, for once, laboured under any illusion insofar as what the SADF, the SAP, and the leaders of South Africa are about. Nor was the invasion of Tembisa any surprise. Only, now and then, when this deeply-held knowledge suddenly manifested itself as a reality, it was after all, human, to be shocked. Steve was trying to visualise what would happen if the people of Tembisa were to emerge in the morning and find the corpses of soldiers and police scattered along the streets. He wondered what Mlambo would say if he posed that question to him. Would the people be jubilant? Would this make them feel defended, and ready to fight? What else, after all that had happened, was needed to make the people ready? Would this bring the day of liberation any nearer? But, have the oppressed people of South Africa not used everything they could, to fight? Why is it that the day of liberation still seemed so distant, so far away? How was it possible, that after so much blood had been spilt, Botha still had a word to add as to how oppression was a good thing for the oppressed. Steve thought about Lucas. Why did Lucas, who was black, who was oppressed, think the way did? He lived and saw misery and suffering around him every day – why couldn't he think like Mlambo? Steve felt frightened to think that skin colour does not always make people think alike.

He heard a sound. At first, he was not sure, then he heard it clearly – Thabo, with both hands clutching at a branch, was quietly snoring. By now, the ears and the heart, having absorbed the soft thunder of the Tembisa night, experienced it as familiar for whatever its effect may once have been, this was now lost.

"Mary, are you sleeping?" Steve asked.

"No."

"Jacob?"

"No."

"Billy?"

"No, I'm listening to the sounds of the night."

"Thabo is," Steve said.

"No, I'm not, the police are here, you know."

Everyone laughed.

"They are here, they have come to search and to take some of us, and to kill some," Steve said.

"Yes," Thabo whispered.

"We came here to work out a way of surviving. As far as I can see, this is a way of life now, we have to live as hunted people, how are we going to do this?"

"We must find a way," Thabo said, "I do not buy the idea that we should go to other locations, as if there are no police and soldiers there – soon they will even be going to the rural areas."

"No, but we should go to places where the police do not know us," Mary said.

"They don't have to know you – it is enough just to be young," Jacob wryly pointed out.

"Well," Mary said, "we have to change our way of working, maybe work at night and sleep during the day."

"Or work twenty-four hours," Billy said.

"Let's be practical," Steve said, "does anyone here know people outside Tembisa?"

"Ja, I do," Billy said, "in Alex."

"I know some in Katlehong," Mary said.

"Would they protect you?" Thabo asked.

"Ja," Mary said.

"Ja, but I think they would be over-protective, they wouldn't allow me to move out of the house," Billy said.

"I can go to Pietersburg," Jacob said.

"That's far away."

"Look," Steve said, "we are merely exploring possibilities – we have to know where there are places we can go to, near or far, then we can work out the practical details. We can also work out and agree on who should use them and what for. Okay, so we have Alex, Katlehong, Pietersburg – I can add Orlando. Anywhere else?"

"Sebokeng," Thabo said.

"Katlehong, Sebokeng, Alex, Orlando, Pietersburg – is that all? Rebecca, anything?" Steve asked.

"I'm thinking of Chiawelo, I have an aunt there, she's alright."

Just then, the darkness and silence of Tembisa shattered, there was machine-gun fire. Among the tree dwellers, there was a brief silence. There were sounds of cars and trucks, shots, and yet another explosion.

"That comes from the direction of Moeding," Steve said.

"It seems so," Thabo agreed.

"Anyway there are about six places we can work on, I suggest that when we leave here, each of us should move towards the places you have mentioned. We'll give each other a week, Jacob will go with me to Orlando," Steve said, "we will reserve Pietersburg for now, do we agree on that?"

Silence.

"No, comrades, in the places we are going to, we have to find out how the people there will receive us, without revealing our plight. We want the people to protect us by giving us places to stay and information about the area regarding safe streets, politically active people, means of transport, and also to tell us about informers, agents, police and army personnel; this should be what guides us as to whether we are still going to work in Tembisa and what work we will be doing." Steve searched the darkness for his comrades.

"Are there any of us who will leave the country?" Jacob asked.

"If we have to, we will," Steve said.

"What do you mean, if we have to?"

"I mean if we can no longer work."

"We are not trained and we need to be trained," Jacob continued.

"I know that we are not trained. I'm suggesting that those who feel they can still do work here should think in the direction I suggested, and that those who feel that they want to leave, should say so."

"I want to go," Jacob said.

"I want to go," Rebecca said.

"Anyone else?" Steve asked.

Silence.

"Both of you want to leave at the same time?" Steve asked.

Silence.

"Ja," Rebecca said.

"Before we work out how you will leave, can you introduce us to the places you said may be safe?"

"That will take a long time," Jacob said.

"But can you?" Thabo interjected.

"Ja, but that will take time."

"How will it take time?"

"I want to leave," Jacob said in a hard manner. There was a brief silence.

"I can introduce you there, Steve," Rebecca said.

"Jacob, it is important that you are not impatient about your leaving," Steve warned.

"Why is it that when the issue of leaving comes up, people become touchy?"

"Jacob, that, as you know, is a sensitive matter."

"Lots of people have left – why does it become special when we are involved?"

"What is the time?" Steve asked.

"Four-thirty," Mary said.

"Jacob, I'm cutting you short, but can you and I deal with this matter later? I'm thinking that we should organise our departure from here."

"We must talk on that matter, you know, I've tried to raise it all the time, and all the time it is avoided."

"We will talk about it, I promise," Steve said. "Today is the 17th of September – when will we meet again, and where?"

"You said in a week's time," Thabo said.

"Does that give everyone enough time?"

"Ja," Mary agreed.

"Ja," Billy added.

"Okay," Rebecca said.

"No, why not meet in two weeks?" Thabo suggested.

"Okay, let's meet here at ten-thirty at night on the first of October," Steve said, as he climbed down the tree. There was a rustling of leaves and branches as, yawning, one by one, they carefully climbed down the tree.

13

THIRTEEN

"Where have you been all this time?" Lindi asked me.

"I've been around," I said.

"Where?"

"Tembisa."

"I've been looking for you, you know," she looked rushed, "there's something I must talk to you about," she lowered her voice, "there's a woman, her name is Nomvula, she has been seeing me, she wants me to help, do you know her?"

"Yes, I do."

"Do you trust her?"

"I have no reason not to trust her."

"She wants me to hide some children."

"She talked to you?"

"Yes."

"And?"

"I said I want to think about it."

"And?"

"I think I can help, but I want to be sure there will be no trouble."

"You want Nomvula to assure you that there will be no trouble – she can't do that!"

I had not seen Lindi in a long time indeed. The troubles of my town had seized me. No-one had not been touched by what was going on in our land – perhaps many of my white countrymen and countrywomen felt that our troubles were remote from them, but then, even they would never ever be the same again. Their streets were not as bloody as ours; perhaps they, unlike us, slept peacefully at night, but certainly, strange sounds at night left them restless. Some slept with guns under their pillows, most never forgot to switch on the burglar alarm, to secure their gate, to watch all

92

black people carefully. The ANC had by now called on all of us to take the struggle to the white areas. The call among us all hung like a thick dark cloud in the sky just before a heavy downpour. We were all pensive about this. We were all talking about it. Even our enemies agreed that South Africa would not be the same again. They were strange days, those. Every time one walked the streets, in one person there were two people: one dealing with life, the other with death. Esther had left the country. I had refused to leave. I had not been to Tembisa in a long time. I do not know where I had been, or to put it another way, I do not know where I had not been. South Africa, a big country indeed, had become at times too small for me, at others too big. In a sense, this is what had made me refuse to leave it; I did not think it was small, although in everyday life it almost always proved itself to be so, and then, when it did seem to be big, it threatened life, it seemed to give no sanctuary. But I knew, it could be like a lover, very possessive, and I said it must possess me, or I would possess it.

Here, then, I was with Lindi. I did not know where she had been, and she did not know where I had been, but we already, each, possessed a struggle vocabulary, which slowly, yet with great care, made us listen to each other very carefully.

"She can't do that!" Lindi said, looking away from me at the distant trees, flowers, fountain, and people, white and black, all of them walking their different ways, through the one-time segregated park, a bloody park. There was a sadness in Lindi's eyes, but also anger, also confusion, also a hurriedness, impatience, but also, something told me, she was struggling to harmonise the turmoil. I had seen this in many faces of mothers and fathers. I had seen this in many young faces.

"That is true," Lindi said, "Nomvula can't assure me of that!"

"Can you hide the children?"

"I think I can."

"They will need food, they will need to walk around, they will be very secretive, they will not want you to ask them where they have been, what they've been doing. They will also want you to be secretive about their living with you. Will you hide them?"

She looked at me, straight in my eyes.

"I will hide them," she said.

93

A great sorrow held me, at this point. "Tell Nomvula," I said.

I saw tears roll down Lindi's face – she took out a handkerchief, wiped her eyes, blew her nose, coughed lightly, and then sat back on the red park bench.

"Where have you been?" she asked.

"Lindi!"

"Okay, you don't have to answer," she said, "how is Esther?"

"She left the country."

"There's too much trouble in our country," she said.

"Yes," I said.

"I went to see Skopendonner," Lindi said.

"How is he?"

"He asked a lot about what is going on in the streets."

"You told him?"

"It's difficult to talk through those bars, but I tried, we sometimes have to talk at the top of our voices. I felt uncomfortable, but he urged me."

"What did he want to know?"

"He wanted to know if even in Soweto there was fighting. Then he asked me about Sebokeng, East London, Western Cape, Umlazi and many other townships. But the guard kept threatening us, and eventually he chased me away."

"Have you been singing?"

"Yes, I went to sing in Tembisa. I thought I would see you there."

"I heard the police and army stopped the concert?"

"Yes, they did."

"They killed lots of people on that day."

"Yes, they did."

"Are you still going to sing?"

"I want to."

"How can you if now you are going to become a hen with chickens under its wings?"

"Chickens eat, so I have to fend for them."

I laughed.

"You laugh?"

"No, well, I can't cry."

"I know," she said.

"How have you been though, where are Billy, John and the others?"

"They are there. They are fine. We have become a makeshift band now. We meet when we can, sing when we can. But otherwise we go out grazing like cattle, at times far from one another. I think it is because of the times, you know, the tension, it's difficult to get an audience."

"Where's Job?"

"He now and then plays at white or multiracial night clubs, he's okay too," she looked at me, and then, something which made her look as if she was uncertain, cleared: "How come Esther left?"

"Well, the police were looking for us."

She turned quickly to look at me.

"Are they still looking for you?"

"Yes."

She was quiet for a while. It seemed her mind was racing, she looked, once more, in that thoughtful manner of hers, into the distance, at the trees ...

"You have been hiding, then?"

"Not really – ja, perhaps you can say that."

"How did you know that we should meet here, then?"

"Well, you told Lungi, didn't you?"

"I did, yes, but was that okay?"

"It worked, that means it is."

"It's okay?"

"Ja."

"Is it okay that we are seated here, then?"

"We should not overdo it."

"How long are you going to live like this?"

"I don't know."

"I think you must leave the country."

So many people had said that to me. Sometimes this made me sad. Especially if they were people I knew, and loved. Somehow I had thought we would want to know how we could assure our not having to leave, so we could fight the boers. People saying this meant, sometimes, that they were very eager to disassociate themselves from the troubles, which could also be bloody; but at other times, they meant pure love for me and had full knowledge of

95

what the process of this act might be. I had learnt I had to sniff out the two positions very quickly; I had also learnt to take quick action accordingly.

"Why must I leave, Lindi?"

Lindi was quiet for some time, then she looked at me.

"Do you feel you must stay, then?"

"Yes, I do."

"Why?"

"You answer a question by asking another."

"I want to know," she said, "it is a serious issue, and I must not rush to conclusions."

She was quiet for a while, then she began to fidget with her dress as she shifted around on the red park bench, and then: "You'll have to be very disciplined."

"I agree."

"So what will happen to you and Esther?"

"I don't know."

She shook her head from side to side, "Well," she said, "there you are!"

"Have you worked out where you will hide your chickens?"

"Ja. I've talked to Lady," she said.

"Don't tell me anything," I said.

"I'm in love with Billy," she said. It was very sad the way she said it.

"Billy?"

"Ja."

"What of Skopendonner?"

"I don't know," she said.

"When did you go to see Skopendonner?"

"In December."

"That's five months ago."

"Is it? Ja!"

"And Billy?"

"I see him now and then, all the time."

"Well, there you are!"

She laughed. Then, suddenly serious, she said, "Everything is so difficult."

"Yes!"

"So many children have died!"

"True!"

"I thought I would never see you again," she said.

What was it? It was very difficult to say, but something kept nagging, urging that one try to articulate it. These days we were living in, the minutes, hours, days, months, even, had taken their toll, had made their impact, had held us by the arm, as a people; these were long days which were now saturated by a past which had hidden itself, brooding, within our hearts and minds and blood. It was deep, deep in us; its heat was intense, we had all been anxious that we hatch or be hatched. This present we were living in had, without our being aware, erased our survival vocabulary, and burnt into our tongues a language which Lindi and I, seated on this red park bench with its erased "Europeans only" sign, were consciously trying to articulate. If we did articulate it, we would have to become new friends, living in a new time. I was wondering how it was possible that Lindi could part with Skopendonner. How Skopendonner could part with Lindi, despite the iron bars which he was behind, despite the bars she had held in front of her as she shouted, her voice hoarse about what was going on in the streets. I also remembered the look in Esther's eyes, which she may also have seen in mine, when eventually we acknowledged that we would part, that beyond that, we did not know what would happen to either of us.

But then, I thought, where I had been, while there, I had been aware of another thing: Once, it was a matter of pride to have been a member of the Movement, but now, the days which were unfolding before us were like a torrent, mercilessly washing debris away, carrying it in floods along its route to a despicable destiny. On the other hand, we knew that beyond the torrent there would be sprouting, blooming, sunshine and fresh air. However, at this hour, nothing was tangible.

I had been to Sebokeng, where Lindi's message had reached me and brought me to her here, by her side, on a red park bench. We had disposed of what was a matter of life and death, as Lindi had now said. She was going to become a hatching chicken. She looked at me, stared at me, searched into my depths as I answered every question about the role she was about to assume – well, there she was. She was reading the distant blue horizon. She was reading above and beyond the blooming tree tops, and listening to the many, many footsteps of domestic servants, one-time madams and masters and hobos passing through the park.

"I have not done much," Lindi said, "but I feel very tired." She sighed, "I think a lot these days. I don't understand my life. I don't know what is going on."

"In battle, that is called combat fatigue," I said. I may have been talking about myself. There were many things I wanted to tell Lindi, I was trying to find a way of saying them – perhaps she had something to tell me as we sat there, carefully approaching the unknown.

"If I may ask," she said, "what have you been doing?" She had read my thoughts. "It's very difficult to know," I said, "I have been doing many things, but you know, since there is so much happening around and about us, what one does always seems so insignificant."

"Insignificant?"

"Yes, you know, doing is no longer measured in terms of life."

"It is measured in terms of deaths, then?"

"It is measured in terms of cutting, link for link, the chain of oppression, whatever the cost."

"When you say that, you know, I keep thinking, how does one do that, can singing do that, can hiding children do that, can throwing a stone or petrol bomb do that, what can?"

"That's the point, you see – not a single act, but a combination of all those can do it."

She looked at me. Her eyes were thoughtful. She looked away, sighed and said:

"No one person can do all those!"

"I have been to many parts of this country. I sit here, I try to imagine how I can relate and understand what I saw, what I helped get done. What I see unfolding. It is so elusive, now here, now gone ... "

"No," she said, "we are at war, it is tangible, because it takes what you may have touched away. It is elusive because we call it war – not blood, not corpses, not burnt houses, cars, shops, you see ... "

"No, Lindi, I am not concerned with that, you know, I have been to what the newspapers call the Vaal, I have been to the Eastern Cape, the Western Cape, to Natal, Umlazi, Edendale and many other areas. I see, I hear the same things which you and I have seen and heard and lived. I don't see what the newspapers say. I see, I feel a force stronger than any steel or diamond. It is unleashed, and I hear America, Britain and France, and I think, how come they don't know that this force exists, that this force is strong? Why do these countries talk as if this force is not in motion, as if they do not know that it will crush everything before it? Why?"

"But you are talkng about white countries."

"Yes and no. Yes, there are white countries, but this is important only because the whites believe they are a master race; no because even here, now, there are blacks who are talking like America and Britain. But you see, there are two forces now; whenever South Africa is talked about, there will be two languages, one defending the oppressor, the other defending the oppressed."

"Are there blacks then who talk defending the oppressor?"

"Defending their interests, which are not the interests of the oppressed, you see!"

"That is heavy," Lindi said.

"I saw this, I felt this, you know, I was walking around Evaton, discussing, driving, burying the dead, listening and running and evading bullets, teargas, sneeze fumes, and, now and then, when the noise was dead, I would walk past the killers, boys who are not yet men, and I would ask myself, what do they think they are doing?"

"They are dogs – murderous dogs!"

"No, they are defending someone's interests."

"Someone?"

"Ja, you know there are three companies, Anglo, Barlow-Rand and Sanlam; these three own the wealth of this country, and they are being defended, by America, Britain, and by the Government, by the police and the army, they are being defended against this force I was telling you about."

"No, but they are defending baasskap."

"Ja, baasskap, but you see, these three I mentioned have made whites the master race so that the whites will defend them; the wealth of South Africa is white private property."

"But Botha shouts at the business people now."

"He does, but that is all he can do."

"No, he can send the police and the army after them, can't he?"

"No, he can't; you see, if he does that, they may take their money and their skills with them, and then the casspirs stop, the soldiers go hungry, the police go hungry, he would have chaos on his hands."

"I see, so the business people can blackmail Botha?"

"They control him."

"Who controls the business people then?"

"We are about to, you see, that's why there is so much blood, they want to stay in power over us eternally, taking everything and keeping us in control by giving us so little, or making us fight against each other, or hiring a few from among us into their fold. Now, what has been happening in the streets, is a direct challenge to the power that takes all and gives so little, or plays the oppressed against each other ... "

"We are fighting for power?"

"Yes."

"So we can control?"

"Yes."

"Control who?"

"Control the wealth of our country so that there is no oppressed or oppressor, white or black, but people building a country which is liveable."

"How do you know that is going to happen?"

"We have the ANC."

"Why would the ANC not do what the boers are doing?"

"The ANC, Lindi, has a history, it is a movement of the oppressed majority who are now challenging the power of Barlow-Rand, Sanlam and Anglo-American. The ANC says South Africa belongs to all who live in it, black and white ... "

"But there are so many organisations, UDF, Cosas, Azaso, and that one of women – Fedtraw, so many!"

"That is our history, that is how we have defined our interests, and how we are going to fight for them, but more important is that the ANC, with its long history and experience and its composition, defends the oppressed, and will defend South Africa against the oppression of any other race."

"You sound so certain."

"I am certain."

"You mean that all the kids who are petrol bombing and stoning are ANC?"

"That is not important, what is important is that they know that the ANC is their leader and they listen to it."

"I must go now," Lindi looked thoughtful, she looked tired, and she sighed, "you must not disappear, you must come and see us."

"You and Billy?"

"Yes, and the children."

"Okay," I said.

She stood up, fixed her dress and slowly picked up her bag.

"I will see you," she said.

"Be careful."

"You too."

I saw Lindi walk away and become part of the many many people who were now emerging from the buildings and pouring into the streets. It was lunch time. I saw her join them, and, I thought, I have not told her my story. That, when I was in the Vaal, I had sensed a deep triumph. I had walked past SASOL, now seemingly intact, steel, wire fence, police, the army and all, looking formidable. I had seen it, and also seen the workers emerge from within its gates, past the police and soldiers back to the troubled townships, some to their compounds. SASOL was not their pride; the townships were Botha's pride, but they were not the workers' pride, nor were the compounds. It was strange to walk past it, feeling dwarfish because of its fence, its size and also because of what it is. But, looking at it, I also remembered how once, not so long ago, we had watched when MK struck at it, when it stood dwarfed by flames which it seemed to release at great speed, around and about itself. It seemed to thrash about like a mad, badly hurt snake which keeps poisoning itself as it tries to heal its wounds. We had seen it engulfed in raging flames which

101

rendered the fire brigades, the police, the soldiers – the whole efficient communication system – helpless before its self-destructive might. Not only that, but also, we who watched, who stood by as spectators – I should, I must one day tell Lindi this story, when I see her again and when I understand its significance more fully ... I was feeling very weak, frightened and uncertain as I stood up to go.

14

FOURTEEN

Mlambo was walking up and down the street. The moon was bright. The breeze blew and soothed his clammy skin. It was silent. He thought of days gone by, of long-ago days as a school-boy, a mineworker, and a factory worker. The days of the trade union, of congress, of jail, of coming back to Evaton to a banning order, rejection by his wife, attachment to his children whom he had to learn to love in silence, watching, listening and carefully asking questions. He came back after the noise, when everything had been broken. Evaton had shrivelled like a dry orange peel that was discarded in the dust; too many houses were broken, there were too many empty patches where once there had been houses, friends' homes, drinking places, barber shops, garages – all these had been erased. Other townships, more regimented, barren, monotonous, were sprawled in what had once been empty patch-es. Children had become men and women, old people had gone – only a few remained, and of that few, a few had waited for him. They had, with great patience, opened their eyes and faces for him to read. They had told him of the quietness, the mad noises of the young, the despair of the dead, the thoughts of the living. Mlambo had listened with great care, his hope being those he had left behind, on the Island. Their strength, their hope, their courage, their determination, were what he had brought with him to those who had lived first under Verwoerd, then Vorster and now Botha. Most times he had asked the questions. He had listened as the sto-ries of a people were told and as they unfolded from their mouths, stories from bygone days. He had listened and watched – and then his questions were answered when one day, Orlando Police station was attacked, then Booysens Police station, Soekmekaar Police station, and then it became an everyday expectation that, when sunrise came, one asked, has there been an MK operation?

He moved, one day, here, to Tembisa. He was ready. He built a zinc shack in the yard, and every morning, every early evening people came to the shack to buy newspapers, to exchange a word, to tell of what they had heard, what they knew or what they had seen. Now, events had taken him away from the shack. Tonight, walking up and down, he was also thinking about where he would sleep. But more, he was waiting for Cynthia. Many times when he thought about her, he would smile, he would laugh. Cynthia, now tall, thin, pretty, could also at times be noisy or stubborn, but what now and then really perturbed Mlambo was when she was impulsive; otherwise he watched her, with a sense of nurturing her. Cynthia appeared from the shadows of the moon. She was wearing, as always, a black track-suit. She walked swiftly across the yard, crawled under the fence, strode into the street, to the corner, looked this way and that way, then proceeded to the tree. Mlambo was watching her.

"I greet you, father," Cynthia said in Sesotho.

"Where are you?" Mlambo answered likewise.

"I'm here," she said, "I'm sent by Ntate Monnakgotla."

"I know."

"He said to tell you the shoes will arrive tomorrow."

"Is that so?"

"Yes."

"And how have you been?"

"I have been alright. We have managed to settle Lentshwe, Thabiso, Nomathemba and Kgathatso."

"Where?"

"Attridgeville."

"Are they staying at the same place?"

"No, two in a place."

"Have you heard from Steve?"

"Yes. He is worried about Jacob."

"What about Jacob?"

"He acts strangely."

"Is it about his leaving the country?"

"Yes."

"And Strike?"

"He's okay, he still talks about it."

"We want people to go out, that we want, but it must be the right people. How is Lungi?"

"She's fine, she managed to get a group of professionals. She is now in Alexandra."

"Are you going back to Krugersdorp?"

"Yes."

"Fine. You see, Botha is acting like a madman now. As we expected, he has become a self-appointed policeman for southern Africa. His army is once more in Angola, he cheated Machel – we expected him to, although we do not know if he will undo what the people of Mozambique achieved through sacrifice – and now he's putting new pressure on Botswana and Lesotho. I am worried about those grenade attacks in Lesotho, but Jonathan has shown that he has brains. But you see, what all this means is that there is no permanent rear base – better then to create it here inside the country. This is what we have to understand, that as you settle people in Alexandra, Evaton, Orlando, this is what you are doing. You are creating a base for our organisation – and so, who, where, what they are there for, whom they are with, all these are very important questions which we have to answer. Wherever you are, you are representing the organisation. Never forget that, it is what you do that will determine what support the organisation will receive from the people around you. These are standing issues which must occupy our minds all the time. What we do is very important. We know what we must do, we agree on that; we must be co-ordinated in how we do it, this is the most difficult task at this hour. Our people have taken a position against white domination, they reject it, they are prepared to pay the highest price so that they can do away with this domination. So, what to do is the issue, how and when are the vital questions. As you settle others, as you settle yourself, as you relate to those who are risking everything they have so they can settle us, let these questions be paramount in our day-to-day life and discussions; our people have accepted armed struggle with all its consequences. So, when Strike or Jacob say they want to leave for training, this is the background we have to bear in mind to guide us as to how we implement their wish. It is correct that young people are demanding that they go for training, it is correct, and we must facilitate it. I am not undermining your fears and your suspicions, all I can say is that the ANC has held the bull by its horns many times, many, many times. We can rely on this if we remember also that we are the ANC and it is us. I do not want to waste your time, you must go."

"You have said so many things!"

"I'm thinking aloud," Mlambo said, "take that with you, we must discuss again some time."

"Anything for Ntate Monnakgotla?"

"No. Tell him you gave me the message. Go now."

Back into the moon shadows, whence she came, Cynthia disappeared. Mlambo walked down the street slowly, he looked at his watch and saw that it was one in the morning. Lucas wants to see him? He cannot deny him that. The Movement must meet those who want to talk to it. He was trying to work out who he would take with him to go to see Lucas. Lucas was playing at bending backwards, he was experiencing serious difficulties in tearing himself from the boers. Why? Mlambo wondered if he should go to see him: why? He suppressed his anger. He heard footsteps coming his way. He stopped awhile, looking in the direction from where the sound came and humming a liberation song which he had heard at the last meeting of union stewards.

> *How will it be that day*
> *when I sit with Tambo*
> *to tell him*
> *the boers have been run over?*

"Evening, father," the voice said.

"You are late!" Mlambo responded.

"I was late for … "

"You must not be late, you must keep time!"

"I am sorry … "

"You must not be sorry, keep time, that is all!"

There was a taut silence.

"I have word from MaNhlapo."

"What is it?"

"She says she does not think that you should go and see Lucas."

106

"Okay. Anything else?"

"Strike is ready to leave."

"Fine."

"Rebecca thinks she can handle Lucas."

"Why Rebecca?"

"She wants to."

"No! No! Someone else, not Rebecca. Also, I think Strike should leave with Jacob. And pass the message to Lungi, I want to see her. Tell MaNhlapo that we have received the shoes. Good."

Steve walked away. He was exhausted and sleepy. He had come with many questions in his mind which he had thought he would ask Mlambo. But he knew better. He let them pass. He wondered as he went down the street where he would sleep that night.

Mlambo had crossed three blocks, and was now turning into a gate. He stood a while at the door, thinking. His shadow was elongated and fell over the fence into the street, the night was peaceful, brightly lit, a soft breeze blew gently over the sleeping Tembisa. He knocked on the door.

"Who is that?" a woman's voice asked.

"It's me."

There was a brief silence. The door rattled and opened. Mlambo walked in slowly, adjusting to the darkness of the house. He stopped awhile in the middle of the room. He could make out that there were people sleeping on the floor; he could hear someone snoring in the other room. The house being four-roomed, he guessed that there may be at least six people there.

"You sleep very lightly," Mlambo said.

"Yes, I do," Nomvula agreed, "have you come to sleep?"

"Yes, if there is space, I am very tired."

"Okay, you can use my room, I will join the children in the sitting room."

"Are you sure?"

"Yes, no problem, I like sleeping on the floor, shall I make you food or tea?"

"No, I'm alright."

"Are you sure?"

"What do you mean am I sure. I tell you I'm alright. How is

107

Thuledu?"

"She's fine, they have stopped going to school, she is asking many questions."

Mlambo, while standing in the middle of the room as Nomvula was preparing bedding in the dining room, began to hum his song once more.

"You heard about Lucas?" she asked.

"What?"

"He told the newspaper that he will not be intimidated by children. He says three boys came to his shop and asked for him and wanted to talk to him about the struggle; he says he will not do that."

"Lucas is a fool. Let him be. I have been so unfortunate, I can't lay my hands on newspapers, the radio or even TV. I must buy myself a small radio to keep in my pocket. Are you through?"

"Yes, you can go in."

"Thank you, please wake me up at six, I hope I will make it in time to Benoni," he shut the door, and it was not long before Nomvula heard him snoring.

Nomvula had to move house from where she, Sipho, Thuledu and little Themba were living. After Sipho's death, Nomvula had kept by the side of MaNhlapo and MaMorula. They had visited her often, had tea together, and visited other bereaved families, especially spending time with women. There were many women wearing mourning clothes in Tembisa. Nomvula began to know them. She realised she was not the only one who had lost a son, and so she became aware of Tembisa. It was after Sipho's death that she began to become aware of his world, the world which he lived and died for. It was a world of many people who came and went; who today one hears about, tomorrow one talks to, and then one day they are gone; they may come back, they may not. Nomvula sensed that this world which she now found herself part of was spreading, she felt it was fathomless and endless like the sea. Every day she was learning new things, more than she had learnt in all the thirty-seven years of her life.

In the short time since she had entered Sipho's world, she had been to the remotest parts of Tembisa, parts which she never thought existed. She had lived a quiet life. Ever since the time when her girlhood boyfriend, who later became her husband and father to her two sons, died in hospital after a fight in a shebeen. She had felt robbed, she had felt the world had been very cruel to her, she had not been able to forgive, nor forget, and she had, without thinking, shut herself behind the doors of their house, between this and the buzzing machines at work where she had come to learn, since Sipho died, that even there, a world underneath the world, existed.

Nomvula's Realization
world underneath the
world existed

① Nomvula - feeling world
of her & Sipho after
his death — world of
canvts' - going - uncertainties

15

FIFTEEN

Lucas woke up that morning, having decided that the city is a cursed place. The people of the city are ungrateful, are mean, are not worthy of being called people. He also hated, feared van Niekerk, and wondered why it was not possible for black people to know and understand that they cannot fight the white man, that they had a lot to learn from what the white man knows and has done. He hated van Niekerk because he seemed to have lost any human touch. He talked about the dead, the communists, the agitators in the same way a priest would talk about the devil, but also, Lucas thought, van Niekerk hated black people. Van Niekerk always made it clear to Lucas that war does not allow for betrayals; those who betray, pay with their lives.

Every time van Niekerk said this, Lucas felt and knew that van Niekerk meant that he would not hesitate to mete out the same punishment to him if he thought Lucas had betrayed him. Van Niekerk also always told Lucas that he must remember that the mad little boys and girls would not hesitate to kill him, so Lucas had no choice but to do what he was told. He told Lucas that if he were not able to keep secrets which they shared, he would not hesitate to leak to the boys and girls what Lucas had told him, and the results of this information. Lucas feared van Niekerk. He also feard his people. Lucas's wife, Mabel, had become quiet, unresponsive. Looking at his wife, watching her daily as she went out to the shops and came back to the house, taciturn, with a faraway look in her eyes, Lucas remembered how, when he was on the mines, a friend of his from Pondoland used to say, the love of a woman is like the life of a sheep, you feed it, it grows, becomes fat, and will fetch you a good price. You neglect it, it will become leaner and leaner and leaner and with time, be mean to you. This thought became his preoccupation. It also said a lot about what

110

was going on around him. He felt these were lean times for him, and somehow he had to find a way out so that the times would not catch him and be mean to him. But what to do?

Tembisa had become, for him, a very small place. It had shrunk to the size of his house. The streets were, to say the least, unkind. In Lucas's life, as in those of everybody else in Tembisa, the simple things of life still went on on a daily basis, people laughed, visited each other, went to work, bought soap, bread and still enjoyed a drink, maybe a Coke, beer or brandy. But the smell of teargas and gunsmoke, certain sounds, and also, the looks on some people's faces, reminded people of the changing times. Lucas was aware of these things and reacted to them like everybody else. However, everybody else did not have friends like van Niekerk. The relationship between Lucas and van Niekerk was defined in very strange terms. They laughed. They shook hands. Sometimes they ate together or shared a drink. Van Niekerk knew Lucas's family, though Lucas knew nothing about his friend's family. At times though, van Niekerk talked about his wife, but Lucas feared, never dared to ask about her. He wondered why – he just knew he should not ask for more than what was volunteered. Lucas had no idea where van Niekerk lived, he dared not ask, but dared not withold such information about himself.

Lucas despised van Niekerk. Van Niekerk suspected this. In cunning ways, now and then, van Niekerk tried to confirm his suspicions, but the trouble was that if these were to be confirmed, their relationship would have had to change. So it remained on the sharpest edge of the knife. Van Niekerk held the knife, Lucas lay on his belly, at its edge. Mabel was aware of this, and Lucas was aware that his wife was aware; in time, this brought a great piteous silence between them. Lucas thought that it was not only Tembisa which had shrunk, but his house, also, had become that corner at the eating table, that space on the bed, and the sofa in the sitting room.

The people of the city are mad. The old people are being controlled by children. They kill each other as if it were people killing snakes. Mabel was right, they must leave, they must go back to the country. The problem here was, every timne Lucas tried to take this decision, he could not come round to telling Mabel. He felt it weighed heavily on him, on his heart and mind. No matter how he tried to tell himself that whether things worked out or not, everything depended on what he and Mabel had once done, he suspected that this was not true. This made him go round and round and round like a mad fly whose wings have been clipped. Van Niekerk suspected that Lucas was not himself. Which pressure was he responding to, that of Tembisa or of Pretoria? Lucas, because of the way van Niekerk would look at him, talk to him, treat him, felt that he was being slowly lured to a snare. But why him, why should all this happen to him? Something about van Niekerk suggested to Lucas that, though thin, he was as strong as a steel wire. Van Niekerk, tall, thin and immaculate in his dress, spoke softly, firmly, making very small gestures, and all the time looking whoever he was talking to straight in the eye. He had a beautiful smile, shining green eyes, and often adjusted his tie. Lucas felt that now and then van Niekerk looked puzzled by something that he said or did. Perhaps it was because even though both of them were men, one was white and the other black, so Lucas thought. But why did van Niekerk think that he was always right, whatever he said or did? Lucas had on many occasions attempted to correct this, but he had to give up, he had to despair. He realised it was because van Niekerk had might that he was always right. Lucas feared this might. But he did not think the way to fight it was through stones and petrol bombs. Through wanton killing of black by black. Through boycotts or strikes. Through the bombing of buildings.

He had not told van Niekerk that Strike and two other boys had visited him. That he intended talking to Mlambo. Somehow, he felt, van Niekerk would not be able to handle this. He was white and this was a black matter. Van Niekerk had proved this many times. Van Niekerk was unable to listen, was unable to have confidence in him. Lucas had already made a mess of things. This was why that group of six boys and girls got killed. Van Niekerk had spoken with him, had told him what to do, and when Lucas hesitated, van Niekerk had told him, "leave it to me"; what followed was a high explosion which left six young corpses mutilated, and Tembisa very angry. Tembisa blaming the tragedy on van Niekerk. Tembisa saying the youth will be avenged, van Niekerk saying to Lucas, "you find out who made the pamphlet and I'll deal with

112

them", Lucas saying, "No! No, no, leave this thing to me." Lucas feeling things had gone too far, were out of control, and too bloody. Van Niekerk saying, with people who allow themselves to be used by communists, one had to be ruthless. Lucas saying, although he knew nothing about communists, he did not think the madness of the youth had anything to do with communists. It was just that parents had lost control over their children. And that was no reason to punish them by death. Van Niekerk had sat back, unblinking, and told Lucas, very calmly, "If that is what you think, you hold very dangerous and naïve thoughts." Upon which a great silence followed. And Lucas pleaded, "Leave this matter to me." "What are you going to do, what can you do?" Lucas replied, "I do not know, but leave it to me." Van Niekerk said, "If you think I will leave this matter to you, you must be out of your mind," he stood up, extended his hand, and they shook hands. Van Niekerk then left.

Three days later, Tembisa was invaded at night. The police and the army came, searching, swearing, beating, raping. When Lucas read the newspapers, it was said that the invasion was a regular search for criminals and hooligans. The police and army never found out who had produced the pamphlet. They had, in their search for criminals and hooligans, left behind a few corpses of school children. Lucas felt sickened by the shootings and grieved for the corpses. When he expressed this to van Niekerk, van Niekerk had said, "Perhaps you are entitled to your naïvety, but for now, I am looking after South Africa …"

Strike, Jacob and Sipho had come to see Lucas.

"We would like to talk to you about the deaths of our comrades," Strike began, his calmness influenced by the way he had seen Mlambo carry himself during moments of crisis. "You are aware that we are very sad about what happened. We know, though, that there is no struggle without casualties – but we must not allow this to go on as if we don't care. So we have come to talk to you."

"What do you think I can do?"

"We think that all of us must do something about this."

"What?"

"We are calling a mass meeting, we request that you give us

113

money for the hall, to print pamphlets and to organise transport."

"Meetings are forbidden, are they not?"

"Who forbade them?"

"The government."

"Whose government?"

"The government of South Africa."

"It is not our government, we will not listen to it, we are organising a mass meeting. Will you help?"

"All this is wrong. Besides I want to talk to someone older, not you."

"But why?"

"Frankly, I don't want to talk to children about such grave matters."

"We may be children, but your government does not treat us as such."

"Mass meetings and stones will not stop these killings … "

"Father Lucas," Strike said, "why does it seem as if you have no confidence in your people? If you don't, whose confidence do you enjoy?"

"You know … " Jacob was about to explain.

"Wait, Jacob, wait," Sipho said.

Lucas looked at them, each in turn. He thought about van Niekerk.

"I will talk with Mlambo. I think you must go now," he said and stood up. Strike, Jacob and Sipho left the house. They did not talk to each other. Each went to his hiding-place.

It happened after the mass meeting. The army and the police were there, and it was said, they were at strategic corners of the township, keeping a low profile. I don't know what that means. All I know is that we walked out of the hall, poured into the streets, our wet rags in hand, knowing that any time, the familiar sound could come. The familiar smell could come. Nothing happened, but, having become familiar with the history of our death and our life, this made us know and understand that soon, we would have to be ready to fight. Except for the sound of cars and a train in the distance, we were surrounded by silence, a disturbing silence. We passed the young policemen and soldiers on their trucks, casspirs and hippos, with their inevitable luggage. We watched each other,

114

not as countrymen, but as strangers ... We walked on, mo
fathers, boys and girls. I saw van Niekerk. No-one had not see
him. Far away, in the distance, I saw thick smoke rise to the sky,
in slow, thick curls; it shaded the light and created a shadow over
Tembisa. We walked on. I heard the cars and the casspirs roar and
move. Some remained behind, others followed us. Behind us,
another pall of smoke, the size of a mountain, loomed in the sky.
It was strange to see how, in a short space of time, as the smoke
thickened, the streets became deserted. Even the hippos, trucks,
casspirs and police cars responded to the smoke which now, on
both sides, was the colour of flames. It was not long before we
began to hear shots in the distance, in the direction of the two
places from where the smoke and flames had emerged.

Once the police were gone, I heard, not far from where I was,
a freedom song. This song, like the smoke, like the flames, like the
quiet of the streets as they were deserted, created for all of us there
a moment of atonement. It was a moment when, quietly, secretly
and with great hope in our hearts, we knew that one day, Botha's
high place would come crumbling down. Tembisa knew, as we
moved from the mass meeting where Monnakgotla had talked and
the people of Tembisa had talked, and talked and talked, as if to
say, now that we have earned our right to talk, through our own
sweat and blood, we shall talk and flood the sky with our hopes –
Tembisa knew, that now, at last, its will would be put into practice.
I saw Lucas appear from the opposite direction. He was followed
by Strike and Sipho. Lucas's hands were bound behind him. He
had only one shoe on, and seemed to have put on his trousers in a
great hurry. His shirt was torn, he was saying something. I do not
know what. Strike and Sipho flanked him. Behind them were a
few girls and boys, singing our song:

> *We have never wanted bloodshed,*
> *but if that's the colour of freedom*
> *it is our blood which will wrap it,*
> *Beware sellout*
> *Beware apartheid police*
> *Beware apartheid army*
> *with our fingers we will tear you apart.*

never wanted bloodshed
at's the colour of freedom
r blood which will wrap it.
e Botha
re Thatcher
re Reagan
With our fingers we will tear you apart.

The boys and girls were singing and dancing, and in the distance, there was rapid gunfire. Strike, Sipho and Lucas reached an empty patch where once had stood a house which sheltered six young boys and girls who were torn to shreds by van Niekerk's grenades. A young girl emerged from the singing crowd, pushing an old tyre soaked in petrol. It was put around Lucas's neck and lit. Lucas fell. I had seen so many people wear the necklace. It was not long when, from the direction of the raging flames of the burning tyre, I heard two dull, very dull explosions. The flames raged furiously. There were now three huge pillars of smoke that hung over Tembisa. From where I was, I could hear the casspir, the hippo and the trucks coming towards us. Soon, the streets were empty, and the smell of burning tyres hung over them.

Eddy Monnakgotla and James Mlambo had known each other a long time. Whenever Eddy introduced Mlambo to people, he would say, "Please meet the man, he and I have been pushed around a lot, and we have decided, enough is enough. Eddy was born in Dinokana, a small village near Botswana. He has lived in Sophiatown, Evaton, Alexandra, spent many years in jail, after which, for a while, he stayed with Mlambo, then went back to Alexandra, where he remarried, he has a son from his previous marriage and another from his new wife's previous marriage. He is well-known and liked, whether he is in Alexandra or Tembisa or Evaton, places he finds himself going back to often."

Eddy is tall, well-built, handsome, wears a short-trimmed moustache, and has a bright, warm smile. His eyes, when he talks, tell you you are being watched, searched, assessed. He speaks in a soft, careful manner, most times asking questions and then giving short, precise comments which warn that one has been heard, that what one has said has been noted, it will be thought about.

116

One thing he never ever does is commit himself, especially with strangers.

Eddy has simple, neat tastes in clothing. He says it is jail which made him develop a taste for good clothing and neatness. He forever told himself during his eight years in jail, that besides fighting the boer government, one other thing he would do is have a simple home, neat and meticulous – apart from enjoying good clothes. He came out of jail a qualified accountant, and worked in Johannesburg at a bookstore. When he was arrested in 1968, besides being an office bearer in the South African Congress of Trade Unions, he was also an underground worker in the people's army, MK. He was then, in 1968, arrested for sabotage, he and Mlambo. Mlambo was given some eleven years, but Eddy had come back from Robben Island, smack into June 1976. He did not wait; arriving in Alexandra, which erupted on the 18th of June 1976, he found that his wife had changed her mind about their marriage, since now there was another man in her life. Which did not surprise him. He laughed at Mlambo and himself, saying, well your wife and mine were very alive while we were away, we will have to make up elsewhere, old boy. Mlambo was eventually saved by this – knowing Eddy, Mlambo knew that this was exactly how Eddy would grapple with life, unlike himself who had spent the year sulking, unhappy, trying to fight to get his wife back. After Mlambo's release in 1979, Eddy moved to Tembisa, stayed together there a while and Mlambo set up his newspaper business. They talked a lot during those days; about what the children were doing, about what they had talked about while in jail, and how to adjust what they had then imagined about the outside to what it really was. More important, school children and those who had been active during the days of June, 1976 came to them for discussions and advice. They noted the role of that period in the struggle for liberation, and defined their role accordingly. Their decision then had been correct, judging by the roles they had to play now, in the eighties. Eddy still felt strongly that their role should be a background one, but events had pushed them right into the open. Early in the fifties, while a young man in Dinokana, Eddy, a favourite son of his father, had learnt the skills of political warfare, mobilising and tactics from listening to him.

His father was close to the then chief of the Zeerust area, Abraham Moiloa, who with calmness and skill had fought the Bantu Authorities Act, which had been responsible for the displacement of so many black people throughout the country. In the early fifties then, the village gave birth to the 'Sons of Dinokana', who opposed and fought the pass books for women. Eddy was among the 'Sons of Dinokana'. It was during this period that he learnt about the boer Government and its evil laws. He was shaped and chiselled by the long discussions in his father's house about the school boycott, the burning of the houses of the tribesmen who were collaborating with the boer authorities. The boers overcame the fighting villagers, but the villagers never forgot how they were humiliated.

Eddy carried this anger with him, to the mines, to the factories, to Sophiatown, where, once more, the Group Areas Act caught up with the residents of the one-time lively township. They were moved from that township by force of arms. Eddy went to Alexandra, and it, too, was soon threatened by removals through force of arms. Soweto, Tembisa and other areas were being born out of the rubble, debris, anger, and humiliation of the townships where people had had freehold rights; they were moved to the regimented, monotonous-looking townships, where one owned nothing but one's clothes, where there was no hope of ever owning a house, let alone land, where rent was paid until one could no longer pay, in which case, then, the vicious street awaited one. Here, one owned nothing. One's life depended on a pass, a work permit, a house permit, the signature of an employer, poll tax, and a section of a sub-section of a law, whether (a), (b) or (c); (i), (ii) or (iii), and according to the letter and the number, one could be tossed from area to area and back as a way of living. That was Tembisa. That was Katlehong. That was the so-called Vaal. And they spread and spread the length and breadth of South Africa, filled with fear, anger, humiliation, despair – and now they had erupted. Eddy knew many of these areas well, his work had taken him to places where he had met people, young and old, men and women, and had come to know that, now, the boer government would fall.

Eddy had, through Steve, sent a message to Mlambo, "Shoes

118

have arrived." He knew that once Mlambo received the message he would travel to Benoni, then back to Tembisa, and that in three to four days Mlambo would come and see him. Six days had passed. He thought there was something very wrong. If Mlambo and the trainees who had just arrived had been caught, then he must move. He thought that he should move out of Alexandra, but then work held him, and also, he kept hoping that Mlambo might turn up. What he did not know was that the boer government, faced with total rebellion, international pressure, and stubborn panic, had formed hit squads throughout the country. All hit squads had lists of 'communist terrorists' who must be killed. They were not to be arrested, detained, banned, banished or exiled, they must be killed. Eddy moved around cautiously, preparing to leave for another area as soon as he had completed his work in Alexandra. On the seventh day, when he had still not heard from Mlambo, he walked out the door, out the gate, into the street, knowing he would not come back to his home for a long time, but telling no-one. He walked out as if he was going to the shop, as usual, to buy a newspaper. It was in the morning. He bought the newspaper, held it under his arm, and walked down the steps. He noticed, then, van Niekerk's car pass. He walked down the steps. He walked down the street, into the dust left by the killer's car.

He would, he thought, go to Nkuta's house and ask to be driven out of Alexandra. There were soldiers, police and special branch all over the streets. Nothing unusual. Another car passed, stopping by the side of the road. Inside were Raymond and Thabo. Eddy passed the car and turned the corner of the next street into what used to be 4th Avenue. That was a mistake. There was no-one there, only a hippo, with soldiers. He looked behind and saw Thabo and Raymond's car, and not long after, van Niekerk's car arrived. Eddy was quietly bundled into Thabo's car. He was tired when the car parked in the yard of a house in a suburb outside Pretoria. He was handcuffed and led into the house. The house, four-bedroomed, dirty, looked like a place where people came and went in a hurry. The doors were shut. Thabo and Raymond sat on the sofa. Van Niekerk went into another room. No-one said anything to Eddy. He chose a sofa away from Thabo and Raymond, and sat down. He immediately began to look around the house. There was blood on the walls. He thought, well, this looks very bad. No nice things happen here. Is this where Mlambo is? Why did they bring him here? Why have they said nothing to him? Had they been watching him? Why did they abduct him? It was then that it occurred to him that they may have killed Mlambo, and that therefore they may kill him. He settled his mind on the worst possibility – they planned to kill him. Just then, van Niekerk appeared from the other room and Raymond and Thabo shot up to attention. Van Niekerk ignored them and went straight to Eddy.

"Monnakgotla, have you heard of the helicopter?"

"What is that?"

"You have not heard of it?"

"Why have you brought me here?"

"To show you the helicopter!"

"I see."

"Now, everything depends on you, there's just one or two things we wish to know. You can give us this information if you wish, if you don't that is your own problem … "

"I have no problem. You look like you have many on your hands."

"To be honest, Monnakgotla, you are correct, and as you will realise later, I have the reputation of solving them. Now, who is in, and where is, your high command?"

"You have silly ambitions van Niekerk. There is a revolution taking place, and you think you can stop it?"

"You are touching a subject which interests me a lot – revolution – who is in, and where is, the high command?"

"The people."

Eddy did not know what hit him. He felt a sharp pain in the solar plexus. He bent forward, slowly, in great pain. Van Niekerk kicked him repeatedly in the kidneys as he fell from the chair. Then he smashed Eddy's head against the cement floor.

"Don't stand there and look at me!" he screamed at Raymond and Thabo who had shifted slightly as van Niekerk was busy kicking Eddy. Both of them leaped into action, rushed forward, lifted Eddy, and rained blows and kicks, and smashed him against the walls. As if in a dream, a nightmare, Eddy thought, this is how they make blood on the walls. He passed out.

His eye opened. There was an awkwardness about him. He tried to look around. He saw blood on the carpet. He was upside down, dangling by the knees, his legs bound together. He saw the brown stick jutting from between his folded knees, to which his bound arms were tied. He realised he could only use one eye which ached and ached and ached. All of his body throbbed with pain. He heard something move, shoes squeak, then a chair creak.

"Who is in the high command, and where is it?" It was Raymond.

Then the creaking chair. Then footsteps. Eddy took a chance.

"I am the high command," he said.

"You are the high command!"

"Who are you commanding?"

"The revolution."

Something hit him from behind on the ankles, and then, and then it was as if his fingers were bursting like balloons, one by one. He began to groan. Something was pulled onto his head and face.

"Who are you commanding? Who else is in the command and where are they?"

"That, Monnakgotla, Mr Necklace, is the helicopter!" van Niekerk said. Hell broke loose, then, on Eddy.

Steve arrived thirty minutes after Eddy had been picked up. When Jane, Eddy's wife, told him he had gone to buy a newspaper, Steve rushed to the shop. Ndlovu, the shopowner, told him he thought Eddy had gone to Nkuta's, he had gone down the road. Steve went to Nkuta's house – Eddy had not been there. Steve went back to Tembisa. He knew he should not, for he was known there, and van Niekerk was looking for him. Nevertheless, he went – he felt he must. He felt he must go to see MaNhlapo.

"I can't find Rre-Eddy," he said to MaNhlapo.

"Did you see his wife?"

"Yes, she said he had gone to buy a newspaper, I went to Ndlovu's, he said he thought he had gone to see Nkuta, I went to Nkuta's, he had not been there."

MaNhlapo looked away from Steve, through the window. "Look here, Eddy knows how to get hold of me, we must not go looking for him. This Mlambo thing worries me. You must not come back here anymore. We will contact you. Ask Lindi to come to the hall on Thursday at nine in the morning."

"I have to go now," Steve said, and walked out, a worried young man. He hoped and hoped that he would see Eddy.

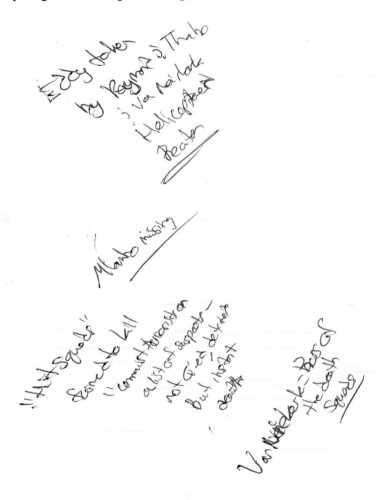

16

SIXTEEN

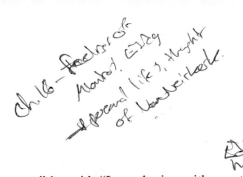

Ch.16 – feelings of Mantor, enemy. + depend like ?, thought of Vanderlerk.

Ddg tells him the reality

"I am not threatening you," he said, "I am sharing with you the reality of our struggle for a non-racial, democratic South Africa; van Niekerk, I know you are unable to understand what I am saying, but just in case someday something may make sense to you, I say to you, the masses of our people, the workers, cannot be oppressed forever. We have always known that you are the boss of the death squads. You have slain my people in the Eastern Transvaal, in Duduza, in Johannesburg, people have disappeared as if they were needles lost in a haystack. My last word to you is that the more vicious you become, the more you make the people aware that they should be heading in a different way."

exposed torture

Van Niekerk had now sat back, and as an experienced torturer he knew that with each one of his victims there comes a time, a moment, especially when they realise they are going to die, when they cross over from the living, when their grip on life slips – it is then when they seem to resolve to say their last words. It shows in their eyes. It shows in their faces. Their breath, their sweat smell of death. Yes, death does smell. It is then that van Niekerk knows he has to listen very carefully, it is this moment which gives him tips about his future work, it is the most reliable moment. It is the moment when his victims pour their hearts out. It is at this moment, when he listens carefully, when he notes detail, that he knows he must listen, for this is the only time he is able to swim across the gulf which time, experience and interest create between the slave and the master.

Some, at this moment, fight with everything in them, clinging to life. With such types, van Niekerk knew, all he had to do then was to dangle the carrot, make the victims believe that he would save their lives, wait, wait, and then, names and places would pour out of them; but then, if one reaches this stage, it is because systematic methods of dislocating life have been used, methods which in the end leave the victim physically torn apart, beyond repair, mere evidence for the communists and liberals to use against the State. The victim is better, more honest and patriotic as a corpse than it ever was when alive.

"We have always known that you are the boss of the necklace," van Niekerk said. He hoped, at this late hour, that his victim would now, when death was holding him close – for he could see death in his eyes and face and in every gesture – he hoped that his victim would, either out of desperation, intense emotion or bitterness, say something, anything, that might be useful.

"For the fact that my people created the necklace, your stubborn government and your likes must take full blame. We are fighting for a just cause, we are fighting to end apartheid, which has caused great suffering among my people, which has made this great country of mine notorious. You are, like me, a very knowledgeable man, van Niekerk. How many people have died at your hands? For what? So that white domination should be maintained? Why? So that, while the wealth of this country makes the whites some of the wealthiest people in the world, millions upon millions of blacks must be illiterate, homeless, forever hungry, and must die like flies trapped in a pool of dirty water from diseases of squalor and the violence of your government? No, we will not allow this, we will do everything in our power, including the use of arms, to change this state of affairs. This is what you are killing me for, but this country, van Niekerk, this country will join the ranks of great countries of the world."

"Eddy," van Niekerk said, walking away from the tree he was leaning against, "I have no interest in Soviet Union propaganda. Do you understand that? I am a South African, ready with everything in me to defend my country against communists. We will smash you everywhere you show your heads, we will smash you ruthlessly," he looked around; Lewis, Raymond and Thabo were sitting smoking, listening. When he looked at them, all three stood up. For a while, they did not exist for Eddy, nor did they exist for van Niekerk.

The three of them had once been ANC members, MK combatants, who had now defected. They were used to doing the most brutal work for the boers, which was a way of keeping them loyal. Van Niekerk had never trusted them. He always made it clear to them that they must never ever think they could win his trust. He never said anything. Like now, when he looked at them, and they stood up.

"I want information from this man, not communist propaganda, can we get it out of him?" van Niekerk's eyes swept quickly across the three.

"Yes," Lewis said, walking towards Eddy, whose hands were cuffed and tied to a tree. Lewis, Raymond and Thabo prepared Eddy for the "helicopter ride". Van Niekerk was watching. Eddy's hands were handcuffed. He was made to crouch and a pole was put between his bent knees and outstretched, handcuffed arms. A rope was tied to both sides of the pole, they lifted him up, allowing him to dangle upside down from a tree. Raymond took a pistol from his holster, and with its butt he bashed at Eddy's knees while Thabo held a wet bag around his head. The bag covered Eddy's head and face, making him suffocate. With a pair of pliers, Lewis crushed, one at a time, Eddy's fingers. They did not know whether the old man was screaming or not. They saw his body shake and wriggle as if he were an animal caught in a snare, bewildered by a sudden loss of freedom, sensing death, fighting with all its might to re-enter the free space and air it knew so well. They maintained the pain by crushing his fingers and pulling out his nails. Then Raymond removed the bag. Eddy was struggling desperately for air.

He was covered in sweat, tears and mucous. What were the sounds he was making?

"Where is Steve?" van Niekerk asked. "Where are Strike and Cynthia?" He moved back. Thabo put the bag over his head again. Eddy wriggled in an attempt to reach for the bag and remove it from around his head. He could not, his hands were cuffed. He was upside down, a position which disorientated him. They did not know that now, in desperation, Eddy produced the sounds of a wild animal. He felt the pain in his fingers, and fresh pain, again, in his toes, and pain in the knees, and a fresh throbbing in the ankles, and then a sharp stab in his private parts. His mind kept trying to use his hands. His hands were useless. His mind kept trying to use his legs, but they, too, were useless. Strangely, he thought, at that moment, so this is why they call this a helicopter. He thought van Niekerk will never lay his hands on Strike and Sipho, not now; he wondered where Steve, Cynthia and Lungi were. This man must never lay his hands on them, he must never ever … he passed out.

"And you must tell us where that little whore, Cynthia, is, Mr Necklace, you must also tell us who you came to see here in Benoni, and for your own interest I want you to know, soon, Monnakgotla will talk and talk, he will tell us where the terrorists are, where the guns are, which targets Tambo wants hit, we will get that from him soon. He will disappear. You want to save yourself? I can get you off, if you tell me."

It was Lewis who felt Mlambo stiffen. He knew from experience that Mlambo must have passed out. They removed the bag, they poured water on him, and when he came to, he heard van Niekerk say, "Mr Necklace, you must also tell us … "

"I, I lose respect for you, you go on like a small boy, do you really think I can tell you that, after what you have done to me – I am ready to die," Mlambo said.

Van Niekerk, Thabo, Lewis and Raymond, the four of them, and, from the sky, the stars looked at Mlambo. They knew there was very little they could do now. Unconsciously, van Niekerk was rubbing his hands as if to remove something sticky from them.

"Give Mr Necklace the necklace," van Niekerk said as he took out his pistol, aimed at Mlambo's head, and fired twice. This act, during times like these, always made the three, Raymond, Lewis and Thabo feel as if the world had shrunk, that the world had no holes to hide in, for it expressed in detail who van Niekerk was. For, once he had performed it, leaving them with a corpse, van Niekerk, without a word, would walk away to his car and drive off. Thus he defined their relationship. The act defined clearly who was boss. It also told them how little he valued a black life, and he had never defined how he thought they might differ from other black people. Indeed, under apartheid they were not allowed to see how he treated white people he thought were blaspheming against apartheid, nor did those whites who felt protected by him

know that, in fact, this man had become a danger to the lives of
their children.

For a while, Lewis, Raymond and Thabo would remain there,
listening to the gathering silence as the sound of his car faded. It
was a most frightening moment for them. Because, for some reason, at this point, they thought of MK. They knew, they just knew,
that one day they would be face to face with their one-time comrades who would ask them about the helicopter ... but it was this
realisation, this knowledge, which created in them a hatred that
could not be cured.

First there was the smell of the burning tyre. The smoke, thick
and black, curled slowly up to the sky, away from the tyre, rising,
rising up and up, slowly. Its colour changed as the flames began
to devour the tyre. The red flames leapt up in fury, with speed and
viciousness; the tyre cracked and sputtered and disintegrated in
the penetrating flames. The flames caught Mlambo's clothes. He
was embraced by the flames now, flames like water, seeking holes
to enter, flames that stuck to the dead man, licking, searching, and
entering his dead flesh. It was only the sky and the trees and the
day which watched in amazement, expressionless and unable to
articulate to anyone or to themselves what they were witnessing.
Something exploded within the flames. It was followed by sounds
of something being squeezed and squeezed and squeezed, and
then the drip, drip, drip of grease and oil and juice. Indeed, the
juice began to spatter and spill from the corpse to the ground.
Again something exploded. Finally, the flames, the fire seemed to
sigh.

Thabo and Raymond stood there, silent. They had hardly
looked at each other. They had hardly said a word to each other.
Both of them stared and stared at the burning corpse. Their eyes,
the way they looked at their corpse, their burning corpse, seemed
to rivet the flames to the flesh, and the flames danced and danced
and danced on their faces and eyes. Raymond took out a cigarette.
Thabo, without thinking, did the same. The nauseating smell of
burning flesh was very familiar to them.

The heap of flesh, the one-time corpse, once blood and soul,
crumbled now underneath the furious flames. It crumbled and
shrank and its texture changed from solid to fragile to brittle and

soot-black, leaving the vague shape of a human being: shoulders, feet, hands, head, a mere heap of ash. Raymond and Thabo walked away to their cars.

Van Niekerk drove the car into the garage. He uncocked his pistol and put it back into the shoulder-holster after putting the safety catch on. He took his jacket from the back seat and slung it over his shoulder as he walked into the warm setting sun. Barbara met him at the door. She hugged him, kissed him and held his hand as they walked into the house.

"How was your day?" she asked, caressing him lightly over the shoulders.

He tightened his hand around her hip, and brushed his cheek against hers, "Okay, sweetheart, though I feel a little tired and I still have to go back to work. How was your day?"

"Fine. One of the Aids victims died today," she said.

"Ag, they're scum, bloody homosexuals!" he said as he let go of her hip, threw his jacket over the sofa, and walked to pour himself a drink. "Do you want something to drink sweetheart?"

"A finger of brandy, thanks." As they settled on the sofa, she moved very close to him, seeking his eyes.

"You know, Aids is not a problem of homosexuals only." His eyes had not met hers.

"Ja, but they brought it here!"

"Sweetheart, you cannot say that."

"Well, even so, Aids is for scum, homosexuals, communists, kaffirs and baboons."

"Derek … " she began to say.

"Sweetheart, I don't want to talk about Aids and scum, I am sure we can talk about something else … "

"It's just that I feel so sad inside … "

"Why?"

"Derek, an Aids patient dies so painfully!"

"They deserve it, that's what I say, they deserve it," he said.

"Do you know what it means to have Aids?" Barbara was looking straight into Derek's eyes. There were many things that he said which she did not agree with, but since these were things he knew more about, she had not challenged him. But then, she knew about Aids. She knew that as long as he thought this way about it, both

128

of them were in danger. She was ready to take him on about this issue. He caught something in her voice. He heard something from it that told him something was wrong. He turned to look at her.

"You sleep with another woman who has Aids, without a condom, both of us are gone, that is what it takes to contract Aids," she said.

"Why are you saying that?"

"Because, Derek, Aids has nothing to do with whether one is a communist or a kaffir or a baboon!"

"Don't you know that communists sleep with each other and everyone and everywhere?"

"So they may, but so do those who are not communists." He looked at her. She seemed to be determined to talk about this subject, indeed, she seemed not only determined, she was fighting him.

"You are in the mood to talk about Aids, heh?"

"I don't want us to die because you are ignorant!" she said. She stood up and walked towards the kitchen. The sorrow that she had carried with her throughout the day, since she had stood before the bed of the dying patient, came upon her. She could see the protruding eyes of the patient. She could see the face of the patient, brow and cheekbones and chin protruding; she could hear him try to say something as his voice, at first pitched high, then fading as he tried to control it, bacame a whistle, whistling and whistling as if forever. She stopped at the table, held onto it, and, unable to stop herself, she began to cry.

Derek walked up to her. He held her shoulder lightly, leaning so that he could see her face.

"Sweetheart, what is the matter?"

"Oh Derek, Oh God, I …," she stopped crying abruptly. She began to wipe her eyes, her nose and mouth and she walked straight to the kitchen. He followed her. He could feel his love for her swell his heart. He wanted to protect her from whatever pain she seemed to be going through. As she stood before him in the kitchen, he gently held her hand in his.

"Do you want to rest?" She shook her head. "Do you want a glass of water?" Again she shook her head. "Come and sit next to

129

me," he pulled her hand gently, but he could feel that she was resisting. "Sweetheart, what is the matter?"

"Nothing," she said, turning away.

"Come with me, then, come and sit a while on the sofa," there was fear in his voice. She pulled her hand out of his, very gently, and walked towards the stove. He followed her. She began to fidget with the knobs on the gas stove and flames popped up. She took the apron from where it was hanging, put it on, and began to prepare a meal for him.

As they sat at table, she drinking and he eating, there was a silence as both of them searched their minds. She had seen James struggle to live for three months. But today she had seen it, felt it, heard it as it slowly slipped away. All of James's suffering, pain, courage and battles seemed to have remained with her. Derek could feel that she was far away. She was a fathomless distance away from him. He pursued her in his silence, in her silence, searching, and searching. The sound of the clock was as loud as the chime of a hundred bells. For a while, for a short while he thought about Mlambo. Then he thought a little about Aids. He thought about death. He looked at his watch. Brigadier Smith must be moving to their meeting point now. He stood up, went to the sofa, and picked up his jacket. He came back to her as she sat at the table and kissed her.

"I must go," he said.

She looked at him, briefly. "Do you have your key?"

"Ja."

"Bye."

"Don't drink too much," he said, as gently as he could.

"I'll go to bed right away."

SEVENTEEN

The bar was noisy. There were cigarette fumes in the air. Van Niekerk could smell beer and the stench of sweat and urine. His eyes darted above the many heads and faces, holes which opened and closed, making sounds, unintelligible sounds. He spotted the Brigadier, who was waving quietly to him.

He stood to attention very briefly and lightly, then pulled out the chair to sit down. They exchanged greetings and moved immediately to business.

"We got nothing out of him," van Niekerk said.

"Where is he?"

"He must be ashes by now."

The Brigadier thought a bit. "I see," he said, rather absent-mindedly.

"We have Monnakgotla, and I think we will get something out of him."

"What have you done with the ashes?"

"We buried them," he lied.

"The Minister is worried that we seem to get nowhere with these arrests. We hear there is a plan for a stayaway by Cosatu and it seems the ANC is also planning some terrorist activites, what do you think we should do?"

Van Niekerk thought for a while. He knew that the Brigadier had already made up his mind about what should be done.

"I suggest a swoop," he said, hoping his guess was right.

"Swoop on whom?"

"From MaNhlapo downwards."

The Brigadier looked at him. "I think you must see Sithole tonight," he gave van Niekerk a sheet of paper, "you know him?"

"Pascal? Yes I do."

"Read on."

131

"He has links with the ANC?" van Niekerk asked.

The Brigadier merely looked at him.

"Sithole must teach him a lesson, one that will become a lesson for all those that you say should be picked up. Come tomorrow to my office to pick up the arrest warrant for them." The Brigadier stood up and left. Van Niekerk felt uneasy. Something was wrong. The Brigadier was a cold man. But when he acted this way, there was trouble. He thought about Mlambo. He thought about his lie to the Brigadier. He must get those bastards, Lewis and Raymond and Thabo. He ordered a shot of brandy, slugged it down and walked out into the hot night. He called Raymond – he was not there. He called Lewis – he was not there. He called Thabo – he was not there. The brandy, the fear, the uncertainty all seemed to burst at the seam, at the seam of his life, wherever this was. He had slipped into a rage. At that point an idea hit him. They say Aids is passed through needles. Barbara must know how to get needles which have been used on Aids patients. He would order Thabo, Lewis and Raymond to be injected and to sleep with all those whores in Mlambo's group, they would die soon, very soon. He would detain all of them, and then order these bastards to rape them. His car skidded as he stopped just in time at the red light.

His mind went back to Barbara. Something was worrying her. Why did she worry about Aids? Why did she worry about a bastard who had died of Aids? Why would any Afrikaner worry about Aids? He remembered then, how, during interrogation, a young Afrikaner woman had told him she was a lesbian. She had also said that she knew of many Afrikaner gays. He had also heard that there were gays in the Cape among the Coloureds. This was to be expected. It was also to be expected that in the mines, among kaffirs, there would be gays. But why would an Afrikaner worry about that? This was all the more reason why there had to be the absolute protection of apartheid, not so? Why, why would any Afrikaner ever want non-racialism? Such Afrikaners must be shot! As he was thinking this, for some reason his mind went to Skopendonner. When he had said to Skopendonner that Lindi was in love with another man, he saw him crumble. He saw his eyes fall to the floor. He saw his shoulders sag. He saw him struggle for air, to sigh.

132

Although van Niekerk was now travelling at 120 km per hour, he was in full control of the car. He must find Sithole. Sithole must find Pascal. Pascal was his passport to the Brigadier. Why did the Minister think that they were getting nowhere with arresting communists? Had the Minister not himself intervened to request that some of them be released? Had the Minister not intervened to complain that there were too many deaths in police cells? Why did the Minister respond to pressure from Britain and America? All of those Americans and British were communists, did the Minister not know this?

Van Niekerk entered Alexandra. He could smell dust and smoke. The streets were deserted. How do people here know where they are going? There are so many ruins and squatter patches and streets that seem to lead into each other from anywhere and end nowhere. He was fortunate, he knew Alexandra so well. His instinct told him where to go, and he never went wrong. Maybe instinct was what they, too, used. No, this was their home, that was why. He stopped at what resembled a gate. Although the streets were empty, and although there seemed to be no-one about, there were sounds of people in the dark. In some way, somehow, Alexandra felt like the bush, he thought. In his escapades into neighbouring countries, many times he'd had to walk distances in the bush. The feel was the same as here. Unconsciously, seeking assurance, he squeezed his armpit and felt his gun. He searched the back of the car, all the while keeping his eyes on the dark of the wires haphazardly put together to make a fence, and he felt the familiar shape of his rifle. He could see a figure walking towards him. He knew it was Sithole – his instinct again. Sithole got into the passenger seat and van Niekerk drove off slowly.

"Do you know Pascal?"

"Yes, baas."

"Do you know where he stays?"

"Yes, baas."

"Get your men; by tomorrow I want him dead still, you hear what I am saying?"

"Yes, baas."

"How are the men?"

"It would be good to increase the money for them."

"Why do you say that?"

"It will shut their families' mouths."

"I will see you, Sithole. Do you want me to drive you back, or are you okay?"

"Drive me back, baas."

"Sithole, are you becoming afraid?"

"No, no baas."

Van Niekerk did not believe him. But he kept quiet. Something was wrong.

"Sithole, I want Pascal dead, I want his house brought down to ashes, you hear?"

"Ja, baas." Van Niekerk stopped the car, Sithole got out and disappeared. As van Niekerk drove off he wondered where Raymond, Thabo and Lewis were. He must search for them. For a moment he had a conflict in his mind – Barbara or them? But now, he must look for them. They must bury the ashes. He hoped they had. Soon he was in the bright lights and neon lights of Louis Botha Avenue. Except for the sound of a car in the distance, it was dead still on the Avenue. He was beginning to feel a little agitated because he had to search for Lewis, Thabo and Raymond. Also, he was a bit worried about Barbara. He would, if it were in his power, rather go to her. It was eleven-thirty when he checked the time. He stopped at the telephone booth. He dialled, but the phone kept ringing. He held the receiver to his ear, his mind searching at great speed – where could they be? He was not going to call again. He would look for them. They should not have been released from the "Spook House" – it was true that there was no way that the ANC could forgive them for what they had done, but that was not to say they could be trusted. Somewhere up there, someone was going mad. The kaffir policemen were now armed; the kaffirs were eating in certain restaurants, they could marry white women …

"Hello?"

"Why do you take so long to answer the phone?"

"I was in the … "

"Get the others – let's meet in thirty minutes," van Niekerk dropped the phone before Lewis could say anything. The car took off slowly. How could he get a needle? He thought about Sithole. Something was not right there. The men want more money so

134

their families will keep quiet? What shit was this? Van Niekerk was beginning to feel that he was alone. He felt tired. The streets were deserted. He was anticipating war with Barbara. And then the fucking kaffirs – Sithole, Lewis, Raymond and Thabo. He felt a heaviness in his chest. Anger. Bitterness. South Africa was coming down on him now. It was coming down on him and he did not know that it was. He kept on driving slowly, the odd car passed by, the street lights danced the same way children hop and jump when they play hopscotch. The lights seemed to keep rhythm with the pace of the car, it was as if they kept pace with his heartbeat, also. He had the sense of being a doormat. Something which everyone takes for granted and treats with absolute contempt, wiping their dirt on it. He had thought that when they gave him this position, when they gave him responsibility for the repentant terrorists and the poor scum of the townships, and the responsibility to kill as he wished and report to the Brigadier, that now he had made it to the top. But the "Tops" treated him like a small boy and the "Bottoms" kept pushing for more space, leaving him to say no. It was tiring, all this was tiring. What, really, was the future of South Africa? Did anyone know? The Minister, did he know what the future of South Africa was? The President, did he know?

A little English girl, curious, ambitious, had ruined South Africa for him; she had come, had taken someone who had given South Africans back their whiteness, their might, she had taken him to bed. He had slept a long time and now the people were leaderless. Why, if he had needed a woman, didn't he get himself a beautiful Afrikaner girl? Why? Why did he have to go for an Englishwoman? How can you trust someone who sleeps with an Englishwoman? It is a step towards sleeping with kaffirs. The people are right not to trust the sleeping leader. It is said that it is not only what one says, but what one does, also, that tests the mettle of a person. Give it to the sleeping leader – he spoke well. He touched what matters to many people, what matters in the heart of hearts of pure Afrikaners: South Africa belongs to the Afrikaners! The sleeping leader did not say this only, nor did he say it in this way – he was a poet. He spoke, and as he did so, it was as if he were caressing one's insides. But now everything had crumbled. The sleeping leader had the police and the army and most of

135

Afrikaner business behind him, he had had all of the farmers – or almost all. Had this not satisfied him? Had this not given him access to many Afrikaner women? He saw the car. He slowed down.

It was one a.m. He was heading home now. Thabo stank, he must have been drinking van Niekerk thought. The burying of the ashes would sober him up. Van Niekerk sought consciously, to think about Barbara. When he eventually entered the house, it was two-thirty. The house was dead quiet. He poured some brandy and threw himself on the sofa. Sipping his brandy, he felt Barbara should be here, next to him. But the house was silent. She must have been drinking too much! What was the matter? He stood up and went into the bedroom. She had barely covered her naked body with a sheet, and she was fast asleep. He shook her lightly. She looked at his glass. She looked at her watch – it showed three-thirty a.m. He sat on the bed next to her.

"Are you alright?" she asked.

"I'm alright – are you?"

"I'm fine," she kissed him. She did not smell very strongly of brandy. Something eased in him.

"Why are you drinking at this hour?"

"Are you offering to put me to sleep?" he asked. She noted mischief in his eyes and on his face. He watched her wake up, get out of bed and walk to the toilet. Fire was rising in him. As he sipped the brandy, its touch sharp on the tongue, he felt it shake his whole body. They made love against the bedroom wall.

Barbara was gone by six a.m. Van Niekerk dragged himself out of bed, into the bathroom, into his car, on the road. The traffic was thick and moving slowly. Van Niekerk had become part of the force which makes South Africa work, which makes it its peculiar self. But he felt different from everyone on that road. If they knew what he knew. If … if … if, but the funny thing about all this was that in doing his work, he was also protecting the scum of the whites – hippies, homosexuals, lesbians and … every time these words and their meanings came into his mind, at times to his mouth, his whole body reacted to them. The filthy-rich English-speaking whites, the filthy-rich kaffirs, the Jews, the Indians with their hot arse holes … he, van Niekerk, was protecting them – all

136

because of his responsibilities and what did he get out of all his hard work? Stupid Ministers, stupid Brigadiers ... he must move now, he thought. He put the blue light on top of his car, unflapped the police sign on the windscreen, and put the siren on ... power, power, power, the cars began to peel away as if something was slicing them from the front of his car. Soon he had left many of them behind.

When he reached his office, the death dealer met other death dealers. A black man was waiting for him. He looked at him. He remembered how often when he saw Solomon, his heavy frame, his tallness, always reminded him of Tshaka. Harry was there, too – fat, moving lazily, so that one was reminded of Dingaan. He treated Harry with contempt. He had a slight respect, very slight, for Solomon. Solomon smiled when he saw van Niekerk.

"Sir, how are you?" Solomon grinned.

"I work hard, but I am paid little," van Niekerk replied, "how are you?"

"I can't complain," Solomon said. "Just a little thing – look at this."

Van Niekerk took the piece of paper from Solomon.

"This is the bastard who escaped from the church that was attacked?"

"Ja, ja, that is him."

"Can you get him?"

"Easy, oh yes I can. I can because he thinks he is in hiding, so he will be very relaxed when I get him. He is staying with a young girl, a daughter of a distant relation of Gumede's mother's sister."

"Listen carefully. You know, this is our cheese, we should leave it there. Many of these other rats will go there, or he will lead us to them. No-one must touch him, no-one must get near him, no-one must frighten him. In fact, we should make sure that he stays there. If there are any needs in that family, don't hesitate to get in touch with me; money, anything, we must make it easy for him to stay there. One day, we know we will pounce."

"Ja, ja, I thought of something like that. That is why I thought I should check with you just to make sure."

"The bloody bastard! He must not get out of our sight now. We must keep him in focus from a distance. When we pull him in, we will throw his mother at him. Otherwise, Solomon, what goes on in Springs?"

"It is quiet now. I think we have flushed all the shit out now. It is quiet. The police wear their uniforms, they are no longer afraid. We are trying to find out how to break the rent boycott," Solomon said, "I have been talking to people, soon I will know what it is they think, what it is they fear. It needs that we act, it should be like a large fist hitting at them. That will teach them a lesson."

"Your group?"

18

EIGHTEEN

Steve and Jacob knocked on the door. She opened the door still wearing a track suit.

"Steve!" she said.

"Barbie, how are you?"

"Steve, come in, where do you come from?"

"It's a long story. Please meet Joe."

"Haai, Joe!"

"Hullo," Jacob, now Joe, said.

"I'm Barbie," she said, extending her hand.

"Joe," Joe said, shaking her hand.

They sat down on the sofas.

"Would you like tea, coffee, milo or something else?"

"Tea," Steve said.

"Anything," Joe said.

"What?"

"Anything," Joe repeated.

"Tea? Coffee?" Barbie insisted.

Joe looked at Steve.

"What Joe?"

"Anything, alright, tea!" Joe said at last.

"Are you sure?" Barbie asked.

Their eyes met. Barbie flashed her pretty smile. Her hazel eyes, glittering in Joe's eyes, shifted from Joe to Steve and back to Joe.

"Yes," Joe said. Barbie walked out of the lounge. Joe was sitting at the edge of the sofa, Steve, almost lying on his back, was sprawled on the sofa. He felt very tired.

"What is that?" Joe asked, pointing at the wall.

"A painting," Steve said.

Joe was staring at the painting; he looked at each of the four

139

paintings, across the wall to a bookcase filled from ceiling to floor, with books.

The morning sun splashed across the lounge floor, on a maroon wall-to-wall carpet, refracted on a long, wooden coffee table in the centre of the room. A cupboard containing china stood in the corner, watching the large french window opposite it.

"Does she live alone here?"

"No, with her parents."

"Where are they?"

"Ask her."

"What do they do?"

"Ask her."

"Do you know them?"

"Yes."

"Have you met them?"

"Yes."

"Are there only the three of them?"

"Yes."

Joe looked around, as if to experience how it felt to be there and live in such a large house. Barbie came back with a tray with three cups of tea, toast and orange juice.

"I hope you're starving," she said as she bent to put the tray on the table.

"I could eat an elephant whole," Steve said.

"Where have you just come from, then?"

"Home."

"Home?"

"Yes."

"I see," she said. Now she was wearing a simple white T-shirt and jeans, with takkies. She put the cups before them. She sat next to Steve.

"Joe wants to know who you live with here?"

"My parents, Joe." She looked at Joe, waiting for another question. Joe kept sipping his tea.

"Joe, ask all your questions!"

"No. It's alright," Joe said, feeling betrayed.

"What do you want to know, Joe?"

"Well, do you live with your parents only, here?"

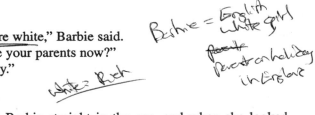

"Yes, we are white," Barbie said.

"Where are your parents now?"

"On holiday."

"Where?"

"England."

Joe looked Barbie straight in the eye, and when she looked back at him, he looked away.

"Don't you know that white parents have everything they want in South Africa?"

"I know."

"Well, here it is," she touched her bosom lightly, "all of it. I can take you on a house tour if you want."

"What is a house tour?"

"To look at the house," she said.

Although Joe wanted to be taken on this tour, he did not know what to say to make it happen. When he looked at Steve, Steve was snoring lightly.

"You are Barbie who?" he asked softly.

"Barbie Levy," she said.

"Levy."

"Yes."

"Are you in the struggle?"

"I want to be."

"Why?" Joe asked. The way he asked, the manner in which he was conducting the discussion – looking now and then at Steve as if to ensure that he kept snoring – his eyes darting about as he almost whispered, made him look uneasy, like a cat sensing hostility as its ears twitch and its eyes rove while it sits on its haunches.

"Are you in the struggle?" Barbie asked.

"Yes."

"What do you do in the struggle?"

"I struggle," Joe said, rocking on his haunches.

"You struggle? What does that mean?" Barbie insisted.

"Can I smoke?" Joe changed the subject.

"Sure, please yourself," Barbie said.

Steve stretched, sighed loudly, and sat up.

"Your tea and food sends me to sleep," Steve said, yawning

again.

"Is it that easy to send you to sleep, then?"

"Plus this comfortable rich people's sofa," Steve said.

"Suit yourself," Barbie said.

"I'm going to leave you here," Steve said, turning to Barbie, "he is preparing to leave the country."

"Oh, he just told me that he is in the struggle, struggling."

"It should be about a week or so before the people who will take him away, come."

"Okay by me if that is what you want," Barbie shrugged.

"Joe, is that okay?"

"Yes, but, er, am I the only one going?"

"Yes," Steve said, making it obvious that he did not want to be asked any further questions. He stood up, stretched, and reached for his light jacket from the back of the sofa. He moved towards the door. Barbie stood up to let him out. They walked outside briefly. She came back to sit opposite Joe.

"The news has been saying the East Rand is up in flames," Barbie said.

"Yes, the army has been there for four days now."

"Are there lots of killings?"

"Yes, and burnings and necklacings," Joe said.

"But this necklacing is so awful!" she shuddered.

"Comrades burn you alive if you are not in the struggle," Joe said.

"But it's such a ghastly way of killing people and of dying," Barbie said, lifting her legs up, shielding herself with her arms as if she did not want anyone to touch her, as, grimacing, she said, "Have you ever seen anyone being necklaced? I don't want to see it!"

"You know, you tie the person's hands behind him, like this," he stood up to demonstrate by putting his hands behind him. "You take a tyre – if you really hate the person, you use a tractor tyre, it is so big," he showed the height of the tyre by lifting his hand above his head. "You walk the person so that everyone in the township must see him, you put papers and petrol in the tyre, you hang it around the neck of the man, he will fall down, you light the petrol and the papers, he screams and screams and tries to

142

stand up to run, to get his hands out of the wire; you know, when death is here, you want to live, you fight to stay alive, that is why he screams and screams … "

"I don't want to hear that!" Barbie said.

Joe laughed: "The sound of the fire goes voooooooooo on the person as he screams. Have you heard a person who is burning, who knows that he is going to die, have you heard such a person screaming and screaming? It's like a pig when you hit it with a four-pound hammer on the head between the eyes, it screams – nothing can scream like it … "

"You are so awful, so sick, Joe, how can you say that with a smile on your face?"

Joe laughed again, it seemed nothing could stop him from finishing his story. "Then there is no more scream. Then you see this – it's not a person anymore – you see it shaking and shaking, like this," he demonstrated by wriggling his body, "and you hear a small sound. I think the person still thinks he is screaming and later the skull goes boooo – what do you say, it 'splodes? – and the stomach gives a sound like that of wind going out the backside, the eyes have also 'sploded, have you heard the smell of burning meat? It's very funny, and then you hear the smell of a bone, and then he smells like everything which burns because nothing is left, maybe the buttock and the thigh, but now it can be anything burning, he smells like that … "

Barbie sat frozen on the sofa, watching Joe. His face was distorted, he looked as if he was hypnotised, eyes bulging, unable to stop himself talking. He seemed to have a great need to talk.

"After that, all you see is ash, black ash, shoulder and body is lying there as ash … " He sat down. He was breathing heavily. Barbie was crying. He looked at her. It was the first time he had seen a white person crying. He had seen this only in movies. He saw her as a woman at that point. He wondered whether she was a virgin. He wondered whether Steve, maybe Steve sleeps with her. He wonderd what she was like, what she looked like naked.

Barbie somehow knew that this was what he was thinking. She felt looked at. She saw his eyes focus between her legs. Their eyes met. A silence fell in the house.

19

NINETEEN

Skopendonner emerged from the office, walking slowly. He knew that the chief warder and the strange white man in plain clothes who had just talked to him, who, with his hard eyes, seemed to know everything about him, he knew they were standing at the door looking at him walk away. He felt humiliated. He felt laughed at. He felt the distance between the office and the prison yard was too long. He walked the whole way, since this was the only thing he could do in the world.

Someone was singing. A dog was barking in the back yard. At that point, as he was walking in the sun, with the purple jacaranda flowers dangling from the tree, and throwing their perfume throughout the years in the prison yard, Skopendonner felt a great sadness grip him. He walked past the wall with the barbed wire above it. Past the first, second, third, fourth and fifth iron gates into the open courtyard where other prisoners of his grade were busy with their different chores. He looked at them. Fits, Panga, Drizzle and Lefty. He saw them, knowing they were the only sanctuary he had. They saw him come. They noticed the way he was walking, and when he joined them, they stood up out of respect. They greeted him. He looked at them, saying nothing. He sat down.

"Drizzle, bring me water." Drizzle walked in the direction of the tap.

"Lefty get me a cigarette." Lefty walked away to fetch some.

The others sat down in silence, next to Skopendonner. Each one's mind went haywire ... What could have happened?

Another charge – murder, robbery, a further charge, of what? Killing a white, raping a white woman? Perhaps killing a policeman? No matter how they tried, they found no crime to match Skopendonner's apparent despair – escape from prison, stealing arms, armed robberies, killing a white child? Killing a white woman – what has he done, what have they just said to him?

Yes. Maybe someone, Lindi is dead …

"Boss, is it news about Lindi?" Panga dared ask. Skopendonner looked at him. His eyes filled with the fire of hell. Panga could feel the heat of this fire, of this anger, of this hate. He did not know how to say it, to say how sorry he was to have asked the question. His friends looked at him, as though to ask, how dare you?

Drizzle brought a mug of water. Skopendonner looked at him. Drizzle sipped from the mug, wiped it, and extended the mug towards Skopendonner. Skopendonner looked at him, not moving an inch. Again Drizzle drank from the mug, taking a large gulp to demonstrate that there was no poison, nothing in the water. Skopendonner took the mug and drank. Lefty brought the cigarettes. He took one out of the packet, lit it, and gave it to Skopendonner, who gestured to all but Panga. Lefty gave each except Panga a cigarette. They sat puffing in the loudest, most threatening silence in the world.

"Why are you still here?" Skopendonner said, looking at Panga.

"I was asking because I was worried about you, boss," Panga said. "You looked unusual."

"To whom?"

"To me, to all of us."

He looked at all of them.

"Yes," Drizzle said.

"Yes," Lefty said.

"Yes," Fits said.

"How unusual?"

"Worried," Panga said.

"How do you know then about Lindi?"

"I thought that's the only thing that can worry you like this."

"What do you mean?"

"What do I mean? I mean … What do I mean?"

"What do you mean?"

Panga became worried.

"I mean, boss, I mean you looked very worried."

145

"What do you mean?"

"Er, that … you … I mean you … what can I say?"

"Are you asking me?"

"No. Me."

"But I asked you, how can you ask you?"

"I'm asking me to answer you."

"Answer then!"

Panga was now desperate.

"I want to answer you."

"Do you know that Lindi is living and loving somebody else?"

"No, no, no I don't boss."

"What did you mean then?"

"I wondered whether she had died."

"I see." Skopendonner stood up, hugged Panga, and gave him a bit of his cigarette.

"Gents, I have just met a very funny white man … " he said.

Funny. That is all he could say to describe the white man he had met. For the first time he came to know, once he met this white man, he came to know what he had not known. What he could not have, no matter how he tried, understood. He had seen fear. He had seen despair. He had seen sorrow. He had seen hopelessness and helplessness in many eyes and faces when some people, who were fathers to many children, who were husbands, who were adults, who were men. He had seen them struck, their faces, their eyes, their whole being struck to the ground by the mention of the word white man. He had never understood this. He had never understood this in his life, in his being, no matter how he tried, he never knew why they were so fear-struck. White man. That is also because he himself was used to being feared. He did not know why people feared him. He knew though, that they feared him. He knew he had power, but did not know why other people did not know that they had it too. He chose to be kind, when he wished so. He chose to be cruel when he chose to be. Those who dared him, he took them on. He did not care who they were. He took them on, and as a result he knew so much, about life, but more about death. Death, he knew, was nothing. Because it was nothing, he did not know why people feared it. He understood that life, like a see-saw, depended on being itself because it

146

could be. Not death, death is a moment. He knew this. If the people he killed had not struggled to perpetuate life, death would have been short, brief as blowing a candle out, or crushing a cigarette in an ashtray. But he had met this white man. This white man made him want to come out of prison before his time was over. This white man made him want to spare himself, to preserve himself, wait for the time he was to come out of prison. For the first time since he had been in prison, for the first time in the timeless time of his prison life, he did not want to be here. He always knew that he did not belong to prison. He knew that no one belonged there. So this once, why not struggle to be out?

"Who wants to go with me?" Skopendonner asked.

They looked at him. A simple question became difficult to understand. Realising silence, he asked again.

"Who wants to come out with me?"

"What's the deal?" Fits asked.

"To kill."

"That's okay," Fits said.

"Fine," Panga said.

"I will," Drizzle agreed.

"Fine," said Lefty.

Skopendonner stood up, and without looking at them, he walked away. For days, he would wake up, knowing he had to wait. He woke up, washed, went to the rose gardens, watering them, tilling the soil, pruning them, plucking some for the chief of the prison. The chief was the only one who told him what to do. In fact, whatever it was he wanted done, he discussed with Skopendonner.

The white man came at last.

"What have you decided?"

"I'll go," Skopendonner said.

"And ... ?"

"I know what to do."

"What will you do?"

"I will go to Lady's."

"And?"

"I know what to do."

"No, you don't. We will teach you what to do."

"Teach me what?"

"How to do that work properly. I know that you want to do away with Billy, badly. That is your business. Not mine. I have my business, and we must understand each other well on that score. I will teach you how to shoot, how to make bombs. But I am the boss, you don't do what you like, you do what I tell you. Is that clear?"

"It's clear."

"So, first you go for training."

20

TWENTY

Alexandra

Moscow = Name lady gave House

They called this house Moscow. Everyone knew that this was the name of the house. The whole of Alexandra knew it as such.

It stood in a yard, sandwiched between two yards, each of which was a miracle, containing so many little houses! Each house had so many people and all of those people, like mosquitoes, like flies, bred and bred and bred – there were so many children.

Lady's House

Moscow was crowded from all sides not only by people, but also by houses. It stood alone. Something about Moscow gave the feeling of its being dust-packed. It had this grey cement colour which seemed to embrace it completely. It had this rusted tin roof which declared it had stood the test of time. The windows, abnormally many in number, hundreds of them slabbed into the great cement walls, gave a feeling that thousands of eyes were watching in all directions, staring and blinking.

Lady was still there. Bitch-never-Phela had joined her once more. Lady seemed always to be sitting outside on the verandah facing the gate and the Avenue, Second Avenue, or what was left of it. She sat there, and, like the many different people who walked Second Avenue, thoughts travelled through her mind. Something about Lady was impenetrable. But also, something about her was so vulnerable. At her age, she was a long-surviving resident of Alexandra, which meant that she had been to many, too many funerals, and, being Lady, she had seen to it that, rather than be dragged by dogs in the streets, corpses should be buried.

The coffin was simple. It was made of planks, a sheet of white cloth, nails, handles with flowers and leaves engraved on them; there were a few men, a few women nearby, and the corpse was ready to be buried. This was the image that Lady had. Besides the fact that Alexandra had not resolved how her husband had died, what it was that had killed him, how innocent Lady was, there was also the fact that most things she had done, her courage to clean up Alexandra, her ability to be kind – these things had left her with an aura demanding respect, and so she kept a distance, and a certain aloofness. She was also feared. When this township did not know what to say or do with her, she seemed to know what to say and do in this old township. She seemed to sit on that verandah for ever, but also she seemed to be everywhere. Very few people in Alex knew anything about her, though she seemed to know a lot about everyone else. Lady had come here as a girl, had grown up here, and it seemed she would die here.

When she heard that her house was called Moscow by the young people living in it, she was touched. Lindi wanted to ask her why it was that she gave this big laugh. But she did not ask her, for she sensed why. Once, this house was known as 'The Palace' and later it was the 'House of Sorrows', and now it was called 'Moscow'. When it was 'The Palace' its floors glittered like mirrors. It had stood at the edge of Alexandra, near to the two main tarred roads which separated the people of Alexandra from those who were not of it: Indians, Chinese and a few white merchants with their stores that sold groceries, vegetables, and, it seemed, anything that could be sold or bought. Besides the Catholic and the Anglican and different 'Zion' churches, 'The Palace' also buzzed with life during weekends. Though 'The Palace' stood, as it did, at the edge of Alexandra, it was of it, and it was because of this, because so many people came to it, that Lady knew so much. Many people came here. Lefty, Lady's late husband, a man born and bred by urban life – Orlando, Sophiatown, Alexandra – was one of the few black matriculants of the time, and Johannesburg was where he worked as a clerk in a law firm. The lawyers, some of whom were known white lawyers who had acted in the political trials of the fifties and sixties, were men whose views and actions provided the hopes of many men and women in the township.

Lefty had brushed shoulders with men and women who had inched their way out of the penned-in townships, into defining the hopes of South Africa. Lefty had met Fischer and Slovo. He had met Tambo, Mandela, Resha but something in his make-up – not

150

despair, not doubt – had made him maintain a distance; Lefty had clinical manners.

When he was alive, all of these people from different parts of South Africa had come and gone in this house. Then, it was a typical Alexandra house with two bedrooms and a room which served as kitchen, dining room and lounge. He extended the house; it grew to become a six-bedroomed house, with a kitchen, a lounge and a dining room. It earned the label, 'The Palace'. This was not because it was a big house, nor because anyone associated with it was thought to be a queen or king. It was dubbed 'The Palace' by Alexandra to claim it, and for Alex to pride itself on what was its own, respected and loved. Alex had an instinct that 'The Palace' would articulate its needs. It is not easy to earn Alex's respect. 'The Palace' did not. When Lefty died suddenly, and Lady was thrust into a role she had never wished to assume, Alexandra could only indict her, so that she earned its respect. Alexandra did not notice that, as it disintegrated under the impact of the apartheid system 'The Palace' also disintegrated.

Once there were people in Alexandra who, like other people in the world, cherished hope. They bought property. They started businesses. They built houses. They sought a future, a future for their children, by dreaming dreams. Malan shattered their dreams. Malan manifested the ideal of an exclusive white Western civilisation, having learnt well from the British before him, that social existence determines the thought of all peoples. To Malan, the only people worth considering were Afrikaans people, for he said: 'Die kaffir op sy plek!' Blacks had no room in his scheme. Soon, from all over South Africa, millions of blacks were removed and resettled. Soon, black people were hunted for pass offences. Ensnared. Caught and 'sold' as farm labourers. Others were recruited like ants and sent below the earth to nibble at it for riches. Black children were educated to know their place in South Africa was to work for whites. Tambo vanished. Mandela vanished. Very few, very few people indeed talked at all about the African National Congress.

Alexandra, like a sponge, had absorbed all this. Its people waded through this muddy social existence, they died as flies do when trapped in a flood; they floated in despair as debris floats

151

endlessly on the surface of a flowing river – and 'The Palace' became the 'House of Sorrows'. It was here where journalists, doctors, lawyers, teachers, priests, nurses, singers and actors drowned their sorrows. They drowned them in sordid acts and existed from one day to the next. When Alexandra saw its priest, Zulu, being taken out of the 'House of Sorrows' in a wheelbarrow and carted to church to give a sermon, hardly able to hold onto the barrow or sit straight because he was so drunk, it focused on Lady, asking in silence for an explanation. When it dragged Lindi out of the 'House of Sorrows' to sing at a festival, and word went round that once, late at night, under a bright moon, she had stood outside peeing and singing the song 'Nobody Knows The Troubles I've Seen', Alexandra stared in accusation at Lady. Alexandra sighed in despair. But also because Lindi, before singing her song at the festival, said, "I hope those who organise the festival will pay me so that I can buy myself a panty. I am not wearing one now."

Alexandra had gone mad on its horror and sorrow. Minute by minute, inch by inch, it sought the best and worst ways of twisting, distorting and eventually achieving living cruelty. The sun went down, and when it came up it was to illuminate corpses, bodies which had been struck and clubbed until there was no more fluid in them. Queues, long queues of men and women, women with children on their backs and hips, every morning of every day for many years headed for prison, for pass offences: men and women drank as if they were rehearsing to find the best methods to finish all the alcohol of the world.

When life is so sordid, who can judge the present so as to be able to predict the future? In prisons, in exile, in banishment, in the remote parts of the land, life was lived in the present, it was lived viciously. The young, in their blindness and deafness to danger, because a future is not real until it is lived – the young with their strong legs and arms and curious minds, were thrust into the present to judge it.

Day and night, Lady and Lindi reminisced. When Lindi was not there – for, like a bitch she had to fend for her puppies – Lady sat on the verandah, seeking answers from Second Avenue.

'Moscow' was a dangerous name in South Africa. Where else

but in Moscow itself is it not dangerous? With bare hands, the youth clutched at the name, and hung it on the house.

Late one night, a car stopped outside 'Moscow'. Its lights died. Its engine died. Two men, one white, one black, held their peace a while in the silent night, watching.

"Do you still remember this place?"

"Yes, I do," the black man said.

"Lindi and Billy are in there," the white man casually remarked.

Skopendonner lit a match, then lit a cigarette.

"Don't," van Niekerk said.

Inside the house, Strike whispered to Lindi, "One is white, and one is black."

*Outside Lady's
house
1 white ♂ van Niekerk
&
1 Blk ♂ Skopendonner*

21

TWENTY-ONE

"On two occasions, he left after I went to bed: once he was gone an hour, the second time, two hours."

"Did he say anything about it in the morning?"

"No."

"Did you?"

"No."

Steve looked at Barbie. "You did not ask him where he had been?"

"No."

They looked at each other again. Barbie stood up and began to pace the room. Steve watched.

"Have you searched his room?"

"I have. There's nothing."

"How have your discussions been?"

"Well, I acted the innocent white liberal girl. I think he believes it."

"But how have your discussions been?"

"He has been very curious about me. My parents. The house. My movements. He has tried to sleep with me. He thinks you sleep with me. Steve, there is something funny there ... "

"What?"

"Well, one of my photographs is missing. I put it there deliberately. Also, I wrote down the phone number of my grandmother. I left it on the kitchen table. Next, for a split second it was not there, and then it was back on the kitchen table." She stopped pacing, examined her nails, bit them one by one – thoughtful.

"He has also searched the room I sleep in."

"When are the owners of the house coming back?"

"In two days."

"We must delay his leaving. Tell him – what's today?

154

Thursday? Tell him I said he is leaving on Monday, and tell him that on Sunday night I'm coming with someone who will train him how to use a pistol in preparation for his departure!"

"Okay," Barbie said, still busy with her fingers, "what's the news about Mlambo?"

"No news."

"Monnakgotla?"

"No news."

A silence fell. Time can be kind. It can be kind when it bestows experience, which enables people to read the writing on the wall and to understand it.

"You look very tired," Barbie said, changing the subject.

"I am," Steve replied.

"Have you eaten?"

"I have."

"Are you going to lie down to rest, then?"

"I should, what is the time?"

"Eleven-thirty."

Silence.

They could hear the breath of the bulb. They could hear the whistle of the wind and the wings of the moth and their own breath. For a moment they felt peace.

"Do you have tea?"

"Yes."

"Can you make some?"

"If you want it."

"I do."

She lit the gas stove. Cups chimed. He could count her footsteps as she walked around the room. He was aware of her, and aware of her being aware of him.

"It is lonely to be a guerilla," Steve said.

"I was going to ask what it is that makes people like Joe be agents."

"Not Joe. Jacob. Yes, for money, ambition, ignorance – a combination of things."

"But ... "

"Barbie, don't be a racist!"

"Why are you saying that?"

155

"Over and over we have experienced this. It is not because one is black or white that one becomes an agent."

"If you are black what's in it for you?"

"You are being a racist."

"Am I?"

"You are."

"Why?"

"It is not the colour of one's skin that makes one an agent."

"What is it – not that I think it's one's skin colour – but what is it?"

"I have just told you."

"Do you understand what I'm asking?"

"I think I do."

"I can understand a white agent. But I can't a black one."

"Fear? Ignorance? Money? Does it make sense?"

"It does, but in this case it is not fear, nor is it ignorance. Maybe money, but even then he must know it cannot go on forever like that."

"Ja, but then a combination of them becomes addictive, one creates a habit. You know, hope is human."

"Hope that it will go on forever?"

"Ja, and that he will not be discovered."

"But there is evidence of loyalty also. Look, this man plans elaborately to do his work."

"If he does not, his handler will tell him in ever so many ways."

"But he knows he can handle him in ever so many ways, he has said that to me."

"He hopes we will not find out."

"He hopes also that he will live long you mean?"

"Ja. But more, that we won't."

"It's twelve-thirty, you know!"

"Yes. Can you set the alarm clock for two?"

Barbie strolled to the bedside table.

She sheathed herself in the sleeping bag. He lay on the bed. He began to snore. She remembered how many times when they had spent the night like this, she could not fall asleep. Steve ground his teeth. He talked and screamed in his sleep. They had talked about

156

this. It was not fear or despair she experienced. She searched for
an answer. She had come to know over time, his fears. She had
come to know that he was flesh and blood: she had seen him
afraid. She had come to him, as a human being. But she was
searching. She did so, and found nothing. Still she searched for
something to hold onto, something to know. She did not know that
what she wanted to know was who she was. She herself was
afraid. She was afraid, for she knew that his and her lives were
woven in this word - 'comrade'. It meant at times you do not ask
questions; it meant at times you do what you are told; it meant that
you could expect, and it would be expected of you; it meant agree-
ment; it meant to trust and not to trust; but she suspected that she
did not live it fully because she was white. She spent time, lived
time, where this word was not used, was not heard, was dangerous, among whites. She could not dislocate herself from this forever unless comrades took over. Nothing said they would in the
near future. Did it then mean that she was to live her womanhood,
her youth, her time, torn between comrades and her community?
No, it was not impatience, nor despair, not being negative, nor not
believing in the justness of the cause, but time is not timeless for
life, nor is it kind. How could she accept death? Why could she
not live in a life and time and a place which she had fought for and
sacrificed for? She, Barbie, who had been told and had come to
know that she was beautiful. She was intelligent and had been told
so many times, over and over again. Of what use was all this if it
could not be used? How could she share this with Steve?

Steve was snoring.

She felt tired. She felt answerless. She felt alone in this room
filled with Steve's snoring. And the bulb breathed, breathed.
Perhaps the moth had gone to sleep. The silence of the night was
invisible. She twisted inside the smooth sleeping bag which made
everything more intangible, textureless, and she yawned for the
millionth time. She saw herself, the Barbie she had unsheathed
from not so long ago. She was young. Youth at times is how
you feel, how you walk, what hopes clutch your heart. She was
young then, and studying at Wits. She read the classics of the
world and got bored. They stuck in her head. She wrote rhymes of
her views and knowledge and emerged from third year, Honours

and Masters with pieces of paper written on in letters and language that were not everyday. She framed them and froze them, and what next? She was to become a white South African woman. But before that she lived as a student-teacher – until one day she entered a police station in her youth. They asked her: "Do you speak English?"

"Yes."

"Are you a Jew?"

The way they said the word frightened her.

Barbie was [?] by police in her youth

"Why are you partying? And are you fucking with blacks?"

Since she knew she was the one to know if she had fucked, and since she knew she alone, if she wished, would tell this, she had looked at this boy, with his crewcut, red-checked shirt, sheathed gun, and moist eyes. "I'll fuck you to hell and back if you are not careful," she had said to him. He looked startled. He looked as if he did not know what the word meant, let alone what one does to enact the word. She was not drunk when she said it. She looked like she meant it.

He did not know what to do.

"May I go home?" she said

He looked at her. "You can only be English and Jew to befriend them," he said, pointing at the 'Bantu' side of the police station where some of her party mates were.

"Since you won't fuck me, can I go?" she repeated.

"No. We are charging you."

"With what?"

"You are very rude," he said, "you don't behave like a white lady."

White lady. White lady. What is that? She wanted to tell him that she did not intend to be a white lady who was fucked by the likes of him. But she said nothing. Something told her not to speak. She knew what she was going to do. Because she knew, she kept her silence, looking at him looking at her and telling her about white ladies.

And when she eventually emerged from the police station to which she had been brought by the police who had raided the party looking for drugs and illegal sex – the supposed diversions of wealthy white South Africans – she stepped into black morning

158

Jo'burg streets, which soon would be white. Johannesburg was coming alive. First there were the unintelligible languages of the workers who, with their milk bottles, their rubbish bins, their trains, their trucks, their fast footsteps, broke into this silent Jo'burg.

She walked the great streets. Though busy, unlike during the day, they seemed to be peaceful. She decided she was going to walk the seven kilometres to her flat. She walked alone, dressed in a navy and red floral mini-frock and highheeled shoes with a red band on her head. She felt a foul taste in her mouth from the red wine. She felt weary from not having slept. She felt tired, her mini-frock seemed to expose her, and her high-heeled shoes added to this feeling. Now and then she wanted to cry, to laugh, to scream but she did not. She walked on and on to the flat. She saw the black men, who now and then stole a look at her. The black women, who seemed to stop to look at her. But all of them seemed in a hurry in the morning Jo'burg streets. She felt so white and so alone, more so than she had ever felt before. She walked on, listening – for there seemed to be nothing else to do – to the sound of her heels hitting against the cement pavement; she also heard the cars and the hooting train. She heard the sounds of languages which seem only to be spoken in loudness. She walked on. She could do nothing else but walk, listen and look. No one had prepared her for this ordeal. She had obeyed all the rules and laws. She did not want her parents pained, so she hoped for, looked for and wanted to choose a Jewish boy, now she could say, to be fucked by ... But those who came her way struck her with fear. Either they were flippant, or too confident, which made her suspicious, or they looked like they were going to experiment on her, to find out what they were supposed to do with her. They came flaunting cars they drove like hell-chariots, or taking it for granted that she thought they would give her heaven. Some wanted to take her to Israel, but it did not sound like a real country to her. She had tried to please her parents. She tried. She had her framed certificates. She was ready. And now she discovered she did not want to be a white lady, an ornament for white South Africa. She walked on, wanting to look straight at these black men. But they walked on, they walked and walked. They were on their bicycles, or running after trucks filled with rubbish, getting out of buses, turning corners in a hurry, sweeping the streets, hardly looking at her. She walked on and on. She thought about how she would lie in her bed awhile, then take a shower, dress, walk to the university, into her class, face to face with white boys and girls who were poised to be white South Africans. She felt the wine inside her ferment. She felt the upheaval in her stomach. But nothing came out. All that was a long time ago. She lay, now, in her silky sleeping bag, listening, listening, listening, even to the fact that she was still a virgin. The ring of the clock frightened her. It was two o'clock in the morning. Steve cleared his throat; he looked at her.

22

TWENTY-TWO

[handwritten: Vigillantier - V. Brutal]

Her mind was reeling with fear, agony and ignorance. Now and then, she felt the lively kicks of her seven-month old foetus. She recalled how, when the door burst open, when the shrill whistle tore the thick darkness and silence of the house, the foetus had kicked and kicked and kicked. Her heart pounded in her chest as if it were jumping to her mouth, wanting to escape. Then Pascal had screamed, "Please! Don't harm my wife, she is seven months pregnant." When she heard that, she knew who these people were and without a second thought, without thinking, she leapt out the window. She didn't know how. But she did – naked, for she had taken off her clothes to keep cool in the searing night heat. But also, Pascal, who had not seen her for some time, having been on the run, hiding and sneaking back to his Martha whenever he could, had wanted to see her body, to touch the throbbing, bulging stomach, and nibble her toes. *[handwritten: Martha - Pascals wife. pregnt]*

[handwritten margin: Pascal House Raided]

Neither knew when it was they had fallen asleep – and then this thunder, made by the vigilantes. Everyone knew about the vigilantes. People would say, either they are the unemployed or off-day policemen. Everyone was fearful of them. They killed people brutally; they burnt houses down; they stoned, almost to pulp, the cars of their victims before burning them; they necklaced the leaders of political organisations, everyone knew this. Martha knew this. And so, when the door burst open, she knew she had to save their baby. And she did!

Now, she was without Pascal. She was without a house or a home. She had gone back to her mother who worked in the white suburbs of Johannesburg as a domestic servant. Almost all day, all night, she stayed in the little servant's quarters, sometimes crying, unable to understand why everything was as it was. Sometimes she lay there dreaming dreams about her coming baby. What

[handwritten: Martha escape - Pascal didn't]

would the baby be? A boy? A girl? How would it come out? She would smile; she would close her eyes; and she would feel so joyous when she thought about how she would hug her child and hold it to her, watching its tiny mouth as it suckled.

And then Pascal would come into the picture, very briefly, in a glimpse, smiling. She and he had agreed that if it were a boy the baby would be called Mandela, if a girl, Tamana. He had told her who Tamana was. She had asked about Dora Tamana in her literacy class. Vino, her Indian teacher, had not only told her, but brought some articles with stories about the ANC and SACP leader. It was her inability to read, her inability to grasp the new information about her history, which so many times kept her quiet, silent, merely watching and listening.

The room was very hot. The bed, which stood on old paint gallon-tins, stood as high as heaven; while comfortable to sleep on, it was a nuisance when she had to climb down for her frequent trips to the toilet to relieve her bladder. And Jesus, with his strange red heart, which shone yellow rays in all directions, and his two fingers pointed upwards in a peace-sign, forever stared at her, without winking, always about to open his mouth, his eyes staring straight, nowhere else, seemed to promise an answer, always just that, a promise. At times during the day when she was alone Martha talked to Him, laughing at herself all the while for talking to a picture.

The traffic outside was endless. Sometimes it sounded like the sea. At times one got so used to it that one did not hear it, and then one would hear it, not as the sea, but as a car or a truck roaring past. Now and then, the dogs barked. Also, one could hear a woman, a black woman, somewhere, talking to someone else at a distance, talking loudly, very loud, a near scream, a conversation at a high pitch. It sounded out of place, something not belonging to the quiet white suburbs. Martha would laugh, smile or be embarrassed by what she heard as she followed the conversation. She longed to be out there with other people. And then the night Pascal was necklaced would come flashing back at her. Her dreams shattered, then.

It is fearful to know the power of the vigilantes. That they came. That they beat up Pascal and took him away; that they burnt her house before leaving; that they could have killed her too, like many, many others, and nothing would have happened to them. It was frightening. Many of Pascal's friends had gone that way. Many people she had made tea for, had eaten with, laughed with, even about the vigilantes, had been taken away and had never come back. These thoughts made her fearful. Who will stop this madness? How? All her thoughts reeled as she spoke to herself, thinking all these thoughts all by herself. And this made real the fact that she would never ever again see Pascal. It was also at this point that she thought about the swimming, moving little life inside her. She would have to help it arrive. She would have to look after it. How? By herself? She would have to, even for Pascal's sake, look after it. More so, since Pascal would never again walk the streets, or smile his smile. She had always known that something like this, some awful thing like this would happen. She had always known and feared and been apprehensive but would never talk about it lest it became real. And Pascal would not, anyway, have listened. He would have asked what she thought he should do, and knowing him and his work, he would not have had an answer. She fell asleep with her thoughts and began to move in the heat of the sun and the stuffy smallness of the servant's room; there were many cul-de-sacs she reached in her thoughts. Perhaps the baby, too, fell asleep and rested.

The two arrived in Orange Grove at midday. Martha did not know who they were. But she tried to read from what her mother had said, "There are friends, your and late Pascal's friends, who want to see you." She knew to keep her cool. They shook her hand. The young woman was smiling warmly, with shining eyes, a likeable face and a loving and wise expression. Something told Martha that Pascal's friends had found out where she was. She sat on the bed, balancing her stomach. They squeezed onto a bench close by. The man seemed determined to be very quiet. He simply stared.

Lebo, the woman, spoke softly. She spoke about Pascal. About the date of the coming baby. About the vigilantes. About the UDF. About SAYOCO. She spoke. She asked questions. She laughed happily. She smiled and shone her sometimes happy eyes, sometimes sad eyes, sometimes angry eyes. She drew Martha to her.

163

She seemed so knowledgeable. She had said one very important thing in the end, that Pascal had been a freedom fighter.

Martha fell asleep with a sore heart after they left.

23

TWENTY-THREE

I arrived in 'Moscow' in the morning. The sunlight in the spring was soft. The breeze still had a bite. The leaves danced gently on the trees, at times seeming to be about to stop their dance, but then they went on and on. There were very few trees there. Even grass seemed to struggle to grow. The shadows belonged, somehow, to the walls they were on; they fitted, they bent, they were of the flavour of the ruins which were all over Alexandra. In the streets, in the weariness of the broken walls and scraps of cars, in the untouched, brimful rubbish bins, the shadow in this soft light of spring, and the biting breeze, belong here. My reaction was to burst into eternal laughter when I saw 'Moscow'. 'Moscow' with Lindi in it. So much had been put under so much pressure, something had to move, something had to shift, something had indeed given way, something was changing. When I entered the yard facing 'Moscow' its windows told me I was looked at even before I touched the gate. The windows, reflecting the sun, blinded me. It was like searching for eye-contact with someone staring at you from behind dark glasses. They are fortified, you are not. They see you, you don't see them. They know how you feel, you do not have an idea of what they are going to say or do, their words are empty without their eyes. I knocked on the door. Someone said, "Come in."

They already knew who I was. I went in. It seemed they hardly even looked at me. I sat down, Strike gave me a chair. The other people, young people, walked around, young boys and girls performing their chores. From the kitchen with its massive stove came smells which made me feel hungry, and someone was humming a revolutionary song in time to the rhythym of her sweeping. Someone was running water; another was applying a brush to the already shining red floor. I felt others were somewhere, doing

165

whatever …

"Comrade Lindi!" a girl I had never seen in my life called out, "someone to see you!"

"Tell that comrade I will be there just now," Lindi called back from some room along the eternal passage.

I almost laughed. Strike put a cup of coffee before me. He brought bread and eggs on a plate and lay them in front of me. He noticed that I was laughing. My secret laugh was contagious. He smiled. It was a gentle, knowing, loving smile.

Lindi emerged. She was still putting the finishing touches to her dressing. In one hand she was carrying sandals while her other hand pulled the dress this way and that in front and at the back as she buttoned it up and fixed the belt. She took years to reach me.

"Comrade!" she said, and in the way that only she does it, she opened her arms, she lay her red lips bare. I fell into her arms, I lay on her large bosom, and she kissed me full on the mouth. She pushed me gently backwards, looking me up and down. She said, "Where have you been, comrade?"

Where have I been? I laughed. I laughed at Lindi. I laughed at the ease with which she called me comrade, as if she and I had called each other that from a long, long time ago. I sensed that there was someone else in the room. I looked back, there she was. "Do you know comrade Nomafa?" Strike asked me. Our eyes, my eyes and 'Lady's' eyes met. She, too, had a massive bosom. She stood there beaming her smile.

"Lindi never stops talking about you," she said.

"Don't give him a big head, don't spoil him," comrade Lindi said.

We sat at the table. We ate eggs and bread and drank our coffee.

"Where have you been?" Lindi asked her question again.

"All over," I said. She laughed. I looked at Nomafa. She was watching us. The other people in the house were watching us. Lindi and I came from another time. A time no-one here had been in. We were in 'Moscow' now, all of us.

"I'm here, though," I said.

"Don't be funny!" Lindi insisted. "Don't come here and be funny!" She repeated, "Where have you been?" The others laughed. "Are you alright?" She helped me out of the corner.

166

"I'm fine."

She laughed, looking at me as if she had never seen me before. Billy was now there looking at us, looking for a place, for a chair to sit on. So many other people were there, around, standing, cooking, working, watching, listening.

"Billy, there's a chair. You know this comrade?"

"This donkey? Remember how you imposed him on me?"

"Shut up," Lindi said. She rattled off the names of the people there. I don't know, but there were so many names, both girls and boys. Some were still half-dressed. Others almost naked. Some were running water to wash. Some were eating. Strike seemed to go in and out of the room, talking to this or that person. I saw a heap of newspapers piled in the corner of the lounge. Mandela's face on the wall. The Freedom Charter. UDF. COSATU. COSAS. FEDTRAW. On the front of their T-shirts. On the back of their T-shirts. On the walls. Only Billy, Lindi and Nomafa, among all the people in the house, were not wearing T-shirts. Maybe there are no sizes large enough to fit Lindi and Nomafa's bosoms. T-shirt or no T-shirt, Billy was alright. He talked endlessly. He is the type of person who, if he kept quiet for a minute, everyone looked for him, asked if he was alright. I wondered where his shining trombone was.

"Do you see my children?" Billy asked me. He laughed. "Watch out, you must watch out," he said, "where have you been?"

"You don't answer – where is Strike? Hey, necklace this man, he does not want to answer me!"

"Shut up!" Lindi said.

"Are you going for rehearsals?" Nomafa asked Billy.

"Shut up! Go to rehearsals! I get the ANC, but I will eat first," he said, taking fork and knife and beginning to eat. We sipped our coffee.

When eventually there were just the four of us in the lounge, the room feeling empty, Lindi looked at me. "Where have you been?" she asked.

"Lindi, what do you want him to say? Hey, Lindi, Lindi … don't break conspiracy!" Billy laughed. "You want him to tell you? Lie to her, mister comrade, tell her anything!"

167

"I went to the COSATU Congress," I said.

"Ja!" Lindi exclaimed.

"You are not a worker, you, man, you were an uninvited guest, gatecrashing!" Billy said.

"Billy, shut up!" Lindi said.

"No, I did not gatecrash, my street committee sent me."

"Street what? You think you are the only one with a street committee? We have yard, block and street committees. Watch out, where have you been? I withdraw my permission now, don't lie, tell the truth!"

I expected Lindi to come with her "Shut up" but she did not. Instead, she laughed, "Oh this man of mine!" I looked at Nomafa. She moved in and out of our conversations as she wished. She looked thoughtful. But also, somehow expressionless.

"Tell him about the car," Billy said.

"Yes, yes!" Lindi said. "Wait, Strike! Strike! Strike!" she called out. He walked in quietly.

"Tell this comrade, Strike, about the car."

"No, you tell him, comrade Lindi," Strike said, walking away.

"There is a car which comes here at night. A black man and a white man. At two in the morning, three, late at night."

"Early in the morning, stupid, not late at night," Billy growled.

"And then?" I asked.

"It comes, stops and after some time, it goes away," Lindi said.

"It's the police," Nomafa said.

"Do you have a bazooka?" Billy asked me.

"No," I said.

"No! Again you have gatecrashed, we need visitors with bazookas, nothing more, mothing less!"

"How was the COSATU Congress?" Nomafa asked.

Billy and Lindi sat facing me, so that they would miss nothing of what I was about to say. It was so difficult, I wanted to share with them what I had experienced. I wanted them to know that something had happened in South Africa. How was I to tell them? About the songs? About toyi-toyi? About slogans? No, not that, not that this did not matter, it mattered. But how was I to tell them? How do I tell it? How was I to tell them about the men, the women, the youth and what was said and done. How was it said

168

and done, how was I to tell them, what language could I use to tell them? Was it enough to say that the men and women and youth came from all parts of South Africa? That did not seem enough. Was I to say these men, women and youth were simple citizens of South Africa? That felt so empty! What could I say? That there were a thousand delegates? That all the languages of South Africa had been used, including Shangaan, Venda, Zulu, Xhosa, Tswana, Afrikaans, English? That over ninety resolutions had been passed. Was I to tell them that until I went to the Congress I had not known what democracy was, that I saw it, I touched it, I felt it at the Congress? I had not known the seriousness of what voting means. I know now. What was I to say? I tried a metaphor. I said that the giant's weak spot was his balls. That the hand of the workers was reaching for the balls of the white giant. The giant knew this. The giant could no longer go on as if it did not feel its balls being squeezed. It felt the grip, the slow tightening. It was lashing out, at times blindly, at times in anticipation of the next squeeze, the next grip. This metaphor seemed so bland, so banal. I told them about the problems of organising farm workers. I told them that COSATU could not resolve the issue of sexism, that it could not decide whether it should form a women's section. What would the section do? How would it relate to other women's organisations? The unemployed were planning to be organised. The youth were militant. I told them all this, but still I felt I had said nothing. They listened carefully; they did not interrupt me. When I finished, they had no questions. Everything felt so incomplete. Even Billy was quiet, he held his hand on Lindi's lap, and listened staring somewhere on the wall. I felt … what? I could not say …

[handwritten annotations in margins:]

[right margin] a "all languages of S.A." · Congress · Democracy

[handwritten below text] COSATU · Congress

You don't ask — "Where have you Been?"

· Problems articulating exp.

169

24

TWENTY-FOUR

The army had been there. The community was preparing for a funeral. The corpses of boys and girls were still sprawled in the mortuary. But people there, having become familiar with such circumstances, while mourning, felt something other than despair, and created an atmosphere which cannot easily be associated with death or mass funerals or even with the numerous distorted corpses of young people. To become familiar with whatever circumstance is to consecrate it. But in this instance a culture was emerging, which, because of the frequency of such events, could easily have been associated with madness, were it not for the fact that something bound the people together, moved them as a whole, inch by inch, as in their eyes a glow seemed to glitter which illuninated their ability to absorb the grimmest of events, for they seemed to have made certain decisions about their lives. They seemed, indeed, to have gone beyond the beyond of beyond.

The stench of the army; of the wheels of their trucks and casspirs, of the hooves of the horses they arrived on, of their boots, all of which, as the community had come to know, could crush bone, could crush and turn flesh into a mere smudge, could crush skull to pulp – their stench, the stench of these things which move and carry the army, of these things which roll and grind, hung everywhere on the streets. The stench of the green uniforms, of blue eyes, of eyes the colours of rainbows, the stench of the steel of the guns, the stench of gunsmoke which, as it were, still hung on the collective mind of the community of Sebokeng. It disorientated all of us, it made us unable to see the houses or the streets as they had once been, not so long ago, and which now had become death traps. We moved around corners and the edges of houses, in the shadows of houses and streets, carrying our lives in our hands, carrying all that we had come to discover was all that

we had here on this earth. We had seen it snatched away so easily. Our lives were very easy to carry in places where ordinary people do not walk. I saw so many people, children, old ladies, old
men, the young carrying a shame in their eyes, a look with which
we watched the life we carried as we walked the valley of death
as we went about our business as people who had brushed shoulders with the strongest army in Africa, an army commanded by
raving racists, and we, the community were black, and the army
was not long gone, we had just brushed shoulders with it.
Watching us, I thought, as they say, this was the last straw.
Something said so. I knew. I knew because I listened to people
talk, I knew I listenend carefully. I was searching for allies. I had
no time to talk nonsense. Many of the communities in Natal, in the
Orange Free State, in the Cape had informed us what we as a community would pay if we continued with our banned mass funeral.
I did not meet anyone who did not want a mass funeral. We were
preparing for it. People had little to say about this. We worked –
as hard-working people would say – our arses off.

I was standing in a crowd; many, many, many people spread
over the graveyard. I had never seen coffins fly and dance as the
twelve or so did, carried aloft by hundreds of people, millions of
hands above so many heads, dancing, singing hands. We all abandoned the cars, trucks and buses which had carried us to the cemetery. Abandoned on the side of the streets, and in the gutters, they
looked like litter under the sun. We surged forward into the street.
Someone, like the first bird to take flight, sang a song; the song
took to the sky, crowding the sun and the air. At first we walked.
Then we ran. Then we began to toyi-toyi. Flesh being weak, it
made the hair stand on end as bodies stomped and shook under the
weight of the song. We entered the cemetery. We entered through
the gate, through the fence, between trees; cemeteries are usually
large, quiet places; we occupied every space, our song taking the
quiet on. When the song stopped, in great uneasiness, the quiet
quivered in the air as we put the coffins down. I was standing
among this strong crowd which had become unbelievably quiet,
when I heard a voice, a single voice whose strength held this large,
strong, angered crowd; the voice took a song, and for a while,
being soothed, being told what we knew in a brand-new way,

toyi-toyi 171

being held by the hand, we dared not interrupt the song except through a sigh, a cough, the shuffling of feet – she was standing on the truck. She stood as if she had been standing there for many years, standing above the heads of the crowd in a long black dress touched with a sparkling yellow ribbon as she sang Nkosi sikelela iAfrika. It was the national anthem. It's not, it never has been one person who sings the anthem at any of our funerals, rallies, demonstrations – but she did for a whiile, while we listened – how we listened! It was late in the anthem when we finally joined in. I cried. I walked through the crowd towards Lindi. She saw me come, and smiled at me as the hands reached up to her, and carried her down from the truck.

A woman looks so vulnerable when so many hands touch every part of her body, lifting it and then carrying it down, holding it up to stand on the ground. I reached her as she was fixing her black dress. I hugged her, and kissed her, and she pulled me close to her as if to show her vulnerability. I felt myself swallowed by her large bosom. She sighed. Again she adjusted her dress.

"How are you?" she whispered.

"Im fine," I whispered back, "you sang well."

"Thanks," she said, her eyes briefly looking straight into mine, and then away. Many people were whispering into her ear. She kept a bright smile, looking this way and that at those who were saying something to her. She held my hand tight. The sweat of her hand and the sweat of my hand kept our palms wet under the hanging heat. I, too, held on to her. Someone said something loudly. All heads turned in the direction of the voice. It was now quiet and still. Mokone was saying something. The birds sang above his voice; the crickets chirped, and somewhere in the distance, a cow mooed. The crowd was still, straining to listen to him. A soft breeze blew, cooling the red-hot heat. I let go of Lindi's hand. She moved slightly, anchoring herself.

A young boy, with an extremely beautiful smile and laughing eyes looked at Lindi. She caressed his head, running her jewelled fingers through his hair. He was very, very shy, and as a result, remained beautiful because he kept smiling. Lindi looked backwards sharply.

"Shit!" she said in a hard whisper.

172

"What?" I asked. She looked back again.

"They are standing there like vultures waiting for th... a carcass."

I saw them. They had dismounted their trucks; their hats, their faces, their eyes, their uniforms, their boots and their guns said they were poised. The young boy walked away.

When Lindi turned to look ahead, feeling that the boy had gone, she began to search for him with her eyes, but he had gone as he had come. I saw a sprinkling of young white men and women in the crowd; they looked like students, dressed in what appeared to be deliberately torn denims. I saw, near them, an Indian man and an Indian girl. I realised that Lindi had noticed them too. The Indian man and the girl, a very pretty girl, had dressed up for the funeral. I remember feeling very, very tired. I was tired of noticing white people. I was tired of funerals and see-ing coffins. I felt angry for being tired. I got angry about every-thing, about Lindi, about feeling close to anyone, about life – what is that?

"Shit! There are so many people here," Lindi said.

I wanted her to leave me alone.

"Are they really going to shoot because we came to a banned funeral?"

How could I know? What could I say? How does she not know?

"Where is that little boy?"

Good Lord, what must I say?

"Where is that little boy?"

"But Lindi, how should I know?" I said. She looked away. Someone called her name, and without moving an inch, she start-ed a song:

> "How will it be when I sit before Tambo
> To tell him the boers have been defeated?
> Answer to your name
> when your names are called mine will be there,
> how will it be when I sit before Tambo
> To tell him the boers have been defeated … "

173

...hen there was the sound of soil hitting ...ent. More song. Lindi took the song. Her ...voices of the thousands of people. She led ...e pace of the rhythym. The people began to ...it afraid. I waited and waited for that dreadful ...o hear it, if I would not become part of the car- ...were waiting for. Dust rose like a cloud, curling into ...iling into the sunlight, hanging on the heat surrounding ...Lindi's voice flew on and on and on. Sweat ran down her face, into her eyes, down her neck. She kept wiping it, instinctively, unconsciously; her mouth caressed the words:

> *"Barayi says we must fight*
> *Tambo says we must fight*
> *You say we must fight*
> *Mdluli says we must fight"*

The song, like waves in an angry sea, rose, declined, rose, declined, rose, led by Lindi, going on and on and on, and as if it were a long, long scroll of names, it unrolled and unrolled:

> *Viva ANC, Viva!*
> *Viva the SACP, Viva!*
> *Viba COSATU, Viva!*

A young voice intercepted the song; the crowd replied. Another song. I realised then that there were fathers and mothers in the crowd. I realised that I had not understood what it was when I kept saying the community, the community – everyone was here. They came from Natal, OFS, and the Cape – many, many shades of blacks. Young men, young women, singng in line, in rhythm with the chant, with the slogan. And these kept them close together with old men and women. Workers, I thought, are here. They must be here because they are the community! For a while I felt safe. Just for a while. For in truth, whether we made it beyond the gate, beyond the fence, beyond the trees – would we make it home, to our mamas, to our streets? I wondered.

I heard a bang. The crowd scattered, the crowd panicked. It ran in different directions. Someone poured water into my face; it soothed my eyes. I saw him, he was wearing a blue overall with the word 'Phillips', printed in red on the chest. I don't know where he got the water from. I began to run. I felt people running behind, in front, and next to me. I saw some people disappear into the empty graves: a woman, women, men. I ran. I heard another bang. For as long as I was able to hear, I would in time find where Lindi was. I ran, and ran and ran. I knew that trees and fences were tearing at me. I was feeling wet, maybe from sweat, maybe from blood, maybe from water. I ran. There was a rapid, very rapid, many, several rapid bang, bangs, – I panicked then, I ran to carry my life on my legs, on my hands, running and running and running. I ran …

Police !, Army opened fire.

25

TWENTY-FIVE

There is something very similar about all townships, no matter where you are in South Africa. They are either demolished, or brand-new like a new coin, or old, dusty heavily-peopled shantytowns. They are dangerous to life. In this time, they all share a tangible loneliness.

Lindi still alive, back in Alexandra

I packed my bag. It was time to leave Sebokeng. I had heard that Lindi was alive, that she had gone back to Alexandra, to Billy, to hatch her chickens. Sebokeng, in her folornness, had readied fourteen young people for the noose. Nothing there remained the same – people, children, houses, streets, all had changed. Sebokeng had gathered its people, itself, together, as if it were kindling readying for the fire. An instinct of the time overcame me. I had sensed enough, and since Esther was not here, since I

instinct to leave

had no property but a toothbrush, wash rag, two pairs of trousers and two shirts, it was easy to obey that instinct. I packed and left. I left behind men, husbands, women, wives, children, small, old people in a dangerous present. They hung onto a hope which soon would abandon them, to become internal refugees, families which drag with them a bit of what they own, and their children, and so carry their lives in their hands and move away. Rebecca and the others from Tembisa decided to stay. Cynthia had been to the funeral, had run and run and run and saved her life. When I met

Cynthia

her, she seemed changed. Something told you that she had grown up. It was not the way she talked. She talked in a hard murmur. I should come back to that later. It was not the way she dressed, for while she was still neat, she displayed an attitude of arrogance, her clothing and manners presented her as defiance itself. She flaunted it, to match, to dare the norms of the youth of the time. Her clothes gave one a sense that she had patched them together. In size they didn't fit, and in colour they were far from matching.

176

They seemed to be picked up in a hurry, and put neatly on the body to cover it. It was the way she wore them which indicated she still cared for herself. Oversize as they were, her clothes were cleaned, ironed, and put on the body with care. I think it was her eyes and her face which told one that she was still young. When she laughed, you sensed that she was lonely - which she was - and that though she was a youth, she was missing out on all the things which the young do. She said that she and the others were in Mamelodi. She talked about the police, the army, the landmines, the shootings, about rent, school and transport boycotts, and finally about her youth organisation. Then she talked, in passing, about those who had been killed, the shootings at funerals, necklaced collaborators, as if in a hurry to conclude so as to talk about the youth organisation. What struck me was that, in fact, she had put all her young life – all that something which now and then glowed, revealing her to be a loveable person - into the youth organisation. But she did not want this questioned or examined or faulted. Then she got angry.

"Where is Sipho?" I asked, changing the subject.

"Sipho has left the country."

"When?"

"Two months now," she said after pausing for a while.

"You did not leave with him, then?" I felt I was teasing her.

"No," she said, "I am commander of barricades, Mamelodi is at war, I cannot leave yet," she said, looking into my eyes. She spoke in a responsible manner, in a manner which could not be questioned.

"Have you been back to Tembisa?"

"Yes."

"Where is Strike?"

She looked at me and said nothing.

"Where?"

She shrugged her shoulders, and I sensed that she was about to tell me that she must leave me.

"I've been here in Sebokeng awhile, what you told me about Mamelodi, the rent boycotts and all that ..."

"Why do you say, and all that?"

"No, it's a manner of speaking."

177

"Have you been to Alex?"

"Yes. I was also at the COSATU Congress." She smiled. As she did so, she lost her grownupness, she became a daughter, someone's daughter.

"I hear they could not resolve the issue of the women," she said.

"Yes, but they did many other things."

"Com, you know, South African blacks, we must address the women's issue."

I agreed. She was still smiling. Something about the way she kept smiling told me that she had been to the COSATU Congress. How do I say this? Cynthia looked older, in her slightly oversized skirt and blazer. The way her clothes did not match, told one that she had borrowed them, but her confidence, the way she looked one straight in the eye, said something else about Cynthia. She smelled of cleanliness. But also, very quietly, she gave one a sense, something about being confident. She smiled easily. Cynthia had grown up in the short time that she had been away. I wondered about her, although she had told me what she had been doing. She had a very beautiful smile. It brought out her youth, revealing that she was a young girl, but something about the clothes, abut the way her face, her eyes snapped, listened and watched, told you that she was not a youth, nor was she an adult, nor did she behave as girls her age would: showing that they knew something about themselves, their breasts, their thighs, their legs, their faces, always concious of them; no, she knew all these, she had, it seemed, come to know what to do with them, and when. She seemed in a hurry, although she kept still. She looked thoughtful, but missed nothing that was said to her. One felt protective towards her, but also, one felt affection for her. She seemed to know that she had this effect, when to use it or when to refuse. Somehow, you knew she was in control, as in control as one could be, in this day which left nothing unilluminated, in this night which had become so perilous.

"COSATU showed that we have a long way to go on the question of women," I said.

"We must separate certain things," she said, "we must also take tradition into consideration. It is not just a social matter that there

178

should be equality between men and women, it is a political matter. How we eventually win all our people to this position, is very important. COSATU must find a way. If it does, other organisations will also." She was leaning against the body of the bus, parked not far away from the gate from where the 14 or so coffins had been lifted, carried and flown over the millions and millions of hands, to the cemetery. Many people were going by, to and fro; you could hear some still crying, there was a noise about us, which made the air uneasy, you could still smell gunsmoke, tear gas, and you sensed the smell of blood. I was struck by Cynthia's calmness amid all this. I held my plastic bag, with my clothes in it; I know I was listening and watching carefully, but then Cynthia seemed not in a hurry. I stood there with her. Now and then someone greeted her. In the time I was with her, from people who now and then came to talk to her, I knew, she had travelled extensively around the country; I knew some people, like me, loved her; some had lots of respect for her. Cynthia smiled.

"I saw these men from the rural and urban areas, they are different and they are the same;" she laughed, "they think of their women with big behinds, and you can see their eyes glitter, hungry, longing – what's wrong with that? They can expect that if they want, but that has nothing to do with the rights of women."

"But then there is sexism," I said.

"Yes, if the women have no choice but to be as men expect them to be, then there will be trouble," she said.

"Sexism is when men expect women to be what they want."

"Yes. They must be fat because men want them fat. They must forever bear children because men think that's all they must do. They must be talked to and be related to as nothing else but those who lie on their back and give sex, then there is everything wrong."

"I find it difficult to draw the line ..."

"There're attitudes, and there're political rights. We should fight for political rights of women, in the process we will be fighting sexist attitudes. But to fight attitudes in a confrontational manner can alienate men. Imagine the traditional men. I was looking at them at the conference, their air of authority, slow, taking their time to do, say anything, not used to being answered back by youth and women. But COSATU puts them in a challenging position. They discover in discussion that often people, irrespective of age or sex, know what they do not know, have their own experiences, and since it is through the union that they have been able to increase their wages, change working conditions, and be treated with respect on the work floor, they have come to know the strength of unity."

"Yes. You know, to see them, all of them, hundreds, discussing their work conditions, the education of their children, their community, the next tactic against the bosses, is to sense power."

"Also change."

"Yes, change, things are changing."

"Why are you carrying that roll of plastic?"

"I have to move from here."

"I see."

"I'm working out where to go."

"I never thought I could live in Pretoria. Those white people, those boers there, I wonder if there is any place for love or care in their hearts. They hate black people."

"Pretoria is a very frightening city."

"No, comrades in Pretoria have fought for space in it. They walk in it and are in it as their own."

"I have heard about toyi-toyi in the city, I can't imagine that."

"We break glass, we put barricades in its streets, we have controlled it, as councillor after councillor, black police after black police have resigned."

"Oh God," I said, as I thought about the battles I had heard about, fought in streets where it was expected no black could work.

"Many informers and agents have confessed publicly, they have apologised and are part of the struggle. Now we are planning a consumer boycott against the white business people, we want our comrades out of detention."

What could I say? More and more, as if recognising that you cannot walk if you do not breathe, my mind was drifting, as it did whenever I found myself in such discussions. I do not know when and how it happens, but I thought about leaving the country to look for and find MK. We had dislodged the councillors, the

180

agents, the black police, we were even making the streets crime-free. But death was always present. The army, the police, the murder squads ... they brought death into the townships. You listened to the sound of the gun, and as your mind and your flesh listened, got frightened, became taut, snapped and became numb, to find you were alive the next day was to stand up immediately and do what had to be done. Drive a car. Throw a stone. Talk with comrades. Stop cars. Make someone drink cooking oil. Whatever had to be done, you went out to do. To stop and think; to miss someone; to look closely, to examine - this came when one was alone, when time seemed plentiful, and then you realised, change is as tough as steel.

"Change is as tough as steel"

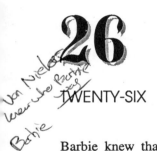

Barbie knew that van Niekerk knew who she was. Daily, she planned each day with great care. Each house, each person she used and knew, in each case she concealed everything about herself. She knew many people from her university days as a student and as a lecturer. She stalked them with great meticulousness, cultivating them according to what each could afford, but also ensuring that she left no tracks.

She lived many lives. It all started in the house where she and Jacob had lived for two weeks. Jacob started by asking questions. Then he started disappearing for short periods. Then he started to warm to her. It did not confuse her; she was lonely and so acted, at times, purely from emotion; and then she would run. He would chase. Partly he was lonely, and also curious, but more, he wanted to have the upper hand.

But Barbie and Steve had counted each step; talked about every move; watched carefully for anything that was not consistent. Each began to know that there was more than met the eye. Jacob did not know, but only because he was under test. Who was Barbie, was the main question. A photograph disappeared. Barbie and Steve moved. Barbie arrived that night with blood-shot eyes, a stagger, and a slur on the tongue. She came in, went to her room, took off her jeans, remained in her T-shirt. Bare foot she walked into the lounge.

"How are you, Joe?"

"Fine. Where have you been?"

"Drinking. I feel drunk."

"Where?"

"At the canteen at the Y, with some stupid students. What have you been doing?"

"Here, I've been here. Thinking."

"What?" She stood in the middle of the room, her knee on the table. She could feel him looking, watching, examining, devouring her.

"Nothing in particular, just my mind wandering."

"You revolutionaries are too serious. You hold onto life with a grip that kills every good thing about life," she said.

"What do you mean?"

"Actually, you're right, what I'm saying is meaningless. All I wanted to say is you are too serious." She threw herself on the sofa, sighing.

"You are correct."

In the two weeks that Barbie lived in this house around Jacob, the world had gone upside down. We think; we imagine; we are told; and, at times, we see. But reality, the actual experience, always has a surprise, at times a shock, and it can traumatise. Yet, Jacob's reality in the two weeks had also changed. Do people change? What is it about life which changes, which promises, which creates optimism, which gives hope? What is it - that which can say, once and for all, hope is not futile?

Both Barbie and Jacob had come to walk, to see, to listen as animals do in their environment where other animals are strong, agile, have sharp teeth and eat meat. They walked the streets of the suburb when few of the inhabitants of the suburbs walked them; they watched lest they be watched. They talked as little as possible, and whatever they said was not loud whenever they met neighbours. They slept each night to its end with a great sense of achievement. Each sunrise which brought a day into being weighed heavily on their minds. It could be a day with unpleasant surprises. They talked about this to each other, and the more they did, they sensed there was much which was not being said. There was this suspicion between them. Each watched, concealing the watching. Each wondered how much the other knew. Each pretended, and the other suspected.

On that day, as she sat back on the sofa, almost sensing the smell of wine on her breath, and somewhat dropping her guard, a sadness reached her, which she fought. She thought of Steve. Steve, in his meticulousness, was also vulnerable; in his honesty, he seemed so revealed; in his coldness at times, his utter loneliness showed. He knew. She knew. They kept an unexplained aloofness. At times it got so complex and so boring. Was there nothing a little – just a little – simple, available, harmless? She felt Jacob stand up, go to the kitchen, and expected him to come back to her shortly, which he did, since he had got lost. She knew he was going to touch her. She was going to allow him. She felt sad. She waited. He sat next to her. For a while there was a large silence. And then he hugged her. She did not move. His cheek was near hers. She turned away. His hand lost itself inside her T-shirt. She longed for Steve. He touched her stomach, her thigh, her knee. He was about to kiss her. She gently, very gently turned her mouth aside. She could feel tears in her eyes. He saw them.

"I love you," he said.

She was not about to respond.

"No, maybe I would like to make love to you," he said. "I have never been this close to a white woman," he said with great honesty.

She looked at him. She felt her emotions confused.

"Don't confuse me," she said.

"No, I don't want to confuse you."

"Shall we drive up, and buy a bottle?" she asked.

"Yes." He knew he had lost the chance. He let go.

They walked out in silence. Just as they were about to walk out the door she stopped, looked at him, and remarked, "I've lost a photograph in the house." Even as he said, "Really?", the way he looked, and what he said, did not correspond. There was a silence. She persisted. "Have you seen it?"

"What? The photograph? No," he said. He had regained himself.

They walked out into the dark, to the car. Slowly the car slid out of the garage, the yard, into the street. There was uneasiness. Silence. The car, climbing the hill, squeaked. Whatever it was that had made one touch the other, and the other allow the touch, did not exist now, under the full moon, indigo sky and twinkling stars. She eased the silence.

"By the way, Steve is coming for you – when?"

"Tuesday."

"Where are you going?"

"What?" He looked at her.

"Sorry, that's none of my business."

He was feeling frustrated.

"One minute you say revolutionaries are too serious about life, the other you are about to give in to me, and then you are asking me about Steve …"

"All of those are related," she said, teasing.

"No, they are not."

"They are."

"How?"

"Really, you want us to discuss this?"

"Well, no …"

Oppression is cruel. Barbie had seen Jacob, almost overnight, change from being illiterate about electricity, about the phone, about the kettle, from being uneasy in the comfort and massiveness of the house, to being a master. He walked differently now. He spoke differently.

As they drove into the main university gate she felt confused, utterly confused, there was little she felt she could understand now. She swerved, braked and got out of the car. When she came back with the bottle in her hand, she said, "How does a township boy drink wine, and not a beer?"

"I'm in a white area – do as the Romans do," Jacob said.

"Too many Romans," she smiled, "you will become a chameleon, with many, many colours, you will confuse me."

The way she said this made him look at her carefully, he was a little confused as to what she meant, and whether she was implying what he suspected she did – or was it simply a manner of talking?

"A chameleon?"

"Yes."

"What do you mean, many Romans?"

"Well, you couldn't be anything else but my servant, or garden boy, but everyone knows I'm not from here. I'm so young, also, you couldn't be my servant, so who are you?"

"I see," Jacob said, "where are you from?"

"Ask nothing, and you won't be told any lies," she said.

"Oh, I see. How old are you?"

185

"You see, I told you, too many Romans, I'm not telling!"

It was a little frustrating. Barbie was behaving, responding as a woman would to a man she knows is not just being friendly, but rather means business, is about to touch, to come closer … but this was also because she had come to watch him closely now. She and Steve thought they had evidence now … Jacob was about to eat from their palms.

Jacob had lost every point of reference. The fact that he had to speak English all the time made him feel as if he was learning everything from the beginning; also, he was in a white area, with its tarred, treed, clean streets, its tangible silence, almost unpeopled, even though you sensed that there were people around. Cars started, roared and drove on to the road. A dog barked. You saw, now and then, a boy, a girl, on a bicycle, at peace with the world, cycling up and down the road. You saw a domestic servant, now with an empty basket, going one way, then coming back, with the basket filled with all sorts of goods, in dapple-coloured covers. All this made him uneasy. But, besides the fact that Jacob had no permit to be in a white area, as an activist here he was hiding, hiding too many things from himself, from everyone, and at the same time, he was not hiding anything. And then, here was Barbie. He looked at her now, under the avenue lamp-light. The darkness was not very far from them, behind the buildings, under the tree, in a car, the avenue light touching them softly, and so the fact that it was Barbie's suggestion to come here, provoked him, but something in the way Barbie held herself stopped him from making a move. Steve? The thought angered him.

There is terror, terror is not a word. Terror arises also out of something understood. No, it is not terror. There is sadness, not sadness, because that, too, is a result of something understood. In this situation, where one has no access to a language, where one hurts, but does not know how to say it, where one wants, but has no words to express the desire, where one wants to know, and is left instead to watch, to gesture, to struggle because one cannot speak the language, one is left empty.

TWENTY-SEVEN

Steve shows up in a car to pick up Jacob.
Heading for Magaliesberg.

It was when he saw Steve that he got a fright. Then he saw someone he had not seen before. Then another, and then the two stood on each side of the van's back doors. Steve asked Jacob to come to the back. He got in, and the strangers sat on each side of him. The silence and the darkness were terrible. Steve said something to Barbie. She got out from behind the wheel as Steve got in. Another person appeared and occupied the passenger seat.

"Jacob, I hope to see you," Barbie said, still holding the bottle of wine in her hand.

"Okay," Jacob managed to say.

The vehicle took off, leaving Barbie standing in the dark. It was after a long time, when everyone knew that they were heading for Magaliesberg, that Steve talked.

"These comrades also want to go to train. Comrades, this is Jacob."

Steve had broken the silence which had left Jacob's heart pounding and pounding. He had felt his saliva dry in his mouth. He swallowed often. He suspected he looked scared, and thanked the night and Steve for breaking the silence.

"Haai," he exclaimed to the figures around him. Only one person responded. This pushed him back to his dreadful, fearful feeling.

"Does anyone have a cigarette?"

"Ja," Steve said, searching his jacket and handing the packet to Jacob. He lit one, and handed the pack back. Somehow he knew he was not to talk to the others. But he tried.

"Cigarettes?"

"Are you offering the cigarettes from my pack?" Steve asked.

Jacob sensed hostility and mockery in Steve's voice. The uneasiness in the car was similar to that which he had sensed when he was with van Niekerk. They crossed the border.

As Jacob was about to enter the door leading to the plane, he spotted Barbie. She had a bag slung over her shoulder, and held up an air ticket. He wanted to weep. He wondered why he had not died. He walked through the door, up the stairs, into the plane. He was sweating. His mouth was dry. He could hear the sound of his heart. He closed his eyes for awhile. When he opened them, he saw Barbie standing over him.

"We meet again," she said.

"Yes," he smiled.

"We will meet in Lusaka," she said as she walked along the aisle to her seat.

Two young men were waiting for them at the airport. They took their bags. Jacob observed how warm the two were towards Barbie, how they hugged - it was clear that they knew each other from another time. Jacob sighed loudly and visibly. He felt alone in a world which seemed somehow smaller and aloof towards him. They got into a car. He did not see Lusaka or the road from the airport. He felt the car stop after what seemed years of driving. Sipho came walking slowly towards him, hands in his trouser pockets.

"Haai," Sipho said, smiling at him. He wanted to run and hug him, but he stopped himself. They went into the house.

Everything about the house showed that it was thoroughly lived in. The chairs, the tables, the cupboards, the beds, the blankets, indicated that many come and go here. There was the smell of food. People came in and out. There were notebooks, ANC journals, pens, and a sense that no-one really belonged to this house. Barbie threw herself on a chair. Sipho looked at her.

"How's home?"

"Home is home is home, we should all be there," she sighed.

"How are the comrades?"

"I saw one or two."

"Jacob, how are you?" Sipho asked.

"I'm well," he said, "how are you?"

"Okay, the boers and their agents are making us work twenty-four hours a day."

"Ja," Jacob agreed.

"The Movement must allow me to see one," Barbie said, "I would really like to see one, what an agent looks like."

"They look like you and me," Sipho said.

By now, Jacob had watched and listened as many came and went, as cars came, stopped, dropped people and drove on. All had come, greeted him, talked to Sipho or to Barbie awhile and left. In between, Barbie and Sipho had gone on with the subject.

"Why do people become agents?"

"You must ask them when you meet them."

"I'm serious, Sipho, why?"

"I can't talk for agents, they have mouths, they can talk for themselves," Sipho said.

While he hoped he would not be pulled into the conversation, he was painfully aware that he was deliberately left out of it. His fear became many demons. He thought, just for a while, he thought, if a chance comes, he must run.

The two young men who had met them at the airport came back.

"Can you come with us?" one of them said.

Jacob had noticed that when they talked to each other, or to Sipho and Barbie, they called them by name or referred to them as comrade, yet they seemed to avoid his name and never once, since he'd been there, had anyone referred to him as comrade.

He stood up. "Shall I bring my coat?" he asked.

"Yes."

They walked out to the car. Jacob looked at Lusaka. It had the features of many townships he had seen. He could see and feel poverty. The people were like people in the township. What had he expected to see? People sold their goods on the corners of streets. There were many people in the streets, just as in Alex. Some of the houses looked like shacks, and some like those he had seen in the rural areas, and some were like the small matchbox houses in Soweto.

It was as the car stopped and he tried to open the door that he realised that he could not open it from the inside. One of the young men opened the door for him and seemed to escort him while the other flanked him. They went into a house. An old man who sat reading a newspaper lifted his head to look at them.

189

"Is this Jacob?"

"Yes," one of his escorts said.

"How are you Jacob?" the old man said, extending his hand.

They shook hands. The old man showed him to a sofa, and sat next to him.

"How is Alex?"

"Fine!"

"But you have just come from the suburbs," the old man said.

"Yes."

"Was Barbie good to you?"

"Yes."

"How's Steve?"

"He's alright."

"When last did you see him?"

"Er ... three days ago."

"Yes, yes, you know, there is a boer there in the townships, he is a menace to our people; by the way, did you know comrades Mlambo and Monnakgotla?"

"I knew Comrade Mlambo, I did not know Comrade Monnakgotla."

"Do you know that they are dead?"

"No, when?"

"Not too long ago they were killed by this boer who is a menace in the township, his name is van Niekerk, do you know him?"

"No, I don't know him."

"Have you heard about him?"

"No," Jacob hesitated.

"It's a pity you do not know him. Maybe after you have trained and gone back home, you will encounter him. He has finished our people."

Jacob sighed.

"Dan, when is Jacob leaving for Angola?"

"Tonight."

"Okay. I will see you, Jacob, have a good trip," the old man said. "I hear that some people at home say we kill people in Angola, have you heard that?"

"No," Jacob said.

"Some say so."

The old man stood up to go. Jacob looked at him, as he was gathering his newspaper from the table. He was tall, thin, with very grey hair, immaculately dressed, and something about him showed strength and wisdom. Was it his eyes? He walked out the door, and drove off in a car which had been parked in the yard. Jacob looked at the car as it drove out the yard. Dan, one of the young men, was looking at him.

"That is the deputy-chief of our security," Dan said.

"Yes," Jacob managed to say.

"You don't know van Niekerk?"

"No," Jacob said.

"Well, you are the first activist I meet from home who does not know van Niekerk ..."

Just then, Jacob remembered that he had met Sipho, and that he and Sipho knew van Niekerk.

"I don't know why I thought I didn't know him, but now I recall that I do."

"Are you nervous?"

"No, I'm not nervous."

"Many comrades do become nervous when they come here, I do not know why," Dan said.

"A new place can make one nervous," Stompie, the other young man, said.

"A new place?" Dan asked.

"Yes," Stompie said.

"Why would a new place make one nervous?"

"Well, it does, if you do not know people, the place, it can make you uneasy."

"No, it is the many things which people say about us. We kill people, we arrest people, people vanish, we rape women, all these ..." Dan continued, "We do not rape women, but of course we arrest and can kill if need be."

"No, what I am saying," Stompie said, "is that people mystify the ANC."

"They don't mystify it, they undermine it."

"What's wrong with you, Comrade Dan? Are you in an argumentative mood?"

"I feel evil!" Dan said.

191

"I see."

"You see what?"

"I understand what you are saying."

"I dislike agents, me, I must ask the leadership to put me in units which shoot agents."

"No, you are alright here, you are the first one captured agents meet, they get the sense from you of what is awaiting them," Stompie said as he looked at his watch. "We must prepare to go to the airport," he said, standing up as he gathered his bag and parcels from the table. It was as Stompie stood up that Jacob noticed that he was armed. They left for the airport.

28

TWENTY-EIGHT

Stayaways

There was a stayaway in South Africa that day. While the heart of this country, its industry and manufacturing sector had almost ebbed to a standstill, the townships were filled with people. Streets and yards and houses were peopled to the brim. It was the first stayaway, when people were in houses with family and friends, careful to make it a success. They had seen the army and the police. They had carefully got out of their way.

Khehla walked into a house in Tembisa to wait for Steve. In Alexandra, Snyman met with Strike. In Mamelodi, Cynthia was preparing to leave for Durban, for a women's meeting. Rebecca was coming back from a youth meeting in Soweto, to Sebokeng. Everyone watched the TV and listened to the radio and discussed the newspapers. All reports indicated that the stayaway was ninety per cent successful. It felt so, men and women were at home *90% success* everywhere. There were house meetings and meetings in churches. Most townships came out into the yards, lawns, streets, into shebeens, and the atmosphere was created by men and women and children, not in a hurry for anything, not having dressed up, going outside wherever there was space; music from turntables, from radios and combis – always the busy ants of the townships in their ups and downs – all these, although it was a weekday, gave the township, the streets and the people a festive feel. Everyone was easy.

The hippos were there. The police vans were there. The trucks were there. They had come to find out who was intimidating who, and to protect the intimidated. The trucks, hippos and vans, rushed up and down the streets, making lots of dust, hurling it into the sky. With aloofness, with a touch of careful watchfulness, but also with readiness, the townships observed all this, from a distance. It was not a distance measured in space – it was an attitude. The

193

distance could not be reduced, it was far and deep, it was aimed against a mighty force. And they could see it, hear it, and somehow they knew its restlessness. The uneasiness, the confidence of this intangible force made the mighty insecure. Something had happened. Something which could not be touched, had happened. It had never before been experienced.

Then some reports began to reach the townships and the little rural towns. The reports had been heard on radios, seen on TV and read in newspapers. They had not been believed. No one believed anything from the media, least of all the people who gathered the information that was turned into news. The news began to walk the streets, arrive in kombis, and was spread by phone from township to township. It was news of MK. About how in the early morning South Africa woke up to the first successful stayaway which MK had quietly defended. Houses of black police and councillors had been grenade attacked – the sign, was the call. The bloody news reached the squatter areas and alleys of the ghetto, turning uncertainty to conspiracy and visions of ice, of fire, of fathomless depths, of steel. The police sensed this everywhere they went; and the townships, as the first day of the stayaway went by, sensed the restlessness of the police. When, by experience, by what people have seen and heard and touched, they ignore threats and dare the unknowing, and without saying a word, break all understood rules and even, when they hear footsteps, they don't look, and when they sense presence and do not acknowledge it, or when, even in their deep sleep and beneath their skin they know and feel danger and yet ignore it – what can be done? The stayaway had brought this to the country of the white might! In the townships and the small rural towns, while the people there stood by, as they went on with the business of being home, with friends, family and neighbours, sharing without knowing, a new set of rules for their lives, rules to relate to the new state they had achieved, they also forged new relations. They knew that, for the first time, they had agreed, they had come together to fight in silence for the future. Amid the loud music and songs and vigorous toyi-toyi, danced as if it were a means of hit-and-run from the patrolling police, a silence, thoughtful and searching for meaning and possibilities in the future, persisted. It was an eerie silence for all.

194

The first day of the stayaway, when the workers agreed to tell the mighty white government that its army and police had rendered the lives of black people cheap, and that this must stop, and when they still, in stealth, defended this, without knowing it or suspecting it, the townships and rural areas held power in their hands. Splashed mauve in the colours of the setting sun, the first day of power of the oppressed gathered shadows as the darkness of night fell. There were no kombis coming back from the cities and white areas with loads of workers. There were no taxis, and there were no buses or trains or cars coming back in a rush and roar of dust, in a hurry to get back to the resting place of deep darkness and ruin. Everyone in the townships and rural dorps noted this quiet, packed with defiance. There were still two more days to go. The news came in the only manner it could come to the ghettos of the city and the rural areas. An old woman had been burnt alive for being a witch; a young boy had been hacked to death for being an agent; all in all, eighty people had been killed in various parts of the country, and more were injured. Among these, ten police and councillors had been killed. Beneath the news, which could not be verified, within the uneasy night, filled with rumour, and the unsaid, uneasy, trying preparations for the second day of the wrestling and wielding of power by the victims against the mighty white victor, in whisper, in song and dance, as meetings ended and gatherings dispersed in many townships, people felt the burden of being free, as questions about the future were posed and the capability of the oppressed weighed, everywhere a new energy and restlessness began.

Steve arrived in 'Moscow' just before midnight. As he knocked gently on a window, his comrades who had accompanied him with cocked AKs lay in the dark in watch. He heard the soft creak of the back door. He quickly went to it, and Lady, in a silk gown, stood there, seeking eye contact with him.

"Everyone must wake up, quickly and get out of the house," he said.

Without a word, she turned back into the house, with Steve close behind her. In the darkness there was movement in and out of rooms, into the yard, over the fences. 'Moscow' was empty in no time, as dark as any house in Alexandra in which people were sleeping. It was at twelve forty-five that the soft sound of the wheels of a car were heard, not very far from the corner of Second Avenue. The car moved without lights. Two people got out, while one remained behind the wheel. The two walked very fast. They went into the yard next to Lady's. They scaled the fence into 'Moscow'. Dogs began to bark. The men moved swiftly around 'Moscow'.

They hurled grenades. They opened automatic fire. In no time, they had scaled the fence into the next yard, into the street, and the car purred, moving to meet them halfway. They got in, and the car reversed, U-turned, and was taking off fast when it was hit on all sides by automatic fire and grenades. Like a great wild horse, it seemed to raise its chest, readying itself for a great gallop, but then, like a balloon deflating, it sank. Three doors were simultaneously flung open. Each of the occupants tried to get out of the car. One ran and fell, struck down. Another staggered maybe one or two paces, and fell. The third had managed only to open the door.

After all this, there was a great silence. And then, as always, a speeding car in the dark of night, waking fear among those who were listening to it, but there was not only one, there were many cars, coming from different directions. The Alexandrans came out into the darkly lit ruined streets. They did not put lights on; they used the shadows of the night and of the ruins that surrounded them to conceal themselves, and to watch. The assaulted car and its occupants were surrounded by the police and the army, and 'Moscow' was also surrounded. An old woman walked out of one of the yards, straight to the police who were examining the car and its occupants.

"Who is your leader?" she asked a soldier.

"What?"

"I said, 'who is your leader'?"

The young soldier looked at her from top to bottom, looked behind him, then back at her. "Why?"

"Don't ask me why! Where is your leader?"

"There!" The young soldier pointed behind him.

The old woman walked to the man in camouflage. "Sir, good morning!"

196

"Good morning, old lady, what are you doing here?"

"What is this?" the old woman asked as, in one sweeping gesture, she pointed to the car, the bodies lying in the street, and 'Moscow'.

"Madness, just madness!" the captain said. "Do you know any of the people here?"

The old woman walked closer to each body, two of which still had life in them, while the third sprawled in death, face down on the earth. They turned the corpse over, she saw the face.

"What is your name?" the captain demanded.

"Mrs Kgosil," she said.

"Do you know any of them?"

"No!"

"Who lives in that house?"

"Lady."

"Lady?"

"Yes, Lady."

"Lady who?"

"Lady, everyone knows her as Lady."

"Where do you live?"

"Number hundred and nine, here in Second."

"Why are you up so early?"

"Can you sleep in all this frightening noise? What is all this, just tell me that, what is all this mess?" She stood facing the captain, looking him in the eye.

"If you want to know from me, I'd say absolute madness."

Just then the ambulance arrived. Van Niekerk arrived in one of the Landrovers, and went to talk to the captain.

29

TWENTY-NINE

When the news reached them, fear and anger choked them. It was summoned strength which enabled Rebecca to sit quietly and to listen as her comrades talked about and tried to understand what had happened. The news was taking on different versions. Rebecca's mind dwelled on what it meant that 'Moscow' was attacked by grenades and AKs. How could anyone have come out alive? What remained of her comrades? Her mind was filled with familiar images of twisted corpses, of missing limbs, of smudges of blood and grey bits of bone on walls and floors. She had seen all this in the past. And now, in trying to think about Strike, Lindi, Lady, Billy, Thuledu, Shakes, Noma, Diana and the others, she could only see smudges of red and grey, her eyes staring forever. She became fearful, she became depressed, as her mind stuck on the images.

"But someone also said the people who attacked were killed," Jersey said.

"Killed, by whom?" Dorcas asked.

"By MK."

"MK"? Dolly asked. "How did MK know this was going to happen?"

"Maybe they were just around," Lucas said.

"Around doing what?"

"MK is everywhere, by the way," Thabo said.

"No, maybe the agents died by accident," Lucas said, "it has happened before."

"We must get a newspaper," Jersey said.

"But you will not get any truth from the papers," Dolly said.

"One of us must go to Alex," Thabo said.

"And do what?" Dolly asked.

"And find out what happened," Thabo said.

"How?" Dolly asked.

"Ask people."

"No, let's wait, we will be told," Dolly said.

Rebecca said nothing. Thabo, Lucas and Dorcas had become very quiet. Dikeledi, Thabo's grandmother, busy cleaning in her bedroom, was listening to this conversation. "Are you through with cleaning?" she asked.

"We are still cleaning," Dolly replied, "soon, soon we shall leave this house and furniture shining and smelling like a palace."

"I hear more talking than working," the old woman said.

"Did you hear what happened in Alex?" Dolly was standing, leaning against the door-frame of the bedroom.

"Yes, yes I've heard. But they found no-one in the house, the comrades had already left when the boers attacked."

"You know that?" Rebecca stood up from her chair and joined Dolly at the door.

"I know that, yes. Three people were killed, they were boer agents."

"Who killed them, then?" Rebecca asked. By now, all of them were crowded at the old lady's bedroom door. They watched her, as she moved with her heavy, limping walk from one piece of furniture to the other, feather-duster in hand, dusting the tops, legs and sides of each piece of furniture with great care.

"One of the agents is the singer's lover, what's her name?"

"Lindi?"

"Yes, Lindi, it is her boyfriend."

"But what about our comrades?"

"All of them are alright, they escaped."

"Who killed the agents then?"

"If I say anything, I will be telling a lie," she said. "Look at you, to see your eyes popped out like that, and your ears on edge just reminds me, you should finish your chores."

There was a silence as all of them watched and as each weighed what they had heard from her. How does she know all this? In the past, their past with her, her character, her confidence, her calmness had told each of them to trust her, to respect and love her. Mamolady they called her. Com Mamolady they would say as she objected persistently, especially to Com. But she had lost that battle.

"Mamolady," Rebecca said, "is 'Moscow' destroyed?"

"Yes, it is destroyed."

"Where are the comrades, then?"

"They must be far out of Alex, I hope, looking for another place to stay."

"Where?"

"I don't want to tell lies!"

They looked at each other; in their eyes, in their faces there was no answer to the question.

"Rebecca," Dolly said, "you look ill!"

Rebecca smiled, she also cried, and Mamolady limped towards her, hugged her, caressing her hair as the others watched in silence, their minds groping for answers.

"You must go to the bedroom and lie down, my child," Mamolady said, "rest yourself and think about the good things that happened. Your comrades are okay. The evil people will do no-one any evil anymore. That, all that, is very good." She held Rebecca by the hand, leading her to the bedroom. The others followed each other like sheep, each going back to their chores.

"I want to leave the country," Rebecca said to Mamolady.

"I hear you, but if I were you, I would keep that to myself."

"I have to talk to you about it," Rebecca said sharply.

"I hear you, I'm saying keep it to yourself."

"If I keep it to myself, how will I leave?"

"I said I heard you," she began to walk out of the bedroom, her eyes flying over the neat though crowded bedroom. There were three mattresses neatly packed on top of each other in the corner, and a heap of blankets neatly stacked; skirts, dresses and blouses hung on hangers on a length of string nailed to the walls, and there were also several pairs of women's shoes. Mamolady opened the window wider, and also the curtains.

"Some of you must sleep in the lounge," she said, "it is not so nice to be so crowded when you are resting. I do not know why you people refuse to share space with me in my bedroom."

"But we like being with each other," Rebecca said.

"No, you like talking throughout the night, that's what you want to do, talk all night."

"Are you going to do something about what I asked you?"

"What?"

"Going!"

"I said I heard you, leave it at that," she began to walk towards the door. She closed it behind her gently as she stood awhile, watching the others – Dolly ironing, Thabo washing the dishes, Lucas on his knees shining the floor, and Dorcas sweeping outside. Mamolady was humming a song as she limped to her bedroom.

"Is Rebecca fine?" Thabo asked.

"She's a sensitive one, that one, she will be alright, she is a nice little girl." Mamolady cut the conversation short by disappearing into her room. She left the door ajar.

Rebecca lay on her back with her knees up. She must go. She must receive training. Her mind went to those far places – Angola, a word which in many townships was changing lots of people. It was said with watchful eyes and carefully listening ears; Lusaka, a word which in the townships and rural areas was re-shaping attitudes, creating courage, and making people dream dreams; Soviet Union, the name bestowed hope, and thrashed atonement and forgiveness in many young hearts. The struggle had by now taken Rebecca to many areas of South Africa, and this, for she had indeed come to know it, was all she knew. In her young years life was not life as it is normally known. She had disowned her parents, and had packed her suitcase and left home. Now her deep feelings for her brother and her sister were overcoming her. She had heard that her father had been necklaced, but she had not had time to think about it. She now and then wondered where her mother was, but just very briefly – all that had been replaced by the weight she had put into the word 'comrade'. She believed it was all she had in this life and this world.

And then Thabo. She had not yet understood why being near him threatened her ability to control herself; her ability to be in control, her strength of being in control. And in her fresh life, she was fearful of what happened to her when, at night, they took a walk to the shop for a talk, or when she was involved in the struggle with him. There was much she could not sort out in herself.

And now, she discovered that inside her, she was hurting. She hurt at the thought of the 'comrades' having been wiped out; she hurt at being unable to imagine what she and the others would have done if Mamolady's place had been the target that night – what if she had survived and Mamolady had not? Then she thought about the many places she had been to. To funerals, to meetings, witnessing death, brutality and ruthlessness. She thought about the maze of squatter camps she had seen and the conditions of life in them, the filth, the squalor, the hopelessness of life and the emptiness of it all in the vastness and derelict reality of these camps. She was afraid to feel helpless. She felt, as in the beginning while they were searching for a place to live, how she was threatened by ending in a shack, by ending her life without a reason for its presence and continuation. She had seen the men and women of these camps, aimless, with devastated facial expressions – lacking life, devoid of a smile or anger or a cry – as if they were waiting, in long and massive queues, in life – for death! She began to weep in her deep melancholy; she began to weep, unable to sort out the myriad images and tapestry of disastrous feelings in herself. She wept and wept, quietly, afraid that her comrades might hear her cry, and that they would think her weak. When could she go? When could she train? When could she then come back, to fight once and for all? The unclear pictures and images in her mind of Angola, Lusaka and the Soviet Union made everything seem so far away, so distant, so unachievable. And then she began to be fearful for herself, because, for a moment, a slight moment, she saw it as a reality that she could take her life. Could kill herself – now she was afraid! What must she do? And then she screamed. And then she saw Mamolady, Thabo, Dorcas and Dolly in her room, around the bed, looking at her. It was Thabo who held her, it was Thabo who pulled her, gently, without a word at first, towards himself and said, "Comrade, what is the matter?"

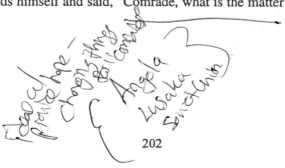

30

THIRTY

The comrades from 'Moscow' wanted to leave the country now. Strike and Steve met, and Strike told Steve.

"There is no problem," Steve said.

"When can we go?"

"Are you sure that this is the only thing to be done now?"

"Yes," Strike said, "we all feel that way."

Steve looked away. He looked at the distant blue-black sky of the horizon, to where the stars twinkled.

"I must go now," he said, "Comrade Strike, I will see you."

"When?"

"I will see you," he repeated. Strike decided to hold on, to clutch at him.

"What must I say to the comrades, then?"

"Tell them what we talked about."

"What?"

"That they will go," Steve began to walk away.

"When?"

Steve stopped, looked at Strike, and then looked down. Strike saw that Steve was very tired.

"Sorry about this, but when?"

"No, don't be sorry about anything – I will let you know when."

Steve walked away casually into the dark street, into the street barked at by dogs. Strike was left standing under the street light. He did not know what to do after what Steve had said to him. A car roared in the distant night. Dogs barked. Stars twinkled. The moon, shaped like a semi-circle, glowed as if it was patched onto the almost black, almost blue sky. He began to walk away in the opposite direction. Steve got into the car. Barbie engaged the gear.

Strike began to drift, barely hearing his lone footsteps. What must he say to his comrades? What would he tell them Steve had said to him? He imagined them walking, tired, worn out by the road leading to faraway lands. He imagined they were in Angola, in Lusaka, in Botswana – where? He imagined these lands, the bush, wild, where many young people were training to become guerillas, shooting, crossing rivers, crawling, shooting ... he imagined that they were engaged in battle, they were shooting, there was shooting, and the soldiers, white soldiers were shooting, running, they were pursuing them ... why was Steve so evasive? Why did he seem to be so reluctant to talk about their going? Had they not been shot at? Had they not heard gunshots, had they not run, ducked under fences, had some of their comrades not been killed? Couldn't Steve understand that they wanted to go, to learn how to fight? Why was Steve so aloof?

"The comrades at 'Moscow' want to leave," Steve said.

"Why don't they?"

"Tell them Justice can."

"Why don't you tell him?"

"I'm asking you to tell him," Steve said sternly.

"No sweat," she shrugged.

Silence fell in the car. They were now on the M1 highway towards Pretoria. The highway was deserted.

Strike tried the handle, and the door opened. Billy was at the table, a glass in front of him. Lindi was smoking, sitting with her head tilted to one side.

"Skopendonner was going to kill the whole bang shoot of us," Billy said with a slur, talking as if to himself but looking at Strike. Strike stood in the centre of the lounge. The recently repaired wall, door and windows stared at him. He became afraid. He could see that Billy was dead drunk. Maybe Lindi, too, seemed to be asleep because she was drunk. Where was Nomafa? Where were Thuledu, Diana, Noma, Shakes, Tshabi, Annah, Tebogo, Peter and Mike, where was Obed? The names seemed to reel in his mind like horses on a merry-go-round revolving at an insane speed; he held on.

"Why are you standing like that?" Billy asked.

"Where are the others?"

"Who?"

"The others."

"Sleeping; why are you standing like that?"

"Nothing!"

"What do you mean, nothing, where do you come from?"

"Third Avenue."

"Third Avenue?" Billy asked as if he did not know what this meant.

Strike sat down opposite Billy. He saw that Billy's eyes were red like liver. His eyelids drooped from tiredness, from drunkenness, from fear.

"You people must explain yourselves. You must not go on as you want, you must report."

"Report what?" Strike demanded.

"What you are doing."

"To whom?"

"To whom? Are you being cheeky?"

"No, I want to know."

"Know what? Don't you know that we all nearly died?"

"Would you remember if I reported to you what I'm doing?"

"You think I'm drunk?"

They stared at each other in silence.

"You think I'm drunk, or I'm stupid, what are you trying to tell me? Who do you think you are? You are a small boy who thinks he knows something about politics, who imagines that he is MK – MK is not made of stuff like you ..."

"What?" Lindi asked, lifting her head up.

"What do you mean, what?" Billy said. "Why are you still here, did you not say you were going to sleep?"

"Me?" Lindi blinked.

"You, who do you think I'm talking to?"

"How can you go and sleep?"

"How can you go and be drunk?" Billy sneered.

"Maybe we are just two fools playing with fire," she sighed.

"You are playing with fire!"

"It will burn you!"

"Who?"

"It will burn you while asleep, at least I will see something of it."

"Shut up, see something of what?"

"I'm going to bed," Strike said standing up. He felt depressed.

"Where have you been?" Billy asked.

"Hell, you are only asking that now?"

"Asking what?"

"This man, this boy has been here for an hour now ..."

"Fuck that hour ..."

"You must be careful of your tongue." Strike walked away. When he got to the bedroom he was met by snoring and someone talking in his sleep. He shut the door. He stood there looking at the five or so bodies breathing loudly, mumbling in their sleep. He wanted to cry. He was afraid. He felt angry at Steve. He began to unbutton his shirt, unzip his trousers, and take off his shoes. The door opened, it frightened him. Billy stood at the door, staggering, swaying like a pendulum.

"You going to sleep?"

"Yes," Strike said.

"Who's guarding now."

"It should be Thuledu."

"Where is she?"

"I don't know ..."

"You don't know, but you have just come?"

"I want to sleep, please ..."

"Sleep? What is that – sleep? I'm asking you about guarding, you tell me about sleep?"

"Don't talk too loud, you will wake the comrades up."

"What?"

Strike looked at Billy. This is absurd, he thought. He wondered what it would be like if he went for training. But what was Steve's problem?

Steve, Barbie and Cynthia were sipping tea now, their umpteenth cup.

"I think we should send Sizakhele there."

"I have no problem with that, besides he has just arrived," Steve said.

"That's not a reason to send him there, that's a reason to get him arrested."

"Don't talk nonsense, he is trained, he is here to train comrades, we must stop this eternal retreat, we must advance."

"Don't throw slogans at me, I'm raising the issue of security. That 'Moscow' is hot!"

"The hotter the better, he must go there. He did not come here to hide, he came here to fight."

"Not to be thrown into jail," Barbie insisted.

"Comrade Barbie, Sizakhele is trained, he is here to train others, he is here to fight. I know that 'Moscow' is hot, I know that. But what about the other comrades who are there, who are not trained, who sleep there?"

"That's not a reason to get Sizakhele arrested!"

Steve ignored her. "Cynthia you must brief Sizakhele about 'Moscow', about the comrades who are there and his mission there, he should be there by tomorrow night. I don't want to debate this any more."

"You are mad!" Barbie said.

Steve stood up and went into the other room.

"If he's armed, if he trains others, if the boers get there, they must know that every place they attack they come back to at the risk of their lives."

"What if they get wind of him before he does any training of the other comrades?"

"He fights!"

"All the other comrades will die like sitting ducks."

"I'm not asking for debate on this issue, it is an order. Those comrades want training, they want to fight, they are ready, we must not encourage them to think that those who fight come from outside only. Also, besides building on the fighting spirit of the comrades, we must inculcate the spirit that the best way to retreat is to advance."

"Don't give me those slogans!" Barbie banged on the table. Steve disappeared into the bedroom.

"We already have so many casualties."

"Comrade Barbie, I'm going to sleep," Cynthia said.

207

31

THIRTY-ONE

Sizakhele made contact with Strike, and then with Thuledu, and then with Peter. Strike was sceptical about going back to 'Moscow'. He thought that the brief he had been given was inadequate. He did not know whether he should trust what he had been told; he wondered about the manner he had been trained. As he walked down the road, back to nowhere, perhaps, he experienced deep sorrow, a sense of despair and regret that he had taken this path. It was a dangerous path. Having held an AK-47, having gone through handling a pistol and a grenade, having listened for all those hours to Sizakhele, he wondered, as he walked, whether he should go back to him the next day. He wanted to pray. He wanted to be left alone. But the seriousness, the earnest manner in which Sizakhele had spent every minute they were together, his systematic handling of every minute, every lesson, every word, made Strike feel he had a strength and knowledge he had never before possessed. He did not feel innocent. He envied the people he saw walking in the streets, talking, laughing, playing with each other. And then he wondered whether any of them had been through what he had just gone through. He decided with a heavy heart to go back to 'Moscow' after all. He turned up Selborne Street and Eighth Avenue towards Second Avenue. When he got to 'Moscow' he was told that Thuledu had left, and so had Peter; Lindi said they had left at different times; she said, from what they were carrying, it did not seem they were coming back. Strike, Annah, Tebogo, Obed, Tshabi, Shakes, Noma and Diana were there, in the bedrooms, on the verandah, in the yard …

When Strike saw them, when they spoke to him, he held on to what had been happening to him in the past week. In the past, only a week ago, he would have talked to them about everything in his life, now he could not, now he was ready to lie … and then he wondered whether they, too, had been lying, hiding things from him. Even as he thought it a possibility that they, too, may have had their week with Sizakhele, he stood aloof, something about him made the others realise that he was now outside of their circle. Billy had told him once that he carried himself like a peacock. Strike came and went with a silence, a concentration about him which made everyone around him feel cautious before approaching him. And then, one day, he disappeared. Diana and Noma also disappeared from 'Moscow'.

Strike had picked on Diana because something about her which was difficult to place made people want to talk to her. She now and then said things about people which left them revealed, which made them known. Strike had picked up this quality in Diana from a long time ago. He himself had, on many occasions, confided in Diana. She listened, gave back her view long after it was expected, and when she gave it, it was by probing further, and suggesting answers in such a way that they never appeared to come from her. When Strike told Sizakhele about this, Sizakhele had expressed interest in meeting Diana. At that point, Strike became protective of her without even knowing that he was. Strike, Diana and Noma found a backyard flat in Yeoville, Johannesburg, and there they stayed.

Diana, in her twenty-third year, at times seemed much older. Her youthful face and penetrating eyes always startled people, even those much older than her found themselves being polite to her. She was very dark, to the point that her teeth seemed snow white. She was tall, with a slight stoop at the shoulders which seemed to accommodate the short people she met and talked to. Strike was aware that he was slightly taller than her, and that Sizakhele was shorter than both of them. Without knowing why, he felt that this was an advantage over Sizakhele.

In Yeoville, in a backyard flat with three rooms and a gate to the street, they settled. Slowly each gave character to the room they occupied, and slowly, they built ways of living together as each slotted into their roles in their work. It was a relief to be there. It seemed there was more space to occupy and there was more room to breathe. In the beginning, each left their space. Sizakhele now and then came to see them. They ate, drank and talked. They talked about everything, but most of all about their work.

Noma wrote things down. She had a stealth about her, which made one forget her presence. She seemed to know how to emerge and retreat without rocking any boat. She struck one as being extremely shy. So shy, that one felt talking to her caused her pain. Unlike Diana and Strike, she was very meticulous, not only in the way she dressed and kept her room, but even in the way she walked. When she was taught how to use a pistol, Sizakhele noted the careful manner in which she followed every step of its dismantling, of preparing to put a target in sight, and even how she concealed it. Learning weapons, and developing a conciousness of how to use them, transformed them all, and Sizakhele imparted his commitment to them.

It was Noma who shot and killed Thabo, van Niekerk's best right-hand man, and from then on, Sizakhele disappeared. They remained, the three of them, with eyes of a wolf, ears of a springbok and legs of a hare.

Diana was now working in a hotel in Berea. Noma found piece-jobs everywhere. And Strike came and went, criss-crossing borders. Whenever he came back from wherever, he would say, "let's look at this closely," and they all knew when he said this that he had been in touch with someone, and that now they were to do the work.

Noma, with her broad shoulders and slight limp, struck one as being a young mother. Something about her was very mature, and only when you were face-to-face with her did you feel it an ordeal which must pass quickly. It was Diana only who could slip under that and reach her. If it were not the authority with which Strike talked to them both, which he consciously maintained, he, too, would have had great difficulty in talking to her. He made his encounter with her brief and to the point, looking her straight in the eye.

Strike had seen how Noma approached Thabo. Thabo got out of the car and was about to open the gate, when he noticed her. He dropped his guard when he noticed the casual walk with the limp, and eyes which seemed uninterested in him. As he turned towards the gate, Noma shot him thrice before he fell; in the head, back and between the buttocks. Strike, Sizakhele and Diana were covering her. The three of them each took one guard. The two guards fell before they could lift their guns.

With evil in his heart, van Niekerk arrived and did not uncover the two corpses which lay at the gate. When he came to investigate the scene, he looked at Thabo and noted that he had been shot at close range. He had absolute contempt for the dead guards, and hatred for those who had committed this act. He had put the pieces together by now. He knew that there were four people who had done it. He knew a woman had shot Thabo, and that, possibly, another woman was involved. He had, without connecting the two issues, noted also that some people had disappeared from 'Moscow'. It was two weeks later, when Solomon was shot, again by a woman – though this time covered by two people, a man and a woman – that he thought more information was needed. He raided 'Moscow'. While Thuledu escaped being caught in the net, Shakes, Tshabi, Annah and Tebogo were caught. Pretending that he was not interested in them, Billy, Lindi and Nomafa were left behind for a later date with the man. He emphasised his presence by going away, and then four days later coming back for Obed and Mike, though leaving behind Lindi, Nomafa and Billy.

Thuledu made known what had happened in 'Moscow'. Diana pieced together that van Niekerk was reacting, seeking information and leads to them. She sent word that the three must leave 'Moscow'. Billy's reaction was that she must not send messages like a thing in the dark, she must come and explain. Van Niekerk pounced again a month later, taking in the three. He more or less had a picture of what was going on at 'Moscow'. He resolved to close it, once and for all.

Squatters moved in. First into the yard, and then into the house. When Nomafa, Lindi and Billy came wearily out, they found they had nowhere to go. No-one listened to them. They were now considered terrorists by officialdom. Lindi had become quieter. She was finding ways now of handling her bitterness and anger. Billy, it was obvious, was broken. The three moved into a shack, fighting for space for their shoes and their heads. Lindi was stern, staring and abrupt. Billy could not get near her. When he died in his sleep, drunk, six months later, the two women were clinical about his burial. It was brief and there were few people. The trombone went to the top of the wardrobe to gather dust. Lindi saw this, but felt she could do nothing about it.

"You are so base," Lindi said once when van Niekerk came with Raymond to see them, "you can even eat the rotting corpse you make." Van Niekerk noted the yellow anger and bitterness in Lindi's voice; he noted also that Nomafa was done, she had had all her fights now. She was not even going to struggle not to die.

"You thought we would not find you and your nest of terrorists?" he asked Lindi, provoking her. She looked at him with dry, staring eyes and said nothing. Nomafa hardly looked at van Niekerk or Raymond, it would have used too much of her energy. Van Niekerk noted all this, and decided he would need to think about it.

"I'm sure we will meet again," he said to Lindi, "then we shall see ..." He left them.

Lindi watched van Niekerk go. She wondered if she would have the strength to meet him again. She wondered if she would have the strength to resist throttling him. She felt the fire, the rage, the hatred in her, rise. But she knew she had to control it. She still had to look after Nomafa. Besides, the comrades still needed her. She would wait. She would wait, as she used to, for her cue in music. She would wait ...

32

Van Newkerr's wife Barbara — knows He kills — is scared of him now

Today, when he came home, he found her sitting in the lounge. The TV was on, but silent. She wore a short navy-blue skirt with a slit on the side, a white blouse and navy sandals. Her handbag was lying on the floor, and her jacket was carelessly thrown on the sofa opposite her. Derek noticed all this, and when their eyes met the gleam of aloofness in her eyes struck him. The flame of desire began to rise, spread and kindle his body. He stood in front of her. He looked straight into her eyes. He saw how her face changed as it was engulfed by a fathomless resentment.

"You hate me and I love you," he said.

She looked away through the large window to the tall jacaranda trees, the blue, blue sky and the wide space beyond their garden.

"Barbara, did you hear what I said?" *Barbara*

"I heard you."

"And then?"

"Derek, why are you unable to listen to what I say?"

"Barbara has said I must leave my job, and I must do this?" he softly asked, controlling his emotions. *— She knows he kills*

"Now that I know that you kill people, I'm afraid of you, I resent you, you make my blood run cold," she said.

He looked away to the opposite window; he saw the jacaranda trees and the hill beyond merging with the shadows of the setting sun, the red, yellow and mauve splash of the departing day. He had said before that his work was to save the Republic, to save the white and black nations; he had said to her before that if one knew what he knew about the ANC, the Communist Party and all of those organisations in South Africa, if she knew what they were planning to do, she would agree with him. She would agree with him that everything possible must be done to stop them. They

white SA ideology Re white rule

would bring chaos to the country; they would unleash violence which could not be stopped; the economy would collapse, the political system would collapse, and the people would be left to the mercy of killers, ruthless killers … He could not say this to her again. There was no point. Yet, by the day, he knew she was slipping out of the grip of his love. The unimaginable then overcame him. Barbara would leave him, she would go away. And then, first the house, and then his and her friends would go, too, and then he would have to look for someone else, she would have to look for someone else. He felt the flame in him now, it rose and rose. No, this was weakness, why would he desire someone who said she hated him, resented him, felt he was filthy, someone who said every time he held her, she felt terrified, afraid … his mind went to those days when they had been happy, when they easily fell into each other's arms, would laugh, would cry in each other's arms … he looked her way. She was looking out towards the trees and to the blue, blue sky. He moved closer to her, and as he embraced her he felt with both his legs the space between hers. He touched her hair lightly and then withdrew. No, he must control this flame. He walked away into the passage, into the bedroom, he threw the jacket on the bed, walked out and went to the kitchen. He took a pan and prepared a meal. His mind drifted to his work, to the food frying, to Barbara, to the flame. He focused on the meal. He set the table for her. He took his plate to the lounge to watch TV.

"Your food is in the oven," he said.

She did not look at him. She did not say anything. She watched the view from the window.

Surely, the only reason she thought about Patrick was that she now felt empty, having lost someone she dearly loved. But another voice inside her said, no, you have always thought about him. She felt confused.

He watched the figures on the screen. Once, twice Janet flashed into his mind. He began to plan how he would approach her.

"Are you not eating?" he asked her. She shook her head. He felt anger rise in him. He could have bashed her, smashed her. He continued to eat, not tasting the food. No, no, he must leave her alone. He would go to the bar as soon as he had eaten. He felt

214

confused, lost, angry, filled with fire. She sat there, hearing Patrick, afraid now that she was going to give in to him. She looked at Derek. She was surprised to feel that if he had said, come, at that moment, she would not have been able to resist him. It was not because she had changed her mind, no. What was it now? The image of P.W. Botha came on the screen, his mouth was moving but silent, his eyes were fiery, his finger was wagging at the viewers. Derek increased the volume.

"... the alternative cannot be contemplated," the white leader said. Barbara stood up, took her bag and jacket, and vanished into the passage. Derek followed her. He grabbed her, and kissed her. He felt her dry and then wet and then still. He lay on his side, looking at her skirt, his trousers and shoes, her blouse and bag on the floor, and he felt sad and depressed. She was weeping. He buried his face in the pillow. The weekend, he could feel, was going to be too long; why had he taken the weekend off ...?

He got out of bed and put on his trousers. He could hear her weeping. He dressed and went to the mirror. He brushed his hair and sighed. He picked up his car keys. He, too, wanted to cry now. He walked out of the door. He drove slowly, his mind racing this way and that, unaware of the other cars and drivers. He stopped from habit at stop streets and traffic lights. He wanted to die. Nothing that came to his mind made sense. He stopped the car, parked it and walked toward the door. He could hear voices and the laughter of people drinking. He sat down, hoping that no one would come to him. Ordering a double brandy, he looked around and caught glimpses of people he knew, heard fragments of their conversations. He saw one of his seniors talking quietly to a colleague. He felt a great urge to go to him and talk to him and tell him about Barbara, but he knew what he would say. This would not help anything. God. Purity. None of that rubbish would help him. He ordered another double, knowing that this, too, would not help him. Nothing could help him. He felt the alcohol go down and its flame rise inside him. He would have one more, and then he must go. After gulping it down, he put some money on the table and left. He stopped at an autobank, drew some cash and drove off. At the Holiday Inn, he filled in his code name out of habit, paid and went up in the lift. He felt drunk now. He felt like

215

crying, he felt he should perhaps call Barbara. Unlocking the door, he entered the quiet room, smelling the usual smell of hotels. He looked at the painting of an owl, which seemed to stare at him as he was undressing. He got into bed.

Barbara had heard the door slam as he walked out of the house. She heard the car start and drive off. She got out of bed and into the bath. She must not allow Patrick to get near her. She thought about Linda. Linda had held her once, around the waist, and had put her thick thigh between her legs and had pressed them hard against her, sending a sensation up her body. She had then looked her in the eye, with her drunk eyes, and said in Afrikaans, "You beautiful thing!" She had then smiled. Barbara noticed that she was very beautiful, and without knowing why, in her nakedness, in the warmth of the water and the rising steam, she smiled. But she wondered at herself, how was it possible that she could think all these thoughts in the state that she was in? She should not think that she was mad. No, she was not mad. She was tired, she was sad, she was depressed. The water was getting cold now. She dried herself, looking at her nakedness in the mirror. When she saw the bush of hair on her groin, she thought once more about Patrick and about Linda. This thought frustrated her. And in her silence, she said, "Look after yourself, be careful." She walked out the door into bed. She switched the radio on. Music. She lay still.

Van Niekerk woke up feeling dizzy and awful. He picked up the phone, called room-service and asked for breakfast. He lay in bed, on his back. This was the end. He would talk to no-one about it. But then he thought about his mother-in-law. He was very close to her. In this time, in this long time of trouble with Barbara, often when he went to see her, she reminded him, when she laughed, of the happy Barbara he had known.

Barbara sat in the sun in her blue bikini. She had come out of the house, thinking she would swim. Instead, she sat there, feeling that she was sorting her heart out. Her mind went backwards and forwards. She must go. Not to Patrick. Not to Linda. She must go. The house seemed large, too large. She wondered a while where Derek was, whether he was alright, wherever he was. She was surprised at her caring about him. She sighed, feeling the sun burn into her. No, he must never touch her again. She must never allow

216

him to. He would come back, she knew, with that look in his face.

Saturday dragged on, dragged him along with it, relentlessly putting him face to face with his life without Barbara. And so he sank, further and further into depression. He began to drink brandy again. It was now sunset, he had not left his hotel room. He prayed that he would fall asleep, sleep forever. His thoughts raced on and on …

She had slept peacefully. When her eyes opened and she emerged from sleep, noting the sunlight on the wardrobe, the ceiling and on her body, she sighed a deep sigh, a sigh which relieved her of her sorrow. She had made up her mind that this would be a good day. She got out of bed, put on her swimming costume, and went out into the quiet of the bright, warm day. The quiet, the warmth and the brightness of the day lifted her heart. She plunged into the cool water. She moved slowly up and down, just beneath the surface of the water. She would go to see her mother. And then take a walk through one of the shopping centres in the suburbs. She would then come back home, to pack her things. Where would she go?

He woke up drunk. His chest was aching from smoking. He picked up the phone and dialled. The phone did not ring long. It was a man's voice. He recognised it.

"Etienne?"

"Ja!"

"It's me," he said.

"Where are you?"

"Can I see you?"

"Yes, where are you?"

The answer to that question would break his solitude.

"I will call you," he said, and hung up before Etienne could say anything more. He lay in bed, feeling the white sheet on his skin, feeling his nakedness, and then, consciously, he held his manhood.

"Shit!" he said. Barbara, where is she? Janet? His life will be a mess now. Etienne must be wondering, what, why did he hang up like that? Why did he not say where he was? Etienne would wait for him to call back. Call back? No. No. That would be to allow fear. He searched his mind, what day was it? Sunday!

217

Tomorrow he would have to go back to work. Solomon. Thabo. Alexandra. Tembisa. Katlehong. Attridgeville. Something was getting out of hand in those townships. He picked up the phone. He ordered coffee, lots of bacon, and all the Sunday newspapers. He would have to take control now. He must look after himself. He must get back to rigorous exercise. This reminded him of Etienne. He would be waiting for him to call back. It was unfair. Etienne was a very good man. He was good as a man, as a policeman, and as a husband. He thought of Barbara, what had gone wrong? Barbara wanted him to leave his job. Why? He picked up the phone. Etienne was on the other end.

"Can you come?"

"Where are you?"

"Holiday Inn, Braamfontein."

"I'll be there!"

Etienne probably thought this was about work. How was he going to tell him?

The papers and his breakfast had come. He chewed while he read. Alexandra. Attridgeville. Uitenhage. Port Elizabeth. All in the thick of it. The police were being blamed. He checked who had written the article. As expected. He would like to meet her soon. This one, this one must have ANC connections.

She had been lying on the soft grass, in the quiet of the hot day. She had cried. She had wiped her eyes. She had laughed at herself. But she knew it was the end. She had to find a new life. It was then that this thought struck her that she thought how short life is. Why did Derek stick to the work he was doing? Why couldn't he see that he was not going to succeed? Couldn't he see how evil he had become, how callous, how cruel and tense he had become? She could no longer reach him. She lay on the grass at the swimming pool, listening without knowing to the purr of the lawnmower coming from the garden next door. Her head began to pound. Her vision began to blur. Nothing seemed to make sense or to have meaning. She must go to see her mother.

Etienne arrived at the Holiday Inn. Van Niekerk was as white as a sheet of paper, his eyes were bloodshot.

"What's going on?" Etienne asked.

"I'm sorry to take you away from your family."

"Not at all, what's going on?"

"I don't know where to start with this!"

Barbara's ultimatum

"What?"

"Barbara wants me to leave my job, or she's leaving me!" They looked at each other. Both got stuck with these words. Neither knew how to approach what had been said. Etienne liked Barbara a lot. He thought her sensible, a good woman, warm. He had known her a long time.

"Where is Barbara now?"

"I don't know. Maybe at home. That's where I left her on Friday."

Etienne looked away. He saw the empty bottles of brandy on the floor. He saw the half-eaten meals. He felt the stale air in the room. He looked out the window and saw the looming skyscrapers.

"Do you want me to talk to her?"

"No."

"What do you want me to do?"

"I had to talk to someone."

"Okay."

"Do you think I should leave my job?"

"No. But I don't think you should leave Barbara either."

"Well, I'm not leaving her, she's leaving me."

"But perhaps something can be done."

"Like what?" Let me talk to her."

"No."

"You are on good terms with her mother, why can't you talk to her?"

"Tell her I cannot leave my job? I'll also tell her that I love Barbara. And that's all I can do Etienne."

"Do you want me to come with you?"

"Okay."

He got off the bed and went to the bathroom. As the shower water poured over him, his mind traced the maze of his life. He had an appointment with his seniors. He also had to meet with Raymond and with Jakes from Botswana; Jakes seemed to know what he was about, he could give good leads. He also had to meet Lydia, so that they could go to Swaziland. His life was packed. He must meet with Barbara's mother. He had not seen her in a long time. He must go and talk to her. That was all he could do. He dried himself and walked out of the bathroom, and put on his stale clothes. He left the hotel with Etienne.

33

THIRTY-THREE

Lungi, Bongi and James arrived with Tholo in a little village outside Zeerust. On the way, the land had Tholo talking endlessly. They crossed through farmlands, mountains and hills in a landscape which stretched for many kilometres, interspersed by large and small houses, orchards and fields and empty patches; on the horizon, mountains splashed the sky with a green which rose and fell far into the distance; all this kept Tholo talking as their car raced along the tarred roads.

"All these towns and rivers and mountains and farms, all of them still have their original names," Tholo was saying, "these Afrikaans names you see on the signposts are a sign of blood, pain and the terrible defeat of our people. Afrikaans is a bloody language."

"English too," Lungi said.

"What is going to happen to these languages when we get freedom?" Bongi asked. There was silence in the car; the wheels purred against the tarred road as the car drove up and down the slopes and inclines and curves of the road.

"Language is the blood and life of a people, it is their life. A people and a language must not, and cannot, be separated," Tholo said, "so if we say South Africa is non-racial, English and Afrikaans should remain as South African languages."

"But you have just said they are bloody."

"Yes they are, because in South Africa these languages talk about how to oppress, how to exploit, how to humiliate, how to repress, and they are used to distort truth, to lie, to deceive, you see? That's why they are bloody!"

"But ... " Bongi began.

"... They have dominated mercilessly the lives of the majority over a long period."

"But you are not saying what we will do with the languages."

"Well, if you are asking me to give a blanket answer, I can't, but I am saying Afrikaans and English, as they have been lived here in South Africa, they have been languages of racism, of exploitation, of domination, and because our struggle is aimed at abolishing racism, exploitation and white domination, we want to change the power-relations in this country. If Afrikaans and English begin to express – because they have no other choice – if they express a South Africa which is non-racial, democratic, what must we do with them?"

"But how will they do that? What is it that the struggle must do to ensure that they do that?"

"There are many languages in this country. Here, in Western Transvaal, there is Setswana, in Northern Transvaal there is Sechankana, Sevenda, Sepedi, in Natal there is Sezulu, in Eastern Cape there is Sexhosa ... English and Afrikaans must, like all these languages, become one among many. You see, if you work in Unions, as I do, you see this development of languages as a reality. We conduct meetings in languages of the workers, and we negotiate with bosses using these languages; the languages must be given power by the workers themselves in a power-base like the shop floor. We must all give these languages this power, but it is especially when the workers have power, and use their power, that the languages themselves will have power, you see?"

"No, I don't," Bongi said.

"With power and with negotiation we can make Afrikaans and English equal to all the other languages," Tholo said. He was seated, puffing his pipe, and eager to talk as he was driving.

"I was telling you the history of this land where we are," he said, pipe between his teeth.

"No, we can go back to that, but let's finish this thing about language," Bongi insisted.

"Lungi, you are very quiet!" Tholo said, taking a look at Lungi in the rear-view mirror.

"Listening!" Lungi said.

"You are beginning to miss Tembisa, heh?"

"I do, actually."

"James, what about you?"

"I'm far from Cape Town," James said, "but I was going to say, by the way, the only language I feel free in is Afrikaans."

"Tell Bongi, that's right, tell Bongi you speak Afrikaans – she wants to do away with Afrikaans. How can she do that without getting rid of you? Do you want to get rid of James, Bongi?"

"But that is an unfair question. I am talking about Afrikaans which dominates, which is bloody, as you said."

"Are you saying there is Afrikaans, and there is Afrikaans?" Lungi asked.

"Maybe."

"But that's what I'm saying, language is politics, just as politics is language, and politics is also power, that's where our answer for language is," Tholo said, emphatically.

"You are still avoiding my question," Lungi persisted.

"No, I am not. Maybe we disagree, maybe that's why you think I am not answering you. You must not be like whites, when they disagree with you they do not say they disagree, they say you are a terrorist or a communist, and like that they prepare to get rid of you, they say you are inarticulate, they justify their disagreement which must lead to action, by making you a target, by isolating you from other ideas and people," he said.

"I am not disagreeing; you seem to know the answers, and I'm asking you to explain to me how you see this one. How have other countries dealt with it?" Lungi asked.

"Russia promotes all the other languages, and Russian is supposed to be spoken by all," James said.

"And India too, everybody has the right to speak their language anywhere," Tholo added.

"I also heard that mother-tongue must be the language of instruction in the beginning classes," Lungi said.

"In South Africa that is going to be very difficult because apartheid is doing that to oppress and dominate," James said.

"Ja, but that does not change the fact that if you teach in mother-tongue – the language children hear, learn and imitate at home – then in school they will have access to what they are taught more easily than they would if they had to learn a language as they learn a subject," Lungi continued.

"But you are not answering the question raised," Bongi said.

223

"This is being done in South Africa, but it is done to divide and rule."

"If you create one national education, and you create in the nation an attitude of respect for all South African languages, and you also create a positive attitude among people towards the diverse cultures which exist in South Africa, and you use the diverse cultures to build a single nation, first there will be respect and tolerance for differences, and then there will be a positive attitude towards building a single nation. What this may lead to is that two people may converse in different languages, and still be able to communicate, but it also means that the languages may influence each other, and begin to form common grounds, for instance, all the languages may adopt the word 'helicopter', and use 'lobola' instead of 'dowry'," James said.

"You are being very theoretical, James, it sounds so easy the way you say it, but in life it is not, and will not be like that," Bongi objected.

"Well, Bongi," Tholo said, "James is talking about something which can be started and encouraged and which will take a long time, of course; but you are right, there are many difficulties. As you know, there's nationalism and nationalism. Some will resist, some may even take up arms to resist this, but it is a possibility."

"The possibility is brought about by struggle," James said.

"But there's resistance to struggle," Bongi responded sharply.

"That does not stop the struggle, the struggle keeps gaining ground," Lungi said.

"Bongi is right," Tholo agreed, "she's cautioning against us thinking that this is an easy issue; it is not easy at all. But no-one said it is easy. Also, this does not mean we should not attempt to resolve this difficult issue."

"I am not disagreeing with you. All I am saying is that we should, as we seek to resolve the issue, look at possibilities, but we must also realise that we have to attend to the problems." Tholo suddenly pointed, "You see that mountain, that is Mogale's mountain, but now it is called Magaliesberg. Mogale means fighter, what does Magalie mean?"

"Is that where 'Magaliesberg' comes from?" Lungi asked.

"Yes. Our people fought battles of resistance here. They fought

224

for the rivers, the mountains, the farmlands, the catle, the sheep, and goats, they fought for a place to live in, and now the boers call this place Magalies, a meaningless word, a word which distorts lives and history," Tholo said.

"I have never seen such a stretching beauty," Lungi said, "such eternal pleasantness."

"My child, this place will make you speak in tongues. It strikes the heart with pleasantness, and pleases the heart, but it also has a history which can break your soul."

"Everyone is speaking in tongues now," James smiled.

"Here, I met my childhood sweetheart; it is this beauty which has, since I left it, left gloom in my heart," Tholo said.

"Tell us about your sweetheart," Bongi said mischievously.

"I ran up and down these slopes, I lay on the banks of the rivers. I ate fruit here, peaches which, when you hold them in your hand, promise you in their largeness and ripeness that you will never be hungry again, but also that life is a great joy," he said, laughing.

"You have said nothing about your childhood sweetheart," Bongi came again.

"I have said all that needs to be said," Tholo said, "If you have not heard me ..."

It was at this point that they slowed down and drove along a dirt road; what was before them cut Tholo short and brought silence to the car, as he cajoled it over thick sand and potholes. Ahead of them lay their new home, a small but spread-out village.

Transformation was taking place here. It was invisible. It was slow as pain. It touched everything before it; people, land, houses, even the trees and grass bowed to it. Change is change when things of the past are known, remembered, or still exist.

James had been struggling to understand. By now, not knowing what it is that was pushing him, he had been to many places and had met many people. He came from far and it was the place he came from that made him who he was, but he was no longer of that time and place, he could not go back there, although many times he found he longed for it. He asked and missed so many things about it.

This evening, as he sat at the fire, knowing that everything

225

about him smelt of smoke, as fishermen would smell of fish, he was trying to understand why he thought a transformation was taking place. His thoughts were interspersed by many others which drifted in and out, making him smile with fondness to himself; at other times, he caught himself laughing aloud. God. He thought about Him, no longer with conflict in his heart, no longer with shame as at times, in the not so long ago past, he used to. He thought about his brothers and sisters, who were making a living as Coloureds as Cape Town can make its Coloureds do; he, many times, longed for the sea, for the large, vast space of water and a splash. He thought about his friends, seeing them as good and trusted friends, though he knew that they were not only that. That they were also something else, which he did not like or care for, but for now he thought of them, fondly, missing them, as he missed the mountain, the sea, the days on end, gloomy and rainy. He was also attached to his present life; he felt he could not exchange it for anything else.

What is a village? Farmlands are not villages. No. This is where he is now, a village. What is a village, what is a rural area? Is a village a green place, with huts, sheep, goats, pigs, cattle and peaceful people? Is a rural place where poor and uneducated and landless people, who are victims of apartheid live? Is this a village? He had not been to one, anywhere as he criss-crossed South Africa. They told him here's a village, and the first thing he smelt was poverty, disease and a life of hardships. They told him here's a rural area, and he met sly people, rich, ruthless people running small but vicious businesses. What is a village? What is a rural area. The people here pretend to be shy and polite, but that is their way of getting into you; no, one must not generalise, but it is true he found people here sly. Maybe it is because he is Coloured. No! No! He had seen this even when people talked to Bongi or Lungi or Tholo. He had seen it. The eyes like looking away and down to the feet, the penetrating questions, the watching when they thought they were not watched. Maybe that's the way of relating to people. No, maybe that is self-protection. What is it? The mirage here is untrustworthy. It reflects intense heat, it is aloof but present, like an eternally watchful eye. It covers everything and emerges from the ever-present, thick sand. But you cannot touch it. It emerges with the cry of the crickets and rings and rings in the air. It tells of the absence of water. It tells of the absence of plant-life. It is as parched as the skins and lips of the people here. It shines like their eyes shine. It is elusive as everything here. Is this which transformation?

The village where he and the others were going to before leaving the area, was like a township except for the number of cattle, goats, chickens, and something in the manner of its people. The same music; at times the same dances and the same languages; the poverty and the cheapness of life; all these abound here, in the village. There are huts here; still thatched and made of mud; but there are also houses here, with tiles, bricks, shining stoeps and servants and even the odd Mercedes-Benz. The trees with white thorns, and grass covered with cow dung, and goats and sheep were there together with the birds and the sounds of their whistles; there were streets and street-signs alongside reed, grass; and wire fences; but there were brick walls too. This was not a village, nor was it a township. What was it?

In the past when people talked about a village or rural area, James had thought that this was where he should go to leave the city behind. But it was hard in these places. Not for him; he could see hardship in the aimlessness of the youth, the lost look of the children, and the eternal waiting of the old people. Here, the sun was like the winters, merciless. It beat down on one's head, amd parched the rivers, wringing the greenness and life out of plants. The sun whipped the animals to a standstill. For him, this place was a strange, temporary sanctuary. He was here now. He might not be here tomorrow. He was living here illegally, hiding while he made war. This place could only be temporary for him. Soon, it would eject him. But now, he had come to know and understand. There were people who had given everything for him to be here. He met them, with a stare which no-one could forget as they spoke in whispers and listened to him, and watched. They had put the hope of their lives in him. All of these people also knew that if he were found here, if the white farmers, and the police, and the soldiers traversing the hills and hillocks, the bush, the footpaths – if they found him, there would be no more people here. They would wipe them off the face of this earth with fire. He knew this. They knew this. And the silence of the terribly poor place kept the faith and the secret. The people were giving their sons and daughters to him to cross the border to learn how to fight. It always happened at night. The trees and the rivers and the darkness of night kept the deal and held the price.

James was becoming accustomed to this place. No sound coming from the night was meaningless, he came to know, and nothing just happened. Everything happened for a reason. That the people were faceless and at a distance from him, was so for a reason. If they were faceless, he was also faceless. It was Tholo and Bongi and Lungi who were not faceless. He watched them, they watched him, amid the red earth, dry as a plank; amid the rocks, and thorny trees, in a space where cow dung dried as soon as it fell from the arse of a cow. The smells here were becoming familiar. The rubbish was familiar.

Bongi and Lungi were working with the women. Tholo worked with the men. James seemed to work with everyone, and as a result, alone. In the time that they had been here, the boers had come to the village twice in a week. The farmers, and the police, and the soldiers came. They came and walked around the village. James could smell the tobacco of their pipes, and when they left, he observed that the rubbish that they left behind was more civilised than the rubbish they found here. When they were long gone, he followed their footprints and read them on the sand; he saw how their trucks broke leaves and branches, and observed how all this told the direction the boers had taken. The people of the village walked and talked differently when the boers were here. He saw and heard them. The boers had come and walked around and said nothing to anyone. They came with their trucks and dogs and kept talking to each other and looking and watching. Last night some young people went away, they had left the country.

228

34

THIRTY-FOUR

It felt as if a secret had been revealed. James and Tholo were going down the rocky mountain slope. Ahead and behind them lay Gamogale, also known as Magaliesberg. The flatness and the hilliness, and the vastness of Gamogale's landscape spread out, challenging the eye to see its farthest edge, to discover more of the beauty concealed. It was that time of the year, when here, everything seems to be in place. The heat is in place. The sunshine. The shadows. The lush green. The red of the soil. Even the million colours of flowers, grass and trees, stand there, and together with you and the shadows and the mountains, and the trees, and the rocks, they seem to stand and stare in amazement. For James, in this restlessness of his youth, in the restlessness of his race, and in the restlessness of the time, in a sense, nothing, not even this stillness, was new. Nor was anything new for Tholo. He had been here before. You could see it in the manner he shook the hands of people here. You could hear it, as, without in any way faltering and with great ease, he called this place Gamogale. You could see the way he plucked grassblades and stuck them between his lips; how he plucked the wild sour berries, and sucked at them – even how he looked and talked to the women here, with mischief and familiarity, and that riveting smile of his, that this was a familiar place. James had watched Tholo. He had listened to him. He had asked him. And at one time, he had treated Tholo as a father figure. But Tholo, in his age, with his grey hair, in his dwarfish height, and his quick gait, was too rebellious to be anyone's father figure. His whole being, everything in him, was charged with fire – it even showed in his grey eyes. It showed more since he had come here. His eyes danced like a floating cork on the river water; his arms and his legs and his body, expressing his soul as he traversed Gamogale, made him seem like wet soap in one's palms. He

229

allowed no-one a tight grip around him.

James had searched this land. He had searched this country, looking, listening and wanting to know. As it was now, he was far, far away from anything which was familiar to his childhood days. Although he was still very young, he was no longer a child like most of his countrymen and women. Between him and Tholo existed war, peace and a search. The search was for him. Tholo watched him. Long ago, in that time when blacks were said to dirty the sidewalks, Tholo had felt that at times a man can go mad. In the mine, in the compound for men only, in the fight to stare back at the bosses' green eyes in the depth and darkness of the earth with its clanging machines, darting rats, and invincible running water, and later in the union, and in the ANC, and in MK and now, back here, to the old, old time – Gamogale – Tholo had become a butterfly. He had even turned the printing press he had founded on the streets of Tembisa into a leaflet and pamphlet press. It had, by now, been destroyed. Derek van Niekerk had touched it. It was in the eye of his eye, what Tholo was looking at. Monnakgotla and Mlambo (Zuluboy, as Tholo had called him), they had gone. Tholo knew, somehow, from deep inside him, how they had gone. You saw this in the manner he looked at and listened to you.

James had come to sense all these things, and he kept his distance. Their peace held. No-one now laughed at James when he attempted to speak Setswana. Everyone gently corrected him. At times he said 'you' for 'me'; they quietly said no, 'me' not 'you' in Setswana. He plodded on. The children in their frankness, their honesty and innocence hugged him, cried out at him when he did not understand them, and played with him since he was almost like them in his speech. He fought, in the circumstances, to be patient in their world. He tried the words. They laughed at him, slapping him with all their childish might. Many times he felt stupid. Many times he felt he had been here too long; and many times he wondered why he was here; especially when he longed for the gloomy sky, for the slow, soft rain, and for the mountains and for the water, the sea, and for the honey-skinned boys and girls of his town, and for their laughter and the gutteral sound of his language. When he longed for these, and when he felt like crying, and when

230

the people laughed at him, pulled at his long hair, and looked at his eyes with amusement, and touched his skin and laughed their naïve, innocent and mocking laughter, then his pain asked, for what? But James stayed on. Soon, they said, his skin was going to be thick, as thick and rough as that of an elephant; as tough as that of a giraffe. So he listened and watched. Now he and Tholo, carrying their large bags, walked down the rocky slope in the early hours of the morning, accompanied by the chime of the songs of birds, and the silence of the moonlight, and the quiet of the mountains and trees and leaves. They walked with ease here, down the footpaths, carrying their cargo. Soon the place would wake up. It was a poor place, this. But it was also a place of plenty. The land and the slopes that stretched and climbed far into the distance, as far as the eye could see, had been quiet a very long time indeed. The quietness here resided in the rough hands of the women and men who tilled this land. With their bare feet and their poor dress and their tired eyes, and their wise faces and naïve English and Afrikaans, it seemed something terrible was being concealed. The whites here, sensing this in times long past, thrashed at it. They thrashed at this unknown with loud blasts of rifles, with crying whips and sjamboks, with spades and pick handles, with electricity at groins and loins, and the air and the clouds and the trees hung with terror and guilt and disbelief. It was quiet here. The children walked the long, stony veld roads to school. The little boys and the little girls walked, rode on the back of bakkies, watched with care and fear, and waited for the bakkies and trucks to stop at their destinations. The mealies, the wheat and the tall sunflowers in rows upon rows, stand and stare at this human activity.

It was at the base of the mountain, near the trees, not far from the country motel, that Tholo and James unloaded their cargo and buried it in the earth. They got back to the village in time for soft porridge and tea, and hot water for washing. James noticed that Matshidiso seemed strangely aloof. She did not smile. She did not even look at him. She went about her chores, merely acknowledging his presence. He had said to her a while ago she must wait until he could get money and then they would do something about her brown teeth. She had said, "Well, you don't have your front

231

teeth, you pulled them out so you can give me sweet kisses, I will pull mine out and our kisses will be sweetest." They had laughed under the mulberry tree, as they lay in the tall tall, grass under the blue and bright sky. He had wanted to take her to the place where the rain falls softly, where the sky and the mountains kiss, and are watched by the vast blue sea. She said, "I never ever thought I would touch skin this colour, or hair this texture, it frightens me." He had felt sad. He had not known what to say. She had asked him why he looked so sad, as if he would cry at any time. Did he not know that she loved him? He caressed her large breasts. He said, "It's okay."

"It's okay?"

"Yes."

"In Setswana we say 'Gosiame', she said. He tried to say it. She corrected him again and again. They gave up for now – yes, in time it would come right.

"I know swear-words now," he said.

She put her hand to his mouth. "You will say none of those words," she said.

"Why?"

"Because you will swear at me, you are so naughty."

"What is this, then, in my language?" he asked, gesturing downwards.

"You sound like these white men here, don't say that!" she whispered nervously.

"White men?"

"Yes, the boers!"

"Do they say this to you?"

"Yes, many times." He feared to ask then. "That big one forced me when I was nineteen," she said, looking away.

"Had you?"

"Yes."

"You mean you allowed him?"

"I had no choice."

"Why?"

"I was alone in the house. I was bent over, washing dirty over-alls, and then he came from behind me"… She began to cry. He held her. He thought and thought about this in the silence of the

232

veld. If he said a word, his anger would tear this place apart. They walked away. They had not seen each other or talked since then – until now. He appeared from the morning, after days of not being there. She kept her distance. She loved him. She hoped he loved her. If not, she would fight the love in her heart once more. He longed to talk to her. He wanted to tease her. But he sensed that she was far away.

She loved him

– Talked of her
  newspaper –
  He asks her
  she said had no
  choice –
  They walked
  away & didn't
  talk for
  dayrafter
  that
  conversation.

35

THIRTY-FIVE

*Don't tell people you are in love with me, if you are
ashamed to be laughed at.
I am.
You crawl out of a door the height of my child, from a
house made of sacks and plastic.
Don't tell people you are in love with me.
Love is not kind
love sees and hears
that is why we cry
love is not blind
Look at you,
in your cap and jacket,
in your baggy trousers, smoking a cigarette to show off.
Who does not know that you steal? Don't tell people you
are in love with me.*

The song moaned and moaned as the kombi rolled on at the speed
of a flying machine, up the hill, down, round the curves. It was hot
inside. It was packed to its seams. Everyone was sweating. There
was a stale smell trapped in the heat of the vehicle, binding the
silent passengers together. The guitar and the words of the female
singer, rang out, her thin voice cutting the silence among the passengers, giving a voice, a word, no longer were they strangers to
each other. Now and then they smiled at each other, as the words
reminded them of where they came from; now and then they
glanced at each other, napping, swinging with the wailing guitar.
The driver was singing along; someone was humming the song,
and the female voice, sharp-tongued with a shrilling cruelty, dug
deep into their experience.

"This is a cruel woman," someone said, "does she not know

234

that no-one must laugh at another's wounds?"

"But today's men are cheap," a woman's voice said. Everyone looked at her.

"They are …" she insisted.

"But there are many women who came out of houses like that … are they cheap then?" a man's voice asked.

"There are cheap men and cheap women …"

"No, women are more cheap, they sell everything, that is why they make you window-shop their bodies. Where have you seen a man window-shop his body?"

"If the buggers want to pay, make them pay, this is Jo'burg you know."

"Who is cheap? Who is cheap?" the woman asked.

"Cheap is not what you buy, what you buy is what you need …"

The kombi kept silent, as if to ponder what the man said. What did he mean?

"You are talking nonsense," the woman said, "don't you know that water, food, clothes, the house, are expensive, are paid for, and people don't work? If you have something to sell and buyers to buy, and you have to pay for what you don't have, why can't you see what others need?"

"I buy nothing if I can also give honey. Why must I pay for giving honey?"

"You need honey, how can you give it if you need it?" she laughed.

"I am not a man who thinks that only women give honey; I know I have honey; that honey you have needs my honey!"

> *If you tell my wife that I see other women*
> *did you pay dowry for me …*

The song cried out from the loudspeaker in the kombi. The heat was merciless. The kombi flew on the M1 from Pretoria to Johannesburg packed with sweating passengers. The traffic sped along the two lanes of the white cement road in opposite directions. The lush landscape flew past, backwards, with its houses, animals, its modern buildings.

I don't know if you paid dowry for me
I don't know if you paid dowry for me
I don't know if you paid dowry for me

The saxophone wailed and cried, chasing the words of the song. It seemed to drag the heat and trap it in the flying kombi.

"All I can say is that honey is honey for men and women," the man said, laughing loudly.

"You are such a silly old man."

"Do you know that honey is sweet, it is sweeter when stolen, not bought!"

"Are you married?" the woman asked.

"Why should I marry? Are you mad! I just told you that I steal honey. Let the mad men get married, I will steal from them. There's always a married woman waiting to steal. Why are you a child?"

"I give up," the woman said, "Jo'burg old men ... what can one do with them?"

"You can see that I'm handsome, I'm healthy, I'm full of life ..."

The words of the song kept pounding and the kombi sped on as if it would lift off the ground any minute. And the young driver held the steering-wheel lightly, using one hand only, his other arm resting on the window frame; he sat with five passengers in a space for three people, they sat as if they were squatters in a camp. His shoulders were dancing, keeping the rhythym of the song. He was listening to the song, and the conversation, and to the humming car, and to his rhythym blend with the song.

 Cynthia watched the outside world. It was flying backwards. The kombi was flying, flying away with her, taking her away. She had no idea as to where she was going. She knew she had to be in a hurry, she had to go away from what she knew. It was only yesterday that she had had a personal life, and now, today, she had to interrupt it, abandon it, maybe even forever. It was the first time that she felt as she did about her personal life. She felt guilty for feeling as she did, almost regretting that she had to fly away from where she wanted to be. And the heat, and the light, unbearable, weighed heavily on her; and the stale smell in the packed kombi, with its frightening speed, increased the weight, and her mind went in and out of the song, which brought with it the township, its dirty streets, its dust and mud, its cramped-up houses, the crowds of its inhabitants, all were pulled along by the flying car. She was quiet and still. Her mind raced at the speed of the kombi, and was dragged by the song and the scattered conversations of the passengers, and the heat, back to where she had come from, from where she was running away from.

Peter had at last said it to her. She had looked him in the eye. She had listened to him, not having anything to say to him herself. She had always known that he felt as he did, though she had never allowed him to get any closer to her. But a week ago, he had come, he had held her hand, no boy had ever done that. He did. And he touched her shoulder lightly. He looked her in the eye. He had started talking and she had listened. She felt many things happen to her at that moment – many things she had heard about, read about and wondered about.

"I am very attracted to you," he had said.

She had wanted to ask him what he meant by this, but she did not. This was because, somehow, she knew what he meant, and since she did not want to be dishonest, and because she wanted him to talk, but also, because she did not know what it was she was experiencing, she let him talk. He said to her that he and she were freedom fighters. He told her he had many times gone to other women instead of coming to her, because he was afraid that if he came to her, she would refuse him. From a long time ago, since school, since Tembisa, even before she had become a commander, before they had separated to look for sanctuaries, he had been attracted to her. He moved closer, dangerously closer; she could feel his heaving chest, and even a slight touch of his manhood next to her thigh, and their foreheads and their noses almost, almost touched. She thought of him from the time she had known him in school as a bright, naughty boy. He was naughty in a restless way, in a nice way, in the way of people who understand things quickly and must wait while others are still grappling with them. Then, he never said a word to her. But she had spoken to him, though he never seemed to give a minute even to look at her. The kombi, the song, the conversation, flew along with her thoughts. She was torn apart, knowing where she wanted to be, but also knowing she could not be there. They had agreed that their life was abnormal. They agreed and they laughed about it, and cried about it, and they promised each other that they would be good lovers, and good fighters. They were young, they had visions which they cherished, as well as their love for each other which burned like a raging fire, just as their commitment to fight for South Africa raged and raged, and many times, both of them together, or separately, would dream dreams. They fought, they loved, they talked, and it seemed they had done so for many, many years, though it had been not so long at all. And now she was flying away in a kombi. She hoped, but also, she knew he would understand. She wanted to be with him, but now, she had to fly away. He would understand. She would understand. Lovers always understand. Fighters always know. She began to cry. The man sitting next to her shook a bit, and looked at her. He did not say anything. He again looked ahead at the cars speeding on the white cement road. She sobbed. He shook again. She was afraid of many things. Not even the old man sitting next to her had been afraid of half of what she was afraid of. Many people had felt her fears. She was not afraid of death. Although that, at this point, was the last thing she wanted to experience. She was not even afraid that she would lose Peter. She knew that if she did, it would be because there was nothing else to be done. At twenty-five, she had lived life at its worst, and at its best. Somehow she knew this. She had seen it in the eyes and faces of many people, people much older than her; they were unable to look her in the eye; they were unable to answer the many questions she raised, and all they could say, as a last resort, for there was nothing else they could say, they said, all youth is like that. It is impatient. It thinks it knows everything. It is always critical of its time. They never asked themselves whether they had been impatient, or asked questions, or thought they knew everything when they were young. For if they had, she would not be in this flying kombi; she would not be fleeing as she now was from the experience of her first lover. She would still, perhaps, be with her parents, or at university, or working; she would never perhaps have come to Attridgeville, she would not be wearing jeans and boots and be armed as she now was; she would

238

have been chasing quietly, and been chased, as birds do before they mate. Maybe she would be thinking about being a chemist or being a doctor, or lawyer, or simply walking barefoot in her house, with her children and her husband. She had never said this to anyone.

She knew, though, that after a certain point, all these adults, with their knowing eyes and faces, and their lust and tricks and playing at being adult, were not looking her in the eye because she was not of their kind. She had nothing to lose, and she had made that decision with her peers, while these people played games. Like this man next to her, who kept stealing a look at her, who kept shifting as if a fire was burning him. He could not even ask her why she was crying.

If ever she found Peter again. If ever. She would touch his beard gently. She would kiss his young beard. She would hold his hand. She would ask him about the latest battle, the latest meeting, the latest hiding-place. She would offer to clean his gun. And then, and then, she would give him what she knew he needed when his eyes glittered, when she heard his voice quiver, and they would laugh from the stomach, and then afterwards, she would ask him to bring tea and to switch on the radio so they could hear the latest news. That is all she wanted. Her life was going to be short, she knew this. She did not think about a home. She did not think about them having children. No.

Steve may not have made it. She had seen him, as he threw himself on the ground and his weapon rattled. She also threw herself down, and fired. But then, after a while, the fire from the other side began to increase. Steve had shouted, 'Retreat!', and she never heard his fire again. She ran. It was luck. She never stopped. She heard, as she ran, fire rage. All she could do, to stay alive, was hope that Steve had made it. She looked out of the kombi window. The empty landscape. The cement road. The cars speeding. And then she heard the music, and she saw the people, and heard what they were saying.

"Yes, MK killed many white policemen," one woman said.

"In Atteridgeville, near the shops, we did not sleep, the whole night guns and guns and guns, the whole place is still filled with smoke, and the roadblocks, the house searches – too many white

239

police were killed – this MK is a witch ..."

"No, those are our children, not witches!"

"No, I don't mean it like that, I mean they are so good ..."

"They are our children," the woman insisted.

"I'm not denying that," the man replied, looking thoughtful.

In spite of the song. In spite of the talk. In spite of the many passengers, Cynthia felt alone in there. Although the kombi was still flying, taking her away from Atteridgeville, if anyone asked where she was going, she would not have been able to say.

Cynthia leaving Atteridgeville.

36

THIRTY-SIX

Barbie stopped the car and got out. The yard was brightly lit, and the rows of trees on either side of the brick-paved footpath threw uniform shadows on the lawn. She walked, listening to her footsteps echo in the night. She could see that the windows of the house were dark. As she walked, her bag slung over her shoulder, she felt the weight of her pistol bang against her ribs in time with her footsteps. She reached the door. She rang the bell and waited. Saxonwold was a quiet Johannesburg suburb. Since Barbie had come to know the township, since, in a sense, she was no longer part of white South Africa, having fought it, having lived the life of the hunted with the outcasts of this country, she was keenly aware of the silence, the peace and the orderliness of the white suburb. But, since she was also aware of the fortification of the houses, she knew that now and then this peace was shattered, that shattering rang all over the land, making the loudest ringing in the world when Lazarus came for crumbs. In the distance she could hear the cars against the quiet of the night. She could also hear the sound of the leaves dancing reluctantly against the blowing wind. She could sense and smell the water of the swimming pool. She rang the bell again and turned around, looking up at the twinkling stars and the dark sky. She felt very tired. She heard the footsteps coming down the wooden stairs. Funny, she knew that it was Jackie from the way she came down the stairs, from the sound of the footsteps.

"Who is it?"
"It's me."
"Who?"
"Barbie."
"Barbie!"
"Yes."

241

"And?"

"What do you mean, and?"

"Where have you come from?" Jackie unlocked the door.

"I've come from far away to see you."

"Come in," Jackie said. Their eyes met when the light went on; Jackie looked Barbie up and down, "Are you alright?"

"Yes, I am."

"Come in," she said, watching Barbie as she gave way for her to come in.

"Jackie, I need help – but coffee first."

"Alright, come up …" They climbed the stairs.

"You look pregnant, Jackie."

"Yes."

"Where's David?"

"Upstairs snoring."

"Weren't you asleep?"

"I was, almost."

"And Jerome?"

"He's fine, he's a lovely big boy."

"Does he know that someone else is on the way?"

"Yes, he's even given it a name, Carol, he says it's a girl."

"Oh, smart boy, he wants a sister."

"Ja." They sat down.

"What help do you want?"

"I need a car."

"Oh, okay."

"And a driver."

"You mind a pregnant driver?"

"David won't allow that."

"I'm here if you need me."

"It's not risky, but you never know."

"As long as I'm not expected to drive at two-hundred kilometres per hour or to shoot, no problem."

"A decent person to drive an injured comrade."

"Where's the comrade?"

"In the car."

"Serious?"

"Sort of."

242

"Drive where to?"

"Advice … a doctor."

"Oh, okay. Coffee first or drive first?"

"Coffee."

"Do I know the person?"

"Steve."

"Shouldn't we take him first?"

"No. He's alright. He said I mustn't rush you."

"Oh, that's because he knows that I'm pregnant."

"You saw him recently?"

"Yes, he slept here … am I talking too much?"

"Yes, you are."

"Oh well, sorry."

"The kettle is boiling."

"Ooh!"

Barbie looked around the kitchen. She sat down on the pine bench. Jackie looked so rested, so healthy, so content. Barbie felt moved by Jackie. She was so dependable. Even more than David. No, that's unfair, David was also so nice!

But he would have asked so many questions. Why? What? Where? First play big brother. And then play the man. Superior, ready to advise and to take charge, mistrustful of women's sense. But he's okay. Maybe she should not mind his playing these roles. Fighting him wouldn't help, wouldn't change him.

"What's David up to now?"

"Poor man, he works so hard. Court. The housework. Even the children. He doesn't complain, though."

"And you sit around like a queen?"

"Nasty! No! I'm pregnant, I'm studying, and here I am, doing terrorist work! What do you mean, a queen?"

"You mustn't ill-treat my brother!"

"Your brother is so domesticated."

"I'd like to meet a white man who is!"

"He is, Barbie, be kind, he is, he tries."

"He mustn't try, he must be."

"I'm not a hardline feminist like you, you know!"

"Am I a feminist?"

"Let's go now. Steve is alone in the car. You didn't even think

243

to give him coffee. Sure he's alright?"

"You think I'd take all this time if he weren't? He's okay. We just want to make sure."

"To make sure what?"

"He's not septic."

"Oh, has he been seen by a doctor yet?"

"Are you mad, you think I'd take all this time without him having been to a doctor?"

"What have you explained to me? Nothing. I have to drag all the answers from you."

You are so disciplined, Jackie!"

"Well, you trained me well didn't you?"

"I miss you so much!"

"You?"

"Yes, me. What do you think?"

"I can't see you missing anyone, Barbie."

"I may be a terrorist, but I'm human. We are human you know."

"I know, but you, I can't think of you missing anyone. That has nothing to do with terrorists. You, Barbie."

"Me?"

"Yes, you. You always play so tough."

"I've become tougher. Maybe that's why men don't even look at me."

"Barbie, you deserve a good man, don't be in a hurry."

"A good man! What's a good man?"

"A good man …" they laughed.

"A good man, hah!"

Jackie looked Barbie up and down.

"I don't understand why these men don't get on your case!"

"I suppose I don't let them."

"Well, if you don't, if you don't …" they walked out the door to the car.

"Steve, what's with you?"

"Jackie, how are you, and the little one in your belly? Where's Jerome and David?"

"Come, let's use the BMW, get out. Can you walk or should we lift you up?"

"Lift me up, two white women lifting up a black man."

"Don't, that's sexist and racist!"

"Please don't go crazy like all these hardline feminists. I'm black. You are white, you are women."

"So we can't live?"

"No, I would not allow you to."

"You are in and ..."

"When I say white, I don't mean white like that, and when I say women, I don't mean women like that."

"What crap, Steve, what are you saying?"

"Obviously I'm too profound for you. Give me a Nobel prize!"

"Last week they shot him in the chest you know," Barbie said.

"What's that supposed to mean?" Steve asked.

"That if they'd killed you these fuckers would have paid dearly!"

"They've done worse things!"

"They have."

"It's the ANC with its peaceful war. But if they'd killed you, I would have let go!"

"No, Barbie, it's not the ANC. It's the workers and the poor people of this country, they've produced a very good army. It fights a peaceful war. That sounds strange to the civilised."

"What's the word we use now, restricted armed struggle?" Barbie sneered.

"I don't know; I'm not English, remember?"

"Our comrades die like hell, we fight a peaceful war."

"You sound so bitter!" Jackie said from behind the wheel.

"I'm proud of MK, it fights viciously, and when we count at the end, at the end of it all, we will find very few corpses made by MK," Steve interjected.

There was silence in the car.

"We must stop this necklacing," Barbie said.

"Yes, we must, but more of it is done by the boers now."

The doctor assured Steve that he was doing well. Steve was very fit. He trained like a madman. You could see it in his eyes and on his face. Even his smile said that he was fit and healthy. Barbie was quiet. Jackie listened to their silence as she drove the car with great care. She felt a sense of achievement, she wanted to cling to the two. She suspected that as soon as they arrived they would

245

want to go. She had not seen them together for a long time. She hoped they would stay. But if they didn't, well, what could she do? They lived this life which only they could know. She wondered if they had ever been in love. Why not? How come? Maybe they kept it secret. They seemed to communicate so well with each other. They had a rapport, as they say. If it were not for the struggle, they would have loved each other. But then, if it were not for the struggle, maybe they would not have known each other. This fucking South Africa, with its whites! Jackie felt that she did not want to be upset. She did not want to become depressed. She did not want to cry. So she said, "Are you going to have coffee when we get home?"

"Ja," Steve said.

"No," Barbie frowned.

"Steve will, you've had yours," Jackie said.

"Do you have brandy?"

"Of course we do, Steve!"

"Steve, you have to rest!"

"Stop making me your baby, you!"

"My baby?"

"You must get a good man who will give you a big baby."

"You are talking shit now!"

"Dirty tongue, d i r t y!" Jackie said.

They talked and laughed about life until David woke up and came to the kitchen. And then Jerome came stumbling in sleepily.

"Look, the whole Steinberg family is up and it's two in the morning," Steve said, picking up Jerome.

"Well, unreal people are here, so everything will become unreal. But remember, we work!" David said, tying his gown.

"David, you work so hard!", Jackie said, caressing David's head and hair.

"Does he?" Steve asked.

"Yes he does," Jackie insisted.

"He makes lots of money," Barbie remarked.

"What lots of money?" David cuddled Jerome.

37

THIRTY-SEVEN

Patrick waited, sipping beer at the 'Yard of Ale'. There were many people, many white clients and many black people in the arts. It was here, in Newtown, Johannesburg, where South Africa played at not being itself. If not at 'Kippies', the blacks hardly listened to music, though Patrick came here often. He liked to sit on the stoep, in the sun; to watch the many, many white people and black people, and hear South African English and Afrikaans. All of them were forging a destiny, and it forging them, a destiny that at times they were unaware of. Often you could tell from their clothing and from who they were with, who they were, where they came from, and what work they did. Once or twice, he had seen van Niekerk here. He waited today; the many times he had come here were beginning to pay off now. It was only a matter of time. Patrick, tall and dark, with a quiet manner of talking, did not fit any mould. It was hard to think of him as a father or lover; it was difficult to guess what kind of work he did. If you did not know him, you would hardly have noticed him, if you knew him you would have liked him and cared for him and respected him.

He could sit in one place for hours. He could listen for hours. Like now, he had, for a long time, been playing with the half-full glass in front of him. He followed, without showing it, all the conversations around him. He reacted to none of them, neither laughing nor smiling. He did not look for the owners of voices in conversations he eavesdropped on. It seemed that even if a fly were to sit on his eye, he would not react. He wore a pleasant facial expression which made many strangers passing by, if they made eye-contact, feel obliged to smile at him, or greet him. He responded in a kind but aloof manner. He knew it was Joan Baez singing from the loudspeaker. And now and then, he followed the up-and-down movements of the waitress as she went from one table to another. He knew her, sort of, because all the time they smiled at each other, she recognising him as a regular, and he from catching her eye at times as he looked at newcomers to the pub.

Barbara walked in. She passed by him, although she had looked many times in his direction and around, searching for him. She had a good sense of who she was, she thought. She knew she was very pretty and looked after that, she wore colours and sizes and hairstyles which brought out all that. The boers and the khoi khoi, and the san san, and the kaffirs, he thought, had made themselves some pretty things, some pretty generations, which went mad. At last she saw him. She flew towards him; he sat there, watching. She sat opposite him, watching his warm smile.

"I'm not late, am I?"

"No you are not," he looked at his watch, and back at her.

"Have you moved?"

"Yes, I'm with my mother."

"Oh, Germiston?"

"Yes."

"Deep into AWB area!"

"I come from there you know."

"I know. How are you feeling?"

"Okay."

"How's Linda?"

She looked at him a while, before saying anything, as if to ask, what do you mean how's Linda. For a brief moment, she thought about what Linda did to her. She thought about the things she said to her in the dark.

"She's fine," Barbara said.

"What does that mean?"

She blushed, her eyes ran this way and that way, she became red.

"She's a good lover, if that's what you are asking." At that moment she had made her decision, that's the way she's going. And yet it saddened her.

"Is she in good health?"

"Yes, she is. She works too hard though."

"Well," he said ironically, "She has to if she needs a lover."

"What does that mean?"

248

"I'm nudging you."

"Why?"

"Because I have lost you," he said. She looked into his eyes.

"You are mad. Derek will kill you, he won't do that to Linda, he will despise us."

"So you are in it for life and death then?"

"No. Yes. No, also I like Linda."

"And me?"

"I like you too."

"So?"

"I don't have to act on it."

"That which is not made use of goes limp," he said.

"It can be used elsewhere."

"And then you won't like me anymore."

"Don't be like that," she said, turning away.

"You are right. Where's Derek now?"

"He's with Etienne. They went to see my mother."

Patrick looked up, as if to the many sounds of the 'Yard', as many, many people, black and white, like ants in an anthole, came in and went out again. Paul Simon was on the speakers now.

"My personal loss must not get in the way, of course you know that I love you."

"I know."

"You have to see Derek, for the last time."

"I will."

"If you walk out of here, past Kippie's, past Fuba, into that street there, you will see a red van with a white woman in it; just open the door and get in, I will see you."

"Okay," she finished her coffee, stood up and left. He observed every move around and about them, without moving. She vanished. After a while, he stood up to go.

"I'm Barbie," the woman in the van said, engaging the gear.

"I'm Barbara," came the reply as she shut the passenger door. The car moved forward. Barbie observed two people walking to a parked car, a white man and a white woman. She U-turned, after pretending to be driving ahead. She sped off, went through a red light and took the nearest corner, arriving at a spot near where they had just come from. She knew she had to cut them off.

He knew they were coming for him. He walked faster into the crowd, as he walk-ran now. This is an arrest, Patrick thought, they had made up their minds now, or had just received instructions to arrest him. He walked faster, turned the next corner, crossed the street and waited to watch. They came running round the corner, guns drawn. He went into a supermarket, past the till, to the door. Nkuta was seated behind the dispatch-clerk's desk. When he saw Patrick he stood up, locked the door and called out for the driver. The truck driver, an old man with a limp, asked no questions; he opened the back door of the delivery van for Patrick to get in; he shut the door and drove off.

That night, as van Niekerk went up to his hotel room at the Holiday Inn, he sensed that he was not alone. He felt for his revolver, just as Barbara appeared outside the lift.

"What are you doing here?"

"I have come to see you," she said.

He held his revolver in his hand.

"Why are you taking your gun out?" she asked.

"How did you know I'm here?"

"Etienne told me," she lied. He put the gun back into its holster.

"When did you see Etienne?"

"Derek, please …"

"Please what?"

"Don't interrogate me, I may be your ex-wife, but I was once your wife."

He looked at her. He had always known that his love for her was his weakest spot. He wanted to cry. He stood there, looking at her.

"Let's go to your room," she said. They walked in. He stood there, after shutting the door.

He did not know what he was supposed to do, here, in this room, with someone who called herself his ex-wife.

"I want to talk to you. Derek, you are doing a dirty job. Please leave it!"

He looked at her. He felt his anger rise inside him. She sat there, knowing that this was the most dangerous moment. She was dead scared. But she held on.

250

"What are you up to?"

"Derek, I don't have to be your wife to care for you, but I do."

"I think you must go."

She stood up. She walked closer to him. "I know you will not believe me, but if once you can, know that I care for you, I think you believe in wrong things, but I know you are a good man, give yourself a chance, there is still time, quit."

He sat down. He was feeling confused. Why did she sound so certain?

She touched his shoulder lightly. He looked at her. The thought crossed his mind that Barbara was a smart woman. Yet he had always known this. He was afraid now. She walked out. He should have stood up, held her, banged her head against the wall. But he did not. He was numb. He knew he must not let her go. But he did not stop her. She walked away ...

He switched on the TV. Several landmines had been detonated in the Western Transvaal near Derdepoort, and six farmers had been killed. In Atteridgeville, two colonels and six white policemen had been killed by a landmine. In Alex, there was a grenade attack on the house of a policeman. Just then there was a knock on his door. First Etienne walked in, and then another man whom he had seen at HQ, and then the Brigadier came in, with his stern facial expression.

"Derek, hoe gaan dit?" the Brigadier asked.

"Dit gaan goed," Derek replied, feeling cornered. He wondered where in hell Barbara was. Why had Etienne brought the Brigadier here?

"What's going on?" the Brigadier asked. "Why are you now staying in hotels?"

"My personal life is disintegrating," he said.

"When last did you see Barbara?"

"Just now."

"What do you mean?"

"She just left," he said, and for some reason thought he should have lied. He then glanced at each of them, the three of them, very quickly. He thought, something is wrong.

"Derek, do you know this man?" The Brigadier showed him a photograph.

251

"Yes, yes, yes, that is Patrick."

"What is his connection with Barbara?"

"With Barbara?" It was, as he asked this question, that so many things fell into place. He wished they would stop asking questions and let him go and look for her.

252

38

THIRTY-EIGHT

Diana had to leave Yeoville. She went to Bloemfontein. Yeoville was a strange place. Culturally South African it was also London, Paris, and New York. All the reflections of Europe were seen in the restaurants and the streets and the people and their hair-cuts and the clothes and the shops. But Diana knew another face of Yeoville, tormented, rebellious South Africa, where the new and the old were forged together in struggle – the political and fighting South Africa. Here she had come into contact with the white ANC. They did not know who she was, but they liked her; they thought her to be warm to the many plans they had. She had come to know them in the time that she had worked here, and she thought, somehow, there is nothing like white South Africa; there were white people who had made the best of growing up here, who were going to die here, but whose lives were a craving and a madness and a clinging to and an embracing of lands far away, beyond the mighty blue waters. It was a problem, this. It was a big problem. When little children and young men and women and old men and women live by the sweat, grow by the blood and flesh and die by the heat and are put into the soil of a land they despise and carry mountains of contempt for, then it is a big, big problem. They got the best and they gave the worst to a country that had made them some of the most fortunate people alive. She felt bitter about this. They felt no allegiance to the fears and anxieties and concerns of this little suburb. Soon, it would all come to pass. She was leaving it; she had work to do and her life to save. She left early in the morning, leaving behind Strike and Noma. The lifespan of a safe house and the lifespan of a freedom fighter seemed to shrink at the same rate. Yeoville, amidst the green hills, was sandwiched between and among poor and wealthy suburbs, and swung in many ways; to politics; to crime; to drugs; to prostitutes and to the poor, sleeping on its streets. Yeoville was young and already it emerged with all the ailments of South Africa, including the illusions of whites, and the bitterness of blacks. Yeoville asked in silence, how, how it was possible to be rich, to be poor and survive? The answer was in the papers this morning. Diana listened to the news, which sounded like a war bulletin; from across the land – marches by workers; demonstrations by students; shoot-outs and road blocks and the mixed mudslinging of words from the international community about this land. She must go. She must reach Bloemfontein, where she would train some young people and then she must go. The time had come. She must go. They had discussed this, she, Strike and Noma, for a long time last night, and all of them said they must leave Yeoville; Strike was torn apart by all this – Diana was leaving. He was to leave too. And Noma. But he was aware that something was pulling them to pieces, something they could not control, something larger than them, tearing them apart. Diana accepted this without a second thought, it seemed to Strike. He had said nothing to her. But he instinctively knew, that a lot had been communicated and understood although nothing had been said. He wondered whether he should speak. But he held back. She showed no sign of wanting to say anything. She hardly looked at him when she left. He had gone to buy a packet of cigarettes which he furiously smoked. Noma noticed that Strike was not himself, but said nothing. She was packing her things. Soon, when Tholo arrived, she would know where she was going. She knew, though, that she would be leaving South Africa.

Strike packed his bag. "I will see you," he said.

"Okay."

He left. Yeoville was out in the streets, walking in all styles of clothes and hair-cuts. But he barely noticed this as he got into the kombi which took him back to Alex.

When Tholo arrived that night in a hurry in Yeo Street, all he said was, "There are changes of plan, you will go to Nelspruit, they will fetch you from your place." He left.

Noma arrived in the Eastern Transvaal early in the morning. Mist hung on the mountains. She was with two other people, a man and a woman, that she had never seen before; their journey was silent, it being night and they being strangers to each other. With the shadows of night melting, and the lush green, and the mountans, the jacaranda trees with their small blue bells strewn on the road like soft clouds, the day came like a dream, slowly revealing the beauty of this area.

Strike arrived in Alexandra, his thoughts racing through a life which seemed, at that point, to have nothing to hold on to. He despised Diana. He felt, he despised all women. He had in the past seen women use their bodies to get what they wanted. He had even seen this with some, who he thought, were respectable. They smiled a certain way. They held their bodies a certain way, and they talked a certain way. He was not sure whether this was a moral issue he was objecting to, or whether it was because it brought out how he, as a man, was susceptible to such temptations. He had seen Diana do this to him. Today, the story which Diana had told him about being cornered by a rapist angered and frustrated him. She had walked to a block of flats. Then, as she reached the lift, she heard footsteps. It was too late to reach for her pistol. The man came to her, took out a knife and said, "Go down the stairs"; she looked down, it was dark, he was close behind her. She said, "Do you have a condom?"

"What for?"

"I may have Aids," she said.

He looked startled, she had said, he looked like someone who was about to unleash all he had into a woman ... She had struck him then. She put the pistol muzzle into his mouth, cocking it, tearing his lips, and had said to him, "If you don't want to die, don't scream, run down the stairs yourself ..."

He did.

She left the building.

Strike was tortured by this shyness. Diana had displayed this many times. And in her work she always showed that her life was a chess game. He resented her. He felt belittled even as he had respect for her. She was a dangerous lover. He thanked himself for not having said a word to her.

Strike had not been to Alexandra in a long time. Coming back now, entering it through Selborne Street, past what had been 'Moscow', he was aware of the many people in the streets who

255

ᴖmed and hovered as if with nothing to do or say. He was struck by the dirty streets, although some women, carrying black plastic bags and brooms, seemed to be sweeping. He wondered what they thought they would do with so much filth. How could they ever remove it? He felt a great relief in coming back here, away from Yeoville, also, never to see Diana again. He got off at Seventh Avenue. Already someone recognised him. He had to stop, give someone a cigarette, and chat a bit. He wondered about this. He had forgotten what it was to be known. No-one knew them in Yeoville. Although he got off at Seventh, he walked through the maze, the many plastic houses and the network of footpaths toward Eleventh Avenue, his destination. All he wanted to do now was to get rid of his bag. To change his shoes. And to sit awhile and think.

The four-hour drive to Bloemfontein takes you through too many empty patches, farmlands and small settlements. Diana watched all this, unfamiliar with so much empty space, and tried to come to terms with what it meant for her and for her work. There are boers here, many of them; there are people here who have been trampled over and over, who have become a rare breed of people because of this. If you asked them any questions, you yourself would answer before they did; they said everything and asked questions. Their Setswana and Sesotho was slightly unfamiliar to her. She decided she would have to hide the fact that she was a stranger here.

Noma arrived in Nelspruit, angered by the fact that many times when she asked, "Who does this land belong to?" she was told, to a boer, so and so. The land stretched for kilometre upon kilometre. It was the most beautiful scenery she had ever seen. She longed to be swallowed by it, to be part of its mountains and rocks and trees. She gave herself to it, from inside herself. She wondered how it felt to grow up in so much space, in so much beauty, which cleansed the heart. A placard said, 'Landmine explodes near Nelspruit'. So much for the beauty, she thought. She knew that the man and woman with her had noted the placard. But no-one said anything about it. They cruised into Nelspruit at eight o'clock in the morning. She began to hear a version of Zulu she was not accustomed to. She felt very tired and dirty and wanted to

Noma's ahead

wash herself. She picked up her bag and got into another car. It
struck her, as she left, that she might never see her two fellow-pas-
sengers again. They knew her as Zini, she had forgotten their
names. After all, she had never really seen their faces. She would,
though, remember their voices …

The heat here was unbearable. She met the type of white people she had many times heard about. If she had met them before,
it would mostly have been police. At the point where a people
have to decide on the degree of racism they can tolerate then, she
thought, the rot was too deep. The whites here, each one of them,
from the youngest child to the oldest, were unable to see anyone
else, on the road, in a shop, in the house where they moved, gestured and talked, for they believed that it was them only that mattered. It was only now that Noma remembered Mapule. Because
she remembered her, she also remembered Marquard. And
because she remembered both, the story of that time – not so long
ago, yet so long ago – began to unreel itself.

"When we fight so that we can walk, we are also fighting so
that we can have a new way of talking!" she said to herself. She
remembered the day so clearly, she could cry. This was because
when she heard this then, she had not known what it meant. And
now her life, and maybe her death, could teach her what this statement meant. How primitive, yet how true, she thought. In a sense
she felt sad for the whites of Nelspruit, but in another she knew
there was no space for them in her life. She straddled this reality,
and many times it reminded her how once, long ago, when she
was beginning high school, she had a boil and it was painful and
she had to walk with her legs astride. She laughed at this, thinking, in my soul I'm made to walk like that by the whites of this
town. One day, to appease her soul, she wrote a poem:

> Plea in my eye
> if this beauty I see
> if it were all of me
> I would grow and grow
> I would be a woman
> filled with life
> of life

257

able to nurture it
I nurture it now
not for me
for my heart which pleads for beauty in my eye
my heart aches
it aches like a large boil filled with pus
oh
how should I say how it aches …

She did not finish the poem. And one day, after she had been shot and killed from a helicopter in the Kruger National Park, among her belongings, in her little room, they found the poem. Maybe she had finished writing it …

Noma shot & killed
from a helicopter
in the
Kruger National
park

39

THIRTY-NINE

[handwritten annotations: Martha had her baby — Pascal's wife named her Mandella]

Martha's baby arrived into the world, with a big cry, on a dirty bed, with bloody sheets, in a noisy cubicle of screaming children, women, and a man crying outside in the dark. Martha felt very tired. She wanted water, but the nurse wasn't there to give it to her; she had not been there to see the small boy, Mandela, come. Martha was very happy that her boy had come, and that maybe tomorrow she would go back to her mother with the baby. Nothing mattered now. All she wanted was water and to wait for daylight to come so that she could go home. She heard the yelling children and a moaning woman, and the crying man and the nurses cursing and shouting. But that did not matter.

"What are you doing?" the nurse asked her.

"My baby came," she said.

"Sit down. I can see your baby came. You were not supposed to give birth here, that bed is so dirty!"

But Martha missed all that. She had not brought herself to this bed. She was brought here, and told to wait. How was she to know when her baby would come, and what she was supposed to have done?

They cut the flesh which joined them. They took the baby away. She wanted to follow them.

The baby was the only thing she had as her own. But she did not even have the strength to follow them to the bathroom. She was grateful when they brought it back. But also grateful because they had washed it. Its shining nose, and quiet kind eyes, and small mouth made her feel deep love for it. She put her nipple into its mouth. She laughed to see it suckle. It was as if it had been suckling for many, many years. She sat there on the wet bed with her baby suckling. They were waiting to go home, she and her baby.

Many other babies came that night, as she looked after little Mandela. They came as if this filthy place was a factory for mass-producing children. At dawn, Martha began to wonder: does this happen every day? Do babies come every day like this? When the sun came up, and the doctors came, and she was discharged, outside in the bright light she saw men coming to fetch the women with their bundles. She was happy to carry hers. She walked to where the kombis were. She was aching. But she reached the place and got to her mother. Her mother told her that there was no point in crying; she too had given birth to her, alone. Her father was in the mines in those days. They would look after the child. If God gave it to them, then they would be able to look after it. Yes, she was going to look after her baby.

But Lebo had said something else to her. No baby must be born in a filthy hospital, she thought. A white baby or a black baby must be born and looked after properly. Who would look after them? In that clinic near Soweto, there were no white babies. And there was no way that a baby could be born properly there. Yes, it would be good if all babies were born properly, but how? And Vino, how could she even begin to think about what Vino was saying. She was aware that her relationship with Vino was changing. It was no longer just student and teacher. They were becoming friends. For Vino it was easy. But for her, it was not easy. Vino had been her teacher; but besides, Vino is Indian. She has this long black hair; she looks properly looked after and knows so many things. No, this is not an easy thing to handle.

"Your baby is so lovely," Vino had said. And Martha had agreed in one word. She had wanted to talk about this. But to think from Xhosa to English takes a long time. To know what someone is saying in English also takes a long time. But also, outside of the single English words, which name things and point them out, how do you get to saying what you fear, feel, understand? So most times Martha was quiet; she said very little whenever Vino came to see her. Vino thought that Martha now and then laughed at wrong places in conversations. She did not understand. More so, because she knew that Martha was an intelligent woman. She wished she could speak in Xhosa.

She had seen how Martha's face and gestures changed when

she conversed with other women in her class in Xhosa. "You know, my bones, and many things in my body, are coming together," Martha once said. Vino thought a while about this.

"How do you mean?" she asked.

"I'm healing," she said.

Vino laughed, looking at Martha up and down. Martha laughed too.

"You have a man?" Martha asked.

"Yes, but I don't know what to do with him," Vino said.

Martha thought for a while. "Love him," she said; "you are lucky to have a man."

"Lucky?"

"Yes."

"What do you mean, 'Lucky'? These men are mad," Vino said.

"They are not mad, sometimes they are like children." Martha wore an amused face.

"I know what you mean. You cook for them. You wash for them. You make up the bed for them, what are they supposed to do?"

"And then they trouble you all night," Martha said, "and leave you with Mandela."

They both laughed. They leave you with Mandela, Vino thought, and laughed again.

"I would not mind if they left me with Mandela."

"But how do you look after him if you are alone?"

"I see what you mean …"

"You see?"

"Yes, I see."

"It's heavy, don't you think?"

Vino laughed again.

"You know," Martha said, her face lighting, "when you give birth to a baby, it is like fire is lit all around here," she said, gesturing to her loins, "and the pain is like a sharp whistle, but large like the sky, and you think, this is the end of the world you know …"

She could see that Vino was listening.

"You know, I was by myself, then, and the bed was wet and dirty. I wanted to go down the bed, up, under, I was afraid to

scream, and I was alone, then, there was Mandela, crying and crying, loud, very loud, I laughed at him. I did not know what else to
say. I picked him up, he was so filthy, but I kissed him, he is my
child."

"Where were the nurses?"

"I don't know. When one of them came, she shouted at me …"

"Why did she shout at you?"

"She asked why I gave birth on the dirty bed."

"But who put you there?"

"This man, I think he is a nurse or something …"

"Why did he put you on that bed if it was dirty?"

"I don't know."

Vino thought about this. The more she thought about it, the
more she could not understand it. The more it angered her.

"So what happened then?"

"They cut this long meat which joined us, and took Mandela
away to wash him. He came back looking at me with his big shining eyes …"

"But they can't do that!"

"What?"

"They can't make you give birth on a dirty bed."

"But they did."

"Which hospital is this?"

"You know, the one near Soweto."

"It's such a long time ago now, what a pity!"

"What do you mean?"

"It is not allowed what they did."

"You mean the dirty bed?"

"Yes."

"Well, if they thought we were people they wouldn't do it,"
Martha said.

"We must fight things like that!"

"How?"

"If I knew about it when you gave birth, we should have gone
to the hospital and raised the matter."

"But I'm sure it did not start with me and it won't end with me,"
she said.

"Actually, you are right," Vino said.

262

There was silence.

They were looking at each other, and Martha, holding Mandela to the breast, kept closing one eye, so that she could focus, and look at him. Through their silence they tried to traverse their world.

"We have always been treated badly," Martha said.

Vino thought about the manner in which Martha said 'We'.

"There is the fact that we all have to bring about a normal life, all of us," Vino said, "and, how and where do we begin?"

"No, I agree with you," Martha said, "and we have to know how to bring people together, but it needs us to know so many things."

"Like what?"

"Like, you see, I am not educated; you are and I am poor and you are not," she said.

"You are right about that, if in knowing that we want to know what it is that must bring us together."

Martha put Mandela down and covered him with a soft blanket.

"Do you want more tea?"

"Yes," Vino said.

"The struggle has brought many people together." She moved about the small room, rinsing the cups, boiling the water.

"That is very good," she said, "but what I am saying is that, for as long as there is a mind, there're blacks, there're whites, there're Indians, and there're those that are educated and those that are not educated, and those who are poor and those who are rich; there is still something which makes us different."

"That is true, but should we not build on what makes us struggle together?"

"That too is true, but what I am saying is also true."

They looked at each other. Mandela sighed, and Martha looked at him.

"To think that you are a mother now," Vino said.

Martha smiled. "What do you mean?"

"No, I mean that you have taken a major step."

"You are younger than me, are you not? That's why you think so."

"I am twenty-six," Vino said.

"I am twenty-eight," Martha said.

Both seemed to think about this for a while.

"I am now a widow," Martha said.

"Pascal," Vino said.

"Pascal introduced me to you."

"Yes," Vino said, "he was such a hard worker. He brought me into the unions, and it is through him that I did adult education and started literacy campaigns for working women."

"I used to feel so funny in those classes," Martha said.

"Why?"

"They make you feel like a small child, you know."

"Is that how you felt?"

"Ja." She put the cups on the small table and poured the tea.

"But why is that?"

"I do not know, but they do," Martha said.

"Is it what you learnt about, or is it because of who is teaching you, or who you are learning with, what is it?"

"I don't know."

"Would you still go back?"

"Ja, I learnt a lot, but it is difficult; the more you know something, the more you know how much you don't know," Martha said.

"But education is like that," Vino said; she was laughing.

"Maybe, but if you are old, and you are learning things which make you feel as if you are learning how to walk, it is not easy."

"Yes, but Martha, what else is there to do?"

"No, I am just saying it is difficult."

"I hear you," Vino said. "I am happy that we talked so much today." She sipped her tea.

"Have you see Lebo?" Martha asked.

"Ja. That one is so busy, I worry about her."

"People in the struggle work very hard," Martha said.

"But that is also because they are few."

"I really never lived with Pascal you know, he was so busy."

"Now he is not here!" Vino said.

"How did you meet him?" Martha asked.

"He came once to our university, to talk to students; after the

264

talk I went up to him. I told him what I wanted to study. He told me it was important. We kept in touch after."

"Now that he is not here, I realise that he and I never really lived together," Martha said thoughtfully, "I sort of know him, but he lived in meetings and travelling."

Vino and Martha had now come to realise the vast unexplored space between them. A space packed with unknowns. And silence fell upon them. Vino looked at her cup of tea as if she had never ever seen it before. Martha was thoughtful, looking at her fingers. The room was small, too small for anyone to shift, and the high bed on which Vino was seated turned into a trap, she could fall from it, and she was looking down upon Martha. Martha was not looking at her, she was looking at her thoughts, at her fingers and holding her cup away from her, in case the tea spilled, which was also a way of saying there was no space at all; the room was too small. She sat on a small bench.

It is a funny moment this. It is a moment when what you wish for, and what is real, conflict. It is a moment for brave people, who are also not afraid of the consequence of love; meaning, people who can also be honest. But then, warriors know, you can't always be honest. And, even if you still love, which is the consequence, you hold on to what cannot be said or done.

"The struggle has been very costly," Vino said, breaking away from the moment.

"But of what use is the struggle if it neglected families?" Martha asked.

"For families to exist, there must be a normal society."

"But normal society is made for normal families."

"Ja."

They looked at each other in silence. Vino wondered what right she had to pursue these issues.

"I don't know Pascal, and Mandela will never know him ..."

When they both lifted their eyes Lebo was standing at the door. She had a white plastic parcel. She was smiling. She tapped her feet on the mat, to remove dust from her shoes.

"Vino, you come to drink tea in servants' quarters?"

"I have come to see Martha and Mandela," Vino said.

"Where's the old man?" Lebo said, as she uncovered Mandela

265

who was sleeping peacefully.

"Lebo, don't wake him up."

"Why?" She lifted the little boy up, kissed him on the cheeks, on the forehead, on the stomach and then held him back, far away from her, looking at him.

"Those cruel people, with their cultural weapons thought they were doing away with Pascal, and here is Pascal," she said, and kissed Mandela again.

"Martha, woman, how are you?" Lebo was smiling.

"I am fine," Martha said.

"Your old lady tells me that she now and then finds you crying, why? A woman does not do that, you know. You don't know that a woman is a thing that holds a knife at its sharpest edge."

"But sometimes it is so difficult!" Martha said.

"What is difficult?" Lebo asked.

"Haai, it's so difficult sometimes."

Vino felt left out of the conversation. Lebo was older than both of them. She had walked in and taken over.

"Hello …" it was Carol, Martha's mother's employer. They looked at her, all of them, from their room. She could not walk in. There was no space.

"How's Mandela?" she asked.

"Fine," Martha said.

"Lydia says he cries at night."

"Not very much, if I give him milk he is okay," Martha said.

"Lydia is Martha's mother?" Lebo asked in isiXhosa.

"Yes," Martha said.

Something told Carol that she must go. She turned to go …

"Martha, I will see you," she said.

"Bye," Martha said.

"That white woman must not call your mother by her first name," Lebo said, "she is a little girl."

"Well …" said Martha.

266

40

FORTY

I am a little angry with Esther. When she left, she was a little angry with me. She wanted to take me with her, but I had already been, and I could not tell her that. She was desperate. She was like someone gone mad with visions, dreams and a spirit that wanted to fight. Many of us have been like that. Many of us are still like that. And many of us have gone; they dreamt, they fought and they died, for what? I am angry with Esther for having left. I know I am being unfair. But then, I loved Esther. How can love be fair? It is not fair. It is love. It takes and takes and gives and gives and takes and gives. That is all it does. She left me here. She left me in a battle; a real battle and an unreal battle and a bloody battle. I still remember when it was that she left. Not the day she left physically, but when she left me. This is because I knew her so well that when she began to leave, having accepted that I was not going to leave with her, having pleaded and pleaded and got angry and then given up – before she left, I knew she had slipped away and gone because she said so very little. I did not tell Lindi this. How could I? It would have meant that I should have told everything. I could not tell everything to anyone. I could not say it to Lindi when I had not said it to Esther. Lindi assumed and took it for granted that she was my big sister; she expected me to know this and she was very close to Esther; women can be very close to each other in a very funny way. Unlike men, they can talk about very intimate things to each other, very close things. They talk about their men, and what the men do to them, and what they do to the men, and how they touch and moan and scratch and groan and cheat and all of that. You can see women who talk like this, and then, you can also see women who don't trust each other. Esther and Lindi had a strange, intimate look when they were together. I know that Ester told Lindi everything about me. I just know. So, even when I was in trouble, I knew not to tell Esther anything. I just kept the hot potato in my mouth. Hot as it was, I kept it between my tongue and my palate. It burnt me like hell. But what could I do?

Esther was fighting me. We must go, she kept saying. We must cross the border. She did not say this just because other people were doing it. No, she said so because she believed it was time. I knew that. I knew that it was time. But I had been there and I still had work to do.

I am thinking about Esther now because I miss her so much. I wonder where she is. I wonder what she is doing. Sometimes I even have the feeling, a strong feeling, that she has trained, she has finished and she is back here. I have that feeling. Esther eats fire. That is why I love her so much. She will not take shit, so we worked it out very quickly that we don't want shit. We understood this quickly about each other and agreed. That's why at times, I think that she's back here somewhere. She may have seen me, but then, if she's in MK, she'll pretend that she has not seen me. I once did this with her, because I am in MK, and I could not tell her. She left me here, then. I wonder what I'll do when I see her by mistake, and she sees me, and there's nothing we can do about it. I think I know what I'll do. I do know. I'll bite her. And I'll eat her up. I'm laughing at myself, really?

I am angry with her. She should not have left me. I was about to teach her, first, how to shoot. Then I would have taught her how to be a guerilla. But first, it took so much time and energy to say to each other, we don't want shit from each other. You can't teach someone to shoot before you finish that fight. It's dangerous. So, I waited and waited. When I was ready she was ready to go alone. I am not angry because she left. No, I am unhappy that she was determined to be a fighter. And yet – I am angry because she left. No. I am unhappy that she was determined to be a fighter. But I am angry that I lost her. I also miss her so much. I don't want all these other women. I don't want them, but, well, what can I do? That's why I am so angry. And maybe that is why I keep thinking I will see Esther. Soon.

It is very lonely here. I read. I watch TV. I sleep. I think. I plan my work. I go out and do my work. I am sometimes very afraid.

The place is so dangerous. Comrades die every day. I do very dangerous work. But then, it is the responsibility of my time and peers. So, I have to do it well. I wish everything was normal. Even though I do not know what it is like when things are normal. I suspect they can be normal. I am thirty-eight now, soon I will be forty; I can sense what it feels like to be forty, as I can sense what it must be like when things are normal. Esther will soon be twenty-nine. We were born almost when apartheid started. It is still here. We are fighting it.

The trouble is that I spend too much time on my own. I don't like it like that. But my work demands it be so. And if I don't, I will get killed. I know that. I see it in the gestures of other underground workers. In the way they carry their shoulders. In their voices and laughter. We are all so watchful and so untrusting. Whichever way you look, you can feel that another is watching you. They are saying, don't fuck up!

I know so many, many people. I have done so many dangerous and intimate things with them. I know I know many people. But, because I have to be careful, and I have to look after myself so that I can do my work properly, I always feel, at the end of the day, alone. Sometimes we work at night, at times during the day, and in between, there is so much time which we spend alone. That's why, at times, I sit and watch mickey-mouse TV for hours. This is when I cannot read; when I am tired of thinking and I can't sleep. I know now what they mean when they say no man is an island, or better still, when they say man is a social being. Man must not be hunted. We must not create a social life which causes others to be hunted. It's dangerous. But then I know why I'm living like this. I also know who is hunting me. They have no chance. Their time is over. That is why they have gone so mad. It is said that the Gods prepare those that they will take; I can see and sense and understand that.

What would Esther and I do with so much time? She is naughty and cheeky sometimes. I don't know what we would have done. Maybe it is good that she went. But I am merely trying to be reasonable when I say so. I do not think that I should have lost her. We had worked out so many, many things. I am sure we would have worked out what we should do with all this time. Even being

269

absent from each other, we would have worked it out. Not absent
and gone forever – absent, but knowing we would see each other
again. That is okay. The other thing is out of the question. But
what can we do now?

I imagine her in a camp. I imagine her wearing an MK uniform
and a cap and carrying an AK; I imagine her in all sorts of situa-
tions. I hope she will look after herself. But what does this mean?
How does she look after herself? I can't answer that question.
Because I can't, at times it makes me afraid, bitter and angry. But
what do I expect? I can only hope that she will be a good cadre.
That is the best I can do. But I have to be very reasonable to say
that. It is so difficult. Does she have the same difficulty as me,
thinking about these things? At times I am absolutely sure that she
must be paining. Then, I feel great concern for her. But at times I
can't see how she can care. How can she? After so many months?
Months upon months? And then, at times I feel that I must forget
everything about her. I must be a good cadre, fight, live, and even
if I die, what does it matter? How do other people deal with stuff
like this?

I really must be careful. Underground is getting to me. It's
painfully lonely. That is why I keep thinking this way; for two
days now, I have been here in this room by myself. I have thought
about many, many things. I have played many games of patience.
Yesterday I finished reading 'July's People'. I am really amused
about this. Not so long ago, I would have thought that Nadine
Gordimer's July was a traitor. But I don't think so now. I wonder
what Esther would say if I gave her my views about July. She can
be so stubborn!

I wonder who Patrick is? I got a message two days ago that
someone called Patrick is here to meet me. The way I was told and
the person who told me made me think that my meeting Patrick is
serious business. What could it be? At times I think that it has to
do with Esther. No, but I'm sure it has nothing to do with her.
People in the underground don't think much about personal things.
This address they gave me is in Rosebank. Rosebank is a rich
white suburb. I know though, that Patrick is not white. If Esther
were to appear now, I would make her watch the twinkling stars
forever …

Reff. to Nadine Gordimer

270

She told me that her name was Martha. I was met at the gate by an old woman who was wearing a very clean domestic worker's uniform. She was at the gate when I arrived, she seemed to have been waiting for me. She then took me to the servant's quarters. As we passed the big main house, I saw many white people, men and women, in formal dress, sitting talking at a massive table piled with food. In the servant's quarters, I met another Martha, and when I asked her what her baby's name was, she said Mandela. Martha was a very attractive, youthful-looking woman. She had a very bright, friendly smile and very watchful eyes. They were the eyes of the people who work in the underground. They looked at one as if they were reading a book. Martha made me sit on the high bed, and she sat on the bench opposite me, carrying Mandela. We sat in silence. I do not know how the Movement taught all of us in the underground to do this. We could be quiet for hours. Just watching and making our minds and eyes and ears work. I wondered what Martha and Mandela were doing here. Come to think about it, there was something similar between Martha and the old woman who had met me at the gate and brought me here. Were they related, and how? Was this the old woman's work place? Where had Martha got that baby from? Martha looked immaculate. She was the type of woman who was very meticulous. She made us tea. She checked Mandela – something about her seemed so alert. She had very beautiful legs. When she passed next to the light, I could see through her dress. She seemed to have very big thighs. Who had given her this child? Why was I in this room with her? How had I come to know her? In the underground, the less you meet with new people, the better. Mandela began to cry and kick and throw his little arms about. I had not been so close to a baby since I had gone underground. Martha talked to Mandela as she fed him. Then there was a knock on the door …

A tall, confident-looking man walked in. He kissed Martha lightly, and held Mandela a while. "This thing looks like its father," he said, kissing it. Martha laughed.

"Don't call my child a thing," she said.

"This thing, this thing …" he kept saying, kissing the little boy all over. Then he turned to me.

271

"Motsamayi," he said, "how are you?"

I was not really surprised that he knew my name though I did not know his. It always happens like that in the underground, and I know how it happens.

"I'm okay," I said.

"You mean you always worry whether you will make it to the next day?"

How true! "Well," I said, "I try to survive."

"Can we talk a little outside?" he said. We walked out, a little way away from the door.

"HQ wants you out of here."

What did he mean?

"Nomvula has been picked up, so have Thuledu and Diana; we have to find a way of saving other structures, one way is that you and others must go," he said.

41

FORTY-ONE

Nomata died

It's terrible. Lindi said that <u>Nomafa</u> died a month ago. She said this in a very calm manner. She said that she had moved out of the squatter area, she was in Yeoville because she was now teaching music and also acting and singing in night clubs.

"And you?" she asked me. She had an aloofness about her.

"I am here," I said. I thought about Skopendonner. I thought about Billy. And in a very funny way, I thought about Esther.

"You must come and see me," she said. She gave me an address. I knew Yeoville. I knew the area where her address was. I thought, at least she has a decent house.

"Whose place is this?" I asked her.

"It's mine. I rent it." She was looking at me hard, straight in the eye. She looked clean and washed and was very neatly dressed. But she made me curious. I could not say whether she was angry, or tired, or what.

"Which night club do you sing at?"

"Neon. Cotton Club, Kippies, and others," she said, "do you want to come?"

"No." It's dangerous, I thought. No. I will not go there. I might visit her house. But I said nothing.

"Did you see the newspaper today?" She asked. *Lindi*

"No, what's in it?" *sings night clubs in Yeoville.*

"They say <u>van Niekerk killed himself.</u>"

"Who is van Niekerk?"

"The boer!"

"Oh yes, when?"

"About three weeks ago." *Van Niekerk dead.*

What could I say?

"Where do you stay?" she asked.

"All over," I said.

"I see. Well, if you want to come to a club where I play, I think the best is the Cotton Club."

"When are you playing there?" I wondered what she meant by the 'best'. I was preparing to leave the country. But I could always disguise myself and go there. I found this very tempting. To leave the country after listening to its music.

"Can you get me a ticket?"

"When will you come?"

"When should I come?"

"Well, tomorrow."

"Time?"

"Seven-thirty."

"The ticket?"

"What name must I use?"

I had to smile. "Robert."

She looked at me, "Robert," she said, "okay."

"I received many messages that you wanted to see me," I said.

"Was that alright?"

"No problem."

"But you took so long to respond."

"I was busy."

"I see. Ja, I did want to see you," she said, "my daughter, Thoko, has left the country. I want to go and see her."

"Do you know where she is?"

"No, but I heard that she left through Botswana."

"When?"

"I don't know, I heard about two months ago."

"Why did she leave?"

"I don't know, is it not to join MK?"

"Maybe," I said.

"Can you help?"

"It's difficult. She may have left through Botswana but she may be anywhere, Botswana, Zambia, Angola, Swaziland, maybe even here," I said. She was very quiet, staring at me as if she did not know what I was talking about.

"A boer came to my house the other day," she said, "his name was Etienne van der Merwe."

"Etienne?"

274

"Yes."

"And?"

"He sat on the chair. He talked about apartheid. About the deaths in the townships, about ANC, about UDF and COSATU, and about the youth."

"Why did he come to talk to you about this?"

"Right at the end, in passing, he asked me where Thoko was."

When I looked at Lindi, she was looking straight at me. She was calm, and something about her told me, once again, that she did not care. She looked like someone who had had it, who had had enough. I was trying to understand what it was that I was observing, what it meant. I knew what it meant, or rather, I knew what might have caused it. But what did it mean?

"Did you tell him where Thoko is?"

"I said I don't know, then he said Thoko may be in Lusaka. I asked why, if he knew this, he was asking me. He said it was because he wondered whether I knew if she had left the country. I said to him, please, he must leave me alone. I said, please, leave me in peace. I could not get angry with him. I did not want to be angry with myself. I listened to him. He sat there as if he was thinking, then he said to me, I'm sorry Nomafa is dead. Then I got angry. I told him to leave. He stood up and left. I got frightened after that. I know he is a very dangerous man."

"You got frightened?"

"Yes."

"Why?"

"Because I know myself, I must not get angry."

"Did he say where he came from?"

"The police."

"Maybe he is taking over from van Niekerk."

"You think so?"

"I don't know. I think so."

"What does it mean, van Niekerk has killed himself?"

"I don't know."

"But that's strange, is it not?"

"It is."

I don't know what a Jewish church is called. At this point I noticed it. I knew it was a Jewish church because I saw the children, the men, and the women who came out of it. They all had clothes on which told me that they were Jewish. I thought about the concentration camps, which I had become familiar with from reading Prima Levy. Forgive but don't forget. This line crossed my mind as I saw the men, children and women. Was it a line from Levy? I was trying to remember it, and its context, or did Levy insist that no-one must be forgiven. I heard the children laughing; I saw the men conferring and the women seemed to walk on. I realised then that we were in Yeoville, near Grafton Road, I think it was Grafton, or Raleigh, I can't recall.

"What are you thinking about?"

"What you were telling me," I said. I realised then, that we – she and I – were clinging to each other. We did not want to part. We talked. We realised our silence. Then we talked again. We must be very lonely, I thought.

"Are you happy with the nightclubs?"

"It's okay. I'm getting old now. I better realise this and make myself a home," she said.

But what I couldn't understand was that Lindi said all this with this face that she wore. I can't describe her face. It wasn't even her face really, it was everything about her. What was it saying?

"How long are you going to go on like this?" she asked me.

Like what? But I did not want to be dishonest with her. I did not want to play games. I knew what she meant. But also, I knew that, as the song says, she meant it from the bottom of her heart.

"Lindi," I said, "I wish I could live a normal life today."

She looked at me. Then she looked down at her feet and she said, "If you think I can help, you know how to find me."

When I looked at her, her eyes stared at mine for a while. Then she looked away, to the traffic, the buildings and the people, black and white, walking the streets, going about their chores.

"I will remember that," I said, "I would like to come to the club to hear you sing."

"Come. You must come," she said.

"I will find out about Thoko." And as soon as it was said, I wondered why I had said this, and why at that point.

"I would really appreciate that."

"I will take some time though," I cautioned her.

276

"Well, what can I do, I will wait," she said.

"I agree with you, Etienne is a very dangerous man."

"I know."

"You must expect that he will be coming back."

"I know that."

"He must have been studying you as he was talking to you."

"Studying me! For what?"

"He is a new man taking a new job and he is feeling his way."

"Using me?"

"Not only you?"

"I don't want nonsense from him, I don't!"

"But be careful."

"He must be careful, I mean it, I don't want nonsense from him," her voice rose.

"Yet you ask me how long I will go on like this?"

"Well, I care about you."

"I care about you myself."

"Well, there you are," she said, "you know I don't like to feel helpless."

"It's a terrible thing," I agreed.

"You should have come home instead of us talking like this in the street."

"I will come."

"I thought I would be staying with Thoko this time."

"Well, she has her own agenda."

"I know. It's terrible to give birth."

"She's a big girl now."

"Even so, she's my baby."

"I allow you that!"

She smiled for the first time that day. "Do allow me that. If you did not, you could go to hell yourself," she said.

"I must go now."

"Okay," she said, "I'll be seeing you, I hope."

"Tomorrow."

"Will you come backstage afterwards?"

"Yes. If you permit me."

"I do," she said, getting ready to go, adjusting the strap of her handbag. She looked at me, smiling.

277

I turned to go. I was tempted to wipe my cheek, where she had kissed me goodbye. It felt as if her red lipstick, which raged red like fire, was still on my cheek.

278

FORTY-TWO

There is something stunning about a voice which hangs like a cloud, like smoke, like a rainbow, like the stars or the moon itself, hanging, holding on – it is stunning when it does this in a space filled with people who are silent, who lean back in their chairs or, hold on to each other, in each other's arms in a dark room, or semi-lit room, with cigarette smells and liquor and sweat and perfume. It felt as if it were the end of the world, or, because of the winking, whispering light, it felt as if the world was just about to begin. The people, in their melancholic poses, forming silhouettes against the voice and against the darkness and the light, came here, sat here, waited here and hung here as the voice drifted with the dignity of a walking giraffe, the voice came, and went, and came …

> *Send Themba to Umtata*
> *Send him on the road*
> *over the hills and across rivers*
> *Send Themba to Umtata*

the song said. Lindi was at the edge of the stage, she was rising, pumping her arms to the rhythym of the song.

> *Why is Themba going*
> *Why are you sending him*
> *Why must he go on that road*
> *Alas, send him to Umtata*
>
> *Themba watch out for the ditches*
> *And Themba watch out for the witches*
> *And Themba watch out for the crocodiles*
> *Why must he go on that bad road?*

279

Send Themba to Umtata
Send him on the road
Give him his suitcase, let him
Why must he go on that road?

Why is Themba going
Why are you sending him?

I know some comrades who, on the night they leave, go to a club
or a shebeen. I am leaving tonight. But this is just coincidence. I
have been on the road which I am about to take many, many times.
On a winter morning, as it will be today, the highway to Witbank
smokes, hangs mist and mirage, as the light and the sun's rays, in
big blades, and the truck on the bridge, against the naked and
sullen trees, hang in space, the truck whispering, up above, on the
bridge and moving like a miracle, it flares its way into the mist.
Soon, you pass under the bridge, and under the moving truck. The
road is moving ahead, as it rises and curls and refuses to vanish.
And the earth is dry. And the grass is dry as it waves at the mist,
the truck, the bridge, and you, the driver. And another car emerges
out of the mist and passes with a speed as if it intended to peep
and hide. The bank stretches and stretches with your sight, for as
far as it can reach into the horizon. Always, this road is quiet and
watchful as it caresses the underside of the clouds and sky. The
sunlight, where it can, dances with shadows and shades of the land
and the grass. The trees, because they are so naked, seem forlorn,
seem alone, and they look at all that comes and passes.

By this time I have joined the shadows. We are absorbing the
song and we are gulping liquids and puffing smoke, whispering
our tears and our joys and laughter and lies and we are believing.
They hang in there. You know we are not waiting, we are riding
on the song. Lindi knows this. And we know that she must know
too. Everyone seems so innocent, and, as a result so vulnerable as
we take in, and ride Lindi's voice which is not virgin at all.

Themba be alright
Themba is going to Umtata

And she breaks out of the words, and the guitar and the piano talk. She is dancing, lightly, moving her shoulders, her hips, and turns slightly into the mike. I remember, I am a hunted man and I'm learning … I wonder where all, all, all of them, who are they, the comrades, what are they doing now in the underground! Soon, really, I must go. I can see that Lindi has been sweating and she is listening to the piano, bass and guitar. She throws her head back, opens her mouth, and calls out, gently,

Themba, Themba, Themba …

I think about the road, also, I realise, the story of this time, is not finished, is hanging too many questions, they hang like many ribbons. I must go now. I think about Mandela, and that's because I thought about Martha, because I thought about Esther. The mind is very funny. Maybe it is also because it controls too many things which are also voluntary. I must go …

As I reach the door, leaving the darkness of the club, and, as my eyes catch the light, the street light outside, I see the youth, black and white, young men and young women, in haircuts I have never seen, in dress, which I am tempted to say is mad, they are laughing and giggling and throwing their heads and their shoulders and talk at the top of their voices. I must go now, this apparent twilight weighs heavily on my heart, I must go now …

ⁱ'The Story is not finished —
to many Q's left
hanging 4